How To Find Happiness In Under Three Weeks

Carol,

To an ex-colleague,
who now has time to read.

Dominique Pfahl

How To Find Happiness In Under Three Weeks

Il faut un village

a novel

Dominique Laurent Pfaff

iUniverse, Inc.
New York Lincoln Shanghai

How To Find Happiness In Under Three Weeks
Il faut un village

Copyright © 2008 by Dominique Laurent Pfaff

iUniverse books may be ordered through booksellers or by contacting:

iUniverse
2021 Pine Lake Road, Suite 100
Lincoln, NE 68512
www.iuniverse.com
1-800-Authors (1-800-288-4677)

Because of the dynamic nature of the Internet, any Web addresses or links contained in this book may have changed since publication and may no longer be valid.

Certain characters in this work are historical figures, and certain events portrayed did take place. However, this is a work of fiction. All of the other characters, names, and events as well as all places, incidents, organizations, and dialogue in this novel are either the products of the author's imagination or are used fictitiously.

ISBN: 978-0-595-48754-7 (pbk)
ISBN: 978-0-595-60832-4 (ebk)

Printed in the United States of America

CHAPTER 1

▼

MIS AU VERT

(Put out to pasture)

What's with all the green anyway? On his mother's head, the whole place looks like a stupid drawing made by a retard with one crayon in his box: big green atomic mushrooms on top, a snaky green squiggle along the bottom, the space in between filled with wobbly green lines and spastic green dots. Not to mention—here the simile drifts, but who cares—the green fingers stuck up over the graveyard wall, pointing at the Infidel god, or the green gunk stuck like chewing gum in every nook and cranny, even on the tiles under his butt, he swears if he stays in one spot too long he's gonna have green sprouting between his toes! And this is only what he can see without turning his head, which he isn't about to do as in his back rises a monstrous mountain, also covered with green, but really dark, and so high its head is wrapped in clouds, and every evening there's a scary racket of thunder and lightning coming from there. Like, it's bad enough to be drowning in green, but to have to deal with mountains?

From the safety of his perch on the bakery's rooftop, Chérif Hamzaoui is giving free rein to his resentment. He isn't supposed to be up there, as round tiles are fragile and the last thing his parents need right now is to have to pay for roof repairs. Nor is his viewpoint entirely objective. Although green is dominant, there are in fact other colors in the countryside around him: some yellow, a little purple, a lot of blue. But it's the green that gets him. For one thing so much green means you're in the BOONIES, where no self-respecting homeboy wants to be caught dead. To a self-respecting homeboy, of course, concrete and asphalt rule. And then, less obvious but just as maddening, there is the fact that unlike the mistreated lawns and bushes of his former HLM, the vegetation here looks like it has nothing to fear from a mere teenage punk. Not wild by any means, but old and tough, with an air about it of knowing things that are way beyond the reach of your boom box and pager and the satellite dish hanging out of your window.

The landscape reminds Chérif of the old Harki that used to sit bent over his cane among the kiddies playing hopscotch and marbles in the courtyard of the project. He still can't figure out what made his presence so unnerving. Maybe nothing more than the ragged scar on his forehead, or the blueish film over the dark of his eyes, like egg white just beginning to cook, that made it impossible to tell whether he was watching you or just spacing out. Anyway, without ever saying or doing anything, the old dude was even better than the teachers and the cops at making you feel worthless. And what gave him that right, apart from the fact that he had once sided with the enemy?

Chérif wonders if he is still alive, if he watched yesterday's incredible deed, if that changed his dim view of the young generations. Think about it. Never since the time of the Prophet was such heroism displayed, never had such a tremendous victory been achieved with such small means. The United States of America brought down by knives! The clip that keeps playing in his head is the one of the second jumbo jet, gliding incongruously low in the New York sky, as if lost, then making that mad, determined turn, visibly gathering speed just before it plowed into the tower, just so you couldn't have any doubt left as to its intention. A witness claimed he could see the pilot's eyes–and Chérif believes him, because in the banking of those wings, in the pointing of that nose, he could himself hear the shout: "Allahu Akbar!"

Ah! suddenly it's a whole different thing to be called an "Arab", which he isn't, strictly speaking, but if they're not going to make a difference, Chérif is willing not to make one either. Not lazy, not dirty, not even *exclu*, but brave, organized, and most importantly, successful. Definitely to be reckoned with. Well, OK, there always were the oil sheiks in their air-conditioned tents, sipping mint tea and puffing on their narguileh while counting the dollars with each thrust of the pump. They do manage to get themselves heard every time they decide to turn the faucet off. But somehow, these, the real Arabs, aren't a model for anyone. So it takes some really crazy act of terrorism for the rest of us grunts to get some respect. And those guys really knew how to get the Americans where they live. It's as if they had pieced their plot together from the best Hollywood scripts.

Twenty four hours after the big news, and despite the deflating greenery, Chérif is still able to nurse his excitement back to a blood-coursing, cheek-burning, tongue-thickening pitch, even though he feels a little woozy after a sleepless night when all his joints seemed to be on fire—growing pains, the local doctor calls them, which is obviously bullshit, as Chérif is hardly growing at all. One meter sixty-five at fifteen. A shrimp. His mother, in her usual quiet fussing style, came in the middle of the night to rest a hand on his forehead, as if he was five years old. The gesture so mortified him, so distracted him from his glorious thrill that it was all he could do not to hurl her hand away. At last, today after school he's managed to escape from both her suffocating female worry and the Father's stony role-modeling to the solitude of the sunny roof, where he is now hugging his knees, shivering in the heat, his heart so full that it seems the only thing preventing him from flying off through the thin blue air is the sight of his sister Nanette, playing house in the dirt down below. She is wearing bright yellow shorts and a flowery tank top, an outfit she wrangled for herself with a well-timed tantrum in the aisle of the *hypermarché* that must have made his mother wish she wore a chador. Talk about female modesty. But does the Father mind? Nooo, he is way too gaga over her to see that at five years old, she is already trashing everything he stands for. So it should up to Chérif to straighten her up. But he doesn't either. Instead, if he was given a truth serum, he would have to confess that he is rooting for her. She knows how to make up her mind about what she wants, and then she goes about getting it. Which is more than can be said about her brother.

Anyway, back to the world of men. Action. Revenge. Sacrifice. One-upmanship. The stuff that makes you feel tall. He replays the clip of the second jumbo jet all the way through the big BOOM! But now there is a subliminal banner running underneath. Coward … Coward … Coward…. That's the word the American president used. What a lame comeback, from a guy who kept on the run for a whole day! Any sixth grade crowd would have laughed him off. Still it rankles, as all insults do. You've got to stick up for your own gang. Chérif dreams of launching his own act of reprisal against the defamation of the Islamic martyrs. But what would he do here among all the green, where the tallest building is the church steeple, and where he already knows all the locals, none of whom, come to think of it, look much like George W Bush? Of course he intends to spin a rap about the whole thing, as soon as his feelings have reached the right level of complication: he's already figured out that there's no good song without a twist. So it's going to take time. Anyway what's the point? The rap will never leave the pages of his notebook.

Unbidden, another page clicks open on the bright screen of his elation. He sees people jumping out of windows, falling in horribly soft bunches through the dizzying height. No matter how hard he tries to steel himself, the memory makes him sick to his stomach, because he can tell those were real human bodies, not plastic mannequins like in the movies. He knows why they preferred to jump to their certain death rather than wait for the flames to char them to a crisp. He saw somebody burn with his own eyes once … but he is not going to think about that now.

Except he can't help considering that there is a flip side to martyrdom. It's all very well to kill oneself for some cause, but what about the mess one leaves behind? What about the other people who didn't ask to get involved, who may have nothing to do with one's problem, who may be misunderstood, but who end up dying too, which is totally unfair? Or else who become heroes against their will by rescuing the wannabe martyr from his own death just to make a point about their innocence? And who, because of the scandal, finally get yanked from their righteous turf by chickenshit parents and plunked down here among the demeaning green, arguably a fate worse than death? Yes, martyrdom is a tricky business. And perhaps even … cowardly?

A loud buzzing has been grating on Chérif's ears for a while. Hidden among the tree leaves is one of those huge bugs, the cicada of La Fontaine's fable, who sang all summer–if you can call that singing: it sounds like a misfiring zap gun in an inferior video game, or like the rattling back and forth of a finger nail on the teeth of a comb. Chérif was amazed to discover that the insect exists outside of textbooks. It's made him wonder–idly, to be sure—whether school has some-thing to offer after all. He has not so far managed to see a live cicada: every time he has poked around the branches, the critter has stopped its racket, so there was no way to find it. He's seen some plaster cicadas at the village store, "Bienvenue à Saint Yves" written on their back. They look like big black flies, but Chérif hopes that's just because the guy that made them didn't know what he was doing. Such a sly, pesky loud-mouth of a bug deserves a cooler look. He wonders if you can get plastic cicadas with your happy meal at the McDo in Orange. He is sure they would be much slicker, day-glow with big eyes and wings that moved … not that Chérif would admit to coveting any piece of American shlock right now.

He finds himself getting really curious about the cicada. As quietly as he can, he slides sideways on the roof tiles, tearing up little mounds of dry moss with the seat of his jeans. When he gets to the edge, the cicada is still buzzing. He gingerly takes hold of a branch and sticks his head into the darkness of the canopy. Silence. Not a hint of movement. Outsmarted again. He snickers softly. And then suddenly, something in the configuration of dappled leaves and twisted trunk gives him a sense he's never had before, of wondrous, irresistible three-dimensionality. He has a brand new experience, one that he instinctively understands to mark an epoch, of feeling part of life, enveloped in the world.

Chapter 2

▼

Mais qu'allait-elle faire dans cette galère?

(Why on earth did she board that galley?)

As she sat hunched over in the dubious bathtub, wet only in patches from the trickle of hot water coming out of the hand-held shower head, the flexible steel hose, about as thick as her pinky, whipping clammily across her back, her arms, her thighs, Franny Laforet had a chilling insight: it was in its inadequate bathrooms that France revealed its true soul. Miserly, uncomfortable, sad. The connection was so clear. Why hadn't she seen it before? She was immediately aware that her characterization would draw blank stares from any of the people she knew, and not given to public contrariness, resigned herself to tucking the thought away in the part of her mind that she shared with no one, where many such thoughts remained under lock. Of course, that small bit of renouncement did nothing to improve her mood.

She looked about her drearily. Indeed, the bathroom was just what she would have expected. Puny, gloomily lit, crawling with exposed pipes, it looked as if it had been carved out of a linen closet as a halfhearted concession to hygiene, its amenities further designed to keep in check any tendency towards narcissistic self-regard—or to curb water and energy consumption, from the curtainless bath-tub that forced you to shower in a crouching position, to the toilet bowl (in a sep-arate cubby, actually, but she already knew what it looked like)–a dark hole one step removed from the outhouse latrine, whose anemic flush mechanism, and its necessary adjunct of a ratty brush in a pool of chlorine, served as catholic remind-ers of the impurity of the body.

How in the world had the image of the French as uninhibited bons vivants ever taken hold? A few hours after landing on the soil of her ancestors, Franny was already feeling their pernicious spiritual influence in the way everything about her body–goose-bump covered flesh, limp strands of wet hair, swollen knuckles and reddened knees–suddenly looked alien and ugly. No, no, it wasn't an intimation of aging, she quickly reassured herself. She had had exactly the same experience on her previous stays, the first, at the age of seventeen, packed off for the summer to some distant relatives for the purpose of improving her French, the second, a graduate semester at the Sorbonne, at a time when for lack of better career ideas, she had fancied herself a scholar in French literature.

It all came back to her now: the *pavillon* in Chatenay Malabry with its Tudor pretensions, the façade of spongy yellowish stones incrusted with tiny fossils, a gingerbread house built for Bouvard and Pécuchet; the squeaky gate and the smothering privet hedge; the green kitchen, the doilies, the heavy furniture that you were not supposed to touch because the dampness in your fingers would leave marks on its waxed surfaces; the lights that got switched off as if magically as soon as you left a room; the endless round of meals to plan, and shop for, and cook, and eat, and critique; the stuck-up cousins, playing at being socialites, already in some kind of Rotary club; and the eternal advice from the aunt and uncle on the only right way to do everything, including barbecuing hamburgers, for God's sake!

The weather had seemed uniformly gray, damp, chilly, thrown like a wet blan-ket over the frumpy suburban landscape, pressing on your soul the conviction that life was hollow at its core. For variety, you had to fall back on the fantastic array of ancient discolorations on every wall, every bridge, every tunnel, every embankment along the train track on the ride towards Paris: soot, oil, rust, mold, saltpetre. This was what made up the charm of the "old country"? Paris itself had been a blur of jostling and jackhammers. It was only in front of the shimmering screen, in one of the many living room-sized movie theaters in the Quartier Latin where she plunged at every opportunity, that Franny had been able to regain her focus, had been able to breathe. If that was Pascalian *divertissement,* so be it. She had pretty much stuck to the formula during her second visit, this time augmented by long sittings at the Bibliothèque Sainte Geneviève and in a booth at the back of some café on the rue Soufflot, the terrace, the locus of every tourist's fantasy of blending in, having turned out to be too exposed to supercilious Parisian glares for her comfort. She had had the obligatory romance with the scion of an upper-class family whose distinguishing characteristics consisted of an unlikely mop of kinky hair, a penchant for swiping hood ornaments from pricey cars, and a curiously detached way of making love. Fleetingly, she had thought she cared for him. Now she couldn't even remember his name. She tried never to generalize from a single experience, still she had become very skeptical about the myth of the French lover.

Franny's sojourns abroad had given her a solid knowledge of world cinema and a strong distaste for the depersonalization of foreign travel. She had been ecstatic to return to the blue skies and democratic artlessness of her native Berkeley. She had hardly stirred from the Bay Area ever since.

So what was she doing in this galley? Why had she let herself be shanghaied into acting as advance scout for an overseas reunion of people she barely knew or liked? Well, in fact, she did know and like one of them, Chuck Fischbein, one of the main clients of the technical writing firm that employed her. But it was his wife Amanda, an irritating yuppie housewife, who had invited Franny to stay with them for free at the "chateau" they were renting for their entourage in the south of France on the occasion of their tenth wedding anniversary. The implied understanding was that Franny, as a fluent French speaker, would pay in kind for her share of the rental by translating Amanda's requests to caterers, florists, maids and other menials recruited to assist in the big bash that was to crown the three-week vacation.

And now, it turned out that the Fischbeins couldn't have picked a worse time to reune abroad, what with all cross-Atlantic flights being grounded after the deadliest terrorist attack in history, and all the guests, who were supposed to converge on the chateau in the next two days, therefore stuck at home. Franny's own plane had been descending towards Charles de Gaulle when the World Trade Center was hit, but she had known nothing about it until the cab driver turned to her with leering solicitude:

"Eh! Bien! Vous devez être bien contente d'être rentrée," he shouted over the din of horns. "Des choses pareilles, ça vous fait froid dans le dos." (So, you must be relieved to be back. This kind of stuff gives you the creeps.)

She realized that he assumed she was French, and instinctively, decided not to disabuse him.

"Que voulez-vous dire? Est-ce qu'il y a eu un accident d'avion?" *(What do you mean? Was there a plane accident?)*

"Un accident d'avion! Oh! ma p'tite dame, bien pire que ca!" *(A plane accident? Little lady, it's much worse than that!)*

He had proceeded to tell her the news, but so incoherently, his attention being split between the difficult depiction of distant horror and the hairy navigation of the Boulevard Périphérique, that all she had experienced was disbelief. A terrorist attack? Without any warning? In the name of what cause? Both Trade Center towers collapsing on themselves from being hit by planes? Impossible. He must be talking about some movie, either that or her command of French had suffered more than she expected from lack of use. She had nearly tuned him out, content to punctuate every new preposterous detail of his account with a weak "Vraiment?" when, out of the blue, she had been slapped in the face by his conclusion.

"Remarquez, c'est peut-être bon pour les américains de se rendre compte qu'ils sont vulnérables eux aussi." *(Mind you, maybe it's good for Americans to realize that they're vulnerable too.)*

His tone had not been particularly vindictive, but tears welled in her eyes. Thousands of people presumably dead, and he saw it as a moral lesson. Was this how the rest of the world would react, without empathy? How did this man presume to know what Americans were like, what they felt, what they needed to learn? Was she herself just an ugly American for all her contributions to Doctors Without Borders, her basically car-less lifestyle and her participation in the Seattle march? For a few seconds, she had had the urge to come out of her incognito and set him straight, until a new blare of horns and a wave of jetlag conspired to push her back down into her seat, defeated. By the time she reached her hotel, all her attention had been focused on the promise of a hot shower. Counting her luggage, paying the cab driver, getting her key from the desk, climbing the two flights of shabbily carpeted stairs had been accomplished on automatic pilot. She had shed her clothes and stepped into the tub. It was then that she had remembered about French bathrooms, and homesickness struck. As she ex-foliated a layer of skin on the grayish towel roughened by Parisian hard water, she desperately wished she was rubbing a magic lamp instead, and that the genie would teleport her back to her own bed this very instant.

As in her past visits, the sky had been gray when she arrived, was still gray when she boarded her TGV at the Gare de Lyon a day later. At least it wasn't cold, the temperature of the sticky air in the train station matching the temperature of her sticky skin so exactly that she felt disembodied, the blurring of her physical sense of herself being echoed by a strange muddling of her mental faculties. In this foggy state she made her way to the ticket counter where she intended to make a daring attempt at using her American credit card. Steeling herself for a bout of red tape, she was shocked to see the railway clerk swipe the card into his machine without batting an eye. He didn't seem any more surprised when the approval flashed pertly after a mere fraction of a second, shrugging off the six thousand miles it had just traveled. Unexpectedly, Franny found this one sign of globalization reassuring.

She spent some time in front of the news kiosk staring at pictures of the catastrophe, but she was unable to squeeze any emotion out of the display beyond a sense of a Hollywood script gone awry. Was it the effect of the language barrier? "Les tours jumelles" sounded like some fairy tale castle, not at all like the pulsating heart of commerce in the world's greatest city. Was it the seeming nonchalance of the pedestrian traffic around her? It was midday, a slack time between the morning and afternoon rush hours, when the echoes of clicking heels and screeching baggage carts seemed to have receded into the steel rafters high above, and travelers, their faces alert with no more poignant concern than the announcement of the platform number for their train, took time to cross their legs and sip thimblefuls of foaming coffee at rickety tables scattered among the potted palms. Was her muted response simply due to the selfish realization that the tragedy did not affect her personally, as none of her acquaintances could conceivably have been in New York at the time? Whatever the reason, it appeared that her capacity to care, like her circadian cycle, was stuck for now in some intermediate time zone. The hollow in the pit of her stomach, the dampness in her back, the vague dizziness she felt every time she turned her head, seemed disconnected from any emotional state.

In the end, she bought the near picture-less Le Monde, a bottle of Vittel water and a brie sandwich (on walnut organic baguette, that was something new!) in case her physical malaise turned out to be nothing more than hunger pangs, and tucking her provisions under her arm—as a sort of French passport, perhaps—directed her steps towards her carriage.

It was her first time on a fast train. She observed anew the French predilection for gaudy "techno" colors, bright orange and glossy blue, as if all things modern were toys. All the same, the carriage was comfortable, with its pressurized doors, its capacious luggage racks at each end, the airline-style trays in front of each seat, and the unobtrusive air-conditioning. The train was nearly empty: a few business people, a military-looking man with his two scrubbed children, two elderly ladies with mod earrings engaged in dignified gossip, three prematurely serious high school students in battle fatigues, one of them a girl, working together on some homework assignment. The passengers were too scattered about the carriage for her to pick up their conversations. Even so she guessed them all to be French. If so, what made them so? Thinner faces, tighter fitting clothes, more erect postures, or just the way their mouths moved, more pucker to the lips, less show of tongue and teeth, perhaps? They looked more prosperous, more relaxed than she remembered from fourteen years ago, yet they still emanated a certain ... was it thoughtfulness, melancholia? She marveled at the human capacity for forming general impressions that resisted the attempt to pin them down on specific details. Of course, this was the source of stereotypes, which as a child of the sixties she had been thoroughly indoctrinated against. Yet, you only needed to travel from Berkeley to Walnut Creek to notice how crowds vary from place to place. Wouldn't it be a worthwhile enterprise after all to refine these impressions of difference to the point where they might yield some actual, perhaps even predictive knowledge? It occurred to her that the State Department, the FBI and the CIA might currently be pursuing this very train of thought with some urgency.

While she observed her fellow passengers, Franny was suddenly confronted with the evidence that she was being observed too: from one of the businessmen, she caught in mid-flight one of those twinkling glances that had so irritated her in the past, more homage than invitation, but unambiguous in its sexual nature. She was thirty-seven now, and more inclined to accept the homage. Still, there was something unnerving about having her curiosity boomerang in this way. She wondered whether, from his penetrating once-over, the man had been able to figure out that she was American. Her physical appearance at least would not give her away: at five-foot two and a hundred and five pounds, with her dark eyes, dark hair and pale complexion, she was just the opposite of the Baywatch babe that she imagined to be the model of the American woman for a Frenchman. Nor could she be identified by a telltale luggage tag—she had torn all of them off in her hotel room the previous night. It was her clothes she wasn't so sure of: the khaki pants, white cotton shirt, braided loafers and patterned socks she had picked for their inconspicuousness might very well be screaming Berkeley Gap. All at once, her native town's laissez-faire attitude towards attire seemed like a handicap.

There were fifteen minutes left before the scheduled time of departure. Franny pulled out Le Monde and settled down to read the news, as much to hide as to bide her time. But every few seconds, she found herself surreptitiously peeking over the top of her newspaper, which her sweaty palms caused to curl away from her face, threatening to blow her cover. She reminded herself that she wasn't in Iran or Somalia, that she did not have to fear for her physical safety. Yet the cab-driver's words kept coming back to her. Overnight she had gone from the privileged position of a tourist to that of an unwilling soldier trapped behind enemy lines.

A barely perceptible lurch in her lower back, like a subliminal anticipation of pleasure, informed her that the train was moving. There had been no announcement, no electric spark, no whir of engine, no release of break steam. The platform was merely gliding backward, as in a dream. Franny checked the old-fashioned analog clock suspended from the platform roof: right on time. Her spine uncoiled, nestling against the back cushion. The newspaper fluttered down to her lap, leaving her face exposed. Thankfully, the other passengers were also absorbed in the thrill of movement. Even the businessman was no longer paying her any attention.

Ten minutes into the trip it started to rain, thin needles of water that pinged against the windows, first a few, then a few more, as if they were not sure what they really meant. But by the time Franny looked out again, they had merged into a misty film, across which silvery rivulets snaked their way randomly towards the window sill. This was French rain, stingy yet tenacious, and it had every intention of getting under her skin. Meanwhile, in Berkeley, it was probably a beautiful day, or would be shortly as soon as the few shreds of fog burned off, a day to ride your bike to Inspiration Point, with a stop at the High Tech Burrito and a visit to the Movie Image on the way back. Again, Franny had to ask herself what she was doing in this figurative boat, when her vacation could have been spent much more peacefully and pleasurably at home. It was true that she had seized upon this trip as a means of escape, but what she had escaped from seemed paltry from a distance of six thousand miles, something she could have handled merely by playing possum, couldn't she?

The ride was so smooth that it was difficult to tell how fast the train was going. Beyond the flying telegraph poles, green hills spread as widely as under an American sky. It was the middle-distance: the bulging confusion of hedges, the narrow canals choked with weeds, the heavy church steeples, the stone farms with sway-backed roofs huddled around rain-spattered yards, that gave the landscape its distinction. The only tokens of wild life were silhouettes of deer on road signs—more wishful thinking than information, it seemed. As in the past, Franny, her cheek pressed against the window, felt the view's atavistic sadness seep into her. At least here, beyond the devouring reach of the metropolis, there was no ugliness. Even the train tracks seemed clean, the concrete ties barely touching the earth, the banks on each side sprinkled with delicate wild flowers. Franny realized that she had never before seen real French countryside, and found in it intimations of something more than sadness: a sense of a thoroughly humane land, used to weathering storms, modest in its abundance, secure in its history–immune to terrorist attacks was what came to Franny's mind.

At Lyon three more teenagers got on the train, and in the careless way they threw their luggage on the rack, shouting to each other as if they were the only people on board, it was immediately clear that they were not the type to spend the ride doing their homework. Two of them were dark-skinned and kinky-haired–most likely Arabs, or Beurs, as they called themselves. There was suddenly a palpable tension in the carriage. Perhaps because they were travelling without tickets, the boys settled down on the floor in the luggage area, which was separated by a glass door from the rest of the carriage, and one of the two Beurs, a skinny kid with scars on his face and a pack of cigarettes tucked into his tee-shirt sleeve, James Dean like, proceeded to blast techno-music on his family-size boom-box. The glass door would have done a decent job of protecting the other passengers' eardrums, were it not for the fact that it would slide open every minute or so, as people went to the lavatory or the dining car. The sudden burst of mindless electronic noise, each time this happened, turned out to be more unnerving than a continuous din. Pretty soon, the other passengers were casting anxious glances at each other, silently pleading for some intervention. The military man, who had just set his daughter to nap on his lap, looked the most agitated, the muscles in his neck swelling each time he turned his head towards the juvenile delinquents. Finally, he couldn't stand it any longer. He softly lay the little girl's head on the seat, and shot into the aisle.

"Non mais, vous allez la fermer avec votre musique de singes, espèces de petits voyous! Ça vous est pas venu à l'esprit qu'il y a des enfants qui dorment ici?" *(Hey, punks, when are you gonna turn off the monkey music? Can't you see there are children sleeping on this train?)*

Before anyone could stop him, he had gone through the glass door and seized Scarface by the collar. Soon the two of them were grappling with each other while trading a volley of insults: "Sale Algérien!" and "Vive Ben Laden!" were the ones that Franny recognized. It sounded like the start of a racial war.

Franny prayed that someone would pull down the alarm or get on their cell phone to call the police. For her part, she felt paralyzed, by fear, but also by her status as a foreigner, which, according to her sense of etiquette, forbade taking notice of problems among the natives, let alone pretending to know how to solve them. Plus, she was not just any type of foreigner, but an American, probably the last nationality at this point whose interference would be welcome.

Strangely though, the other passengers seemed more annoyed than terrified, one of the elderly ladies giving voice to their concerns by complaining:

"Si ça continue, il va falloir qu'ils arrêtent le train. Et ça, ça va nous mettre en retard, que je ne vous dis pas ..." *(If this continues, they're going to have to stop the train. And that's going to make us very late, believe me ...)*

Franny now noticed how ineffective the fighters were. After several minutes of scuffling, their bodies were still upright and none of their jabs had really hit flesh. And then, in the most unexpected twist, it was a woman who intervened to stop them. She was one of the passengers whom Franny had earlier tagged as business people, although from the easy authoritative way she strode down the aisle in her straight skirt and bare legs, her hands in the pockets of her denim jacket, a sort of hip, bemused smile playing on her concentrated face, she was more likely a teacher. She opened the glass door, and with a simple "S'il vous plait", sandwiched her body between the two men.

They went on gesticulating and shouting, albeit with a little less gusto. Soon, however, it was the woman they were both addressing. The soldier, still red in the face, was admonishing her to butt out, obviously disgusted by this female interference. The youth on the other hand was appealing to her in a semi-sarcastic but surprisingly courteous whine: "Mais Madame", "Mais Madame" Franny heard over and over. Faced with this unexpected pleading, the soldier had no choice but to offer his own justification, de facto agreeing to make the teacher the arbiter of their dispute. The teacher, still holding her position, was quick to make the best of this tactical switch. She started responding to each in turn in low but very distinct tones that conveyed a fearless certitude that reason would prevail. At length, she agreed with the soldier that loud music playing was rude and with the youth that being grabbed by the collar was insulting. She advised the soldier to go back to his little girl and the youth to stop looking for trouble. Meanwhile, taking advantage of the distraction, the second Beur had sneaked to the boombox and turned it down to a hum. At last, the military man seemed to take notice that the source of his ire had been removed. After a last invective, he shrugged and went back to his seat. The battle was over. The teacher however, perhaps to ward off the risk of further altercations, stayed in the luggage area with the youths. Before long, she had engaged them in some sort of socratic dialogue, to which they submitted themselves with astonishing good grace.

"Bon", concluded one of the elder ladies, "au moins ils sont polis avec les dames." *(At least they are polite with ladies.)* And with this, peace descended again on the carriage.

The whole scene had been bewildering to Franny. In the US, she felt, the blows would have been real, the hatred would not have yielded to talk. And of course, in the passengers' minds, there would have been fear of a shootout, which would have made the teacher's intervention reckless instead of brave. And this relatively benign, this nearly comic confrontation had occurred at a time when the racial polarization was bound to be exacerbated by the recent terrorist attack. What was to be made of it? A fluke, or an illustration of some national truth? It wasn't the last time that Franny would ask herself this question.

Whatever the cultural context, Franny would have given much to be the kind of woman who could handle a public altercation with such confidence. For she had no illusion that she would have found a way to get involved if the fight had occurred at home. Even in Berkeley, the most individualistic, etiquette-free place in the world, she was often beset by feelings of impotence connected to a suspicion that there were rules of group dynamics she would forever fail to grasp. Perhaps if her diminutive ancestors had stayed home instead of catapulting themselves into a land of giants.... Franny fancied she might have had more guts if she had been surrounded from infancy by people her own size. As it was, from nursery school on, she had always been the runt, without enough beauty, wealth or guile to fit into the social order in spite of her height deficiency. Her parents, in their blundering immigrant optimism, had enrolled her in martial arts classes. It was there that she had learned to respect her best asset: an unpredictable but powerful temper. Unfortunately it was a gift that, outside of judo, she could summon only after a long string of provocation. She had made use of it a few times in the cause of political activism. The rest of the time she saw herself as a mouse and a pushover.

They were travelling along the Rhône valley and there were noticeable changes in the landscape: red tile roofs, blue shutters, pastel façades sprinkled the hills. In the valley, rows of poplars and cypresses were gloriously arrayed to battle the Mistral. Even the sky looked less leaden, as if traversed by faint strains of the Marseillaise. Franny's spirit rose a little. It might have sunk instead had she paid attention to the plumes of white vapor emanating from a handful of concrete silos strung along the river, which indicated the nearby presence of several nuclear plants. Fortunately, like most tourists on their way to Provence, she didn't notice them.

By the time the train slowed in its approach to Montélimar, the rain had stopped–or perhaps it had just been out-raced. The windows facing west framed a faded blue sky with streaks of high clouds, while dark purple masses crowded the eastern panes. Without a knowledge of wind patterns, it was hard to tell which way the storm was going. For her part, Franny couldn't help expecting bad weather.

Then the train door opened, and her glumness was blown away by a great swoosh of moist air, not the icy, nitpicking wind of the Parisian basin, but a warm, muscular flow, vaguely redolent of something besides creosote, some faint herbal scent. For a second she felt transformed, the buzz of jetlag replaced by a delightful sense of being alive. But a nudge from a fellow passenger quickly recalled her to the thorny task of getting herself and her two bags through the narrow doorway and down the steep carriage steps. Propelled forward by the exiting crowd, she barely had time to spot the teenage rowdies getting off at the other end of the carriage. Their shoulders in the thin tee-shirts hunched against the wind, the boom box tucked away in a plastic bag, they looked small, as disoriented as she was.

The car rental place was not in the station itself, but across a large plaza planted with sycamores, too close to take a cab, too far to lug her suitcases without a firm assurance that a car was waiting for her. And of course, this being France, the station's *consigne* was closed, although, as it turned out, not out of sheer bureaucratic unpredictability, but for security reasons, according to the apologetic, computer-printed sign on the door, another new development. Feeling her jetlag returning with a vengeance, Franny made her way to the station's café, where she sat in a gloomy corner, the blue glow of a faraway news broadcast flickering on the marble tabletop, while the bartender polished wine glasses, an eye to the show and an eye on her. At last he sauntered over, and after the obligatory exchange of Franc notes for a cup of espresso, good-naturedly agreed to watch over her luggage while she ran to get her car.

"Est-ce que vous voulez que je mette les valises derrière le bar?" she offered, blushing under the consciousness that her fear of theft might be offensive to him. *(Shall I put the suitcases behind the bar?)*

"Non, laissez-les là, y a pas de danger!" *(No, leave them where they are, it's safe!)* he answered nonchalantly. Was he defending the honor of his bar or of his country, or just wishing to avoid the taboo of letting a woman carry a heavy load while not willing to carry it for her? Unless of course he figured that in case the suitcase contained a bomb, the farther it stayed from him the better.

Driving turned out to be a breeze. Traffic was light, the signs surprisingly familiar from long ago games of Mille Bornes, the roads impeccable, so smooth the tires seemed to lick at them sensuously. At every intersection, there was a traffic circle, its domed center a miniature garden, each one done in a different style: contrasting sections of salvia and marigold here, faded lavender scattered among artful rocks there, masses of riotous petunias further on, as if the circles were the object of some adopt-a-highway scheme. But their best aspect was that they gave her time to glance at her map for directions. It looked more and more like it was going to rain, the areas of blue sky shrunk to forlorn shreds peeping in farewell between bloated cloud heads. Vineyards lay on both sides of the road, flat at first, then ascending in gentle waves over expansive hills, looking in the distance like a sea of green, the precision of their rows revealed only for a brief moment as you reached a perpendicular angle to them. At the speed she was going, it took her a while to spot any grapes. But there they were, hanging motionless under their swinging skirts of leaves, their dark purple still touched with green, nearly ready to be harvested.

Coming around a bend, she discovered a change in the scenery. Above the cultivated hills, there now loomed a series of wild looking mountainous shoulders culminating with an actual peak, a huge cone whose tip was shrouded in vapor, like the throne of some god. And in fact, no sooner had Franny come up with this simile than a flash of lightning rent the clouds over the peak, followed a few seconds later by a loud rumbling that seemed to be the very voice of the mountain. Strangely enough, she wasn't scared. For the second time since she had gotten off the train, she felt lifted out of her jetlagged anomie by a buoyant, responsive feeling. Immediately, she saw the sign pointing to a two-lane road branching off on the right: St. Yves, 2 kms.

CHAPTER 3

▼

LES CLÉS DU PARADIS

(The Keys to Heaven)

Franny darted across the square with the cold bunch of keys clutched tightly in her fist, the homely piece of string that held it together wrapped around her wrist as an extra precaution against its slipping from her grasp and scattering in the water boiling around her feet. For as she drove into Saint Yves's narrow main street in search of the office of the notaire who was supposed to hand her the keys to the "chateau", the storm had returned with a vengeance, bringing with it a premature dusk broken at intervals by a blinding glare, and sending indoors anyone who might have helped her with directions. It was nothing short of a miracle that, having pulled the car into the only space that seemed fit for parking, between two huge sycamores on the elongated village square, she noticed the black marble plate conveniently illuminated by her headlights: Mtre. Gounod, notaire. Without bothering to retrieve her umbrella, which she had left in one of her suitcases in the trunk, she ran across the road only to find that the notaire had left for the day, a cardboard sign protected by a sheet of plastic wrap on the door advising late arriving tenants to address themselves to the bakery next door. At the bakery, the steel shutter had already been rolled down, but seeing a rectangle of rain-streaked light emanating from an open side door, Franny made bold to inquire there. In the low-ceilinged, antiquated room, amidst a confusion of floury racks and bins and baskets, and what looked like state of the art machinery from its slick steel surfaces and LCD displays, she saw a woman in long skirts with a bright scarf tied around the back of her head occupied in mopping the floor while humming a song with some kind of Arabic lilt.

"Excusez-moi!" said Franny softly.

The woman turned around abruptly, instinctively putting up a hand in front of her mouth. Then seeing Franny in the doorway, she broke out in a shy smile.

"Oh! Madame l'américaine? C'est pour le château?", and Franny assenting with mixed feelings of relief at this evidence that she had been expected, and mortification over being so easily identified as American after all, the woman dried her hands on her skirt and with a "Attends Madame" disappeared through an internal door, coming back a few seconds later with the precious bunch of keys. She deposited them in Franny's hand, and then, as if struck by second thoughts, she took the hand back between hers, and squeezing it gently, she cried: "Quel malheur, Madame, quel malheur!"

What misfortune was she talking about? Had the "chateau" burned to the ground or been swept away by torrential rains? Why had she given her the keys, in that case? Finally, it occurred to Franny that the bakery lady was in fact offering condolences for the terrorist attack. It was the first time since her arrival in France that someone had expressed sympathy, and ironically, that someone was apparently Arabic. Moreover, she seemed to feel genuine grief over it, which was more than Franny had so far been able to muster. At a loss as to how she should respond, Franny merely returned the hand squeeze and said "Merci".

"Et où est le château, s'il vous plait?"

This simple question however seemed to tax the woman's command of the French language to the utmost, unless it was Franny's that she doubted. After much stammering and covering of her mouth with her hand, she escorted Franny back to the doorway where she stood while the rain fell in sheets from the eaves over her bare arm, making vague gestures towards the end of the village, among which a recurring bent wrist seemed to indicate a right turn uphill at some landmark that she called a *lavoir*. She improbably concluded her pantomime with another pat on Franny's hand and an encouraging "Tu peux pas te tromper". Given the darkness and the rain, and her own at best shaky sense of orientation, Franny thought it very likely that she *would* make a mistake, but convinced she had exhausted the woman's powers of explanation, she thanked her again and set out running across the square.

By the time she got back to her car she was soaked and water was sloshing in her loafers. She deposited the keys on the passenger seat and turned on the ignition with a pang of worry. What if the engine had drowned? Fortunately the car started without a hitch. Lavoir, lavoir, what was that word? Her French-English dictionary was also stowed away in her suitcase. Well, she was going to manage without it. In fact, jetlag notwithstanding, and in spite of the danger of being struck by lightning or catching pneumonia, not to mention the thousand other scary scenarios that the situation suggested, she found herself backing out of her parking place and getting back on the road with what felt like resolve. She normally had the utmost mistrust of people who traveled abroad in search of "adventure", figuring that thrill-seeking must be proof of a deadened sensibility or of a desire to show off on one's return, either attitude effectively canceling out the terrifying otherness of foreign lands that should in fact have been the point. But now that adventure had found her, she was pleasantly surprised to discover that for the moment at least, she was up to it.

She had just passed the sign with a red diagonal bar across the village name that indicated she was leaving St. Yves when a flash of lightning illuminated a low building on the right, a tile roof supported by stone pillars with water gushing over a low wall on the side to merge blithely with the general deluge. A wash-house! The *lavoir* indicated by the woman at the bakery! By the time she recognized the landmark, she had passed it. She had to pull over, at the risk of getting stuck in the mud on the soft shoulder, which thankfully held firm. Looking back, she glimpsed a one-lane road starting right past the wash-house. That must be it. She backed up carefully and turned into it.

The road wound uphill, a good sign. But the higher she drove, the darker it got. Soon all she could see was a few feet of glistening pavement ahead, the night on each side so thick in between the slackening bolts of lightning that for all she knew she was driving on a narrow crest between two deadly ravines. Then suddenly the road turned, and she was driving under a high stone arch fitted with two long slits on the sides, probable traces of a medieval draw-bridge. The word "chateau" had not been mere touristic hype. She barely had time to slow down before her headlights hit a massive stone wall smack in front of her windshield. She pressed her foot against the brake and heard gravel pop under the tires. She must have arrived.

Now what? She seemed to be in a bare courtyard surrounded by walls on all sides, the only exit other than the arch she had just driven through being a rotten barn door on her right. Considering Amanda Fischbein's expensive taste in decor, it was highly unlikely that this could be the entrance to the place she had chosen as the theater of her tenth wedding anniversary bash. Franny was going to have to get out of the car to investigate.

At least the storm seemed to be on its last leg. The interval between lightning and thunder was now long enough for the two phenomena to seem disconnected from each other. The rain itself had turned to a quiet drizzle, barely perceptible in the headlights. Somewhere far off a cricket was chirping. Franny got out of the car, retrieved her umbrella from the trunk, and gingerly stepped forward on the crunching gravel. As she neared the left-side wall, a light suddenly went on, revealing a stone staircase going up along it. She took it. As she ascended, other lights set into the wall were turned on, marking a trail as in some fairy tale, until she reached a terrace. On her left stood a large three-story façade with a symmetrical arrangement of tightly shuttered arched windows around a double door with a porch overhang. On her right, there was a row of widely spaced trees with high crowns of feathery leaves, then a stone balustrade, below which, from the flow of cool scented air, she could guess the presence of a garden.

After standing on the terrace for a few moments while the rain pitter-pattered on her umbrella, she found herself in no hurry to get inside, and instead walked to the balustrade to peer at the luscious darkness beyond. In the faint glow of a number of tiny lights set on thin metal pedestals under shades that looked like mushroom caps, she made out a sloping terrain with meandering paths and a profusion of plant masses, among which she recognized tufts of lavender and the hand-shaped leaves of a fig tree. Then, as her eyes adjusted to the dark, she perceived some movement among the bushes. As a sort of reverse alarm, the cricket stopped chirping. A huge toad, no, a gnome, no, a human being in a rain slicker with a hood, was hopping from place to place, doing something to the ground. A thief, a murderer? Her first instinct was to disappear behind an urn sitting on the balustrade. But then, reigning in her imagination, she decided it must be a gardener and called out to him: "Hello?", realizing only after her cry had traveled the length of the garden that she had spoken English. As it was, she got no response, and in her embarrassment did not make any further attempt to draw his attention. It seemed a little bizarre, now that she thought of it, to have sent her to the notaire for the key if the place had a gardener on the premises. But the man having disappeared, and the insect having resumed its chirping, she gave up on solving this mystery for the time being.

She now turned to the problem of getting inside the house. There was a light above the carved lintel of the door, but the door being recessed, it was hard to see the key holes of its three separate locks, besides which she now discovered that she had been given five keys. She was too tired to compute the number of combinations she might have to go through before she could cry sesame, but considering the habitual finickiness of locks, it was going to be an exercise worthy of

Bluebeard's wife. Nevertheless, with hands trembling from the wet cold that was slowly seeping into her very marrow, she set to work. She had been thus feverishly occupied for some time when from the edge of the terrace, she heard someone say, just loud enough to be heard at that distance, in a tone that was both polite and a little commanding:

"Wait!"

She turned around and saw the gardener standing in his slicker at the top of the stairs, her two suitcases framing a pair of rubber boots. He had spoken English too. Then again he had only uttered that one word, and there was something in the way his neck seemed to retract into his shoulders as he strode towards her on the wet gravel that suggested it would not do to attempt a friendly chat about the weather. So she did as ordered, simply waiting for him to get close, at which point she was able to catch a glimpse of a swarthy, unshaven, gruff but not evil face under the slicker's hood. She dropped the keys into his extended hand and he went to work on the door without another word. Within seconds, he had unlocked it, and with a push that raised the sinews on his wrists, caused it to screech open. He then reached through the opening and a light came on, revealing a large hallway paved with a checkerboard of black and white tiles leading to a staircase with a wrought-iron banister.

"Voila!" he said, and without pausing, carried the suitcases inside and gave the keys back to her. As she held out her hand to receive them, she overshot the mark and his fingers brushed against her palm. His skin felt hot against hers. She blushed, fearing he might misinterpret her clumsiness. There was nothing she loathed more than the tendency of some women to see foreign tourism as an opportunity for flings with the native help. Fortunately, in his brusqueness he did not seem to have felt her touch, and proceeded to retreat out of the house without further ado. He was at the bottom of the stairs by the time she had rallied enough to say: "Merci!" She realized she had whispered, as if there were people asleep inside the house.

"Bonne nuit!" he replied in the same hushed tone. "Vous devriez prendre un bain chaud!" *(You should take a hot bath!)* It was fortunate that she stood against the light, which gave her full leisure to blush again at the evidence that he had after all noticed her cold hands.

He had talked about a bath, but what she really wanted was a good, full-throttle American shower. Without bothering to explore the first floor, which from the hallway light spreading through a number of opened doors, seemed to consist of a series of living rooms of various degrees of formality, she ascended the curved staircase, pausing at a landing lined with bookcases and curio cabinets, and arrived at an upper gallery that overlooked the hallway. On one side, in the middle of a white wainscotted wall, was an ornate double door that must lead to a bedroom suite. On the other side, a carpeted corridor lined with what looked like a dozen more doors burrowed deep into the building. Again, Franny was reminded of Bluebeard. She gave herself a mental slap on the head. After all, she hadn't travelled this far to have Disney moments! (She laid the blame on old Walt for the often shockingly childish turn of her imagination, although in this case she was being unfair, Bluebeard being one fairy tale the cartoon pioneer had wisely stayed clear from). Opening door after door, she at last found a largish bathroom, with, she couldn't believe her luck, a real shower-stall fitted with a glass door, a giant shower head with several jet options and an adjustable wall mount, a soap dish containing a new bar of soap, a ledge where you could rest your foot while shaving your legs, and even a mixer in the shape of an horizontal tube with separate knobs at each end for the water heat and volume, something she had never seen before, but figured out fairly quickly. The room seemed to have been recently remodeled, from the inset lights in the ceiling to the cheerful expanse of gold yellow tiles. Something had definitely improved in the kingdom of France!

The only thing missing was a towel, the two racks being bare, and the cabinet under the sink turning out nothing but cleaning products. There must be a set of instructions somewhere that would reveal the location of the linen closet, but Franny was too cold and exhausted to go in search of it. Leaving the bathroom door open so that she could find her way back to it, she ran downstairs for her suitcases and threw them on the floor in the smaller of the two bedrooms closest to the bathroom. She figured the Fischbeins would claim the larger room, if they ever managed to get there. She unzipped the suitcases, found the terry robe that would do for a towel, and stepped into the warm oasis of the bathroom, where she had a most satisfactory shower.

When she came out, the hallway was dark. She had a moment of panic, when she remembered how familiar the gardener seemed to be with the inside of the house. She had bolted all three locks after her, but he might have another set of keys. Then she remembered the screeching noise the door, probably swollen by the humidity, had made upon being opened. In the echoey house, she would have heard it even with the water on. And then, from what she knew of Amanda, she must have gotten the most impeccable references before she signed the rental agreement. So the lights must simply be on a timer, the *minuterie* dear to the parsimonious French!

Of the bedroom, she only noticed the tightly drawn shutters and open casement, an arrangement she left intact for fear of making noise or breaking something, and the pretty white coverlet, a little frayed, underneath which unfortunately there were no sheets, not that she was in a mood to care. Dizzy with jetlag, exposure, and the strangeness of new places, she turned out the light, flopped down on the bed, wrapped herself in the coverlet, and fell into a dreamless sleep.

In the middle of the night, she woke up with a need to pee. She stumbled to the bathroom, which was fitted with a toilet instead of the old bidet–but a perfectly nice toilet, expansive and inviting, worthy of the American seal of approval. As she sat in the dark, her gaze turned to the small window, noticing for the first time a glitter of sequins on the lace curtain. They were stars, a multitude of stars, awash a swath of the Milky Way. All was well. Out of the blue, as she was wont to do, she burst out in tears.

CHAPTER 4

▼

COCORICO

(Cockadoodle Doo)

The Chemineaux' house stood at the end of the last cul-de-sac in the Cité des Cadres EDF, a housing development built for its professional staff by the State owned energy consortium twenty-five years ago, at a time when the idea that new buildings should fit within the regional architectural context had not yet taken hold. Indeed, all over France, even before the telltale cooling towers came into view, you could at one time have deduced the nearby presence of a nuclear plant from the incongruous prospect, miles out of any town, of an American-looking suburb of houses all built on one model, complete with composition roof tiles, prefabricated siding, garage-dominated fronts, trim hedges, and a general air of spaciousness and comfort that bespoke the availability of cheap energy. Since then of course the EDF houses had taken on a certain patina while the general prosperity had caused a mushrooming of similar single-home, middle-class developments that fit with varying degrees of success within the country's traditional landscape. Thanks to the expansion of the network of fast trains, the whole of France had to some extent become a giant suburb, with the exception of the original peri-urban belts of highrises built during the baby boom, which now played the role assigned to American inner cities. At any rate, the EDF cités no longer stood out, and the social standing of the engineers and supervisors who kept France from depending too heavily on the whims of OPEC had diminished accordingly. But this was nothing compared to the currently looming threats to their very identity, for the National Electric Company was on the verge of being privatized.

Due to the vagaries of their father's job, the Chemineaux children had lived in four successive EDF cités, surrounded now by alfalfa, now by potatoes and wheat, now by apple trees, now by grape vines, but perhaps taking their cue from the way the beams of the development's street lamps stopped at the exact border between lawn and field, had never learned to recognize any of these agricultural products. One generation ahead of their peers, they had been raised to believe that food originated at the supermarket, usually the only store within easy range of the cité, the best (to them) part of their diet consisting of pizza, Coke and candy bars. In spite of this reliance on junk food–a betrayal of their cultural heritage–they had not grown obese, being all in fact of a lanky build, like their father. In any case they were now in the process of leaving the nest, the oldest having just moved to Paris for his first job as a C++ programmer, the second one away at an engineering school, and the youngest having just started twelfth grade, where her favorite subject, taught through an online course, was Japanese. They would no doubt shortly acquire more sophisticated tastes, as their parents were leisurely doing, for a culture, thank goodness, has a way of surviving and reasserting itself, sometimes with a little unrecognized help from foreigners, such as the California chefs who attended the birth of Nouvelle Cuisine.

On September 13, 2001, at five-thirty in the morning, Gérard Chemineau woke up before the alarm as he did every day. As he did every day, he shuffled downstairs in the dark in his pajamas and was nearly toppled midway by the family pet, a Bulldog as big as a cow and as ugly as J. Edgar Hoover, who, blissfully oblivious to his breed's reputation for fierceness, was so fond of human beings that he insisted on greeting everyone with a hug and a wet kiss, his master, as the first person to relieve the awful loneliness of a night spent on the cold kitchen tile, being singled out for his most extravagant displays of slobbering frenzy. The dog, whose pedigree name had long been forgotten in favor of the more apt "Gros Bébé", was the third animal–the previous two having been a Pitbull and a Doberman–enlisted in what looked like an experiment on the Chemineaux' part to prove that nurture always trumped nature. The experiment's success would have been welcome news to the housebreakers–bête noire of every French household– whom the dogs' purchase was originally supposed to deter. Fortunately, they didn't know.

"Bas les pattes, Gros Bébé" whispered Gérard, causing the dog to slobber over him all the more. "Bas les pattes, te dis-je!", he repeated, with as little effect. A friendly tussle ensued, punctuated by stern commands and terms of endearment, until the dog, tired of standing on its hind legs, resigned himself to expressing his affection by chewing on his master's slippers. Thus attached, they made their way to the kitchen, where Gérard filled the dog's bowl and switched on the espresso maker. There was another exchange of caresses, and Gérard went back upstairs to shave and get dressed. When he re-entered the kitchen, he experienced a familiar relief on finding his wife Pierrette bent over the dishwasher, still in the sexy night-shirt that barely covered her luscious rump. Not once in the twenty four years they had been married, no matter what shift he had been on–except right after the birth of each child–had she stayed in bed when he got up for work. But he had never taken it for granted, even though he had married her when she was only seventeen, a good-tempered, poorly educated girl who could be counted on to concentrate on wifely ambitions. He was aware that if he had been smart, he had also been lucky, succeeding at the kind of marriage where his father had failed. Now with their nest emptying and their twenty-fifth anniversary looming, he was doubly grateful for her faithful attendance to his morning routine. He greeted her with a little circular pat on the rear and proceeded to help her unload the dishwasher.

For the next few minutes they were both conscious of the pleasure of working as a team, moving in sync wordlessly, brushing against each other without ever clashing as they grabbed plates, glasses and silverware from the steaming dish-washer and carried them by the armloads to the Louis Philippe buffet. Gérard couldn't remember when he had started helping her with the housework. It had not been part of his training as a boy, and his status as sole family provider cer-tainly did not demand it. But somehow–Pierrette might have provided more detail on this evolution had she cared–he had come to enjoy giving her a hand even with the more feminine tasks such as laundry and dishwashing. It was one way that he manifested his love, and his lack of assumption that he could rely on retaining hers.

Over a breakfast of brioche and café au lait, they planned the dinner menu, easily agreeing on rabbit with a mustard sauce and tomato salad, and discussed the evening TV schedule, deciding to record *The Devil's Advocate* while watching the latest episode of *Friends*. Then they cleared the table, Gérard pocketed his cell phone, Pierrette stood on tippy toes and offered her warm lips for a kiss, as she did every day. By the time Gérard's Ford Escort roared out of the garage, she already had the vacuum cleaner going. By the time their daughter Chloe got up, she would have completed her housekeeping and would have settled in front of her computer for a day of Internet surfing.

It had been a long time since the children had last seen him off with a "Bonne journée, Papa! Et fais-pas ton Homer!" the Homer referred to being Homer Simpson, whose sloppy work habits at the nuclear plant Gérard was thus enjoined from emulating. The kids had been joking of course. They had never expressed the least fear for their own safety, implicitly trusting their father to do whatever was necessary to avert a meltdown. And they were right. Even now, with the threat of terrorism presented to his imagination as never before, he was not so much worried as annoyed. For of course the attack on the World Trade Center was causing a fuss at the plant. The big boys had been roused from their stock option dreams. They would want to show that THEY were in charge, that THEY were not about to be sideswiped by a bunch of *métèques* with X-acto knives. It would take them two, three days to turn around, giving any lunatic aware of how bureaucracies worked ample time to try his hands at another set of fireworks. Then they would descend on the staff in their Armani suits to propose new security measures that would be exactly the same as the ones implemented during the last terrorist scare, and abandoned after a couple of months: parking lots closed, staff required to wear their badges, visitors turned away. They would be mum about the weakest link in the nuclear chain: the high-voltage, unguarded pylons radiating hundreds of miles around the plant that carried the generated electricity to the grid. A good charge of explosives, readily available from the fertilizer silos that dotted the countryside, thanks to Con Agra, would interrupt the flow and force an emergency shutdown of the reactors. Power to activate the cooling pumps would then have to come from backup diesel generators, which would for a while—how long, that was the question—keep the nuclear fuel from turning into a bomb, but would do nothing to palliate the country's paralysis.

As he sped through the still dark nearby village of Saint Yves, Gérard felt the usual tinge of solemn pride in being the first one up and about. In fact, had he looked carefully, he might have noticed a ray of light seeping beneath the bakery's steel shutters, a faint glow in the church's stained glass windows. But he did not pay attention to these small details. To him, the village was an abstraction, a satisfyingly predictable configuration of church, town hall, post office, war monument, as shot through with meaning as a flag would have been for an American. He hardly ever stopped in Saint Yves, and would not have recognized any of its inhabitants in a line-up. His sense of responsibility towards them was of a more general nature. For even though he had worked with nuclear power for his entire career, it was another thing he had never taken for granted. To anyone who asked, he would have boasted about the safety record of the French system, would have demonstrated how it made impossible the cumulative failures that had resulted in Three Mile Island or Chernobyl. In the privacy of his own head, he acknowledged that France's reliance on nuclear power was something of a Faustian bargain, foisted on his countrymen while they slept. It was his job to ensure that they remain sound asleep and undisturbed by nightmares, the current fad for "transparency" notwithstanding.

But how was he going to do that, once the company had been turned over to the greed of private investors and the megalomania of CEOs unchecked by the State? What was going to happen when after one too many highly leveraged acquisitions, a nuclear firm went bankrupt? Or when the search for the highest rates of profit encouraged maintenance shortcuts? Or when insurance companies refused to underwrite plants? That was what the big boys should have been worrying about, more than the risk of a 747 crashing on the massively reinforced containment domes. The real danger, as far as Gérard could see, was not represented by Islamic fundamentalists, for whom France didn't mean that much, but by the neo-liberal miasma blowing from across the Atlantic, which had infected the French ruling class from right to left–although it was the working man that would feel the pain. These days, Gérard saw himself as a member of the working class. It was ironic how he had reversed his father's political journey, starting where the elder Chemineau had ended, as a Gaullist–his first vote cast for Giscard d'Estaing–and had ended close to the older man's early communism–as a some-time supporter of Arlette Laguiller. This was in no way meant as a rebellion. In all things, Gérard was faithful to his father's memory. He was sure that if he had lived, the old guy would have come around just as he had.

No, it wasn't the Arabs that Gérard feared. At one time, for sure, he had decried the Maghrebine invasion for the way it undermined "western values": those people had too many kids, too many of whom engaged in drug dealing, car burning and bus driver harassment. They wanted to erect mosques right next to catholic churches. Worst of all, they tried to keep their women to themselves, which was what the veil controversy was all about, at bottom. But since then, so many nationalities had vied for his detestation, each one chipping away at the beautiful, fragile gem that was his country. There were the Germans who zoomed past everyone on the highway in their Mercedes, and the Dutch who overflowed the nudist camps, their RVs stuffed to the gills with provisions brought from home so they wouldn't have to buy anything abroad. The British tried to impose cheese pasteurization on the European Union just to kill the competition for their tasteless Cheddar. The Spaniards dirtied our beaches, the Portuguese fished the seas dry, the Albanians pimped, the Romanians led panhandling rings, the Malians had tuberculosis and even more kids. And nobody, nobody, had any realistic plan for making them go away. Even the Algerian French were complaining about the country's deterioration. If you counted the votes for the Le Pen candidate at the last mayoral election in several Southern cities, you were bound to conclude that some of them must have come from Arabs.

Meanwhile, who was the main culprit of global warming? Who refused to ratify the Kyoto accords, the Land Mine Treaty, the Convention on Children's rights? Who was years in arrears in the payment of their UN dues? Who continued to bomb Iraq every day, while even Le Pen's wife had started a charity for its children? Who encouraged Israel in its colonial endeavors? Whose films and music provided the young punks in the HLMs with role models of violent hedonism and the copout of racial oppression? And who was pushing for the dismantlement of every shred of social protection won by generations of workers against the depredations of unfettered capitalism? Who had convinced France's big boys that privatizing the production of energy was a good idea, at a time when Californians were discovering the consequences of deregulation? It turned out that "western values" were not a very useful concept after all.

There was fog on the road, water evaporating from last night's storm. Lost in his thoughts, Gérard was driving too fast. He saw the herd of sheep at the very last second and had to break so suddenly that his car skidded. Catching his breath while the dun sheep, unperturbed, pressed each other across the road, he taxed himself with recklessness. How could he, this family man who in public was deliberate, laconic, a stickler for safety, a model of responsibility, with barely a hint of irreverence, turn into a maniac behind the wheel? It was a mystery he had never solved, even after two serious accidents. All he could do was to resolve to be more cautious, until the next time.

The sheep, about six hundred of them, herded by two dogs and one man, were taking their sweet time. Gérard pushed the window open and leaned back in his seat. The air was cool, clouds of vapor rising from the valley to melt in the transparent sky. It was that early part of dawn when the beginnings of light have not resolved to color. Then from a nearby farm, a rooster went off. "Cocorico", it proclaimed, drowning the bleating of six hundred sheep. Gérard laughed, in sympathy with the bird. Suddenly the sky had turned blue.

The rest of the drive he tried to clear his mind of unpleasant thoughts, concentrating instead on his current pet project—one assigned by no one but himself, being outside the scope of his stated operational responsibilities: he had been pulling together data collected by the plant's various sensors over time, tabulating it in Excel and coming up with some extremely interesting charts. He had found out that many of the equipment tests randomly ordered by the guys in Paris were actually shortening the useful life of the plant. That morning, barring the distraction of a general staff meeting, he was going to craft the niftiest, most respectful e-mail informing his superiors of the fact, with attached proofs, and CCs all the way from the plant floor to the Parisian top. You couldn't wish for higher transparency or better team playing, could you?

But when he got to his office he found that a meeting on security for the professional staff had been convened for nine o'clock. The meeting lasted until ten, giving ample opportunity for the head honchos to strut their superior cool, but otherwise yielding no surprise. Then he had to meet with his own men to pass on the management message. At eleven, a worker coming off his shift set off the alarm at the control gate. There was a mini-panic, with a couple of hourly clerks ducking under their desk. The worker turned out to have a spot of radioactive contamination on his right sock. Two hours of investigation failed to reveal its origin. Gérard had to do without lunch. He spent the rest of the day attending to the treatment of the contaminated worker, writing an incident report and reassuring the clerks, one of whom suspected a plot to spirit away some enriched uranium for the benefit of Al Qaeda, the strength of her argument residing in the swarthy look of the man, who was merely of Italian descent. In the end, the incident had to be dumped in the "shit happens" category, which made Gérard uncomfortable. For there were always reasons for technical failures, and if you did not ferret them out, they might come back to haunt you one day.

He was driving leisurely by the abandoned wash-house on his way home when in his state of hightened alertness, he spotted some furtive movement at the back. Without thinking, he pulled over, got out of the car and tip-toed in the grass around the building. There on the far side, a Beur kid was holding a spray can to the wall. Gérard was all set to yell at him, but then he saw what the kid had written: "LE LACHE, C'EST GEORGE W B" *(The coward is George W B)*. He was mollified. There were a hundred ways he could have accosted the boy, the trick being to do it in such a way as to teach him a lesson without antagonizing him so much that he wouldn't listen. But he didn't have the luxury of weighing his words, and so had to trust in his experience as a father and supervisor.

"Bon," he started in his mellowest, tongue in cheek voice, "j'ai rien contre le message, mais ta manière de le communiquer, par contre ..." *(OK, I have nothing against the message, but your way of communicating it, on the other hand ...)*

The boy pivoted around. He was small and wiry, thirteen or fourteen, dark eyes, cropped curly hair, oversize tee-shirt over baggy jeans, the punk uniform. The startled expression on his narrow face was in the process of turning to hostility, but there was something in Gérard's words that gave pause to his feelings.

"Quoi?" (What?)

"Je dis que je suis d'accord pour George Bush, mais quand même, c'est pas une raison pour défigurer un lavoir qui doit dater d'avant la naissance de ton arrière grand-père." (I said I agree about George Bush, but still, it's no reason to deface a washhouse that must date from before the birth of your great-grandfather.)

"Et qu'est-ce que ça peut vous foutre? Mêlez-vous de vos affaires!" (What's it to you? Mind your own business!)

"Ah mais justement, ce sont mes affaires! Qu'est-ce que tu dirais si j'allais faire des graffiti dans la cuisine de ta mère?" (But it is my business! What would you say if I covered your mother's kitchen with graffiti?)

"Foutez-lui la paix, à ma mère! Et d'ailleurs, c'est pas chez vous, cette bicoque, si?" (Leave my mother alone! Besides, this dump is not your property, is it?)

"Si, c'est chez moi. Et c'est chez toi aussi, d'ailleurs!" (Yes, it is. And it's yours too by the way!)

"Ah oui! Le patrimoine rural, et tout ce blabla. Mais moi, c'est pas mon patrimoine! Moi, j'suis pas d'ici, malheur!" (Yeah, right! Our rural architectural heritage and all that jazz! But it's not MY heritage. Me, I'm not from here, word!)

"Tu vas pas m'dire que tu t'crois Algérien, avec ton tee-shirt de Tupac Shakur!" (You don't mean to tell me you think of yourself as Algerian, with your Tupac Shakur tee-shirt!)

"Non, j'en ai rien a foutre de l'Algérie, c'est tous des sauvages. Moi, j'suis du Neuf Trois!" (No, I don't give a damn about Algeria, they're all savages over there. Me, I am from the Nine Three.)

"Tiens, par exemple! Moi aussi!" (Fancy that! Me too!)

That stopped the kid right in his tracks. The thought had never occurred to him that this sample of the French bourgeoisie would understand what he meant by the number, much less that he might have to share his native turf with him. From the bewildered look on his face, he couldn't decide if he should feel mad or curious.

"Vous m'chantez des balades, hein? Ou alors vous venez d'un bled comme le Raincy, une villa, quoi?" (You're shitting me, right? Or else you come from some place like Le Raincy, a detached house?)

"Non, un HLM, à Bondy. La Cité des Ormes, plus exactement." (No, a housing project, in Bondy. The Cite des Ormes, more exactly.)

"Ah! bah ça alors! Moi c'était les Peupliers! Mais c'est pas possible, c'était pas construit à votre époque, c'est pour nous les basanés qu'ils les ont construits ces cages à lapins!" (I can't believe it! I come from the Cite des Peupliers! But that's *impossible, the projects weren't built in your time, it's for us darkies that they built those rabbit hutches.)*

Gérard couldn't hold back a laugh. He had the kid where he wanted him.

"Là tu te trompes, mon p'tit bonhomme. Ces cages à lapins, comme tu dis, elles ont été construites pour nous, les prolos bien français du baby boom. Et je peux te dire qu'on était bien contents, vu qu'on venait tous de taudis en taule ondulée!" *(There you're mistaken, little buddy. Those rabbit hutches, as you call them, were built for us French proles from the baby boom. And I can tell you we were pretty happy about it, given that we all came from corrugated tin slums.)*

The kid was floored. Corrugated tin slums? That was the kind of sob story he would have expected from his grandfather. And the French boojie dude didn't look that old. He was trying hard to find an angle that, without calling his interlocutor a liar, would still leave intact his sense of victimhood. At the same time, he couldn't help having a flitting vision of himself at fifty, as a possibly respectable citizen with a wife and kids and a cushy job, like this other native of the Nine Three. As for Gérard, he had mixed feelings about unloading childhood memories that he had never shared with his own children. They stirred some pain as well as an unexpected pride, both feelings checked by a fear of theatricality and a scrupulous attachment to fairness. He had pulled the rug from under the kid's justification for being a juvenile delinquent. And now, other memories flooded his consciousness: his own adolescent pranks, including the frequent defacing of school desks, and the theft of a bottle of wine, undertaken as a dare, that had landed him at the police station. For all he knew, the Beur kid in front of him had never done anything worse, and was acting out of the same motives: rebellion and boredom. It was true that in Gérard's days, there had been no spray cans, making the commission of graffiti much more painstaking and much less blatant. And it was also true that Gérard had been French-French as well as lucky enough to have a very articulate–if working class–father. The police had treated his misdemeanor as they would have their own sons', sternly but without contempt. And nowadays, just as the opportunities for mischief had increased exponentially, what with drugs and guns, you couldn't even be stern: authoritarian relations were a thing of the past, for better and for worse.

"Et alors, comment est-ce que vous y avez échappé, à la galère?" *(So, how did you escape the ghetto?)*

"Je voudrais bien pouvoir te dire que je m'en suis sorti en travaillant bien a l'école. Mais c'est même pas vrai. En tout cas, le goût des études ne m'est venu qu'après le lycée. J'ai quand même réussi a décrocher un DEUG technique. A ce moment-là, l'industrie nucléaire était en plein développement. Ils avaient besoin de beaucoup de techniciens. J'ai eu de la chance. C'est tout. Et toi, comment est-ce que tu te retrouves dans le Huit Quatre?" *(I would like to be able to tell you that I studied my way out of it. But it's not true. At least, I didn't get interested in studying until after high school. I managed to get a two-year degree. At that time, the nuclear industry was in full expansion. They needed a lot of engineers. I got lucky, that's all. And you, what brought you here?)*

"Ah! ça c'est une longue histoire! Mais j'peux vous dire que c'est pas mon choix!" *(It's a long story. But I can tell you it wasn't my choice.)*

"C'est pas assez cool, je m'en doute bien … A ton age, j'aurais pensé la même chose. Mais si tu regardes autour de toi, tu pourrais être surpris. C'est très beau, le Huit Quatre. Et puis, c'est peut-être ici que tu vas trouver ta chance …" *(Not cool enough, I'm sure. At your age, I would have thought the same. But if you look around, you might be surprised. It's beautiful in the Eight Four. And then, you might find your chance here …)*

"Ouais! Ben ça, ça m'étonnerait!" *(Yeah, right, I'd be surprised!)* The kid had the blasé tone down cold, but Gérard sensed that underneath, a certain hopefulness was piercing. As a confirmation, he now asked:

"Alors, vous travaillez à la Centrale? C'est pas dangereux? Vous avez pas peur d'un attentat?" *(So, you work at the nuclear plant? Isn't it dangerous? Aren't you afraid of a terrorist attack?)*

"Non, tu peux me faire confiance. Je veille à ça de près. Au fait, je m'appelle Gérard Chemineau, j'habite la Cité des Cadres EDF, par là-bas. Et toi?" *(No, it's safe, you can trust me. I'm watching over it carefully. By the way, my name is Gérard Chemineau, I live in the EDF development, that way. And you?)*

"Chérif Hamzaoui. Mes parents ont repris la boulangerie à Saint Yves." *(Chérif Hamzaoui. My parents have taken over the bakery in Saint Yves.)*

Gérard held out his hand, and before he could think better of it, Chérif had shaken it.

A few minutes later, as he was nearing his home at last, Gérard found himself looking around with a new interest at the countryside that rolled by his windows. Indeed, the Eight Four—in other words the Vaucluse department—was beautiful.

CHAPTER 5

▼

IF AT FIRST YOU DON'T SUCCEED

(Two Business Models)

Franny's first instinct on finding herself trapped in a possibly hostile foreign country after the September 11 attack had been to make herself invisible—but then again, that was always her first instinct. Not every person in her situation reacted the same way. One of the problems with any action undertaken to "send a message" (a form of communication whose medium is so often death) is that it's impossible to predict in advance how the message will be received. Where some people are cowed, others may strike back, and yet others behave as if nothing had happened.

A photograph taken by Patrick Malefoi, tobacconist in Saint Yves, on September 15, 2001 provides evidence for the possibility of this last type of reaction. Monsieur Malefoi had been in the process of locking up his store for the lunch break when an intriguing sight prompted him to go back inside to fetch his polaroid camera, always loaded for such occasions. For if Monsieur Malefoi was a shopkeeper, he was also an artist. Over the years, he had turned the upper part of the walls in his store into an informal gallery where his caustic temperament, necessarily repressed during commercial transactions, was given subtle vent.

The picture shows the village octagonal fountain, dating back to 1833 and lovingly maintained by the municipality, on whose council Mr. Malefoi sat. Looking closely at the central column surmounted by a stone vase overflowing with geraniums, you can see the marble plaque engraved with the names of the sons of Saint Yves who died for their country, and the chipped enamel sign that reads: "ne pas salir l'eau" *(Don't soil the water)*. In the foreground, sitting on the margin with her feet in the water, a hippie skirt hitched up to her knees and her possessions strewn about so that they obstruct access to the basin, is a strapping young woman with untidy hair piled up on top of her head and held in place by a pair of chopsticks. Her face serene under the blistering sun, she is writing with a round hand in her diary, her whole demeanor exuding the kind of comfort that Mr. Malefoi associates with sitting on the john. An American, probably.

A picture is worth a thousand words thought the tobacconist (in English), as he shook the photograph into focus. He wasn't one to voice aloud any complaint about the lack of decorum of tourists, at least not in front of them. Being the sole vendor of postcards in the village–if you excepted the grocery store, but he was working on that–he depended on their business. And there were precious few tourists in this out-of-the-way place that had no restaurant listed in the *Gault Millau*, no hotel, no historical church, no recreational facilities–although Patrick was working on that too. Even the chateau stood on a separate hill a kilometer away as the bird flies, the village having been relocated after the revolution of 1789. It was only a nineteenth century concoction anyway, built on the old site by a general in Napoleon's army, and everyone knew that the Noblesse d'Empire didn't count–except of course the Americans who rented the chateau through the Internet in the summer, for whom it no doubt satisfied covert aristocratic fantasies. That web site had been a good move on the Vicomte's part, Patrick had to admit. But even with twelve bedrooms and a summer that lasted from May to October, the chateau did not generate that much business traffic, although thank goodness the Americans were better spenders than the Dutch. And if the chatelain managed to pull off his harebrained scheme for an organic winery, he was no longer going to be forced to pimp out his home to make ends meet. What would Patrick do with his stock of cuban cigars, then? Fortunately, Degency needed a good ten hectares of additional land to make a go of it, and those he wasn't going to get, not if Patrick had anything to say about it–which he did, since he had contacts within the SAFER. In the tobacconist's view, there were much better uses for the land than the eyesore of a weedy, scrawny vineyard. Let's face it, organic agriculture wasn't *clean.*

Patrick went back inside to stow away the camera. He found a spot for the new picture, next to another one of his favorites, which showed Mr. Hamzaoui, the new baker, wiping his brow on his shirt sleeve, his small wiry stature dwarfed by a huge stainless steel monolith, still shrink-wrapped and crated, the just delivered bi-modal, double-chambered electric oven. In the background, the baker's wife, even shorter than he but more rotund, leaning against the door frame, a hand on her mouth as if awe stricken. Word had it that the vicomte had co-signed the loan on the shop and its equipment, as if he didn't have enough debts of his own. He had had his heart set on refurbishing the ancient wood burning oven–no doubt nostalgic for the days when the lord of the manor had had a monopoly on baking. That may have been why he had decided to give support to an Arab: like his uncle, who had bought back the chateau from some nouveau-riche interlopers with the millions he had made in Algeria, he counted on the vasselage of the ex-colonized. Hamzaoui had humored him, and then purchased the most modern equipment anyway. Patrick rooted for the Algerian there. He himself was on the side of the Modernes, even though modernity was starting to be considered passé. But handling modern technology properly required a good deal of education. And Patrick would not bet on the Algerian being able to read the safety instructions on his new oven. Besides, there was something unseemly about entrusting the making of bread–this most symbolic of national staples–to a foreigner. For all Patrick knew, the inhabitants of Saint Yves might soon have to get used to pita and baklava. Not that Patrick's family was likely to suffer from any such tampering. His wife had been instructed to continue getting their *bâtards* from the grocery store, which also acted as bread depot. Other housewives were following her example, building a fund of goodwill on the part of the grocer that might in time help with the issue of the postcards. Anyway, there were already three other Arab families in Saint Yves: the men worked in the vineyards, the women cleaned houses and babysat, all properly modest occupations that filled a niche in the local economy. Plus, each family had three or four kids, which kept the primary school from closing and Patrick's own children from having to be bussed to the next town. This was all very well–Patrick had never joined in the ill-tempered, impractical rants of those who wanted to kick out all the Arabs. But it would be another thing when there were Arab property owners who could influence the run of commerce and even want a place on the municipal council–not to mention a taxpayers funded Mosque.

No, Monsieur Malefoi couldn't help thinking that Degency had opened another Pandora's box with his bit of noblesse oblige. But it was in his nature to meddle, another case in point being the way he had pretty much taken control of the Cooperative Viticole. Frankly, Patrick wished he had kept his primary residence in Paris, where he belonged. It had been aggravating enough to deal with him in the summer, when he used to descend on the village in his Mercedes to demand that the tobacco shop stock the Monde Diplomatique. But to have to tolerate year round his fantasy of turning the clock back to the Middle-Ages! His wife, now, that was something else, a real beauty, always impeccable in silk and linen, and not proud. She had even danced a tango with Patrick once on the fourteenth of July. She was rumored to have done more than dance with some of the chateau's male guests, but Patrick didn't believe it.

You couldn't blame her for calling it quits after her husband suddenly bailed out of the banking business to become a gentleman farmer. She might have given more consideration to the likely harm of divorce on their two little girls. Still, you could understand her: women like a steady income. But since her departure, Degency had been getting more fanatical by the minute. If he had his way, they would tear up the village's main parking lot, decommission the nuclear plant—which would make a huge hole in the municipality's finances—and keep bugs out of their gardens with stinging-nettle tea.

Thus did councilman Malefoi see the village's ship sailing dangerously between the twin reefs of an Arab invasion and a luddite retreat. But being a philosopher as well as an artist, he did not let pessimistic speculations get the better of him. His own aims were modest: to send his children to the university and to pass the shop on to them as it had been passed on to him by his father. He didn't see anything on the horizon that would thwart their realization—not even terrorist threats, which were only a big city problem. And so he smiled as he looked at his picture gallery. *Live and let live*, that was his motto.

As Patrick Malefoi went up the back stairs to join his family for lunch, the strapping young tourist was still sitting at the fountain, still engrossed in her diary. What adventures could she have been recording? In fact, she had been drawing more than writing. Under the date, the left-hand page of the diary displayed a very deft cartoon of a rhinoceros holding on to a kite. Tears ran down the rhino's face, and the kite, shaped like a house, was inscribed with the word "MALIBU". The style of the cartoon—the way the rhinoceros' head filled the frame, the kite appearing tiny from a long perspective, the clutching energy of the paws on the kite string, the shading achieved with small dots—showed definite talent. The right-hand page for its part only contained a number of self-help maxims written in large letters, the source of most of these bromides being a slim volume improbably entitled Rhinoceros Success by a certain Scott Alexander, published long ago in the eighties and still included in the handouts at some marketing seminars on the evidence that it had made at least one person rich–its author. Victoria McWorruster–that was the young tourist's name–had herself picked it up for fifty cents at a garage sale, and had never regretted her investment. Rhinoceros Success had had the same influence on her as Ayn Rand on Alan Greenspan: it had provided a philosophical, even moral basis for her instinctive outlook on life, which was strictly business. Unfortunately, the book had been lost in her travels, and she was reduced to quoting it from memory. As to her more personal story and feelings, we will have to read them between the lines, since she deemed them too mundane, too dangerous, or too downbeat to be written about.

"Don't be distracted by small problems!" read one maxim. Indeed, being down to her last hundred dollar bill, the one Scott Alexander advised her to keep in her pocket at all times in order to feel rich, that was a small problem. Not knowing where she would spend the next night was another, a third one being the possibility that she figured on the French gendarmes' wanted list. At least they didn't have her picture. And the name they had was not hers, but the woman's whose passport she had found in a purse left in a taxi-cab on a beautiful morning five months ago.

"Shoot and ask questions later!" advised another quote. She had done just that. As soon as she had got to work, she had locked herself in a bathroom stall to examine her find. Apart from the passport and sundry cosmetics, the handbag turned out to contain a driver's license, several credit cards, seven hundred and fifty-two dollars in cash, and an LA to Paris ticket for a flight departing in three hours. Without her papers, Victoria intuited, the woman was unlikely to try and board her plane. And by a remarkable coincidence, the passport picture looked quite a bit like hers. Struck as by lightning with the conviction that this was the opportunity she had been waiting for, and that she only needed to step up to the mark, Victoria alleged a violent migraine to her boss, called another taxi, had it wait in front of her apartment while she stuffed a couple of bags with clothes she had borrowed from the store, and asked to be driven to the airport. Her instinct had been right: her karma was in full ascendency. She had no trouble getting through check-in, airport security and customs, and before long was sipping white wine high above the Rocky Mountains. It was the first time she was leaving the US, a fact which far from giving her any trepidations, did not even register on her consciousness.

"Every six months or so, go lie in the mud for a week". Taking that injunction more or less literally, Victoria had traveled by train to the resort of Biarritz, which, through another karmic coincidence, had been featured on the airline magazine. What had attracted her immediately was the wedding cake look of the big hotels lined along the beach, with the ocean on the left, an orientation famil- iar from southern California maps. Upon further reading, she had learned that the town had originated as an Empress' pleasure ground, and was now a renown convention site and surfing mecca, where the networking possibilities were sure to abound. But what had clinched her choice was the mention of its luxurious spa facilities. She had spent three delicious days at the Hotel Miramar, pampered with massages, seaweed baths and gorgeously arrayed dietetic food. Her face had gained a new glow, and she had even lost a pound. Still, she had made no useful contact, so when the time came to renew her hotel registration, and Myra Brown's VISA card turned out to have been canceled, she was glad to look for other accommodations.

"Associate with the go-getters." It was at a bar across from the little Hotel des Touristes that she met the people on whom she would hang her hope of success for the next few months. There were four of them, three men and one woman, downing big mugs of beer at a table across from hers. They were neither loud nor obnoxious, but in the way they sat as a unit, as if their elbows were welded together, they seemed to have taken possession of the room. From the relaxed bulk of their shoulders and the dusty look of their fingertips it was easy to assume that they belonged to a construction crew, but there was also a certain alertness about their eyes, a certain cosmopolitan aura to their episodic conversation. At some point, Victoria had met the woman's gaze and found herself invited over. The crew turned out to be multi-national: the woman was from Belgium, one guy was Basque, another Swiss, the last one Latvian. They communicated in a mixture of French, German and English that immediately put Victoria at ease. She had had only one year of French in high school, but she remembered enough phrases to make do in everyday situations such as shopping, asking for directions and ordering dinner. Beyond that she knew how to use her hands, and most peo- ple, if you were friendly and enthusiastic, were only too happy to practice their English anyway. Besides, Victoria had the linguistic advantage of not putting too much stock in words. In her experience, it was much more prudent to pay atten- tion to people's body language than to what they said. What she noticed that night was that the woman, whose name was Ruth, liked her, was intrigued by her, was trying to include her in the group. She also noticed the big wad of cash from which Ruth paid the tab.

She ended up spending the next day at the beach with them, and while the guys were surfing, Ruth explained their business: they were recyclers of antique construction materials. They went around demolition sites to salvage roof tiles, flooring, door and window frames, fireplaces, fountains, which they then sold to retail dealers. The overhead was low, the profits were high, the demand was growing, the supply nearly inexhaustible. On top of that, traveling was involved. It was in short an ideal entrepreneurial niche. The crew needed someone who could draw pictures of various structures, then label the pieces after the structures had been disassembled. Someone who could also read maps, keep track of surveyed sites and tutor Ruth in commercial English, because in a few months, she intended to set up a global retail business on the Web, seeing no reason why middlemen should continue to pocket most of her hard-earned money. Victoria easily convinced Ruth that she was perfect for the job.

So she became part of the firm. It didn't have a name yet, and the two women spent a fair amount of time during road trips trying to come up with one, which seemed to irritate the guys a little, even though their ideas were welcome—it's just that they didn't have any. Their business strategy consisted of picking areas on the French map where the web of roads was the sparsest, which indicated that people were still leaving farms to settle into town, which in turn meant there would be many unattended ruins ripe for the picking. They would canvas the area by car, looking through gates and over tree tops. When they found a likely prospect, they sent Victoria to reconnoiter on foot. They had quickly figured out that with her long-legged, gawky-breezy gait and her flowing multi-colored skirts and tank tops, she was the least likely to attract the ire of unforeseen owners or caretakers. If there were other houses in the neighborhood, Ruth would accompany her to interview the inhabitants to make sure they wouldn't object to the dismantling of a local landmark.

Sometimes all that was needed was to sort good tiles from broken ones in piles left on the ground by a collapsed roof, and everyone would participate. The work was easy, but the financial rewards were comparatively small. Sometimes a stone sink could be pried with chisel and crowbar, which was a cinch for any of the male members of the team. The most profitable loot however tended to require special equipment, which they would rent as needed. The Swiss guy was in charge of cherry pickers and backhoes. They would sell their finds straight from the truck, one at a time, to uninquisitive dealers. Victoria was so quick at learning the value of various artifacts that she soon became the haggler of choice. At first she had relied purely on the degree to which the potential buyer's eyes would narrow at their sight, but she quickly augmented this intuitive knowledge with the haphazard perusal of illustrated books on architectural styles that she came upon in public libraries in the towns where they stopped. Ever diligent in the pursuit of success, Victoria never missed an opportunity for self-improvement. While the others slept and goofed off on their days of rest, she got up early, worked on her maps, visited antique shops, made contacts with building contractors. For her part, Ruth kept the books and distributed the profits.

"Prepare yourself for the charge." At last, after three peripatetic months, they found their El Dorado, an honest-to-god chateau in the middle of a forest in a remote part of a region called Nievre. It had obviously burned down a long time ago. All that was left was the façade's first story, the mortar between its bricks so loosened by fire that you could practically wrench the stone window frames apart with bare hands. There were also a magnificent door arch, its keystone bearing a coat of arms, one-piece bull's eyes, sculpted brackets and cornices, balustrade segments, tons of slates and the best, a white marble Louis XV fireplace that Victoria herself had found behind a curtain of clematis. As arch and window frames started lining up horizontally in the grass, their shape intact but for the gaps between each stone, Victoria found herself surveying the prospect with a satisfaction that went beyond the expectation of profit. She was reminded of the strange comfort she had experienced watching the wrecking balls during the demolition of the buildings that would be replaced by Hollywood's City Walk. In her mind, enclosed structures were like families huddled around their dirty secrets. It was a relief to see them dismantled, each piece torn from the whole and laid on its side seeming to regain its innocence by supporting nothing but itself.

There was so much work that the crew had to hire a couple more hands. And then tensions started to mount between the partners. The guys, being now a decisive majority, complained of not getting their fair share, given that they did most of the work. Ruth, as founder of the business, insisted on making all financial decisions. Victoria, who had for a while been the engine of discovery, realized that the time had come to strike out on her own. But as she was going to need some brawn to complement her brain, she cautiously sounded out Heinrich, the Swiss guy, about joining her in her new venture. Unfortunately, Ruth surprised them on the bed in his hotel room where Victoria was putting into practice the principle that "in a free enterprise system, everyone has to sell themselves to somebody". Ruth turned out to be unsympathetic to the spirit of free enterprise. Some words were exchanged, and Heinrich ended up leaving in a huff. Two days later, as Victoria was emerging from the woods after a bathroom break, she saw two police vans parked in front of the chateau. One gendarme was escorting Ruth out of the ruins, while others were moving in on the rest of the crew. Victoria ducked back into the trees. It was a good thing she had taken her belongings out of the truck that morning to make room for a load of cargo. She had stowed them under some bushes, where she found them intact a couple of hours later.

"At times, you will have to adapt your plans to new situations." Victoria spent the next few weeks hitchhiking around the country, trying to regroup, meanwhile spending all her capital on the immediate goal of surviving. She never despaired, knowing herself to be the tough-skinned rhinoceros fated to become rich described in her favorite self-help guide. She kept her sight on her long range goal, which was a multi-million-dollar mansion on a cliff overlooking the Pacific in Malibu. What eluded her for the time being was an intermediate goal.

She was informed of the attack on the World Trade Center from a collect phone call she made to her ex-roommate in L.A. in a moment of homesickness. She listened to Maggie's cries of horror with all due sympathy, remembering that one has to give in order to get. In truth, she agreed with her personal bible that worrying about the world's problems was a counterproductive distraction. She was glad to be spared the orgy of mayhem that would be the staple of every television channel for weeks to come. It seemed that the more people led cow-like, bland and unadventurous lives, the more they wallowed in big-scale tragedies, vicariously going through all the stages of grief, but invariably ending with anger. And it was their anger that would have real consequences in the shape of new tragedies. So what was the point of "being informed"? If Victoria had been granted one wish–after the making of her own fortune, it goes without saying–it would have been to wipe out the past from humankind's memory.

And this is how we find her refreshing herself in the fountain in Saint Yves. It is now mid-afternoon, and her stomach is growling, but she is reluctant to change her last hundred dollar bill to purchase a meal that will be sure to be rich in unsaturated fat and white flour. One drawback to living far from California is the dearth of health food.

Not far from the fountain on the village square, there is a phone booth. For the last twenty minutes or so, it has been occupied by a petite woman with straight dark hair, cut in a shoulder-length bob obviously meant to keep men at arms length. The effect is reinforced by the non-descript jeans skirt and plain white polo shirt she is wearing, and her completely untanned skin, although there is good raw material in the trim body and dewy eyes. Through the gap around the glass door, bits of conversation drift towards Victoria, mixing pleasantly with the gurgling of water and twitting of birds. It turns out that the woman speaks English, American English. "Oh! my god!" and "I can't believe it!" and "How horrible!" Victoria distinctly hears, guessing that the diminutive woman must be talking to someone back home about the recent events. Interestingly, while her words alternately express outrage and sympathy, her posture suggests a mixture of irritation and guilt: wincing, biting her lips, playing with her hair, shifting her balance from one foot to the other, tapping her head against the wall of the booth, she keeps agreeing with the person at the other end of the line, her voice never deviating from a tone of nervous meekness. A person who doesn't know how to say no. At first, Victoria is merely amused. Then it occurrs to her that now would be a good time to re-connect with some of her compatriots, who, after the scary attack on their homeland, may be more inclined to circle the wagons and help one another. So she shakes her feet out of the water, puts on her sandals, straps on her backpack and guitar, and walks towards the phone booth. Within ten minutes, she has been offered room and board by the tiny woman, whose name is Franny.

CHAPTER 6

▼

ON DIRAIT QUE QUELQUE CHOSE SE PASSE, EN FAIT IL NE SE PASSE RIEN.

(It Looks As If Something Is Happening, But In Fact Nothing Is.)

Greeting the day in Saint Yves, Franny has found, conforms to the very essence of mystical practice: a series of awkward gestures that end in ecstasy. First, a jab with the heel of the hand at the bumpy latch, stuck in its iron brace by too many coats of paint. After that a twist of the wrist, up and to the right, all fingers clutched on the unwieldy knob. A slight shudder of release. Then on tip-toe, a push with both palms on the dew-covered slats, upper body projected out in the void. A squeak, reticent at first, then crescendoing, then easing into a sigh as the heavy shutters finally swing wide open, coming to rest against the stucco wall with a clang that echoes across the terrace. "Tada!" the shutters seem to be proclaiming, "Look what we've cooked up for you!" Franny wipes her dripping hands on her night-gown. She blinks, the sudden burst of sunlight tickling her eyelashes. Yes, it's all there, as it has been every morning, this honeyed, indulgent, inebriating expanse, not just offered to her gaze, but lifting her, nestling her. Although she is not religious, she can't help feeling that she is resting in the hand of God.

Why, she wonders, analytical even in her flights of enthusiasm. The landscape here is not that different from the Napa valley: waves upon waves of vineyards, a background of wooded hills, the occasional lavender field. Yet the feeling is completely different. There is no hint of harshness, of ostentation, of hubris. Something about the light, pearl rather than sapphire, its shadows more forgiving. Something about the earth, edible looking in its smooth taffy shades sprinkled with pure white pebbles. The greens softer, tending to yellow and gray as opposed to black and purple. No fans or irrigation pipes in the vineyards. More whimsy in the contours, the sculpting of agriculture done with a lighter hand. Glimpses of dirt paths in every direction, inviting you to roam at ease, not to cover a distance or to attain a view, but simply to be part of that smiling land. In California, come to think of it, it's more or less impossible to hike except in public parks. At this moment, Franny would give all the coastal redwoods for the parasol pines through which sheaves of sunbeams pour onto her offered face. Or the church steeples, airy here with their iron filigrees, several of them visible from any point, the imaginary lines between them weaving a sort of safety net: thou shall not get lost, their bells intimate every half-hour, slightly out of sync, as if time had a certain amount of stretch.

She tries to put her finger on it through comparisons, but she is aware of not being able to account for the most important, something that vibrates through her, as if her whole being was in tune with the harmonics in the air.

From a pragmatic point of view, opening the shutters is a totally inconvenient chore, requiring about as many steps as assembling a piece of furniture from Ikea. Ah! but this chore has a spiritual dimension too. It's like the symbolic parting of the curtain at the beginning of a play, a play that becomes more beloved with each performance. Or a sort of French equivalent to the Japanese tea ceremony, the type of ritual which far from pointing to the mysteries of the hereafter, anchors the participant in the exquisiteness of the moment–a gesture of belonging. For the last three days, in the absence of anything more urgent to do, Franny has been developing quite a repertoire of such rituals.

On her first morning at the Chateau Degency–for this was how the place is named, according to a discreet sign posted at the wash house turnoff that she has since discovered—after opening the shutters and being knocked out by the view, she had decided to drive into town to procure the means of a breakfast. But upon opening the front door, she found a basket on the threshold, loaded with bedding, dishcloths, bath towels (but no washcloth, some things about the French never changed …), a photocopied sheet of instructions for the house, and on top, a brown paper bag with its ends twisted, containing two warm croissants. Besides the basket, as if it had been brought by someone else, a yellow ceramic bowl filled with fresh purple figs. Strange! Was the chateau attended by a retinue of ghosts? At least they seemed to be benevolent.

She went back inside and found the kitchen, a sprawling affair, badly lit and far from spic-and-span, that seemed to never have made up its mind between a modern and retro look: a stone sink and a butcher block counter, wainscotting and a built-in convection oven. She took an inventory of the cupboards, finding evidence of previous Anglo-Saxon guests in the form of cereal boxes, ketchup, brown rice. There was also a tin of ground coffee, some milk powder, a jar of red-currant jelly in the fridge, enough for breakfast. She ate perched on one of the stools disposed around a center island, American style, with the instructions sheet tucked under her plate, a finger nail idly scraping the gunk stuck in the grooves of the tabletop.

After a little sanitary scrubbing of the sink, dish-drainer, stove top, counters and fridge shelves, and a little mopping of the pitted tile floor, Franny finally set out to do some shopping. In the clarity of a sunny morning, and with her jetlag nearly gone, she had no trouble finding the staircase that led from the terrace back down to her rented car in the lower courtyard. There, however, she found that a locked wrought-iron gate was now barring the entrance arch. More friendly ghosts intent on her safety, she had to assume, but how was she supposed to get her car out? Stumped for a few seconds, she finally remembered the big bunch of keys. And indeed, one of them fitted the lock.

The winding road that had seemed so scary the previous night turned out to meander tamely between vineyards and orchards, no trace of a ravine in sight, the only sign of danger being a occasional shovelful of rocks washed across the pavement by the late storm. She took the left turn at the lavoir and in no time found herself in Saint Yves, which was a midsize village with a town hall, a church, a post office, a primary school, its sycamore shaded yard reverberating with the cries of children, a brand new complex in the post-modern style housing a *médiatheque* and a childcare center, and a full complement of shops, including a café, a tobacco and newspaper shop, a *quincaillerie* with an outside display of brooms, plastic fly curtains, lavender soap and ceramic cicadas, and even a bank with an ATM inserted into its stone wall. The whole business district was no longer than five hundred yards, arranged around a village square that was a mere widening of the main road, planted with the ubiquitous sycamores and harboring a fountain and a public phone booth. A few narrow streets branched out from the main drag, up toward a wooded hill and down toward a shallow river meandering among smooth rocks. The houses were crowded together, remarkable only for the lovely shades of their stucco: caramel, cinnamon and butter, the latter color being that of the chateau. Franny would later learn that these hues were obtained from local ochre mines.

There was no supermarket, but the grocery store was stocked with the essential staples, plus a postcard stand and its own collection of ceramic cicadas. Franny also found a greengrocery, a corrugated tin shack on a side street where an phlegmatic looking young man sold organic tomatoes, lettuce, beans, grapes and nectarines. Passing the tobacco store, she briefly considered buying the Monde to see what was happening in New York, then decided against it. At the bakery, she vainly looked for the Arab lady, whom she wanted to compliment for her delicious croissants. A young girl, also of Arabic descent but speaking fluent French, stood instead behind the counter in an unbuttoned white coverall under which she wore tight jeans and a tight knit top. Franny bought a wheel of multi-grain bread, one of an assortment of variously shaped organic loaves scrumptiously arrayed on a separate counter that would have done honor to the Berkeley Cheese Board. As she was paying for her purchase, she heard a clatter of steps tumbling down some stairs in the back of the building. The young girl behind the counter made a sudden move to the side, just as a surly-looking teenager in a Tupac Shakur tee-shirt burst into the shop, filched a couple of candy bars, vaulted over an empty bread cart and disappeared through the front door. The girl shrugged and muttered: "Toujours en retard!", an unwitting note of admiration and envy in her voice. The boy had looked very much like the three troublemakers on the train: aggrieved, provoking, carapaced in hipness, yet oddly fragile. Could he really be the son of the bakery lady, with her warm, humble, archaic manner? Talk about a generation gap!

By the time Franny had put away her purchases, prepared and eaten a lunch of bread, cheese and tomatoes, and perused again the instruction sheet, the temperature outside had climbed into the nineties, although it was cool in the shuttered, thickly walled mansion. She explored the first floor, which consisted, on the right of the hallway, of a dining room, kitchen, pantry, and a small bathroom, and on the left, of three rooms for which the term "parlor" seemed more adequate than "living room", if only because of their number. The dominant impression throughout was one of faded grandeur: stained and curling wallpaper, chipped marble fireplaces, missing pieces of furniture inlay, worn upholstery nap, mismatched chairs registered subliminally on the eye everywhere, countering the luxurious effect of high ceilings, tall windows and intricate parquet designs. There was a baby grand piano in surprisingly good tune in one of the parlors, a pool table with a tear in its felt cover in another one, slightly askew family portraits in oils and sepia on the walls, crystal (or glass?) chandeliers, magazine racks with issues of *Chasse et Pêche* and *Femmes d'Aujourd'hui* dating from the 1960s as well as more recent copies of *Architectural Digest* and *Forbes.* The most precious heirlooms: hand-painted china, gilded and leather-bound volumes on military strategy, a whole collection of antique mechanical toys, were locked away in glass-fronted cases. But many objects that looked to Franny as if they could have fetched a hefty price in any American antique shop were left lying about: ivory and ebony chess pieces, tin soldiers, closetfuls of embroidered house linens, Egyptian statuettes, 78 RPM jazz albums in their brown paper covers. Among these relics, there was one that made Franny's eyes water. It was a tiny travel diary illustrated with exquisite miniature watercolors of Italian landscapes, each one about two by three inches but still managing to suggest vast expanses. The location and date of each painting ("San Giovanni, 9 Mai 1898") was noted underneath, otherwise the diary was devoid of any text. From the vibrancy of the watercolors, it looked as if it had never been handled after its completion. How could such a beautiful object have been disregarded for so many years? And how had it ended in a basket full of commercial postcards? As she reverently turned the pages, Franny felt as if the soul of the artist was crying out to her, a soul that for some reason came off as a cross between Dorothea Brooke and Little Dorrit: a shy but independent young lady dragged by her family on the conventional grand tour, for whom painting had been a refuge from social obligations as well as a means of self-expression that transcended customary female accomplishments. Perhaps she had died of some disease contracted in Italy. Or she had sacrificed her talent to matrimony, as expected in those days, and still rather frequent now. A sad, truncated life either way. But at least it had left this one gorgeous memento, which was more than could be said of Franny's life up to now, for all her health and freedom.

The upstairs was divided into two wings of very different character, although they looked the same from the outside: the west wing, where her bedroom was, was furnished in a somewhat utilitarian manner, the rooms laid out on each side of a central corridor, with the exception of the master bedroom, which occupied the whole width of the building at the end, and which contained its own comfortably appointed bathroom. These rooms seemed to have only recently been occupied by the owner's family. Her own bedroom, with its white wrought iron bedstead, the pink cardboard box in a dresser drawer that contained beads, glitter, barrettes, a hairless Barbie doll and a composition book entitled "Devoirs de

Vacances", and the poster of Britney Spears inside the armoire's door, had obviously belonged to a girl. Across from her room, next to the yellow bathroom, there was an office, fitted with mostly empty bookshelves and a large walnut desk, the wall behind it displaying the telltale pattern of magnetically aligned dust left by a now removed computer monitor. Another room, whose wallpaper was decorated with bunny rabbits, must have been a nursery. The last bedroom, lacking any idiosyncrasy, had probably served as a guest room.

The East wing was a maze of large bedrooms, dressing rooms and rooms that seemed to have no use at all, communicating with one another through a multitude of doors, some of which were imposing, and some hidden in the wainscotted walls. The furniture ran the gamut between white, gilded and gracefully curved (Louis XV? Woman's room?) to massive mahogany with eagle and bee motives (Napoleon? Man's quarter?), and seemed to have been amassed there without any concern for functionality. One of the rooms had a four-poster bed with a dusty chintz canopy. There was also a vast bathroom with rectangular white tiles and ornate brass fittings reminiscent of a fancy nineteenth century spa, but lacking a shower stall. Between the grandiose and the convenient, which wing would Amanda pick, if she ever made it to Saint Yves? Franny betted on the grandiose.

The third story could be reached by a narrow enclosed staircase at the back of the east wing, which also led back downstairs to the kitchen area. These must be service passages, and the top floor, lower of ceiling, must have been the servants' quarters. It was now occupied by several pretty, unpretentious bedrooms with painted and stenciled walls, chenille bedspreads and bird's eye views of the property from their small rounded windows. Other rooms were empty or served as attics. One was yet another bathroom, and two were locked. There was one key on her five key set for which Franny had as yet found no use, but unlike the Bluebeard heroine, she wasn't tempted to try it on either lock. The instruction sheet having failed to mention them, it seemed clear to her that those two rooms, like the locked cabinets, were off limits to guests.

While touring the house, she had opened shutters and windows here and there to let in light and create ventilation. Still she found the atmosphere inside oppressing, suggestive somehow of stale tobacco smoke, afternoon snoring, broken toys, nightstands crowded with bottles of medicine, unpaid bills. She made a couple of forays to the front porch but was each time beaten back by the heat. She ended up going up to her room where she took a fitful nap, waking with a sensation that she had been drugged. By then though the sun was lowering, a breeze was stirring in the feathery trees on the terrace, which seemed to be some kind of acacia. Somewhere in the distance, a rooster crowed out of turn. "Cocorico!" it distinctly shouted with pugnacious bravado, defying the heat to shut him up—like the Gallic bird that he was! Franny laughed, found herself thoroughly awake, ready to resume her explorations.

The garden stretched in a series of tiers buttressed with piled stones and linked to one another by irregular flights of steps, ending at the bottom at a stuccoed wall pierced with a wrought iron gate that looked out on a weed-invaded dirt road, vineyards sloping beyond that toward the village. The garden was otherwise bordered on the north side by the terrace, on the west by the massive stone wall which closed the entrance yard and on the east by a fragrant pine wood. The first tier had rose bushes against the terrace wall and a scalloped, algae-invaded basin in the center of a lawn. After that all attempts at formality stopped, yielding to an untamed profusion of flowers, shrubs, trees, some decorative (oleanders, hollyhock), some functional (fig and olive trees, and even tomatoes and eggplants in a corner plot), some both (lavender and rosemary), many more unknown to her, that seemed to be the legacy of several generations of idiosyncratic gardeners. Hidden among the plants was a network of miniature canals, barred at intervals with wooden dams that could be moved up or down to direct the flow of water, converging towards a large flagstone fitted with an iron ring and surrounded by wild mint and forget-me-nots. A cistern, probably. It was those dams that the gardener must have been adjusting the night before, Franny realized.

When she got back inside, she noticed a tray holding a bottle of wine, a corkscrew and a glass at one end of the huge dining room table. She could have sworn the bottle wasn't there earlier, but then again the house was so full of stuff that swearing to any of its contents was a hazardous proposition at best. The wine was a red Côtes du Rhone bearing the label "Château Degency" and an organic certification. So the place was also a winery. And organic at that. Then where was the cellar? In the huge barn on the side of the entrance arch, derelict as it looked? She would have to check it out later. For now a glass of wine seemed the right antidote to the darkness closing in around her. There was a boombox on a marble-topped sideboard, which she managed to tune in to a classical music station. She poured the wine, held up the glass and gave herself a mental toast. The wine was decent, she thought, not too thick or astringent, with a nice fruity taste that sneaked up on you.

Taking her cue from the place where the wine had been left, she ate dinner at the dining room table, dishes of paté, salads and cheeses and an issue of *Vins et Gastronomie* arrayed around her as a bulwark against the table's immensity. Afterwards, a second glass of wine in hand, she sat on the front steps to listen to the crickets and watch the stars bloom in the sky, and fell to musing about the quirks in her character. In truth, she had undertaken this trip not just to escape a sticky situation in Berkeley, but also as a dare to herself to be more sociable, to loosen up, to go with the flow. For she had lately started to worry that her beloved independence was turning her into a curmudgeon. And what better opportunity to practice sociability and flexibility than spending three weeks in a foreign country with a dozen strangers (with the exception of Chuck of course, whom she had known for years, and who was a dear in spite of highly suspect political views)? But now that a twist of fate seemed to have indefinitely postponed her social experiment, she had to confess that she felt relieved. Dealing with people was such hard work! Talking without offending, listening without getting bored, taking care of unexpressed needs, conciliating incompatible desires, none of it was instinctive to Franny, probably because she had been an only child. Alone she felt whole, at one with the universe, particularly in a beautiful place such as this. And yet a little forlorn too. A part of her soul, which she dismissed as overly romantic, craved for an easier kind of companionship, one based on fearless conversation and deep affection.

Was she drunk? A light was filtering from around a door she had not previously noticed in a recess under the hallway stairs. Suddenly her heart was pounding. Without thinking, she put down her glass and tried the door. It was locked. She got her set of keys and tried each one in turn. None of them worked. She looked for a light switch around the door but couldn't find any. She switched the main hall light on and off–to no effect. She tried to escape to the kitchen, was drawn irresistibly back. The door seemed to be taunting her. She leaned her cheek softly against it. Something cold, subterranean, watchful emanated from the other side. She even thought she discerned some faint sounds, stealthy, but too deliberate to be made by a prowling animal. Once again she fell prey to fairy tale imaginings: trolls with pick axes, witches brewing spells in black cauldrons whirled dizzily through her mind. What was she to do, all alone in that huge house, far from any help? Ah! the instruction sheet. It had a couple of phone numbers to call in case of emergency. Was this an emergency? Was she going to be laughed at? Well, there were a lot of expensive things in the chateau. Even if her fear for herself might be superstitious, it was rational to guard against thieves.

She picked up the hallway phone, put the receiver against her ear and was about to dial the first number when she realized that she did not have a dial tone. Yet the line was live: behind the silence, she could hear a thin hiss similar to the sound of a fax connection. For a second, she thought she was experiencing one of her recurring nightmares, the one in which she desperately tried to make a call and the phonebook kept falling out of her grasp, or she kept dialing wrong numbers, or the line went dead. The next moment, the certitude that she wasn't dreaming threw her in such a panic that she nearly dropped the receiver. There was someone in the house! He had climbed through one of the windows she had so incautiously opened and disabled the phone line by taking a set off the hook in another room. Madly, she clicked on the hang-up button. She heard a dial tone. With trembling fingers she dialed the first number, and got a message from the notaire's answering machine. She dialed the second number, fumbled, had to redial. The phone rang and rang, each ring stretching as if she had been sucked into a time warp. Finally someone picked up at the other end.

"Oui?" It was the gardener's voice, and again Franny heard that slightly impatient, slightly imperious tone melting into empathy within the space of one syllable. She was so relieved she could have kissed the receiver.

"Bonsoir Monsieur, je suis désolée de vous déranger, mais il y a une lumière derrière la porte sous l'escalier, et je ne sais pas comment l'éteindre." *(Good evening, Sir, I am sorry to disturb you, but there is a light behind the door under the stairs and I don't know how to turn it off.)* Unable to voice her fears of pillage and murder, she was falling back on reasons of household economy that she supposed would be more credible to the French. On the other hand, calling the caretaker at ten thirty P.M. to report a waste of energy might be a stretch of the concept of emergency. Strangely enough, he didn't seem to mind, for all his gruffness.

"Ne vous inquiétez pas!" he said. "Je m'en chargerai." *(Don't worry, I'll take care of it.)*

But that wouldn't do at all. By the time he got around to it, Franny might be dead, and all the furniture might be on a truck speeding towards the border.

"Ce que je veux dire, c'est que je n'ai pas allumé cette lumière, et je me demande s'il est possible que …" *(What I mean is that I didn't turn the light on, and I wonder whether …)* Franny was searching for the French word for intruder when he replied, as collectedly as if she had asked for an extra towel:

"Pas de problème, Mademoiselle. La lumière, c'est moi qui l'ai allumée." *(No problem, Miss, I was the one who turned the light on.)*

At the risk of being impolite, Franny could not let the matter rest there. If the gardener had the full run of the house while there were guests, she needed to know.

"Mais comment est-ce possible? J'étais sur le porche toute la soirée." *(But how is that possible? I was on the porch all evening.)*

There was a pause, as if he was reluctant to confess some impropriety. Because of his relaxed tone so far, Franny guessed that he probably had reasons to rummage around the house that his boss would not disapprove of. All the same, he owed it to her to explain.

"Il y a une autre entrée à l'arrière menant à la cave. La porte sous l'escalier y mène aussi, mais elle est fermée a clé pour votre intimité." *(There is another entrance to the cellar in the back. The door under the stairs leads there too, but it's locked for your privacy.)* Again there was a pause. Then he added:

"Je m'excuse si je vous ai causé un effroi. Je ne voulais pas vous déranger, mais j'avais du travail à faire à la cave." *(I apologize for frightening you, but I had work to do in the cellar.)*

"Je comprends. Je ne savais pas, avant de trouver la bouteille de vin offerte par le propriétaire, qu'il était un ..." *(I understand. I didn't know, until I found the bottle provided by the owner, that he was a ...)* Franny couldn't find the French word for winemaker.

"Vigneron?" he suggested. "Oui, du moins il essaie." *(A winemaker? Yes, he is. At least he tries to be.)*

Was he being snide towards his employer? Actually, his tone sounded fatalistic more than anything else.

"Est-ce qu'il y a du vin dans la cave?" *(Is there wine in the cellar?)* Franny continued, determined to exhaust the subject of her fears.

"Oui. Aimeriez-vous la visiter pendant votre séjour?" *(Yes. Would you like to visit it during your stay?)* He was very chummy for a gardener, or cellar manager, or whatever he was. She did not want to sound flirtatious in return.

"Non!" she answered too quickly, immediately fearing that she had hurt his feelings. "Je veux dire ... je ne connais rien sur les vins. Je voulais seulement savoir si il y a quelque chose qui pouvait intéresser les voleurs, parce que j'ai entendu du bruit dans la cave." *(No, I mean ... I know nothing about wine. I only wanted to know if there might be something of interest to burglars in the cellar, as I heard noise in there.)*

"C'était probablement moi," he said. *(It was probably me.)*

"Non, je veux dire il y a une minute, juste avant de vous téléphoner." *(No, I mean a minute ago, just before calling you.)*

"C'était probablement moi," he repeated. "J'y suis encore. Vous m'avez appelé sur mon portable. Mais j'allais juste ressortir. Vous pourrez dormir tranquille. Et puis, ne vous faites pas de souci pour les voleurs, la cave est bien protégée, la maison aussi d'ailleurs, une fois la porte et les volets fermés. Mais n'hésitez pas a m'appeler en cas de problème." *(It was probably me. I am still down there. You called me on my cell phone. But I was about to leave. You'll be able to sleep in peace.*

And don't worry about burglars, the cellar is secure, the house too, once the door is locked and the shutters closed. But don't hesitate to call me in case of problem.)

She barely had time to assure him that he had not bothered her and that she would secure the door and shutters right away before he wished her good night and hung up.

As she went over the conversation in her head, Franny was struck by how articulate the gardener/cellar manager had sounded. He used words like "effroi" and "intimité", he did not drop the "ne" in his negatives, he used the formal interrogative with great ease. She was afraid of having misjudged him for a simple peasant because of the context of their first meeting and his unkempt look. For all she knew, he might have a university degree in enology and be in charge of the whole vineyard. She tried to remember what she had said, searching anxiously for signs of condescension in her attitude, which would have been a terrible lapse for someone as determined as she was to treat every human being with respect, someone who had in addition been indoctrinated early and often by her father into the superior nobility of manual work.

She had been absorbed in these unpleasant reflections for some minutes when she thought of looking at the cellar door. The light behind it had been turned off, and all hints of black magic had vanished from its blank surface. She laughed at herself and went up to bed, taking care on her way to lock and shutter all the chateau's openings.

Lying in the dark, she tried to sort out her feelings towards the strange house. She felt safe now knowing that the person in charge was just a phone call away. She had no idea where he lived, but obviously not far away if he came to the cellar at night to work. And she had to smile at how her perceptions of what lay behind the recessed door had been both accurate and completely paranoid. All the same her sense of unease was not completely gone. It seemed likely from the evidence that the owner's family had had to vacate their ancestral home to make room for paying guests. She could imagine how expensive to maintain such a house might be, and maybe vineyards in this area weren't very profitable, especially if the "vigneron" was not very competent. Renting out to Americans may have been a convenient way to make ends meet, but it must have been humiliating, and she hated to be seen as an invader, the strong dollar playing the role of the armies of the past. She could see now why the keys were handled by the notaire: the owners did not want to have to meet with the crass foreigners who came to feast on the ruins of their past magnificence. And wasn't that precisely Amanda Fischbein's intent, though of course she wouldn't put it that way? Amanda, who was addicted to Masterpiece Theater, whose favorite word was "sophisticated", and who would if she could have insisted on an appearance by the lord of the manor, complete with silk scarf and children in sailor suits, as a provision of the lease?

About the landscape she felt no ambivalence. By the second time she went through the ritual of the opening of the shutters, she was conquered. From then on she spent as little time as possible in the house, which was easy as the good weather continued, and when she was there, kept enough of its windows open that she could fancy it as a massive ship sailing on a sea of green.

The next morning she went for a walk, starting from the back of the house, where, at the bottom of a flight of stone stairs, the arched entrance to the cellar stood locked on its mysteries. A narrow path climbed the steep butte right behind. At the top was an orchard (apricot trees?). She walked through it and found herself in a sun-flecked live oak wood. There the path branched in several directions, none of them well marked, as if the paths might be the work of deer instead of humans. She roamed around for a while, smelling plants and listening to birds. When she came out in the open the view was so arresting that she felt transported again. From the top of the butte, she could see even farther than from the top floor of the chateau: hills and valleys in every size and shape, each with its own pattern of field, chaparral, forest, village, fading to misty blue far far away, where mountains took serrated shapes. She wondered which of the plots of land around her belonged to the chateau, and whether the grape harvest was about to start, but as carefully as she scrutinized the landscape, she couldn't see any human in it to whom she could address her questions.

On her way back the cellar door was still mute, but another door was open, this one on the east side of the house. It was a low door leading to a space under the kitchen, probably the laundry room mentioned on the instruction sheet. The last key on the set must be for its lock. Franny peeped through the opening and was astonished to recognize the bakery lady. Dressed in her customary flowery skirt, loose short-sleeve blouse and head scarf, she was bent over a front-loading washer, retrieving wet sheets and placing them in a basket in slow, energy conserving movements.

"Bonjour!" said Franny softly.

Startled, the bakery lady straightened up.

"Oh! Madame," she blurted out, drying her hands on her skirt. She proceeded to apologize for the use of the washer, swearing in her broken French that she would be done right away. Franny assured her she was in no hurry, complimented her for the croissants, introduced herself. The bakery lady reciprocated by giving her name, first as "Madame Hamzaoui", then, with a little more prompting from Franny, as "Savia". It turned out that Savia, apart from her duties at the bakery, helped with the housekeeping at the chateau. She also did her own washing on the premises. She was the one who had brought the linens and croissants yesterday. She reiterated that she was very sorry about what had happened in New York, opining that the people who did that must have had very bad mothers. She was relieved to hear that Franny did not have any family in those buildings that had crashed, and asked if she needed anything washed. No, not yet, answered Franny, but she would take care of her own laundry anyway. And then, as Savia bent down to pick the basket of wet clothes, and as it looked very heavy, Franny moved to grab one of the handles, Savia protested, Franny insisted, and before long she was helping the bakery lady hang out the laundry on some lines strung across a patch of grass on the side of the house.

She had only vague memories of watching her grandmother hang laundry to dry, but now, doing it herself, she found it a very peaceful activity, meditative and sensual. There was something deeply satisfying about the way the wet sheets, twisted together in fantastic embraces in the basket, indolently let themselves be pried apart and lay on the arm with the cool heft of a pet boa constrictor; something thrilling about the way the taut plastic cord yielded under its load; something neat and timeless in the stretching and smoothing and pinning gestures. And then there was the clapping of the breeze, Savia's dark face playing hide and seek among the dazzling waves of fabric, the chlorophyll-like emanations of detergent, which didn't smell the same as in the US, Franny could swear: less sweet, more authentic. Putting clothes out on a line seemed so much more aesthetically appealing—not to mention more ecological—than stuffing a dryer stinking of burned gym shoes in a dark basement, that Franny resolved to turn it into one of her vacation rituals, which was just as well, as the laundry room turned out to be unequipped with a dryer.

In the afternoon she took a nap, then, as the temperature remained in the nineties, she drove to the next little town where the greengrocer had mentioned the amenity of a swimming pool. She was impressed by what she found: a brand new building, an olympic-sized basin with a retractable roof, a nicely landscaped garden. In the pool, a Scandinavian type was vainly trying to swim laps as French teenagers, under the indulgent eyes of the lifeguard, either lolled in the lanes with their arms resting on the edge of the pool or dive-bombed into the water without any regard for other swimmers. By giving up on the straight line, Franny managed to cool off and get some exercise, not to mention the small competitive pleasure of her superior adaptability.

There *were* hair dryers mounted on the walls in the locker rooms, but they turned out to be out of service—switched off for the summer, the attendant explained with a smirk, for one didn't need to dry one's hair in the summer, did they (except if you were a spoilt American, the smirk implied)? The pool was open to the public every day, this in a town with a population of no more than two thousand, none of them wealthy from the look of the houses. How did the French do it? How did they pay for the impeccable roads, the "mediathèques", the childcare centers, the swimming pools? A combination of high taxes and moderate military budget, probably.

After her swim, Franny had a "panaché"—equal parts of beer and a Seven-Up type of soda—at a café in town, and noticed that sitting on the terrace no longer frightened her, but on the contrary felt like the perfect thing to do at the end of an afternoon, even without a book to keep busy or give herself some countenance. Was she changing? Was there after all such a thing as a French *joie de vivre* and was it seeping into her?

That night, after failing several times to reach the Fischbeins, as the phone either sounded like it was transmitting a fax or was picked up by an answering machine, she had dinner at a white wrought-iron table that had materialized on the terrace of the chateau in her absence. Afterwards, a couple of glasses of wine having bolstered her optimism, she practiced a Chopin etude whose score had been left on the piano. She was not aware of the light having gone on behind the door under the staircase, but then again she had not looked at it all evening. She fell asleep pondering the meaning of the word "intimité", which seemed to mean "privacy" as well as "intimacy".

By the third day her routine was in place: walk in the morning (still no sighting of the gardener, only a pair of work gloves on the balustrade), and in the afternoon a nap, then a drive. There were a number of sightseeing attractions in the area, but Franny felt lazy. Besides, wasn't she already staying in a chateau, didn't she have a wine cellar on the premises, could she find any view more arresting than the ones that surrounded her? She did not want to be a spectator, but to belong. Food shopping seemed as legitimate a touristic activity as a guided tour of a cathedral.

But when she got to Saint Yves that afternoon, all the shops were still closed for lunch. On the village square, a young woman with a guitar and backpack was resting on the rim of the fountain, one of the second generation hippies, distinguished from their parents by their tattoos and piercing, who were integral to the Berkeley scene but whose presence here Franny found a little repellent. The phone booth, however, was free and looked in working order. It must be eight, nine in the morning in Cincinnati (six or seven hours behind?). Franny used the *télécarte* she had bought in Paris and was finally able to connect with Chuck and Amanda.

They were both overwrought, on the edge of hysteria, even Chuck, who was renowned among his employees for his unflappability. All transatlantic flights were still grounded, but even if they were to resume in the next few days, the Fischbeins couldn't think of taking a vacation abroad, not while bodies were still being brought out of the debris, not while they wrestled with the evidence that so much of the world hated Americans, not as long as the Fischbein children ran the risk of being traumatized. All they wanted was to cocoon with family and friends. All they managed to do was to watch TV. They had talked to the other anniversary guests, and they were all of the same mind. So what were Franny's plans, Amanda asked? (As if she had any of her own ... As if her arm hadn't been twisted into this absurd mission in the first place ...) Because if she decided to come back to the US right away, maybe it would be possible to get a partial refund from the owner? (And how was she supposed to come back? On a cargo ship?) Could she make inquiries with the notary on this point? (She would never dare. The lease surely forbade cancelling after the first day anyway.) After all, it was a case of force majeure, an act of God, well, no, actually it was the opposite of an act of God, but Franny understood. (What Franny understood was that even while it rained fire and pestilence, God was supposed to make an exception for Amanda Fischbein ...) Anyway, she was rambling, she was so upset she couldn't think straight. Look, Mayor Guiliani was at ground zero. He had such presence ... He could really pull people together ... He and Peter Jennings ... Maybe Amanda should put Chuck on? What did Chuck think? Chuck thought it was better to make no decision for the time being. They would see their way more clearly in a day or two. Could Franny hang tight till then? Yes, she could. (Indeed, she had every intention to ...)

The hippie was waiting for her turn when Franny came out of the phone booth. She was in fact American. Finally awake to the scope of the horror that had just befallen the world, Franny felt more sympathetic to the young woman. They struck up a conversation, where it transpired that Victoria Brown—that was how she introduced herself—was from New York, and had vainly tried for the last three days to have some money wired. Her bank had been housed in the World Trade Center, where her sister also worked, and she couldn't get hold of either. Silencing her misgivings about this too young, too spacey, too voluble stranger, and squashing her selfish wish to enjoy as long as she could the new, expansive canvas of her solitude, Franny ended up offering to shelter her for the night.

CHAPTER 7

▼

WINE, WOMEN AND SONGS

Let's now turn our attention to the elusive vicomte Degency, the man council-man Malefoi viewed as his arch political enemy—although the chatelain on his side was barely aware of the tobacconist's existence—and the double object, in his split personas as landlord and as groundskeeper, of guilty solicitude on the part of his American guest—a concern he was far from suspecting as in his experience, Americans were much too self-involved to pay attention to others unless they stood to profit by it. On September 16, 2001 around noon, Hughes Degency stood naked in the middle of a clearing rife with fennel and scotch-broom, against a background of oak, cedar and pine trees. At the edge of the clearing stood a tiny square stone house topped by a dilapidated round tile roof, its walls more voluminous than the space they encompassed, its only architectural features being a door in front, a window on one side, and a chimney on the other. Nearby there was another small stone building, this one of conical shape, like a prehis-toric rocket.

A passerby might have fancied he had come upon a nudist camp, but for the lack of bamboo curtain and recreational vehicles, or that sunstroke was causing him to hallucinate a bit of Greek Mythology, if it weren't for the blue jeans and white shirt thrown over a line stretched between the tiny house and the prehis-toric rocket, which was actually a well. And indeed there was something timeless about the bucolic scene, although in fact the chaparral had grown in the last thirty years over what used to be a sheep pasture, reclaimed by wilderness after cheap lamb from Australia made sheep raising a losing proposition, and before that an olive grove, decimated by the 1956 big freeze, and before that a rye field, until even the peasants demanded white bread, and at various times a battlefield between Gauls and Romans, Saracens and Franks, troops of the Pope and troops of the King, Catholics and Huguenots, Royalists and Revolutionaries, Wehrmacht and partisans, etc. etc., and at all times, due to its convenient distance from the village, a meeting point for clandestine trysts which not infrequently coupled members of the then warring parties. Love, war, economic Darwinism and sectarian insanity, a summary of mankind's tribulations inscribed in invisible ink on the smallest plot of land. And yet it was so peaceful....

Hughes drew the chain over the pulley until the bucket appeared above the rim of the well. The water was cold and dark from its subterranean slumber, but as he grabbed the bucket handle, a smile of sunlit stars broke over its surface. "Ouf!" he couldn't help crying as he upturned the bucket over his head, training the outpour on his shoulders, arms and legs. The now gray water, after running under the wooden drainage board on which he stood, was guided downhill by a pebble-lined ditch towards a wilderness of elder and bramble bushes where it would be safely re-absorbed into the earth, the soap in it being bio-degradable. Hughes had to repeat the rinsing operation a second time, then he stood in the sun to dry off, very unself-consciously happy for the time being.

It was something he had only recently learned, this luxury of sensation, the deliberate quieting of all his striving and worries in the absorption of the moment. In his previous executive incarnation, it would have been more than impossible, it would have been taboo. For there was a tacit understanding, developed first in prep classes, and reinforced ever afterwards in that straight and matter-of-course journey that carried you through the Ecole Nationale d'Administration to a high civil-servant post, that the perpetual buzz of over-exertion, over-extension, over-availability to all the intellectual currents and political winds and social issues, quite apart from the amount of work you actually produced, and overriding the banker hours, long weekends and five weeks of vacation, was the price to pay for your class distinction.

But even as a vintner, there were plenty of opportunities to fret, which compromised the rootedness of labor. It was lucky that Hughes had inherited a vineyard instead of a wheat or dairy farm, because at least he wasn't forced to engage in productivism, as wine grape production, in the case of wines that aspired to the Appellation Contrôlée, was limited by ministerial decree. So was the spacing of plants, the types of pruning allowed, the percentages of various varietals going into the blend, the amount of sugar that could be added to the must. You were spared the temptation to increase yield by pumping up the grapes with water or fertilizers, you could live with a certain amount of loss due to pests. If ever there had been a propitious framework for reasoned agriculture, this was it, a textbook example of a beneficial intervention of the State in the otherwise anarchic field of economics.

Still there were long-term issues, starting with a labor shortage. The Spaniards who used to flock to wine growing areas at harvest time now stayed home in their country made prosperous by adhesion to the European Union, and even the new generation of French Algerians wanted computer jobs. A number of vintners in the village had recently cast their lots with harvesting machines, but these shook the vines so much that they reduced their productive lives by half. In addition, they were going to kill one of the last communal, festive agricultural rituals, that of the *vendange*. It was that, more than anything else, that Hughes was resisting. Here again, the State had weighed in on the side of the angels, guaranteeing the RMI for any student, welfare recipient or unemployed worker who took part in the harvest. (Of course, citizens who were not growers were wondering why their taxes had to pay for the wages of farm workers. But Hughes had gone over his accounts, and he knew that if he were to offer the kind of money that could by itself entice ordinary people to camp for three weeks while doing backbreaking work, he would go under in one year.) However, on the eve of the first day of the grape harvest, with his one full-time farmhand convalescing from a gall-bladder operation at a State supported spa in the Massif Central, Hughes was still waiting for a response to the employment offer he had e-mailed to the ANPE.

The Syrah was certainly ready to be picked. Hughes had gone over his two separate Syrah plots that morning to test the grapes' sugar content with a refractometer, confirming the apparatus' verdict by popping the grapes between his fingers and licking the exposed flesh. In fact, he wondered why he had spent eighteen hundred francs on the gadget, the signs of ripeness were so clear, so instinctively grasped. In any case no scientific equipment existed yet to assess the quality of the tannins, so you still had to taste your grapes. As in so many farming supply purchases, the manufacturer's quest for profits had fed on the insecurity of the farmer as opposed to filling an actual need.

Hughes however was no Luddite, contrary to what Patrick Malefoi thought. He did object to machinery that was noisy, polluting or overkill. In all things these days he sought simplicity. But he was too well educated to be afraid of technology, provided it was environmentally responsible. For instance all summer he had submitted for analysis at the Cooperative the grape samples he had gathered from every one of his plots. The results had been tabulated into the Cooperative's database, to which he had access via the Internet on his home computer. From this data, instead of depending on the old estimation based on counting a hundred days after the first bloom, he could predict that the first Grenache would be ripe for picking in about a week, and the Mourvedre a few days after that. Of course, this assumed the absence of any major storm, which could throw all predictions to the winds. As to the weather forecast, it was still completely unreliable more than two days in advance. All the same, the computer maps and charts and columns of numbers provided a useful overview of the entire estate, a way for Hughes to keep his mind unencumbered–to a certain extent.

All water having evaporated from his body, and the midday sun starting to bake his rather sensitive skin, Hughes put on his clothes, leaving the shirt unbuttoned and with the sleeves rolled up to the elbows. He was a slender man of medium height with the spare musculature of someone who gets his work-out from physical labor, a narrow face with a straight nose and gray eyes rather close together, the vertical crease between them giving him a perpetually worried look. His hair, still damp, was of an indeterminate color, dark without being brown, slightly touched with gray. Standing in front of a small mirror hung from a nail wedged between the stones of the well, he drew a comb through it, parting it on one side and letting it fall over his forehead, the drying strands already springing back up, long in front, shorter at the nape, in a cut that had once been stylish but was now overgrown. He had not shaved in several days and wasn't going to bother now, a small compensation for the absence of a woman in his life.

He could have taken care of his present grooming needs in the dingy little bathroom attached to the chateau's laundry room, but it smelled of mildew, and he was reluctant to interfere any more than he really had to with his guests' privacy. Working in the basement office in the evening was bad enough. He had scared the little American the other night. But sometimes he found himself in the awkward position of having to retrieve one of his reference books from the upstairs bookshelves. He had so far managed to make his raids unobtrusive by picking times when the parking lot was empty of cars, but now that there was a car-less guest on the premises, it was going to be trickier. Slinking around his own house, that was what came of his attempts at "self-actualization"–or so Christiane would opine, putting verbal quote marks around the expression, which for his part he had never used, as if to imply its peculiar unfitness as a choice for her ex-husband, even though she had been busy self-actualizing for a number of years before the divorce, and was now determined to self-actualize their children, having just enrolled Héloise in a Waldorf school. When he had tried to oppose it, arguing that the Degencys had always gone to public schools (he realized this was not the most cogent argument, but he would have come up with better ones if she had been willing to listen), she had countered that he should be happy, as the school applied the philosophy of Rudolf Steiner dear to his own bio-dynamic leanings. At that point, trying to explain to her the difference between an interest in traditional methods of soil enrichment and a superstitious belief in the power of the phases of the moon would have just provided the kind of intellectual diversion she had so skillfully relied upon to get around him throughout their marriage, as he had understood much too late.

A rope hung over a second, newer pulley bolted into the arched roof of the well. Hughes pulled on it, retrieving a small cooler which he carried to a molded plastic patio table sitting under the pines on the side of the house. Then he went inside, emerging with a tray carrying a loaf of bread and some silverware. The cooler, opened, disgorged a bottle of wine, some cheese and other perishables that were kept cool just above the water at the bottom of the well. Hughes poured a glass of wine and raised it towards the sunlight. The color was fine, a purple red, intense yet limpid. The first and second nose confirmed his satisfaction. But it was the length and complexity of the mouth that pleased him the most. Overall, the wine came close to what he had had in mind during the many weeks of testing various blending formulas, and the whole year he had aged it in uncle Freddie's oak barrels—against the Cooperative's practice, whose enologist had accused him of trying to create a Bordeaux. To crown his achievement, this wine had just been granted the ECOCERT organic certification. He had been lucky, he knew, three years without any major infestation, no prefecture mandated chemical spraying, and hot, dry summers. In fact, he had had to work to maintain the acidity in this 2000 vintage, the fruit had been so ripe at harvest, as evidenced by the slight jammy taste. The goal, he reminded himself, was not to scientifically produce the same wine year after year, but to improvise from the given of each harvest a series of variations on a theme—to which you might as well give an anthropomorphic characterization: the one he was after was solid, sophisticated without being flashy, generous beyond an initial reserve, with a couple of eccentric surprises along the way, a sort of grit. In the French version of the Cooperative's web site, he could get away with calling it virile. In the English version, of course, it would be a matter of rounded tannins, black fruit aromas and subliminal oak notes.

He remembered the enology class at UC Davis, where under the guise of a minor concentration in wine management, he had played hooky from the drier subjects of international finance. Dr. Noble, his professor, had been intent on revolutionizing the language of wine appreciation, insisting on an "objective" identification of the various aromatic components of any wine as a safeguard against merely "hedonic" and "judgmental" descriptions. But as much fun as it had been to be able to point to a smell of pineapple or wet dog in a beverage made entirely of grapes, Hughes had never bought the underlying philosophy, in which he detected a mixture of scientism and priggishness, with unpleasant whiffs of market populism. As it turned out, the aroma wheel had been a very useful pedagogical tool in the development of a wine culture in the US, for which French winemakers could only be grateful. But now, as could have been expected, some American companies were using it to "create" wines through focus groups, demoting the vintner from the status of artist or craftsman to that of a commodity broker.

In any case, a purely aromatic analysis failed to capture the experience of a wine, which happened in time, each event in it being relative to other events and to the whole. It was like trying to describe a piece of music by mentioning that it contained a lot of E flats or quavers. What was needed was precisely something akin to musical notation, with its ability to plot on one graph combinations and evolutions occurring on several planes.

Hughes drained his glass, ate another piece of goat cheese. It struck him that the kind of notation he had just been envisioning would be useful to understand not only wine but people, by which he meant women. In the case of Christiane, he realized now that he has assured himself of her fitness as a partner by—so to speak—counting her E flats and quavers. His only excuse was that he had met her upon his return to France after two years on an American campus, where, in his memory, all the women were big, blonde and frumpy, with dazzling square teeth too much in evidence, and an abysmal lack of culture for university students—how else to account for the fact that none of them had ever heard of Céline (and he didn't mean Dion)? It seemed impossible to carry on a normal camaraderie with them, as a simple meeting for coffee became a "date", marked by a series of symbolic gestures that were all charged with sexual suspense: the initial greetings, the sharing of biographical details, the picking of the tab, the good night kiss, the follow-up call. A paint-by-number intimacy, devoid of wit or personality, the women reduced to eye-batting dolls, unwilling to exhibit their knowledge, to advance an opinion or to make a joke for fear of being threatening to the man. But then, in class the same women would monopolize the floor to whine against patriarchy in flat, self-righteous voices. It was schizophrenic. Strangest of all, neither side of their split personality jibed with his previous knowledge, acquired through movies and TV sitcoms and widely shared by his compatriots, of American women as castrating. Perhaps that was something that happened after marriage, although his few brief contacts with married couples in the US hadn't supported that view either. Many times on the streets of Davis, he remembered seeing pairs of older couples riding in those big wasteful cars, the men in front and the women in the back, like chattel. It did not suggest that the women were in control.

It was at a party at his parents where he had got a little drunk that Hughes first caught sight of Christiane: a girl with delicately bangled wrists and lustrous black French-braided hair, whose face, vaguely oriental from its high cheek-bones and taut eyelids, glowed with what looked like self-contained amusement. A girl who took the initiative to engage him in a conversation that ranged from the politics of Ronald Reagan to the films of Satyajit Ray, and who did not hesitate to disagree with him, teasingly, charmingly, on many points. A girl whose parents knew his parents, who was just completing a degree in social work, who could distract a crying child by performing magic tricks with sugar coated almonds. A girl whose lingerie soon proved as *soignée* as her tailored skirts and lacy blouses, whose ardor in bed matched the relish with which she relayed her latest bistro discovery. It had felt natural to marry her, as it had felt natural to take a director's post at the Credit Lyonnais. His days as a prodigal son thankfully over, he would never again have to preface any attempt at a witty remark with "Perhaps you have heard of …". In Paris, everyone was sure to have heard of whatever topic he brought up.

So what had he missed? To what pattern, woven through the notes he had found so compelling, had he been oblivious, in his relationship with Christiane as well as in his life? It was too hot, too sleepy a time of day to think about it. Besides, it hardly mattered. He was reconciled to his divorce and profoundly happy with his new vocation, for all its insecurity.

Leaning back in his chair with his arms behind his head, for a while he was only conscious of the sort of Morse code effected upon his eyelashes by the swaying of pine branches across the orb of the sun. High in the tree, a late cicada whirred intermittently, unaware of the approaching winter and the necessity it would soon be under to plead famine with the ant. Even though he spent nearly every minute of his life trying to ensure his family's sustenance, Hughes felt sympathetic to the musical insect, which represented the fanciful, exuberant, free-spirited aspirations of his soul. As Rousseau had said: "Le pays des chimères est le seul digne d'être habité". Hughes let himself fall into a daydream.

What a puzzle was the little American! First of all because she was so little, one meter sixty at the most, delicate but not fragile, the sound of her bare feet on the kitchen tiles above his head very neat, very decided, a preponderance of heel, but then a softer landing of the ball, and even a distinct patter of toes. Her French, remarkably good, a little formal perhaps, but much more fluent than what can be learned in school, her R's with a hint of roll, like Canadian French. Could she be Canadian? No, the group was supposed to be coming from California. Her face, the little he saw of it that first night under the porch light, both shy and intense, straight eyelashes over big dark eyes, a glitter of raindrops caught in them like butterflies in a net, a small mouth, the contour of the lower lip a little blurry, the tips of two pearly canines barely showing when she broke into a smile. So un-American a smile, it seemed to Hughes ...

It was remarkable how much you could learn about someone whose name you did not even know. As a case in point the way she had cleaned the kitchen showed that she was very tidy. Hughes was a little embarrassed by the state of the house at the time of her arrival, but the previous tenants had only left the day before, and Savia had been busy at the shop, her teenage helper having been stuck at home with a sick baby brother. All he had been able to do was to stow away the patio furniture and barbecue, as it was threatening to rain, then strip the beds and run the vacuum cleaner on the first floor, probably not very well, as housecleaning had never figured in his educational curriculum. Nor did it seem to generally figure in his tenants' training, although the terms of the lease specified that they were to clean up after themselves on pain of incurring an additional fee. But according to the notaire, the little American had not registered any protest. She had made do without sheets the first night and put things to order the very next morning. He had to admit that things might not have been so smooth if she had happened to be French.

He wondered how she had liked his special reserve wine, the first labeled bottle of which he had placed in the dining room as a welcome gift. All he could say was that she had drunk it all in a couple of days, as he had found the empty bottle in the recycling bin. As a Californian, she was probably a connoisseur. It would be interesting to know how the wine compared in her mind to her native Merlots and Cabernet Sauvignons. But satisfying his curiosity would require the awkwardness of introductions, which would lead to the further awkwardness of bringing to your guest's attention the fact that they were sleeping in your bed—more or less—while you camped out in the woods, and the worst awkwardness of making conversation with a foreigner who would no doubt have opinions about your culture just as you had opinions about theirs, opinions that were best left unspoken within a business context. No, as Hughes had determined upon first renting out the chateau for the summer after his divorce two years ago, the only way to handle it was to lie low, to interpose the notaire in his dealings with all his tenants.

What else did he know? That she took walks but did not take pictures, stopping to smell and touch things, seemingly content to let the land embrace her. Several times, upon rising from a row of vines, he had spotted her, at the top of the hill, in the garden, at her bedroom window, her face too distant for him to read its expression, but her body emanating a sort of wondering languor. That she read the *Monde*, a page of which the Mistral had blown off the terrace onto the lawn below; that she liked to swim, according to Guillaume, the greengrocer, who sold Hughes' organic figs and tomatoes; that she had been kind enough to help Savia with the laundry; that she ate meat, thank God, the aroma of her barbecue last night having reached him all the way into the basement; that she played the piano a little; that she smelled of Shalimar …

There he went again, making a list of E flats and quavers while completely ignorant of the chord progression! He had paid attention to her because she had been alone, and he had felt some concern for her enjoyment, given the recent events in New York. But now that other guests were arriving, he was free to return to his sheep—in other words his vineyard. As to the new woman, she was too young, too big, too giddy-looking to spark his interest.

In the distance, a church bell rang three times. It was still too hot to fix the dump-bed for the upcoming harvest, too early to go back to the office to check his e-mail for an answer to his ad. If worse came to worst, perhaps he could get Savia to help. She was from Ain-Tellout, a little village near Tlemcem where coincidentally Uncle Freddie had owned a winery until the end of the Algerian war, so she may be familiar with vineyard work, and she and Hacene needed the money. She might even bring her son Chérif along. That would make him miss school, but according to Savia, he was botching his studies anyway, which was not that surprising after what he had gone through. A few days of physical labor might actually be good for the kid. And while he harvested grapes, he wouldn't be defacing local landmarks.

With still a couple of hours to kill, Hughes went back inside to fetch his clarinet and set to work on Brahms' Sonata in F minor.

*   *   *   *

It was three in the afternoon, according to the distant church bells, still nap time, but Franny had to get out of the house, which huge as it was, suddenly felt cramped by the presence of the new guest. At least for once she didn't have to blame herself for her notorious inability to say no, because anyone under the current circumstances would have felt obliged to come to the help of a stranded fellow citizen. But she couldn't help wishing that she hadn't made that fatal trip to Saint Yves the day before, or alternately that the stranded fellow citizen had happened to be a little more subdued. What she had got instead was a cross between Dale Carnegie and Lucille Ball, to use the Valley girl's own phraseology. For a shower and a change of clothes had accomplished this metamorphosis of the fountain hippie. In a lemon strapless top and fuchsia capri pants, she had appeared ready to answer a casting call for Melrose Place. And indeed, during the conversation that took place that night on the terrace, after she had taken possession of the entire east wing, moving furniture around in a way that might not please the owner but that Franny was feign to object to as it at least promised to keep her at a safe distance, and after she had declined to partake of the steak with which Franny proposed to inaugurate the newly discovered barbecue, preferring instead to nibble on raw carrots and cucumber, and in between outbursts of anguish about the missing sister in New York, and philosophical affirmations that anything that happened was for the best, and homilies about the evils of carbohydrates and red meat, Franny had learned that Victoria was from Los Angeles (hadn't she said at first that she was from New York?), that she had until recently worked in a clothing store in Westwood where she had met a number of movie personalities, and that her long term goal was to buy a house in Malibu. In the middle of the night, Franny had been awakened by bumping and crashing noises, followed by muffled cries of pain. Her door had been cracked open, and in a small, contrite voice Victoria had whispered that the east wing was too spooky, and that if it was OK with Franny, she was moving to the room next door. At least she hadn't asked to climb into Franny's bed.

In the morning Victoria was her bubbly self again. By the time Franny came down for breakfast, she had managed to unearth several maps of the area and a complete set of touristic brochures which she had spread out on the kitchen counter and was now in the process of covering with red pen marks. She had also somehow found a small TV set and propped it precariously on one of the stools which she had dragged to the nearest outlet, partially obstructing the doorway.

She had soon turned the TV off, having found that it only had three available channels, all in black and white, not to mention in French. But she had not thought of putting it away. Franny was beginning to feel like a step-parent stuck with a particularly rowdy teenager when she noticed that Victoria had brewed some coffee and buttered some toast, obviously for the benefit of her host as her own diet forbade either. She gave up for the time being on reminding the young woman that she had only agreed to let her stay one night.

After breakfast they had driven to Saint Yves in a vain search for the soy and oat products that Victoria needed to survive. It was Sunday, and a dirge-like chorus floated out of the open church door onto the village square. Victoria expressed a wish to attend mass at a later date. "Oh! you're Catholic then?" Franny had asked, a little surprised. Somehow, the idea of a Catholic Valley girl struck her as odd. But then again, she knew nothing about Southern California, which might as well have been a different country as far as she was concerned. "Not really," answered Victoria, "but I am spiritual, you know. I mean, you can't lose by betting on God, see? Like, if He doesn't exist, you didn't have to pay for anything anyway, and if he does, then he can help you succeed." A valley girl quoting Blaise Pascal, that was even odder, although as it turned out, she thought that the argument for religion as a good bet originated with some guru of hers by the name of Scott Alexander.

Back at the chateau Victoria commandeered the phone, failing again to contact either her bank or her sister, although she managed to reach at least one other person, to whom she whispered excitedly at length in an English sprinkled with French words. (Franny meant to mention the high cost of international calls as soon as she got a chance.) Afterwards she set out on a systematic tour of the house, oohing and aahing at many of the decorative details. In particular, she drew Franny's attention to a couple of fireplaces, one of which, in white marble, with curved sides and a shell motif in the center of the mantle, Victoria declared to be Louis XV, the other one, red marble with carved sphinxes being of the Empire style according to her. Franny was amazed that her guest should exhibit such knowledge, especially as it validated her own confused memories. It transpired that among the young woman's clothing store acquaintances, there was a set designer for United Artists specializing in period movies. He had taken her around to antique stores and given her the basics of various styles. She had then studied on her own with a view of being hired by a studio. Her current trip was in fact partially motivated by business: she was scouting locations for a romantic comedy involving some French aristocrats, and she was starting to think that she had found just the right place. Franny couldn't quite see it. To her the house was too plain on the outside, lacking as it did battlements and turrets, and its interior decor was too decrepit and too much of a hodgepodge, although of course Holly-wood was probably capable of transforming it into a fairy tale palace. As they went from room to room, Victoria took photographs of the more interesting arti-facts, dragging furniture out of the way, removing paintings from the walls, clear-ing surfaces of their clutter of knickknacks. Each time she moved on, Franny would step in to put everything back in its place. This little pantomime had lasted for half an hour when Victoria seemed to finally realize that she was taxing her host's patience. "Oh! you don't have to do that, you know? As soon as I am done taking pictures, I am going to dust and vacuum and tidy up! I mean, this place can use a good cleaning, don't you think? Don't worry, I used to clean houses in Beverly Hills, I know how to take care of precious objects. Why don't you go rest for a while? You look, like, a little tired. I mean, this is your vacation, isn't it? You've got to let you motor cool down so you can charge better when you go back to work. Anyway I would love to repay your hospitality a little, you know? As my teacher says, you have to give in order to get." And she looked so well-meaning, so business-like in her ditzy way, that Franny had no choice but to let her do as she pleased. By the time Franny left the house, Victoria had indeed found a vacuum cleaner somewhere and was gliding it deftly along the second floor hallway. A scarf wrapped around her frizzy hair, a feather duster sticking out of her back pocket, she looked as if she did have a lot of housekeeping experience. At least she hadn't broken anything, for all her gawky, manic demeanor.

Cases of empty bottles were stacked in front of the cellar. They hadn't been there before as far as Franny could remember. Was the cellar staff bottling wine underground while the tourists frolicked upstairs? And how had the heavy cases been brought to the back of the house? Franny noticed for the first time the dirt road that wound down towards the bottom of the property along the edge of the pine woods. The cellar was definitely a place of business. Strange for it to be located right underneath this posh residence! Franny wondered if the cellar man-ager used the dirt road to drive back and forth between the chateau and his own house. That would explain why she had never seen his car in the lower parking lot. In any case, the chateau was turning out to be a pretty porous haven, for all its medieval walls and locked gates.

Franny climbed the steep butte behind the chateau, in which makeshift steps had been carved out of the dirt, held in place here by a flat stone, there by a con-venient root, a very minimalist construction in view of the surroundings. It worked, though, in a sort of appropriate technology way. In the apricot? orchard the leaves were crackling against each other. For the last two days there had been a steady wind, barely perceptible at ground level, but bending the tops of the taller trees. Higher still, the blue ether seemed to be singing. Was that the famous Mistral, the dry, cold wind that was reputed to drive people crazy? Here it was very mild, perhaps because of the big mountain chain that barred the horizon toward the North. It did not so much assault the land as play it like a giant harp … or was it a clarinet? Franny stood still, trying to separate faint reedy strains from the general plangency. The sound seemed to be coming from the woods on her right. She walked towards it, closing her eyes at intervals to concentrate her senses on hearing. It was hard to determine the sound's provenance, or even if it was more than an acoustic mirage. The whims of the Mistral would cause it to bounce about, and a second later it would be hushed by a fluster of dry leaves, or be mimicked by the trill of a bird. Walking along the edge of the woods, she found one of the myriads of deer trails that laced any piece of wild land in the area. The trail burrowed deep into the woods with a sort of purposefulness that looked human. Franny followed it. About two hundred feet from its starting point, sunlight broke through the oak branches. The clarinet sounds came from there. Padding quietly on the mossy path, Franny approached the clearing, focusing on a blue/white dot that floated in and out of the mass of green leaves. It was a man, standing in front of a stone hut, barefoot in plastic thongs, wearing jeans and an open shirt, playing Brahms's Sonata in F minor on an unaccompanied clarinet. He was reading the score on an actual music stand, tapping his foot to keep the tempo, stopping to wait his turn during the imaginary piano solos. Here in the middle of this wilderness, with the wind lifting the corners of the score, and under a shower of pine needles, he seemed as composed as if he had been playing at Davies Hall. He was actually very good.

In one of those coincidences that the mediatic bombardment of modern life make all too frequent, Franny was dimly conscious of having recently run into that very sonata. Suddenly, she remembered where: the piano part had been among a pile of scores in the music room at the chateau. In a flash, all the pieces of the puzzle fell into place. This was the landlord, the formerly rich man who had been reduced to renting out his own home, *and* it was the gardener, barely recognizable in the light of day, his hair lighter and less hirsute, his posture more erect, his silhouette slimmer looking without the bulk of the rain slicker, something even genteel in his rolled-up shirt sleeves. He was not at all the swarthy, gruff looking man she had barely glimpsed on her first night, except for the unshaven chin and the vertical crease between his eyebrows. And his name must be de Gency, not Degency. A French aristocrat! A hero for Victoria's screenplay! The dear girl would be tickled pink. But of course, Franny couldn't tell her. He obviously had no wish to mingle with his guests, and whatever his reasons, which may be quite other than those she could imagine, she had to respect his privacy, his *intimité* as he would say. She was about to turn around when something made him raise his eyes from the score. He frowned more visibly, as if worried or irritated. Then suddenly he saw her, and completely against her expectations, his face relaxed into a smile. He was lowering his clarinet, and seemed about to wave her over when a rude electronic beep broke the bucolic peace. Monsieur de Gency made an ambiguous gesture that might have been apologetic and retrieved a cell phone from his pocket. A second later he was striding towards the middle of the clearing, where the reception was probably better, seeming in his agitation to have completely forgotten about Franny. Unsure of the etiquette of the situation, she waited for a few seconds, but as he was absorbed in his phone conversation, she turned back the way she had come.

CHAPTER 8

▼

SI CE N'EST TOI, C'EST DONC TON FRÈRE

(If You're Not To Blame, Then Your Brother Must Be)

It was too typical. The only proper video arcade—not one of those sissy Internet cafés full of nerds playing Super Mario or worse doing searches for a school assignment—the only video arcade within doable range of this rotten hole was an hour away in a shopping center on the outskirts of Avignon, and the bus going there came only once in the afternoon, right in the middle of his geography class. And even then you had to walk like half a kilometer after the bus dumped you in the middle of nowhere like a sack of garbage, and if Chérif started to think about the hot pavement, and the chances of rabid dogs or gangs of thugs erupting from the out-of-control grass in the vacant lots on the sides of the road, he was going to get discouraged, and now that he had skipped class anyway, it would be too stupid to get hanged for it without at least getting himself a little fun. That he was going to get hanged for it, he had no doubt. Even if the teacher didn't notice his absence, someone else would see him hanging out at the bus stop or at the arcade, and they would rat on him to his parents like they had ratted on him for tagging that ruin of a wash-house that nobody even used. They had eyes behind their heads, those Marcels. In the Nine Three they would never have dared.

It was too unfair, being dragged away from his homies, not for goofing off or punking out (although he had to admit he had done plenty of the former and a little bit of the latter—not that they knew about it, mostly) but for doing the right thing for once. And was he asked for his opinion about the move? Noooo. The Father had laid down the law, as usual. Silent like the tomb, like you were supposed to become a man just by walking in his shadow, and then suddenly his mother was taking down the lace curtains. The Father could never get it into his head that this was not the old country, that people here had rights. After all, Chérif was fifteen, not five, and not a girl, like his sister. But if she hadn't wanted to go, Chérif could bet they wouldn't have left. The Father would have found another bakery to buy in the Nine Three, the girl was that willful, that cunning. As it turned out, she couldn't wait to get out of the project: she figured that once they lived in their own house, she would be allowed to have that puppy she had set her sights on. Chérif suspected her of even more devious motives. You could see the signs everywhere. Like that nickname Nanette, the outcome of her first attempts at pronouncing her real name, which she had adopted in preschool, and soon forced on the whole family by playing deaf to being called Yasmina. And like those yellow shorts. But the Father himself did not object. On the contrary, Nanette had been the only thing that could light up his face on those nights when he had come home more stony than ever after the adult education classes. And yet, it was Chérif that could have helped him, if he had just asked. It was too unfair.

So now he was stuck in this mud hole, without even one friend to skip classes with. The kids around here were just that: kids. OK, they wore the right baggy pants and Nike shoes, they played NTM on their portables, they peppered their talk with Verlan. But that was all show. They didn't have the edge that came from knowing what deals were going down in what stairwell, which dude was likely to pack a gun, how to act with the cops. Even the Arabs and the Blacks were peasants, their faces soft and lopsided looking, like big slow question marks. It was funny when you thought about it, that the place where you just happened to live could have more effect on how you looked than your ancestry. And here, everything lacked an edge: the roads petered out among the rocks and plants on each side, the shops were crammed to the rafters with an overflow of weird dusty crap, the buildings bulged and sagged. In his bedroom, the ceiling was supported by huge twisted beams with notches all over them that made them look like they had been hacked with a blunt axe by some mongoloid mainstreamed into carpentry class. Chérif had assumed this was a mark of his family's low caste, that they couldn't afford a house with proper flat ceilings and planed timber, until he had caught a glimpse of the very same kind of beams in the mayor's house.

Here, everything was slow and hot and confusing, and Chérif felt as if he didn't know who he was anymore. He had been trying to wrap his mind for two days around the fact that a guy like that Chemineau dude, with his good job at the nuclear plant and his doofus plaid shirt, could have come from the projects. He couldn't have been lying, he knew the place too well, and anyway what was in it for him to admit such a thing, now that he was a regular boogie? But how did you go from hanging out, being cool, wanting everything but having nothing, to grubbing away and having a little? From hating Babylon to being part of it? Chérif wouldn't have put it down this way in any of the rap songs he was forever trying to write, of course, but it wasn't the implied treason that flabbergasted him, not even the perspective of having to work to make the switch, but the possibility that Babylon might let you in. Chérif's whole attitude in life, the boredom, the uselessness, the anger turned into an art form, was predicated on the safe assumption that he had no future. If he was wrong, then some lifestyle adjustments might have to be made, like maybe cracking the books. But then, on top of boredom, he would have to face the risk of failure: one thing he knew for sure, and that was that he wasn't very smart. Over the years a couple of teachers had pretended to suggest otherwise, just because that's what they were told to do in teachers' school, but they couldn't fool him. Grammar made no sense to him, algebra–for all its Arabic origin–was like Chinese. Even in English he was no good. He did do convincing imitations of American rappers, contorting his mouth to form words he did not always understand, and never missed an opportunity to watch subtitled movies, although in this dump, all you got was dubbed (it was too ridiculous, the same bored voice for Denzel Washington and Bruce Willis, all the manly wrath toned down to mere peevishness). But the English teacher couldn't care less about a cool American accent, nor about all the gangster and consumer slang that by now had become part of French. What counted was to be able to memorize the past tense of irregular verbs and the poems of Wordsworth. No, the only way out of the projects was as a rapper or soccer player–and in his case, even those careers didn't look very promising. In short, he was fucked.

OK, so the father had found a way. Even after he had been laid off from the auto plant, he hadn't given up. He had gone to the ANPE, he had listened to them with his head bowed. He had got with the program: evening classes, apprenticeship, small business project, a low-interest loan. Chérif was sure it would go nowhere: they were just humoring him, this stony-faced man who barely spoke French. But on his mother's head, there he was, in his own bakery, making organic bread for the Gawris. He didn't look any happier, but with him you could never tell. And what did this make Chérif? A shopkeeper's son? Was he expected to become a baker himself, to be his father's heir? No way, not in a million years. If he had to work under the old guy, he would kill him within a week. They had nothing, nothing in common.

Chérif stepped onto the pavement to peer around the row of sycamores that masked the turn of the road. Still no bus. And now he had melted tar sticking to his sneakers, damn it. He was sweating too, in spite of the anti-perspirant. Plus he needed to take a piss, but there was too much traffic to go behind a tree. It would be his luck to whip out his thing just in time for a stupid girl to giggle at it from a passing car. It was funny, but in the project, where you were always surrounded by ten stories of windows, he had never felt such a lack of privacy. The people here were just too close, and even though they pretended not to pay attention, you could tell they thought they had a right to judge, especially if you were a newcomer, especially if you were the baker's son. The few other teenagers in the village tended to make themselves scarce. They must have secret hang-outs in the hills. But first Chérif would rather die than associate with those yokels, and second the hills were full of wild beasts, which meant they were also full of dudes with rifles, as the hunting season had just opened. They would probably as soon shoot him as shoot a boar. Even from the bus stop, he could hear random pops in the woods all around. It was a little scary.

What was taking so long? If the bus didn't show up soon, it wasn't going to be worth catching it. What Chérif needed right now to relax was a good set of inter-galactical battles. He had never liked the kind of games where you shot at human enemies, but with space aliens, you could let yourself go. That had been the problem with the World Trade attack: no matter how stunning, how brave, how good for Arab pride, it had been ultimately tainted by the fact that it had killed real people. Six days later, the excitement was gone. All the TV stations except CNN had stopped showing the clips of the planes crashing into the buildings. Now all the reports were about dead firefighters and rescue crews and grieving families. It was too depressing. Chérif had tried to imagine an improved version of the deed, one where the terrorists called the FBI right after takeoff to tell them to evacuate the buildings, where the planes made a stop to let out the passengers before continuing their mission. He couldn't work it out. Then he had tried to write a rap song where he would lay out the tragic contradictions in his feelings. But all his rhymes sounded trite. At school, at home, he had kept his mouth shut. Nobody would understand. He would only get in trouble, just like when he threw his brand new leather jacket on that jerk who had tried to immolate himself. Pulled into the principal's office, asked whether it was true he had stolen the kid's CD, the Father glowering, and his mother wringing her hands. The whole thing had been hushed up, and then three months later, a TV crew, looking for the race angle. OK, they may have mentioned something about his self-possession, but did they ask how it felt to see a classmate's face eaten by the flames, to smell the mixture of gasoline and burning flesh, to know you've got to do something otherwise the clown's death is gonna be pinned on you, and at the same time to be sure that you're dreaming? He had watched the clip they had put together for the evening news, and he had not recognized himself in the sullen midget they showed. No, it was no use trying to communicate. Nobody understood, not even himself.

He was throwing gravel at the bus shelter from twenty paces, trying to hit the X in the FedEx ad. No car had passed for the last few minutes. Between the plinks of stone against glass, all you could hear was the wind singing in the trees. Chérif felt himself straightening up, his lungs dilating with fresh air. Again he had this new sensation of being free from the prison of his thoughts, of merging into the landscape. "Je veux vivre simplement avec le calme comme essence," the line from the Akhenaton rap came to mind. To live simply with calm as an essence. Suddenly, he could feel it. In the past, he had dismissed Chill as an over-the-hill sellout. He admired the virtuosity of his language, but he thought his grooves were mushy, his message much too conciliatory. Yet he was a Moslem. In the wistful appeal of the phrase, Chérif sensed for the first time the call of faith, not as a pose, a challenge or an abdication, but as the thing in itself. He had just had time to swear that this year, no matter how his parents would object about its interfering with his studies, he was going to follow Ramadan, when the cops descended on him.

"Eh ben, ça t'amuse de démolir les édifices publics? Tu sais ce qu'il en dit, le code pénal?" (So, you think it's fun to destroy public buildings? You know what the penal code has to say about it?)

Chérif turned around as slowly as his beating heart would allow and was confronted with the telltale baby-blue shirts. They were two of them, the one who had spoken towering over Chérif about twenty centimeters away, the other's face visible over his shoulder, like an extra head. They were both smirking with fake indulgence. For a second, Chérif thought they were busting him for the George W Bush graffiti. In cases like this, all you could do to gain time was to plead ignorance.

"Quel édifice public?" (What public building?)

"L'arrêt d'autocar, p'tit malin! Tu crois qu'on t'a pas vu y jeter des pierres?" *(The bus stop, genius! You think we didn't see you throw stones at it?)*

"Pas des pierres, M'sieur l'agent. Juste des p'tits cailloux, pour me distraire en attendant le bus. Parce qu'il est drôlement en retard, le bus. Vous sauriez pas pourquoi, par hasard?" *(Not stones, officer. Only gravel, to pass the time while waiting for the bus. Because the bus is pretty late. You wouldn't happen to know why?)*

"Non mais, tu nous prends pour la RATP?" said the big one, who had a Parisian accent. "Et pis, même si le bus est en retard, c'est pas une excuse pour bousiller l'arrêt, que je sache." *(You got us confused with public transport agents! Anyway, even if the bus is late, that's no excuse to mess up the bus stop, is it?)*

"Mais je l'ai pas bousillé! Regardez, pas une nique dans le camion des FedEx!" *(But I didn't mess it up! Look, not a scratch on the FedEx truck!)*

"Pas d'histoire, on t'a bien choppé en flagrant déli de vandalisme. Et justement, on recherche un p'tit vandale qui a mis le feu à une voiture à Mirésol la nuit dernière. Ça serait pas toi, par hasard?" *(Don't bullshit us, we caught you red-handed in an act of vandalism. And as a matter of fact, we're looking for a vandal who set a car on fire in Miresol last night. It wouldn't be you, by any chance?)*

"Non, rien à faire, mes parents me laissent pas sortir le soir, vous pouvez leur demander." *(No way, my parents don't let me go out at night, you can ask them.)*

"Alors, c'est p'têt un de tes p'tits copains?" *(Well then, maybe it's one of your buddies?)* The Parisian cop had put a paw on Chérif's shoulder. He was leering at him, trying to intimidate him, just for the heck of it. That's how those teufs thought they could keep the Beurs in line. And here, in the boonies, far from any possibility of rescue by the members of one's gang, it had a better chance of working, Chérif realized. It made him mad. He couldn't just fold, but he couldn't swear at them either, because then they would have an excuse for hauling him off. Suddenly he had an idea.

"Ouais, comme il disait La Fontaine, si ce n'est toi c'est donc ton frère …" *(Sure, like La Fontaine said, if you are not to blame, then your brother must be …)*

"Qu'est-ce que tu dis, p'tit morveux?" *(What you saying, you little snot-face?)*

"Ou bien quelqu'un des tiens." *(Or else one of your kin.)*

The big cop's face had turned red. His grip was tightening on Chérif's shoulder. His partner on the other hand had burst out laughing.

"Peuchère! Laisse-le. Tu vois bien que c'est un bon petit, puisqu'il sait ses classiques par coeur." *(Dang it! Let him be. Can't you see he is a good kid, since he knows his classics by heart?)*

"Quels classiques?" *(What classics?)*

"Bé Le Loup et L'Agneau, voyons. Tu te rappelles pas? La raison du plus fort est toujours la meilleure …" he started quoting. *(The fable of The Wolf And The Lamb, of course. Don't you remember? Might makes right …)*

And then, out of nowhere, this tall woman with frizzy hair appeared on the scene, shouting in English.

"Leave the boy alone, you fascist! He hasn't done anything. And anyway he is with me." And she was pushing the big cop aside, grabbing Chérif's hand and pulling him against her like a mother would do.

"Qu'est-ce qu'elle veut celle-là?" *(What does the broad want?)* asked the big cop, turning to his partner for translation. He looked completely befuddled.

"Laisse tomber, te dis-je. Tu veux nous faire des escagaces avé l'ambassade américaine?" *(Just drop it, OK? Do you want to get us in trouble with the American embassy?)*

In his confusion, the Parisian cop had backed away a little. The other one was standing back with his arms crossed, obviously in no mood to intervene. Taking advantage of the lull, the big woman pulled Chérif forward, saying something that he did understand: "Let's go!"

Her car was parked twenty meters away, a tin can of a Peugeot 206 that in Chérif's imagination metamorphosed into a silver Porsche. They climbed in and pulled away with tires squealing. In the rear view window, the cops stood still like discarded tin soldiers. Man, this was fun, this was better than Battlestar Galactica.

"Hi, I'm Victoria!" gushed the big woman, as she ground the gear shifts. "What's your name?"

Chérif looked at her. She was really tall, with big shoulders and big boobs, a round face with red cheeks, her hair tied in two big fuzzy ponytails that gave her a look between goofy and sexy. It was weird to have been rescued by a chick, and even more so by an American, after what had happened last week. Chérif wondered if she was going to try and seduce him … but that would be too much luck for one day.

"Comment vous appelle?"

Chérif came to.

"Chérif. I speak English … a little."

"Sheriff? That's a nice name! Nice to meet you, Sheriff!" And she thrust out her hand in a big jerky gesture that nearly made the car veer off the road.

"Oh!" was all he could say at first, still in shock over the adventure, and a little worried about her driving. But this was the chance of a lifetime to practice his English and impress a grown woman, and he was determined to rise to the occasion.

"Why you come help me?" he ventured.

That was a good question, thought Victoria, one that, amazingly considering her utilitarian philosophy, she had not asked herself before springing into action. She had been driving towards Orange, having borrowed Franny's car under the pretext of going in search of tofu and rice cakes, but in fact to meet Heinrich, with whom she had finally managed to reconnect. She was bringing him a stack of polaroids she had taken of the appointments at the Chateau Degency. They had not yet made any concrete plan as to what they were going to do about them. The word theft had not even crossed Victoria's mind. All she knew was that the objects on those photographs must represent a lot of idle cash. And as everybody knew, idle cash was bad for free enterprise. Then all of a sudden, a hundred yards ahead, she had seen the two cops get out of their car and swagger over—well, not exactly swagger, French cops just did not have the height, the girth or the bullet-proof vests to achieve that effect—the two cops saunter over to where the kid was waiting for his bus and start harassing him. Her reaction had been immediate and unplanned: charge as hard as you can, her instinct had said, in the complete absence of a long term, mid-term or even short term goal.

She looked at him now. Cropped kinky hair, soulful eyes, full lips, skin tones duskier than hers. In the US, he would have passed for black, or perhaps Hispanic. But here, she realized, the racial landscape was different. The only people that counted as black were the one hundred percent Africans from Mali or Senegal. Once, within the context of a conversation she could not remember, she had laid her own claim to blackness, not that it meant anything to her, for Victoria was instinctively color blind, but simply because it was true: her maternal grandfather, in the one picture she had of him, had been as dark as Sidney Poitier. "Oh! tu exagères!" had been Ruth's surprising answer. The Basque guy, who took no end of pride in his own ethnicity, had for his part accused her of being a poseuse. People here were not trained to identify Blacks or Mexicans, only those they called interchangeably Algerians or Arabs, who looked nothing like the hooked-nosed Saudis and full-faced Iranians you ran into on Rodeo Drive. The kid in the passenger seat was probably one of those Algerians, which did not in any way affect the sympathy she felt for him. As to the origin of her sympathy, we are left to speculate, as Victoria did not pursue any further her reflections on the topic. It is true that the boy was handsome, but she couldn't have noticed that from a distance of a hundred yards. Besides, he looked younger than his age, a mere child in her eyes, too small to be of use to her either romantically or for business purposes. On the other hand, she had herself been a waif in L.A. at the time of the Rodney King riots, and had only recently experienced her own entanglements with law and order.

"Kill the pigs!" she joked in answer to his question. He laughed too at the familiar expression, and they gave each other a high five.

"So shall I take you home? Where do you live?"

"Saint Yves. At the ... I don't know the word ... boulangerie."

"Oh! You live in Saint Yves? That's where I am staying too. At the Chateau Degency. You know it?"

"Yes. My mother, she work there."

"Really? I haven't seen her. Do you want to drive up there now?"

"Not now, it's time for school. My mother is very ... en colère."

"You've been skipping school, uh? That's very bad. You've got to have discipline, you know, if you want to succeed." He could hardly believe it, but unless his English was even worse than he thought, the wild American broad who had basically flipped the cops was giving him the same line as his parents about the importance of school work. She looked at him, half-figs, half-grapes as the French say, while the car slowly swerved towards the left side of the road. Chérif gave the steering wheel a discrete tug before replying. The words that came out of his mouth astonished him. In French, he would never have been so bold.

"I know. I know. OK. An idea. You give me English lessons. Then I am good in school. I cut the grass, I babysit your children. OK?"

"Oh! I am so busy I wouldn't have the time to give you lessons. And I don't have any children. But I'll tell you what. There is another lady at the chateau, and I am sure she would love to help you. Why don't you come up tomorrow after school and I think we can arrange it. Do you have a bicycle or something? It's kind of far from the village."

Chérif had missed most of what she had said. But after a couple of repetitions, he understood that he was invited to come up to the chateau the next afternoon. Shortly thereafter, Victoria dropped him off at the lavoir and did a U turn in the direction of Orange, in the process autographing the pavement with a big loop of rubber. She hoped that Heinrich would wait for her, as she didn't have a cell phone and could not therefore inform him that she would be a little late. But she wasn't overly worried. She knew she was on the right track, and that everything was going to work out for the best. As to that kid she had just helped out of a tight spot, he illustrated the truth that you always received ten times what you gave. If he was too young to help with her plans, at least he could help keep Franny out of her hair. The girl moped too much anyway.

Chérif watched the car speed away, its boxy blue back still a sleek silver in his mind. He was going to take English lessons from a wild and sexy American chick, and who knew where it would lead … First of course, he was going to have to figure out a story to tell his mother.

CHAPTER 9

▼

Does She Dare To Eat A Grape?

(Ose-t-elle manger un raisin?)

Saint Yves, Tuesday September 18, 2001, about tea-time, to paraphrase Monty Python. What brings to the dispassionate observer's mind the opening sequence of *Life of Brian*, where the denizens of Palestine are shown to be blissfully unconcerned about the Messiah's imminent birth, is the extent to which, a mere week after the September 11 tragedy, the rest of the world was able to carry on its business—as it would have after a typhoon had killed ten thousand Bengalis. History turns on the stories we tell, so perhaps it is a valuable thought exercise to view the World Trade Center attack from a distance, on a par with forgotten natural disasters.

   Then again we could be accused of taking an easy refuge from the problems of the world in that little village in the Vaucluse, although honesty compels us to report that even there globalization is proceeding apace. And what about our cast of characters? A bunch of middle-class Californians? A French aristocrat? Why not a beggar child scratching a guitar on the streets of Lima? Why not an Ethiopian ex-prostitute starting a small tailoring business with a micro-loan from an NGO? (But why should we be anthropocentric? How about rabbits, or ants? It's been done.) Six billion life stories out there at any time, and all we have to offer is a bicultural romance? For romance is where we're headed, be forewarned.

A simple trick to ward off incipient depression consists of looking up at the sky. As it is, above Saint Yves, on September 18, 2001 around four PM, a lot is happening in that spacious blue vessel, still stirred, not shaken by the Mistral's fingers: a commercial jet, packed with 139 separate life-stories on a peanut and soda hiatus, visible only through its vapor trail; one of those new motorized kites, as noisy as a leaf blower, manned by a modern Icarus in goggles and kneepads; the black arrow of an Air Force Mirage, tearing the French sky in order to protect it, gone in less time than it takes to name it; ah! and more to our taste, a hawk riding the air currents, quiet and effortless, its sight of legendary sharpness. How lucky the hawk to be able to view the lay of the land from above, perchance to espy some of the people who interest us, and even to predict where their paths will next intersect …

Bingo! For who should be coming down the rocky path with that unmistakable combination of surefootedness and diffidence, in a floral print lavender dress and plain lavender espadrilles—both purchased this morning at the street market in Saint Yves—if it isn't our friend Franny, her nap schedule in disarray due to the continued presence at the chateau of that second-hand victim of terrorism who goes by the name of Victoria Brown? And whose bush hat should be poking above a row of grape vines a mere hundred feet in front of her, if not Hughes Degency's?

The last few days have brought the beginning of a tan to Franny's limbs in spite of meticulous applications of sunblock. In Berkeley, it is nearly always cool enough to wear pants and long sleeves, the best protection against holes in the ozone. Not here. Actually, although Franny is not aware of this, the tan is just what was needed to go with the lavender dress. Her cheeks too are glowing from wind and sunburn, and there are gold highlights in her umber hair. In short, she is a picture of health on a diminutive scale, the muscles in her arms and calves still defined after more than a week away from the gym. Still, her expression is less ecstatic than it has been. A cloud hangs on her forehead, distinct from the shadow created by her bangs. She is not sure why she feels dissatisfied, but it has nothing to do with the landscape, which she still finds entrancing. The uncertainty as to whether Chuck and Amanda will come may be a reason. She talked to them only an hour ago, and they were more coherent than last Saturday, but still undecided as to their plans. The sticking point now seems to be their unwillingness to leave their children behind. Unthinkingly, Franny suggested that they bring them. After all, it is as safe here as anywhere. The suggestion seemed to open a new vista in the Fischbeins' minds. They promised to call back tomorrow. If they come, Franny will have to get rid of Victoria, a task she is not looking forward to.

There is something poignant about the gypsy girl, for all her self-help energy. She seems adrift in the world, grasping at the feeble straws of her elusive sister and vague movie acquaintances. She has a great love of learning but lacks the educational framework that would give meaning to her scraps of knowledge. Her conversation is full of cliches, although her person is far from trite. Her very ignorance, of history (she did not realize that the Louis XV and Empire styles corresponded to different historical periods; to her they were like Ralph Lauren and Donna Karan, different designers), of geography (she had no idea where England stood as regards to France), of psychological or social nuances, is accompanied by–perhaps is the condition of–a complete absence of bigotry. Yesterday she managed to make friends with a local boy who needed a ride home. He is supposed to come to the chateau this evening to practice his English. Victoria would like Franny to join them because she is bilingual, and Franny is happy to oblige, although she hasn't had much dealings with teenagers, because as beautiful as the land here may be, and as attached as Franny thinks she is to her solitude, she is starting to suffer from a lack of human connection.

Apart from Victoria, the only people she has talked to in the last few days are Savia the bakery lady, whom she helped with another load of laundry yesterday afternoon, and Guillaume the greengrocer. As to Mr. De Gency, he has remained invisible, although signs of his presence are everywhere: the cases of bottles have been stowed away, the lawn below the terrace has been mowed, a tractor and its dump-bed attachment, along with two other cars, have been parked on and off in the lower court. Most tellingly, the cellar light was on last night. Franny is just now returning by a circuitous route from a walk up the hill behind the chateau, during which her steps led her as if by chance to the clearing where he was playing the clarinet two days ago. The clearing was empty, the hut was closed up. But through the one window, she had a glimpse of the music stand, an open sleeping bag on a cot still bearing a body's imprint, a white table with an empty wine bottle, a few objects on dim shelves. He lives in the hut, he gets water from that conical building, which turns out to be a well, but there is no trace of electric connection. A practically homeless life style! Does he drink? Is this what has caused his fall from grace? She is curious, but doesn't know what she would have done if she had run into him, and not just because it would have been awkward to account for her nosiness. Her very curiosity is suspicious to her.

She is at the point in life where one starts to draw conclusions from the patterns in one's emotional involvements. What Franny has concluded is that any man she takes an interest in will turn out to be what anyone but her would call a loser: writers with blocks, violinists with DTs, bipolar professors, philandering bosses. She has further figured out that what she assumed to be her spontaneous attraction to these men's gifts, intellectual, artistic or managerial, was in fact engineered over weeks, months, sometimes even years, by the men themselves in a game of seduction probably made all the more piquant by her obliviousness to it. Why men should bother trying to seduce her, she still can't fathom. She is not beautiful, or fun in that giddy exhibitionist way that can compensate for a lack of beauty; she is too self-contained, too honest, too intelligent to stroke men's egos. Why weak, needy, fickle men should precisely be the ones trying is even more of a mystery. At least it is easy to understand why the resulting relationships always end in disaster—usually with the man dumping her. In the last couple of years, she has tried to leave the field on which the battle of the sexes is fought: she has stayed away from parties, declined invitations to anything that might look like a date, given up on most political activism. But then the problem resurfaced at work.

Really, it's just as well that the landlord is playing invisible man. If she ran into him, she would have to be civil. And where Franny is concerned, mere civility can lead to the worst surrenders. In any case, even being civil might be difficult with a French aristocrat. Would he expect to be referred to by his title? Would he think he is condescending by chatting with a commoner? Franny's ancestors did not cross an ocean for her to defer to old world social superstitions.

Suddenly conscious of having been absorbed for some time in unhappy ruminations, Franny looks up toward the sky and sees a hawk gliding through the blue air, as if buoyed by a liquid medium. She remembers that last night she dreamed of floating down a river—one of her most sensual dreams. She stretches her arms and experiences the wind as a powerful current. The rocky path becomes a riverbed, the soft rayon billowing between her thighs has the feel of water. She is propelled downstream.

*   *   *   *

A random bolt of lightning during last week's storm struck a couple of plants in the Mourvèdre plot, bending a metal stake and severing several of the trellis' wires. The patch of blackened wood and shriveled leaves makes the otherwise perfect row look like a mouth with two rotten teeth. Hughes is surprised he did not notice the damage earlier. He has been watching this plot, the first planted under his direction, as a mother hen watches her newborn chicks. It was his idea to add the robust Mourvèdre to the other varietals planted on the property. He likes what it has done for his wine and wants to plant more of it. The problem is that he does not have any land to spare. The cherry orchard would do: it has full southern exposure and excellent drainage. But he can't bring himself to tear out venerable, beautifully pruned trees that still produce an abundance of fine fruit. Last year he thought he had a deal to buy nine hectares of fallow land. He would have planted part of it in Mourvèdre, the rest in Syrah, starting from scratch with row design, organic composting, then new plants that would be trained on trellises as opposed to the still common but less convenient *gobelet* pruning method. But at the last minute the SAFER inexplicably nixed the sale. Now a new opportunity has presented itself. Yesterday, while he was unloading his first Syrah at the Cooperative, he learned from Guillaume about a eighty year-old vigneron in Mirésol who has kept seven hectares of vineyard under his ownership for the sole purpose of maintaining his right to distill alcohol. The right will die with him, and his children have apparently no need for the land. Guillaume quietly suggested that Hughes pay the old man a visit. In retrospect, Hughes is puzzled by the greengrocer's oddly conspiratorial tone. He has an inkling, not for the first time since he settled in Saint Yves, that there are political currents moving under the village's unruffled surface.

But even if he convinces the Mirésol man to sell his land, how is he going to pay for it? Since his last purchase attempt, high-tech stocks have tanked, wiping out thirty percent of his investments—what was left of them. The recent terrorist attack is bound to make things worse. Now would be a good time to convert liquid assets into solid ones, but other pressing demands are weighing on his wallet: the barn needs a new roof, the inter-row plough has to be replaced, the chateau's shutters are rotting away, the plumbing in the east wing is a ticking bomb. Meanwhile, he still doesn't know what his share from the Cooperative for last year's harvest is going to amount to, or what profit he can expect to make from the object of his pride, the wine in his private cellar. How much will he need to borrow? How much will he be allowed to?

Getting a handle on his own business finances has been a humbling experience. And humility is a good thing, he reminds himself each time he has to struggle with his accounts, as he did last night. Hughes rues the arrogance he unwittingly displayed in the days when he could dictate loan conditions to Third World heads of state. How easy it seemed to estimate the cost of a development project, the value of the proposed collateral, the potential for future earnings, when each of these figures was in the billion Franc range. How righteous it felt to hector dignitaries from Cameroon or the Ivory Coast—men who often had gone to the same schools as Hughes—about waste and corruption. How sure he was to be a herald of progress, helping to bring water, roads, energy to the people from France's ex-colonies. Of course things turned out to be more complicated than that: lakes created by dams in tropical countries became breeding grounds for parasites, the construction of roads led to uncontrolled deforestation, fossil fuel consumption triggered global warming. Vast amounts of aid money were stashed in Swiss bank accounts, the underground economy prospered, the gap between rich and poor widened. Still, Hughes wanted to believe that his efforts had resulted in more good than bad. Now he isn't so sure.

He has lived much of his life out of a sense of noblesse oblige, part and parcel of his napoleonic ancestor's heritage, together with the real estate and investment portfolio. It was precisely because of this ethical heritage that he was so shocked by the revelations that his employer, the flower of French banking, State con-trolled Credit Lyonnais, at one point the biggest bank in the world, was in fact led by crooks, people who took bribes from Italian Mafiosi in exchange for a two billion dollar loan against non-existent collateral to purchase a Hollywood studio, and who then lied and cooked the books in order to facilitate privatization. The scandal has dealt a lethal blow to the ideal of the high civil servant as protector of the common good, the elite training ensuring the persistence of nobler values than mere money grubbing. It took over a year for Hughes to act on his disillu-sion, most of the soul searching happening below the level of his consciousness. One morning he was reviewing the week's appointments with his secretary, the next day he was the one taking Clarisse to the dentist. The straw that broke the camel's back had been comparatively trivial, as is often the case: an interoffice memo announcing a weekend wilderness retreat. (Wilderness? In France? Where? To teach the bank's managerial staff the laws of the jungle? The top executives at least had apparently no need for this kind of training.) American style corporate culture had arrived, and Hughes was a goner. Then within a few weeks, Uncle Freddie got sick. Hughes, who had until then only dabbled in the management of the vineyard, mostly to steer it towards organic methods, arrived in Saint Yves and immersed himself in viticulture, thinking of it as a temporary stint. It was Christiane's decision to serve him with divorce papers that cemented his choice of a new career.

A sound of crunching gravel uphill on the path, cool and even, like the gur-gling of a creek. It's the little American, walking bareheaded in this heat. He will mention the risk of sunstroke when she passes by, if she sees him. In the meantime he'd better make a note of the needed repair on the lightning-struck trellis. He squats lower to write in his day planner, his bush hat disappearing below the top of the vines.

*   *   *   *

She has gone too far and lost her bearings. The road back to the chateau should be somewhere on her left, on the other side of a line of trees, but she can't find the path that leads back to it. It would not occur to her to cut across fields as she is used to hiking in California, where wandering off the trails is an invitation to be stung by poison oak or bitten by rattlesnakes. What shall she do? Retrace her steps? She surveys her surroundings, a hand shielding her eyes. She needs to buy new sunglasses, hers having disappeared. Do they sell them in Saint Yves? At the quincaillerie, or the tobacconist's? It will give her an excuse to go into shops and talk to people. She should hurry back, to make it to the village before closing time. She is about to turn around when she notices a brown sunken patch in an otherwise green row of vines. What has happened there? Mildew, or the infamous phylloxera, which destroyed all the French vines a century or so ago and caused them to be replaced by American plants, so that when she thinks of it, she is really quite at home here? She stops in front of the row. She runs a hand through the luxuriant leaves. She notices how the vines have been pruned in such a way that the grape clusters hang free from the green vegetation, like pendant earrings. They are not as big as she would have expected. The grapes themselves are kind of small and tough looking, covered with a purple mist that might be chemical. Is it OK to taste one?

*   *   *   *

Oh! She is right there, on the other side of the row. He can see her bare legs in between two vine stocks, and a small hand with short nails closing in tentatively on a grape cluster. Well, he'd better make himself known, and he'd better do it gently, or she is going to think he is some kind of satyr. The scene at the cabanon the other day has probably already given her the idea. And God knows American women are afraid of sexual predators!

*   *   *   *

"Does she dare to eat a grape?"

"Ils sont trop verts, et bons pour des goujats!"

The response has escaped her before she took note of the language spoken to her, before she recognized the man smiling on the other side of the vine row like a tennis partner about to shake hands across the net. She is exhilarated by her own impromptu wit. He laughs, too, and they do shake hands. His hand is dry and calloused, its pressure brusque at first, then yielding for the briefest of moments. Even in this heat, his skin feels warmer than hers.

"Hughes Degency. We have met in passing."

"Je sais. Franny Laforet," she answers, determined somehow to pursue the conversation in French. After all, they are on his turf.

"Leforay?"

"Non, Laforet. Comme les arbres."

"Ah …" he says, looking pleased with himself. "I see that you know your La Fontaine."

"Et je vois que vous connaissez votre T S Eliot. Vous avez étudié en Angleterre?" she ventures, as his accent is more British than American.

"In the US. UC Davis. But not literature! You on the other hand must have majored in French. You have read the classical authors. So, a Master's degree at least. Let me think … a thesis on patriarchal structures in the tragedies of Corneille?"

"Pas du tout. Qui vous a donné cette idée? Mon sujet était quiproquo et contestation sociale dans le théatre du dix-huitième siècle. A UC Berkeley et à la Sorbonne."

"I see …" he says, and laughs again, but looks a little contrite. "You must have French connections, then."

"Mes ancêtres. Canadiens Français. Ils ont émigré dans le Maine, puis l'état de New York, et enfin la Californie. C'est là que je suis née. C'est là que j'habite. A Berkeley."

"And 'Franny'? A Salinger reference?"

"Un diminutif de Françoise. Mais personne ne m'appelle comme ça. C'est un nom trop dur, trop … autoritaire?"

"OK, then. Franny it is. It's true you don't look authoritarian. Stubborn, maybe …"

"Vous aussi vous êtes … comment dites-vous stubborn in French? Oh! All right, I see that I lost the language contest!"

She has been fidgeting with a grape leaf. But now, as she concedes to his superior linguistic skills, she paradoxically crosses her arms on her chest. He is tickled by this sign of instinctive defiance. Then he remembers being endeared by the same type of reaction on Christiane's part. A subliminal alarm goes off in his head. Does he enjoy power struggles with women? Does he set them up for a fight? Is that what wears them out? No, that's not quite right. But there is something there he should think about, later, when he isn't distracted by the need to respond.

"Don't worry. I will soon stumble too. But remember that the French have more occasions to speak English than you have to speak French."

"All the more reasons why we should speak French now."

"Next time we meet, I promise."

She looks up at him now, the thick straight lashes rising like a shade on eyes of melted chocolate. He realizes with relief that he's got what he was looking for: this attentive gaze, humorous and yielding all at once. He does not see any more to it than that, and he is right. But if Franny could see herself in a mirror just now, she might understand her appeal to feckless men: there is a fervid something in the brown luster of her eyes that could easily be taken either for maternal care or filial adoration—or both—or even naked lust, depending on the viewer's psychological quirks. If her genetic makeup had gifted her with blue eyes, she might have had a wholly different amorous career.

"And now in defense of my grapes. These are not quite ripe, in fact. But even when they are, they won't be very good to eat. They are used to give the wine more tannins."

"How come they are not yet ripe? I heard from the greengrocer that the harvest has started."

"Ah! yes, Guillaume," he muses, looking as if something is bothering him. Does he dislike the greengrocer? But then he adds: "He is a good friend of mine. Anyway, to answer your question, these grapes are called Mourvèdre. They ripen later than other varietals we grow around here."

"What other varietals?"

"Are you interested in viticulture?"

"I guess. I am interested in this place. It's very beautiful, but it's also somehow very comfortable. I feel quite at home."

"That's just how you should feel."

"Why?"

He shrugs, as if the answer was obvious, or as if he hadn't thought of one.

"Because of your French ancestors. Because you are my guest." As soon as he has referred to the nature of their relationship, he regrets it. She is probably going to bring up the missing bedding, the leaky faucet in the kitchen, the lack of a swimming pool, his forays into the cellar and laundry room, all details he already feels bad about. He was hoping for a freer exchange, as between equals. Thankfully, she makes nothing of the opportunity to complain about the lodgings. Did she already know that he is the owner of the property?

"About those varietals?"

"On this property, we also grow Grenache and Syrah, all red wine grapes."

"How can I tell the difference?"

"From the look of the leaves and the shape of the grapes."

"Would you show me?"

"Sure! If you don't mind walking some more. There is a Grenache plot over this hill."

She can tell he is pleased with her request. For the first time since they started talking, his face is free from a certain brooding look. She notices that his eyes are an even gray, happy without a fleck of flirtatiousness or condescension, that he has shaved. She starts moving towards the path.

He can tell that she is actually interested in learning about grapes, and not just humoring him. He had barely assented to her request when she started moving towards the path. From the back, he can see that she has a lovely figure, perfectly proportioned to her height. Those rounded shoulders and calves look like they were made for farm work. Her French blood no doubt. He follows the trail of Shalimar released by her perspiration.

They meet at the end of the row and fall in step quite naturally. He spends the rest of the afternoon showing her around, expounding the tenets of reasoned agriculture, talking about mechanical weeding and *bouillie bordelaise* and pest control through sexual confusion. She reminisces about the summers spent on her grandmother's farm in Quebec, feeding the ducks and gathering chamomile. He tells her about his plans to purchase more land, about his success in convincing Cooperative members to take advantage of the subsidies granted by the government to farmers going organic. She tells him about the Seattle march, about the school nutrition program started by Alice Waters. He quotes from *The Age of Innocence*, she from the *Rêveries d'un promeneur solitaire*. They find themselves in complete agreement about the need to protect the environment, to preserve traditions when they have proven useful, to question the mad rush into the future, to nurture beauty and joy. In fact, in spite of the divides of nationality, gender and class, it is remarkable how much they have in common intellectually, including the belief in the importance of intellectual affinities.

To the more subtle aspects of their interaction: the tendency of their shoulders to lean towards each other, the touch of Hughes's finger on her cheek as he brushes a strand of windblown hair away from her mouth, the messages of trust and diffidence alternately sent by Franny's eyelashes, they deliberately pay little attention, because both of them are past the age when these small tokens of sexual attraction could pass for momentous, and even more to the point because in a few days Franny will be gone. And of course, they each have their reasons for not falling in love. The possibility of a "fling" is in neither of their play-books. All the same, sexual attraction creates its own subterranean channels, while other bits of body language, biographical details, unexpected retorts, marked evasions, are passively recorded to be later fitted into a gestalt of the other person.

To Hughes, the revelation of Franny's French ancestry has irrationally acted as a palliative to her American-ness. (He would be the first to see his relief as irrational, if he stopped to think about it. He is not the kind of racist that would assign any cultural agency to genes.) More than her literary references and environmental convictions, her family tree has led him to be open with her, to see her as on his side in the many-pronged battle he is mentally waging against a tentacular enemy that you could call greed, vulgarity, injustice, aggression, humorlessness, ignorance, or economic neo-liberalism, cultural imperialism, moral relativism, or simply globalization. Franny for her part has laid to rest her imaginings of the landlord as a pathetic, possibly alcoholic character and at the same time as a haughty nobleman. He is articulate, courteous, earnest, qualities that don't depend on a title. But other fears are just waiting to sprout. She has taken note of his possibly misogynistic guess about the subject of her Master's thesis, and of his choice of a quote from Edith Wharton, which concerned the desire of Americans to get away from their pleasure even faster than they want to get to them.

Interestingly, in their quasi-unconscious mutual exploration and testing, they have stayed away from the topic of music. For obscure and differing reasons, neither one of them wishes to bring up the memory of their musical encounter in the clearing.

By the time they part in the lower courtyard, Franny has agreed to meet Hughes on the same spot at seven AM the next morning. The harvest has indeed started, and Hughes' team is short-staffed. What better way to sink one's teeth into the land than to work on it? It will be great fun, at least for a day. They say goodbye simply, relaxed in the knowledge that they will see more of each other and that it will not have to mean anything.

CHAPTER 10

▼

CHACUN CHEZ SOI

(A Man's Home Is His Castle)

It all started on Monday afternoon, when he turned the front door knob, and the door, unaccountably, did not budge. No, who is he kidding, it started much before, it was always there, from the minute he said yes to the mayor on that cold November morning and looked back at his bride in her hand-me-down, unseasonably low-cut dress, her jaw bravely set against her teeth's urge to chatter, her freckles, in the surrounding whiteness, seeming to detach themselves from the surface of her skin to float up tremulously toward him. Behind her were the two sets of parents: her mother, her hair sprayed for a day, in square heels, her big plastic purse dangling at arm's length, her face closed in brute endurance; her father, an alcoholic blur; his mother, in pearls and black stockings, looking very much like the prosperous matron she was destined to grow into, and had after all nearly managed to become, but for her abstracted, pathologically shy air; and his father, debonair and wistful, the air of someone who has seen it all, as he had. Beyond them, the other relatives, their gaze likewise noncommittal. The wedding, for all that it required their presence, was to be the first leap of Gérard and Pierrette's escape from them, from the tawdriness, the dysfunctions, the anxiety, the despair. And until last Monday, Gérard thought that they had succeeded. His peripatetic job had helped keep the families at a distance. A decent salary, spacious housing and three bright, well-behaved children had done the rest.

But you never escape from despair. How else can he explain that after twenty-five years of safe, contented predictability, he should react so strongly to the small disruption of his wife's temporary absence two days in a row when he came home from work? On both Monday and Tuesday, Pierrette showed up within half an hour of his own return, aglow with strange energy, and was so prompt with the inquiries about his day that he never managed to ask about hers. As to reproaching her for her tardiness, it was out of the question: there has never been an explicit agreement that she would be home every day to greet him. It was just that she had always been. So is it any wonder that he read the direst omens in her sudden change of behavior? At any rate he has been able to think of little else today, even as yet another inexplicable goof at the power plant demanded his full attention. This time, it's a crack in the welding of a spent fuel container, discovered by the safety inspectors at the Cruas depot, through which the container was transiting by train on its way to the treatment plant at La Hague. There has been no significant radioactive leak, but that did not stop the Cruas guy from chewing him out on the phone for half an hour. After the brouhaha of a few years ago over the repeated contamination of railroad equipment by the nuclear waste it transported: the parliamentary debates, the interministerial commission, the enactment of a new law, a new safety agency put into place, and Greenpeace activists throwing themselves in front of trains, the last thing Gérard needed was for one of his forklift operators to drop a container, and then to load it on the boxcar without checking its integrity. For that is what must have happened, although no one at the plant will cop to it. With such sloppy workers, who needs terrorists? Because of the new requirements for transparency, the incident will have to be officially reported. Which means that tomorrow, Gérard will have to face the plant director, who, in turn, will have to face a roomful of barking reporters reassigned from the coverage of more exciting disasters. And of course some of the media will suggest that privatizing EDF would put an end to such incompetent handling. It would make Gérard laugh, if he was in the mood for it.

How did he always know that it would someday come to this: his wife, bored with her married life, frolicking somewhere while he is at work and not telling him, preparing her exit towards greener pastures? For today is Wednesday, and again she is absent. He can tell she's been away all day, because this morning he left a love note on her computer keyboard (something he admits he hadn't done in a very long time), and when he came home just now, it was still there, unopened. If she had been engaged in some legitimate activity, such as shopping (but surely not three days in a row), or even volunteering at some local organization, wouldn't she have told him? He might not have liked it: he is so used to her constant presence that without it he feels as if he had inadvertently entered the wrong house, as in the nightmare he used to have as a small boy daunted by the multitude of identical doors in the housing project. But he would never have forbidden her to continue. One thing he promised himself not to emulate was his father's tyranny.

He can see now that all his efforts to keep her happy, and even to help her feel independent, were just a desperate bid to delay the inevitable. He is not thinking of things like a two-story detached house, an American-sized fridge with ice cube dispenser, a new washer every five years, a DVD player, a gold and platinum watch band. No, he is not as dense as his father, who confused his comfort and pride with the desires of his wife. But what about the cycle exerciser, the programmable embroidery machine, the guitar, the English tapes, all the way to her own DSL line? Those were for her and her only. He always saw women as more than wives and mothers. After all, he has three older sisters, each one more ambitious, more extroverted, more ornery than any man he knows. (This is in itself another mystery. How did a couple consisting of a despot and a wallflower raise such independent daughters?) He has intuited, along the years, that Pierrette's life, uprooted every few years by his job transfers, must be lonely in spite of his love and the bustle of three children, and he has tried to compensate for this drawback by encouraging her to develop her own interests. As to the sticky issue of her financial dependency, given their agreement before the wedding that theirs would be a traditional family, meaning that she would never work, he again has been more tactful than his father: instead of granting her a weekly allowance, with its demeaning undertones of perpetual childhood, he has put her in charge of the whole family budget. And she has proved remarkably competent at it, for all her lack of formal education. She is a masterful bargain hunter and a skillful investor: their little nest egg has grown to the point where they have nearly enough for the down payment on their own home. His gifts on the other hand have met with mixed success. Pierrette does speak English, or rather she reads it, as attested by the shelves of British and American detective novels she orders on Amazon.com. Her linguistic skills have helped the children's education. And she does keep in shape, still wearing the size thirty-eight of her wedding day. But other pastimes have fallen by the wayside after a while, as could perhaps be expected of activities that are not shared with anyone.

Frankly, Gérard had been hoping that this would be the fate of her current infatuation with the Internet. Many times over the last few months, she has gotten up from the couch during the commercial break between two TV programs and when she failed to return after an interval amply sufficient for the toilette of the most finicky woman, he has gone in search of her, only to find her glued to her computer. He has felt a little abandoned, watching TV by himself, but has been too considerate to mention it. Now he realizes he may unwittingly have loaded the gun that is going to kill their marriage: she may have joined a dating chat room, she may have started an e-mail romance, and now she's decided to carry it out in the flesh. It will be some middle-aged playboy with a sports car and plenty of cash, who will spirit her to one of those exotic places that Gérard has been too much of a stick-in-the-mud to propose as a vacation destination. And then the cad will abandon her, poor innocent girl that she is, unused to the wiles of men. The DSL line will have turned out to be an attractive nuisance, and she would have a right to sue him for negligence, the way people, under the sway of American practices, are starting to do when their kids fall into the neighbors' swimming pool. Oh! it's no use trying to be facetious. He can't bear the thought of living without her.

He is sitting on his usual half of the couch, as though she were still sharing it with him. But the TV is off, the stereo is off, the computer is off. The newspaper on the coffee table is still folded. Gros Bébé is lying on the rug at a distance, its slobbering chin resting on its paws, its hind slightly raised, its eyes blinking in alarm at its master, as if it wasn't sure it recognized him, as if it was considering making its own getaway. Chloé is not back from school. The alabaster clock on the dresser is ticking away, the gold-plated sun with a face at the end of its pendulum swinging recklessly between the two fluted columns as if eager to dash its own brains. The sound, dainty as it is, fills the hushed room like a roar.

A memory stirs: he is four or five years old and the front door has just slammed. From his refuge under the dining room table, he caught a glimpse of his mother leaving, her face red and puffy, a coat hastily thrown over her nightgown. She is gone, and he knows it's forever, even though his sisters, whispering in a corner, won't tell him anything. Only the alabaster clock talks to him, and it says: bad boy, bad boy. Later that day she comes back, cooks dinner as if nothing had happened. He will never try to learn what it was about. All his life, he has deliberately built a containment dome over the radioactive material of his early years, pouring a layer of concrete on each new episode likely to contaminate his ideal vision of family life. And mostly, it has seemed a healthy alternative to his sisters' tortured psychoanalytical probing. What if he had been wrong? What if the buried anxiety and despair had been building up to critical mass, what if the dysfunctions were about to blow up in his face?

Other shards of the past prick his consciousness: his mother's bare legs in her high heel shoes, that winter when ten centimeters of snow clung to the ground for weeks. She couldn't afford nylon stockings, and fashion prohibited wool socks in rubber boots. The children on the other hand were warmly clothed. The fit his father threw when she ordered a washing machine, the first purchase she made without consulting him. She never understood how poor they were, having come from a well-to-do if delinquent family. But in the end they had been able to pay for the snazzy appliance, and the arthritis in her hands had improved. His father's absence for two years while he worked towards the engineering degree that was to wrench his family from blue collar abjection. And then, as soon as he had stepped on the lowest rung of the middle class, his Saturday escapades, explained as over-time work, later revealed to have been illicit rendez-vous. And all along, the imperiousness, the sarcasm, the tantrums, alternating with sickly sweet demon-strations of love. And his mother, as the children grew and passed her in knowl-edge, sinking ever deeper into abstraction, suffering her husband's touch with passive revulsion, making more and more extravagant purchases. She never did leave him, but she did worse: after he died, she told her children that she had hated him, tried to get rid of everything they had owned together, and moved to a condo in a town far away. The only way her children could hang on to a few scraps of their heritage was to buy them from her. This is how the alabaster clock has landed in Gérard's hands. She died a few years ago, to everyone's secret relief. What was it that they feared so? And why did her death affect them much less than their father's, whom they still mourn, for all his obvious guilt?

These are questions Gérard could swear he never asked himself until three days ago. He had set up a mausoleum of filial respect in his mind, locked it, and thrown the key away. His innate vigilance had seemed to be entirely channeled towards the prevention of nuclear accidents. But all along, he must have had a split self: one trying to prove that his parents' type of marriage could work, the other one alive to all the signs that it didn't. He cringes, thinking of his own con-descension towards his less educated wife, his surprise–a pride mixed with unavowable pain–at her financial wizardry, her ease with computer software, her mastery of English that exceeds his own, even though reading reports from Amer-ican nuclear facilities is part of his work. He remembers his own misogynistic sar-casm, and her often passive acceptance of his caresses, the even temper he has never seen fit to question, not even when it edged into sullenness, as it did occa-sionally: it was so much easier to attribute her mood swings to "that time of the month" than to ask her what she felt.

Most maddeningly, he wonders how they came to the decision that she would be a stay-at-home wife, at a time when that choice was already becoming obso-lete. He is sure that he did not impose it. She had her own fears of going out into a world she had not been prepared for. And there is no denying that her presence at home has benefited the children's education. They have all been at the top of their class, and are on their way to solid white collar careers. But what toll has her constant devotion to others taken on her own sense of individuality? And how is she going to adapt to an empty nest? Is this what her desertion is all about?

He has never been sure how the decision was arrived at in his parents' case. One of his sisters claims that their mother had wanted to work, that it was their father who had forbidden it out of jealousy. Another recalls a conversation she had with both parents towards the end of their father's life, when her mother admitted that the reverse was true. And in fact, the sister argues, the latter makes more sense. It has always been common for working class wives to have a job. It was in the middle class that the housewife model long prevailed. Whatever the case may be, their father took explicit pride in being able to support a wife and four kids. It was part of his dream of social respectability. But what was their mother's share of the bargain? It is impossible to trust her account of it, her confessional bouts, spurts of lurid non-sequiturs erupting without warning out of her normal preoccupied daze, having had little anchoring in objective facts or sober introspection. So what is to be made of her growing resentment as she aged, of her progressive lapse into childish egotism from the self-sacrifice of the early days, and of their father's concurrent blossoming into a generous, indulgent, undemanding man? Was it just her, was it just him, were they just the product of their times? How do their lives bear on Gérard and Pierrette's? Of her parents, he can't even begin to think.

He has gone over the entire house another time, looking for clues of her whereabouts. He has visited every bathroom, opened every closet door. Every object is where it belongs, but it is as if he recognized nothing, as if nothing was his, or hers, or their children's, as if they had all been impostors in their own lives, as if the scam had been discovered, the evidence seized, and he was about to be taken away into an exile from which he would never return. It occurs to him to leave the house for a while, go for a run, mow the lawn, in the superstitious hope that next time he turns the front door knob, the door will open, meaning that the door is unlocked, meaning that she is home, and all his thoughts of the last three days will magically vanish. But he can't rouse himself from the couch, where he has landed again in his distress and where he is sitting so rigidly that his bones seem about to snap.

A car is approaching, it turns into the cul-de-sac, it hiccups over the bump in their driveway, its engine dies with a familiar sigh. It is hers. He hears the key turn in the lock, her step, springy over the tile floor. She is looking down at him, her happy expression turning into alarm. He can see on her face the echo of his own disintegration. She freezes, her freckles disappear in her sudden pallor. He realizes in a flash that her reaction is in no way compounded of guilt, that what she is afraid of is what she has always feared without ever mentioning it: that there has been an accident at the plant, that he has been irradiated. He gets up to reassure her, and falls into her arms crying, which of course only ratchets up her panic.

It takes him a little while to clear her confusion, and then it's her time to explain. She has been bored at home, has felt that she was getting addicted to the Internet, has been thinking of a way to get some air and meet people. So last Sunday she answered an ANPE ad for harvest labor. She has been picking grapes for three days at the Chateau Degency, just outside the village. The work is to go on for the next three weeks, and even though it is backbreaking, she is thoroughly enjoying it. She hadn't wanted to tell Gérard until she felt sure that it wasn't just a whim. She knows how he despises physical labor, and that they don't really need the money. But she would like to continue anyway. Her boss might even need her after the harvest to help bottle the wine in his cellar. And really wine-making is not dirty work, her boss is a vicomte and he picks grapes right along with the rest of them, and you should see what care he takes, how proud he is of his crop. There follows a series of pointed questions on Gérard's part about the age, marital status, physical appearance and other qualities of the Vicomte Degency. But Pierrette assures him that he is not her type, besides his American girlfriend is taking part in the harvest, and they seem very much in love, it is a pleasure to watch. Plus they tend to speak English with each other, and it's contagious. So they are all "practicing the language of Shakespeare while handling the grape shears", as another worker by the name of Guillaume put it. There's going to be a dinner to celebrate the end of the Syrah harvest on Saturday night, and Gérard is invited. He is so relieved by her innocent account, and even more by the way she has thrown her arms about his neck and is leaning into him with lusty abandon, that he consents to everything: the prospect of her continued desertion of their home, her working for money, the stigma of manual labor, and even the Saturday dinner, the ultimate sacrifice for a man who is so averse to going out in public that in a more psychiatrically inclined culture, he would be diagnosed as agoraphobic.

Later that night, he is uncharacteriscally moved to confess all the fears, regrets, questions that have plagued him for the last few days. She pooh-poohs them all in her usual good-natured way while happily registering the evidence that he is not taking her for granted. She responds to his caresses with renewed passion.

CHAPTER 11

▼

LA PAROLE EST D'OR

(Speech is Golden)

How reliable is the information conveyed in a face? Determined as we may be to resist stereotypes, such as associating fairness of skin with fairness of character, thick lips with sensuality, or a high forehead with intelligence, we can't help reading signs there. Sociobiologists, those armchair Darwinists, argue that once upon a time our survival depended on our ability to interpret faces. And sometimes it still does. But what are we supposed to do the rest of the time, when the only danger is the risk of being disappointed? Do we "trust our gut"? That might be dangerous or unfair, as our "gut" is likely to be full of prejudices. Do we reserve judgement until we've had a chance to observe a person's actual behavior? But leaving aside the possibility of the observer affecting the observed–the "it's only with you that I act this way" syndrome–how much observation is necessary to balance our first impressions? And how do we avoid getting hopelessly entangled with the subject of our inquiry in the meantime?

At thirty seven, as could be expected, Franny had been disappointed many times by her fellow human beings. Although she was reluctant to admit the extent of her disenchantment, negative thoughts not being held in high regard in her culture, at times she felt that she had been mostly disappointed, and she often blamed herself for having failed to trust her first impressions. At other times she blamed herself for having trusted them too much. So it was with a mixture of pleasure and wariness that, protected by the near total obscurity of a country road late at night, as well as by Hughes' absorption in his driving, she examined his profile from the passenger seat of his ancient, well-maintained Mercedes.

He had been in her sight almost constantly for the last few days, but always in action, and always among other people. What she had caught during that time was a range of expressions (grateful, protective, stoical, contented, teasing …) that overrode his normal air of preoccupation according to the circumstances—expressions mostly conveyed by his steady gray eyes, and very well suited to them. She hadn't had time to consider his other features, a task she now undertook in earnest.

His nose was fine with her, straight but for the hint of a bump without which no French nose seemed to be complete, and well fleshed out on its entire length, from the bridge to the barely flared nostrils. It was not an aristocratic nose, thankfully, but a simple instrument of temperate sensuality. His mouth was narrow and pale, mostly defined by a shadow of mild pressure along the line where the lips met. It might have been grim without the twist of something ironic or thoughtful in its upturned corners. His forehead was high under the shock of dun hair. His chin was long but rounded. There were indentations around his temples and in the hollow of his cheeks that made his face look both resolute and fragile, a face whose handsomeness needed to be well fed. It looked as if there had been some lapses in this area over the last couple of years, which was how long he had been divorced. He had two daughters, who lived with their mother most of the time, an arrangement he seemed to find normal.

All in all, it was a face she instinctively liked. She felt the same way about his general demeanor, which was manly, albeit in a more subdued manner than she was used to: his shoulders did not roll, his elbows did not swing, he walked with his knees close together and drove with both hands on the steering wheel. He did not storm, nor did he indulge in theatrical mellowness. He occupied little space and appeared unself-conscious. Yet he emanated a definite authority and seemed at ease with everyone, from his Algerian housekeeper to the old peasant they had just gone to meet in Mirésol, from his buddy Guillaume to the socially awkward housewife he had hired for the harvest. How much his low-key confidence, and the relaxed deference of others, owed to his social status, this ridiculous, incomprehensible title of vicomte that Guillaume had let slip under cover of a joke, Franny could not tell, but she suspected there was a connection for all of Hughes' seeming indifference. The only other vicomte in Franny's acquaintance was the protagonist of *Les Liaisons Dangereuses*, who was far from being a recommenda-

tion to the class. But the eighteenth century was long gone, and Franny was willing not to hold Hughes' title against him.

It was clearly his unassuming charisma that had brought together the motley
crew of his harvesters. Indeed, when on Wednesday morning Franny looked
down into the courtyard still plunged in the bleariness of dawn and saw the people assembled there, they had seemed so mismatched that she feared she had
made a terrible mistake by accepting Hughes' invitation to help pick his grapes.

She had immediately recognized Savia by the scarf wrapped around her head
and the long flowery skirt. The bakery lady stood against the wall in a world of
her own, her shoulders weighed down by a lumpy sweater, her hands, normally
her most expressive feature, buried deep in its pockets. She seemed to have materialized out of thin air, the two cars in the parking lot other than Franny's being
accounted for by the presence of their owners. Later Franny would see the old
bicycle fitted with a wire basket leaning against the stone staircase and realize that
Savia rode from the village in her long skirts nearly every day, often with a load of
laundry at her back, often in the most stifling heat.

Another woman was sitting sideways on the driver seat of a white sedan, her
pedal-pusher clad legs dangling through the open door, purple toenails peeking
out of impractical platform sandals. She was clutching a large purse on her lap
and puffing on a cigarette as if her life depended on it. Hearing footsteps on the
stairs, she looked up at Franny without answering her smile, the freckled paleness
of her small pretty face intensified by her hennaed hair and dark mascara. She
appeared to be in her early forties, with that air of carefully maintained sexiness,
quite distinct from self-confidence, that French women affected well into their
middle age. All in all, she was the most unlikely candidate for a grape picking job
that Franny could have imagined. But perhaps she was there for another purpose.
Out of the blue, it flashed through Franny's mind that she might be Hughes'
jilted lover, intent on making a public scene. It was a morbid thought, and
Franny discarded it immediately, but it may have had something to do with her
sudden realization that the air was cold, wet and gray, and her resulting inclina-
tion to turn around quietly and go back to bed.

Her discomfort was relieved by the discovery that the third person in the parking lot was Guillaume, the greengrocer. In bermuda shorts and work boots, he
was leaning against the hood of his van, eating a fig and reading a book, a canvas
hat shading his features. As he posed to turn a page, he raised his head and saw
Franny frozen on the steps. "Par ici, Mademoiselle!" he drawled out, folding a
corner of the page and flinging the book into the van as a welcome gesture, thus
preventing her retreat. Just then, a black Mercedes drove through the medieval

arch and purred to a stop next to Franny's car. Hughes leaped out, looked about and said: "Bonjour tout le monde!" with a very slight but heart-warming nod of welcome towards Franny. Instantly the courtyard came to life, like a scene on a Swiss clock when the hour strikes.

Hands were shaken, introductions were made. The freckled woman's name was Pierrette, and she had only worked with Hughes for two days, but was already on joking terms with him. He had apparently scolded her for working without a hat the previous days, and that day she had brought one, a baseball cap inscribed with, of all things, the logo of the Oakland Raiders. With a flourish, she pushed the hat over her thick curly hair and mugged with awkwardly, claiming she was going to need a raise to pay for a new perm after wearing it. Hughes offered to trade the baseball cap for his bush hat but she refused his offer. The cap was a collector's item, she claimed. It turned out that her husband was a fan of the Raiders. Franny took advantage of this opening to say that she was from the Bay Area, and Pierrette, who had seemed until then not to know what to do with the newcomer, thawed a little toward her. She said that she would like to visit San Francisco some day, if only she could convince her husband. What about organizing a trip around a Raiders' home game? suggested Franny. Pierrette made one of those doubtful French grimaces—raised eyebrows and air blowing through pursed lips—which convey that things are not as simple as that, but her eyes, within their fortress of mascara, registered a flicker of interest.

"Et vous, Franny, vous n'avez pas de chapeau?" *(What about you Franny, don't you have a hat?)* asked Hughes. Franny, blushing from her ignorance, nodded in the negative. "Pas de problème," he said, " la maison a pensé a tout!", *(No problem, the house will provide!)* and he strode towards his car, returning with an old-fashioned straw hat, its rim adorned with silk forget-me-nots, which he held dubiously for her inspection.

"Qu'en dites-vous? Il appartenait à ma grand-tante." *(What do you think? It belonged to my great-aunt.)*

"Il est très joli. Mais je ne suis pas habituée des chapeaux …" *(Very pretty. But I am not used to hats.)*

"Ah! c'est une question de santé du travail. Je ne veux pas être responsable d'un coup de soleil." *(It's a work safety issue. I don't want to be responsible for a sunstroke.)*

"Dans ce cas …" Franny laughed, but made no move towards the hat.

"Bon, si la montagne ne vient pas à Mahomet …" he muttered, and stepping forward, he deposited the hat on her head, pulled the rim back a little, arranged the cord under her chin, and stepped back to judge the effect. The touch of his hand on her neck had caused Franny to blush more deeply. There was a second of profound silence from the rest of the crew, as if the Swiss clock was being adjusted. Then the compliments pealed: "Pas mal!", "Ça vous va très bien!", "Tu as l'air d'une star, Madame Franny!", from Guillaume, Pierrette and Savia respectively. Hughes did not say anything, although his eyes were eloquent enough. It was probably at that moment that the others started hatching their matchmaking plans.

By the time the tractor and dump-bed were out of the barn, the plastic buckets and wheel barrow loaded and the members of the crew had squeezed together into the van, the walls of the courtyard were crowned with sunlight and the morning chill had transubstantiated into a delicious medium of adventure.

During the bumpy ride to the vineyard, Franny learned that Guillaume had just joined the crew that very morning after twisting his mother's arm into covering for him at the shop, in one of those games of musical chairs that seemed an essential aspect of the labor market in Saint Yves. He was doing it to help Hughes, who was still short a couple of harvesters, and only expected to be paid in produce, barter being another feature of the local economy. For all his phlegmatic manner, he clearly saw himself as a fellow warrior in the struggle to establish organic farming methods in the area, and hinted darkly at the presence of enemies in the village's very heart. As to Savia, she seemed to be at Hughes' beck and call, behaving towards him as a doting mother, although she was probably about his age. She didn't talk much, but nothing seemed to daunt her: shopkeeping, housekeeping, grape-picking, it was all in a day's work. She came from a wine-growing region of Algeria, and although she had immigrated to France as a young girl, she was completely at home in a vineyard. Pierrette was picking grapes to overcome an addiction to the Internet. "Accrochée", she called it, and Franny took note of the new word.

When they got to the Syrah plot, they had to wait for Hughes, who was driving the tractor. The sun was just out over the hill, filtering through horizontal bands of dove-gray clouds, as if Nature had pulled down a venetian blind. The weather seemed about to change: the air felt cooler, stiller, damper than on previous days. Among the sea of green, an occasional leaf blazed in scandalous red. As she paced back and forth on the path, Franny spotted a furry-looking brown ball nestled in a dip between two vines. It was a bird, its head tucked under its wing, its down disheveled, its feathers covered with dew drops, asleep on the bare rocky ground. There was something dispossessed about the sight that Franny associated with fall. And in fact, there were only two days of summer left.

Hughes spent a few minutes showing Franny how to handle the shears, how to check the clusters for maturity and health, how to position the bucket for maximum efficiency. Then she was on her own, each member of the crew assigned to a separate row, except for Hughes, whose main job was to push the wheelbarrow up and down the rows, collecting full buckets and handing out empty ones. Being solely in charge of pouring the grapes into the dump-bed parked on the dirt path allowed him to perform a last minute triage, a task for which the cooperative was not equipped. He was obviously a perfectionist, at least in regard to his crop. But Guillaume seemed to back him up fully in his obsession. The two men were in fact in such agreement on the matter that after a while, they alternated in the collection and inspection tasks.

In three days, Franny's feelings about grape picking ran the gamut from exhilaration to boredom to exhaustion to a zen-like peace. From a social point of view, it was a little bit like working in a cubicle: shielded from her co-workers' sight by a green screen, she could make faces and mutter to herself, while the muffled sounds of their exertions kept her working at a healthy clip, and the occasional exchange over the partition took on the free floating, intimate tone of late night conversations. As to the work itself, it was both sensuous and dull. At first, she had been thrilled by the fluttering of leaves around her face while she located the grape stems, and by the neat click of the shears that released the full weight of the cluster in her hand. She had watched with delight the grapes loll against each other as they landed in the bucket, had dilated at the sight of a bucket filled to the brim. After a while, of course, it all became as routine as tightening bolts on an assembly line. After a while, her back, her knees, her wrists started aching, and late foraging bees took an interest in the sticky grape juice splattered on her arms. Franny resorted to motivating herself with competition, checking at a glance how far other pickers were in their respective rows. For even though there were no quotas assigned and no supercilious foreman, it was understood that speed was of the essence, the grapes being on the verge of overripeness, and the crew being small. (Feeling guilty about deserting Victoria, Franny had dutifully tried to recruit her, but the poor girl had untimely come down with some kind of stomach flu.)

Savia was in the habit of humming as she worked. At one point, Franny, who was getting sleepy, asked if she would mind singing louder, and Savia, after a little insistent prompting, obliged. What she sang was not Algerian music, as everyone first assumed, but a Sufi hymn by a Pakistani singer, and the words were in Urdu, a language Savia did not speak. She had learned them from sheer repetition by playing the tape on her boombox. Her thin voice, in turn undulating and screechy, still managed to convey a sense of mystical elation. Intrigued, Franny undertook to learn the chorus. Before long, the whole crew was good-humouredly raising Allah's praise to the Provençal heaven.

After that, music became an integral part of the vendange, with each member of the crew contributing their favorite songs from the Beatles to Maxime le Forestier as inspiration struck them. On Friday, Pierrette even brought her guitar. Hughes borrowed it during the lunch break to play *A la claire fontaine*, and they all joined in, including Franny, who was surprised to find that she remembered the song very well.

Aside from the musical interludes, the work proceeded apace and uneventfully. The Mistral had died, but the heat wave had concurrently broken, the sky turning increasingly hazy, then cloudy as the days progressed. The atmosphere in the vineyard, moistly tepid under the white light, and redolent of organic fermentation, reminded Franny of the gym, so that when her courage flagged, she tried to think of her. monotonous gestures as exercise reps. At other times she mused about the other crew members, wondering how they all fit together. Savia and Pierrette, who had motherhood in common, would chat about the cost of kids' clothes, the necessity of monitoring homework, the pitfalls of the *Baccalaureat*. Hughes and Guillaume discussed the appalling farming practices of some of their neighbors and the machinations of the municipal council. Franny, as a single woman and a foreigner, did not have much to contribute to either conversation. And her companions being French, they showed a typical lack of curiosity about her native land, whether out of pride, respect for her privacy or saturation with American culture, she couldn't tell.

In the midst of such melancholy conjectures, she would hear the rumble of the wheelbarrow. Hughes' denim-clad legs filled her field of vision, his sinewy arms, covered with a fine blond down, reached for her bucket. She would look up, and see his gray eyes settle on her for an instant, full of concern. "How are you?" he would ask, seeming to create a little bubble of intimacy around them by addressing her in English. "Wonderful!" she answered throughout the first day. On the second day, she was just fine. By the third day though, she no longer felt compelled to be polite, and barely claimed to be hanging in there, until at last she bluntly declared that she could see the point of harvesting machines. A smile flickered on his face. She attempted to rise, he gave her his hand to help pull her up, he gazed down on her while she stretched, his shoulders half-turned, as if he was about to move on, but his feet rooted to the spot. "Ah! but harvesting machines don't give recitals ..." he concluded, always intent on having the last word. For the next ten minutes grape picking felt like a walk in the park.

For the most part, though, Hughes scrupulously avoided singling Franny out for any special attention. It was what any good boss would have done, Franny understood, and she approved. The fact that she was not in fact his employee did not enter in the equation as far as she was concerned. She had volunteered, and had to honor her commitment. Besides, as there couldn't be anything else between them, the professional stamp of their relationship was a blessing. She did not wonder how it looked from his point of view. But after a while, she couldn't help noticing that the rest of the crew wasn't impressed by their mutual show of equanimity, and was in fact doing everything in its power to bring them together.

The weather cooperating, the crew being conscientious and the equipment as low tech as it comes, there wasn't much that could go wrong with the harvest. But even in a vineyard in the Vaucluse, Murphy's Law applied. On Thursday morning, the tractor stalled just as Hughes was preparing to drive it to the cooperative with a full load of grapes in its dump-bed. Patiently, he tried for several minutes to restart it. When that failed, he got off the driver's seat without a word, retrieved a tool box from under the wheel, raised the hood, rolled up his sleeves and got to work on the engine. Within fifteen minutes, he had fixed whatever the problem was. "You'the man!" cried Guillaume, who had watched the whole interlude from the sideline with the willfully relaxed expression of a father entrusting his car to a teenage son for the first time. Franny blushed to the roots of her hair, not so much from surprise at hearing the American idiom trip off the grocer's tongue, as from the realization that it fit her sentiments exactly. She wished her own father could have been there. He would have instantly approved of a man with such mechanical talent.

As it turned out, Guillaume wasn't the only one who could trot out bits of American slang. Partly, it seemed, to draw Franny out, and partly to razz Hughes, who flaunted his mastery of English, the others got into a game of peppering their talk with "Cool!", "Whatever!" and "Excuse me!". Even Savia could say "Yes!" like Macaulay Culkin. But Guillaume was fluent enough to make bilingual puns. He had studied hotel management, had worked for Club Med, had even done a stint at a Florida resort. Then he had become disgusted with tourism and had come back to his village, where he eked out a living forwarding the cause of slow food. He was in his thirties, with traces of the beach boy in his seamless tan and crinkled blue eyes, his laconic rusticity probably acquired as an accoutrement of his return to the land.

It was Guillaume who engineered the first few minutes Hughes and Franny got to spend alone with each other since their initial encounter. At the end of the shift on Thursday, Hughes was preparing to take the second load of grapes to the communal winery when Guillaume expressed a sudden wish to drive the tractor, and given that Hughes had to be present to sign the receipt on his grapes, and that the tractor only sat one person, Hughes had to drive the Mercedes, which did have room for an extra passenger.

"Au fait, Franny aimerait peut-etre visiter la cooperative?" Guillaume had asked, throwing the question into the air. Hughes glanced at Franny, his habitual frown much in evidence. She wondered for a second whether he was opposed to the idea, then, in an uncharacteristic burst of self-confidence, decided he was just shy. "Je serais ravie!", she said brightly. "Eh bien! Venez!" he answered, all business, motioning her toward the car. Guillaume watched them get in, looking pleased with himself.

They drove to the cooperative. She was shown the crusher, the complicated network of tubes that transported the must, the wine press, the huge steel vats, the computer consoles, the lab. She learned about malolactic fermentation, endogen yeasts, sulfite treatments (necessary, even in "bio" wines?), barrel aging (not suited to Côtes du Rhone wines, according to the enologist, but Hughes disagreed), flash détente (a no no, as far as Hughes was concerned, and the enologist concurred). What surprised her most was the size and modern look of the operation, from the computerized equipment to the ugly corrugated steel construction of the building. Because the village was small and out of the way, and because of Hughes' attachment to traditional winemaking methods, she had imagined a quaint stone cellar half-buried under a grass hill, with rows of oak barrels and grapes crushed underfoot. How could a handful of farmers afford such a snazzy outfit, particularly as according to Hughes, winemakers did not get any government subsidies? And how could they be so comfortable with both thirteenth century churches and high-tech wine cellars?

Last but not least, as he would have put it himself, it was to Guillaume that Franny was indebted for her current opportunity to observe Hughes at leisure. He had heard of a retired farmer looking to sell some land in the nearby village of Mirésol, and suggested that a woman's presence might induce the old guy to make a deal with Hughes. "And for you," he had said to Franny, "it will be a good opportunity to see how the other half lives." "Which other half?" had asked Franny. "Oh! you know, peasants without a title of vicomte."

Throughout the harvest, Savia's own contribution to the matchmaking effort had consisted in using Franny as a relay for any question, information or food item intended for Hughes. She did this shamelessly, with little pats of the hands and yenta smiles. As to Pierrette, who at first had seemed to claim prior flirtation rights, she took to including Franny in her girlish joshing of the men, instinctively creating a magnetic field of sexual friction into which only Franny and Hughes could be drawn. And even though the pair was aware of what was going on, even though they were both intent on keeping at a safe distance, the very sharing of this knowledge and this intention drew them closer.

✳   ✳   ✳   ✳

What was she thinking about? Was she quietly happy, quietly worried, or quietly disgusted? It was all very well for Guillaume to argue that she was getting a unique touristic experience. Hughes for his part could not help feeling a good deal of compunction about taking her money and then putting her to work. Of course, it had never entered his mind that she would spend more than a few hours picking grapes. But she had returned to the field day after day. Although he would have liked to think that it was for the pleasure of the company, he already knew enough about her to suspect that she had stuck with it out of a sense of obligation. She seemed to have an almost supernatural concern for others: she made sandwiches for the crew, applied salve to bee stings, offered to buy Raiders tickets for Pierrette, was tutoring Savia's son in English. More than anything else, he thought, it was her instinctive empathy that had jelled their unlikely group. Her duet with Savia in particular had been a stroke of genius: the song, with its mixture of sensuousness and transcendence, and its execution, both heartfelt and clumsy, had lifted everyone out of their normal embarrassed solipsism. Here Hughes had to give American showmanship its due. No French woman he knew would ever have dared perform in public, without rehearsal, a new song in a genre she wasn't familiar with.

Did she enjoy grape picking at all? She said she did but of course she would. She had a lot of nervous energy, which it was probably good for her to wear out with physical labor. Her face was normally tense, the depth of her brown eyes constantly changing from keen to warm to inscrutable, her smile slightly crooked, as if caught in flight from some inward pain or private irony. She was prone to flinch, to bite her lower lip, to wring her hands. But there were times, toward the end of a shift, when her features would slacken under a glistening dew of sweat, her eyelashes resting against her cheeks, her mouth gaping a little, her whole body languid with exhaustion, when Hughes had to fight an urge to fall all over her. Guillaume himself was a little smitten, but although he had known her longer, he had gallantly departed the list, yielding to *the droit du seigneur*, he joked, but more probably because he had other amorous prizes to pursue. Not that Hughes saw Franny as a prize, of course.

When Guillaume had suggested that Franny accompany Hughes on his visit to the old farmer in Mirésol, all Franny had said was: "Pourquoi pas?" But really it may have been too much for her, the cavernous kitchen with the fly paper dangling from the ceiling, the chrome chairs upholstered in cracked plastic, the buffet shelves stacked with medicines, the smells of damp plaster, rancid dishcloth, perhaps even urine, and the old man's unintelligible chatter–at least to her–between the Provençal accent and the slur of Parkinson's. She had been a real trooper, biding her time while the men talked business by sipping peach wine from a dubious glass and looking at pictures of Monsieur Rosetti's 1991 trip to the Napa Valley. Her pliancy had oiled the wheels of commerce: the visit had concluded with a tentative deal which would provide Monsieur Rosetti with his quota of distilled spirits. But as an independent American woman, she probably chafed at the decorative role. And how could Hughes repay her for all her help without seeming crass? Certainly not by making a pass at her. From an ethical point of view, the whole relationship was simply impossible.

At least next week he wouldn't have to rely on her for the harvest. He had received three additional responses to his ad at the ANPE and Henri, his one full-time employee, was sufficiently recovered from his gall bladder operation to come back to work. The timing couldn't have been better as the Fischbeins, the couple whose signature was on the lease, were finally arriving from the US with their children the next day. This time, there would be clean and ironed linen for everyone, even if he had to release Savia from grape picking duty. The Fischbeins were going to be at the chateau for only ten days, and they would be eager to pack their schedules with as many touristic activities as the area offered. Franny would no doubt want to join them. The crew would miss her, but life would go on.

They should be done with the Syrah by Tuesday. Ten more days with a full crew for the Grenache, including Saturdays, then four people for a couple of days for the Mourvedre. By the tenth of October, he should be able to escape to Paris for a few days, spend time with Clarisse and Héloise, catch a concert and a couple of movies, browse the book displays at the FNAC. *Le Monde N'est Pas Une Marchandise*, by José Bové, had just come out in paperback and Hughes wanted to check it out. It was interesting how he appreciated Paris now that he no longer lived there, now that he no longer had to insulate himself from its noise, its grouchiness, its pretensions in order to survive day by day. It was also interesting that given the number of people who felt as Hughes did, who also had escaped to the provinces, Paris remained the center of French intellectual life. So far the Internet had made no dent in this dominance. But in Hughes' experience, a few days in the capital every couple of months sufficed to stay abreast of cultural currents. The rest of the time he was fully content to be a peasant: to sweat in the open air, to produce something tangible, to be yoked to the cycle of the seasons. How could have mankind ever wanted anything else?

A flutter of arm brought his attention back to the present. She was putting a hand in front of her mouth to stifle a yawn. She was bored after all, and he was becoming a boor. But what did she want from him? He realized he had no idea.

✳   ✳   ✳   ✳

"A quoi pensez-vous?"

At last he spoke French to her. It gave a serious tone to a question that in English would have been mere conversational filler. The problem was, there was nothing like a request for your thoughts to make them vanish without a trace. On top of that, she was so sleepy that she could barely talk, let alone in a foreign language.

"Hmm! Voyons. Quelque chose sur les apparences deceptives …"

"Décevantes ou trompeuses?"

"Oh! J'ai fait un anglicisme. Mais en fait, les deux."

"So whose appearance did you find deceptive and disappointing?"

"I meant in general …" They were back to English, inexorably, which was a relief to both of them. They had started their relationship in English, according to the rule that between multilingual people, the vehicle of conversation always ends up being the language that is on average the least uncomfortable to all parties, regardless of location. And while Franny felt intellectually diminished by her lack of mastery of French, Hughes had found that speaking English gave him a sort of emotional freedom.

"But specifically? Off the top of your head."

"Are you asking me to free-associate?"

"Pourquoi pas?" They looked at each other. Their faces were shrouded in darkness. With the loss of delineation came a sense that the hard shell of their personas had been peeled off, letting a softer, blurrier medium expand between them. "Why not?" they both thought. They had nothing to lose.

"I am afraid my thoughts have to do with men."

"Go ahead. I like to hear a woman talk about men."

"But it may not be flattering."

"That's all right. Whatever criticism you make, I have the option of thinking it only applies to American men, or at least to every man but me."

"OK, then. This may be as relevant as "hair in the soup", as the French would say, but remember I am free-associating. One thing I have never understood is seduction games. How can a man in conscience put out all the signals of a genuine interest in another human being, when all he cares about is adding another notch to his belt? Please, don't tell me that it's in the genes, the adaptive function of the male hunter instinct and all that Sociobiology ... stuff."

"You mean bullshit? I wasn't about to. I am not too fond of Sociobiology myself. But surely, seduction is about more than satisfying one's vanity."

"You mean sex."

"Yes." He drew out the word, trilling the E and whispering the S. He was making fun of her, in a gentle, surprised way that she couldn't find in her heart to mind.

"Then, why not come right out and say: I want to have sex with you? Skip the meaningful conversations, the protective gestures, the tender looks."

"Because it wouldn't work?"

"Why wouldn't it work?"

"Because women are rarely interested in sex for sex's sake?"

"And men know this, and so they lie to get what they want, regardless of what the woman wants. This is instrumental behavior of a kind that is not acceptable in any other social context. Why is it still *de rigueur* between men and women?"

"You are against instrumental behavior?"

"Of course!"

"I am glad. I had the feeling, when I lived in the US, that instrumentality was *de rigueur* in all relationships."

"Whoa! That's a harsh way of characterizing Americans, but probably as deserved as my rants about men. Have you read *Habits of the Heart* by Robert Bellah, by any chance? It was at the top of college reading lists when you were at Davis, if I remember well."

"Yes." Again, the notes of gentleness, of amusement, of surprise. It was amazing how much meaning he could pack in one syllable. It was also amazing how little defensiveness he displayed while his gender was being attacked. Was he different, or just more conceited than the other men with whom Franny had had similar conversations?

"But let's not get side-tracked into philosophy. First I want to say that I understand your indignation, that I agree that we should strive to keep in mind the full humanity of every person we deal with, that it is wrong to lie to get one's way, that the genetic programming explanation is just a modern excuse for an old type of misbehavior. Do you believe me?"

"Yes."

Her answer had been short and firm, but she had hesitated for a fraction of a second before giving it. She was willing to put her doubts in parenthesis for the time being, a small level of trust Hughes was going to have to be content with. Oddly, he wasn't put out by her diffidence.

"What I have come to realize, though, is how powerful sexual attraction is, how it takes a life of its own, quite apart from our conscious plans, scruples, conceits, rationalizations. I am not going to put it all down to chemistry. I know attraction is often made up of questionable psychic ingredients like power seeking, jealousy, even shame. Perhaps we would do well to question our desires, although that might not be very good for the perpetuation of the species."

"Do you think desire is always based on illusions?"

"Probably. That doesn't mean it is doomed, I hope. It doesn't mean we should yield to it indiscriminately either."

"It seems to me that we are still relying on women to do the discriminating. Sometimes I get tired of being on my guard, of being the one who has to resist, the one who has to decipher intentions, the one who has to think."

"You don't have to."

"What do you mean? Should I let men use me?"

"You don't have to with me. I think too."

What a strange way to arrive at a confession of mutual attraction, they both realized. Franny, who had been inculcated—much against her will—in the dos and don'ts of dating, knew that complaining about gender inequities with a man you were interested in was equivalent to throwing a bucket of cold water on the first spark of a fire. And in a free-associating way, that is what she had been trying to do. She knew that a woman was supposed to leave all her hard-earned experience at the door of a new relationship to spare the man not only the trouble of having to work to earn her trust, but even the knowledge that in general women might have reasons to mistrust men—reasons men claimed to be blissfully ignorant of, though they were detailed in every TV sitcom. Later, after the woman had taken the required leap of faith, and the man had revealed himself to be a cad, he would be the first one to blame her naivete. Hughes's willingness to listen to her criticisms, not to mention his agreeing to their validity, had been a balm to her wounds. She was also intrigued by what he had to say about desire. The possibility that its force might trump our most rational intentions was something to consider. Best of all, she had liked the fearless way he had acknowledged that desire was an issue between them. Of course he had in the same breath assured her that it wouldn't be an issue.

To Hughes, who in fact had never engaged in the kind of seduction game Franny complained about, her generalizations might have been offensive if it hadn't been for the mysterious sympathy, born of the late hour and the certitude that their time together was finite, which had allowed him to see things from her point of view. He was also conscious of unresolved issues on his side around the meaning and power of desire, which he had been glad to clarify aloud. What he had not mentioned was that his own desire for a woman was enhanced by her putting up a fight. For as mild as he looked to Franny, he liked verbal jousting, and particularly in an erotic context. Until recently, he had complacently seen this trait as a sign that he did not fear strong women. Besides, he was pretty sure he could win any argument. Now he questioned both the motives and the consequences of his pugnacity. In any case, he had been pleasantly surprised by Franny's intellectual fierceness, which would have reminded him alarmingly of his first impressions of Christiane but for one crucial and encouraging difference: whereas his ex-wife had used abstract arguments as a tool of insouciant provocation or diversion, his little American argued passionately about matters that were of great concern to her. Just as he had recognized Christiane's provocation as an invitation to come closer, he understood that Franny's polemic had been an attempt to push him away. The cause was the same in both cases though, and the outcome was up to him again. But as he had promised, he was going to think before he did anything.

CHAPTER 12

▼

WHEN THE CAT'S AWAY,
THE MICE WILL PLAY

(Quand le chat n'est pas là, les souris dansent)

"You don't need anyone's permission to charge," Victoria reminded herself as she positioned the drill bit against the back of the mahogany cabinet. Like the writings in her diary, much of her internal monologue consisted of aphorisms, reminiscent of the Bible verses religious zealots mutter under their breath to ward off the devil–though of course the principles she tried to live by diverged widely from the Ten Commandments, for all her guru's claim that the Bible was the original "how to be successful" manual. There is something to be said about her choice of spiritual foundation, since she was more successful than most Judeo-Christians at obeying its dictates. In Victoria's case, the flesh was as willing as the spirit.

All the same, it had taken her three days to get to the present moment of commitment: in one second, there would be a hole in an expensive piece of furniture entrusted to her, and no matter how well she managed to conceal it in the short term, in the long term she would probably have to give up on Franny's friendship. She did feel sad about it: she had come to think of the diminutive Berkeley-ite as a sort of unworldly big sister, the type whose kind disposition towards you rested on a blissful ignorance of your faults, both of which (the kindness and the ignorance) you ended up striving to preserve by being on your best behavior around her. It was another example of how you had to give in order to get, and it was fine with Victoria, at least for a while. But you couldn't make an omelet without breaking some eggs. And so, holding the drill firmly against the wood, she pressed on the trigger. The bit skidded around wildly. She pushed on it harder, and at last it sunk in, spitting out little corkscrews of pink sawdust for a second or two, then whirring freely. She had gone clear through. It was so easy! The hole was not exactly where she had planned to make it, but it would do. Twenty or so more holes at the top, the same number at the bottom, a couple of knocks with the hammer and screwdriver, and the board should spring free, like a postage stamp.

Victoria stopped to listen for signs of disturbance. Even though rain was threatening, she had opened both of the windows that lit the staircase: a small one, looking out the back of the chateau, located on the mezzanine where the curio cabinet stood, and a larger one, overlooking the front porch, situated on the second floor landing. This way she had full command of all the approach routes, which had thoughtfully been graveled for the maximum detection of intruders. Fortunately there was no wind, so the draught was minimal, barely stirring the yellow moire drapes. All Victoria could hear was the plaintive song of a lone bird in the trees along the terrace, and scattered gun shots in the distant woods. She proceeded with her drilling.

Franny's sudden interest in farming had definitely been a lucky break. Left with the run of the house and the use of the car every day between seven AM and three PM, Victoria had been able to concentrate fully on the task of leveraging her providential sojourn among the wealthy. But first, she had had to exert herself to avoid being drafted into the harvest. Fortunately, Victoria was an old hand at faking illnesses. A little stomping to the bathroom in the middle of the night and a little sticking of a finger down her throat had caused Franny to get out of bed and knock on the bathroom door, asking if she was all right and offering some Maalox. The next morning Victoria claimed to be too sick to stir out of bed. When Franny returned from the fields, she found the invalid reclining against her pillows, a cup of herbal tea at her elbow and an issue of Vogue in her lap, the meaning of those props being so obvious that she didn't have to explain what she had done all day.

An additional benefit of the sick strategy was that it had spared Victoria another tedious tutoring session with the Sheriff kid, who the previous evening had not taken his eyes off her, as if the entire English dictionary was written on her face—or more exactly on her chest. From then on, Franny, dear girl that she was, would assume the entire tutoring burden.

Heinrich on the other hand had let her down: after a cursory look at her polaroids, he had declined to be further involved. Too risky considering the potential loot, he had said. Well, he was no expert at antique furniture. Nevertheless, the lack of brawn had strategic implications. By herself, Victoria could not even handle that cute Directoire desk that served as a telephone stand in the hallway, let alone undertake a full scale moving operation. What she needed to find was a small but expensive object that would fit into the trunk of the Peugeot. The trouble was that the value of small objects was difficult to assess at first glance, depending as it did on a knowledge of collectors' whims. At last Victoria had an illumination: why not be guided by how the current owner appraised his own possessions? Among the many knickknacks that vied for her attention, weren't the most precious ones likely to be those kept behind locked doors? When you thought about it, a lock was more or less a sign advertising that what lay behind it was worth stealing. Unfortunately, Victoria was no locksmith, nor could she think of a believable excuse to bring one to the chateau.

"Think outside the box!" she admonished herself, the issue in this case being to think her way *into* one of the chateau's glass-fronted cabinets. For as to the third floor rooms, much as their solid oak doors gave them the allure of pirates' caves in Victoria's imagination, she deemed them impregnable. Of the three locked cabinets, she quickly gave up on those in the dining room and living room, due to their exposure. The third one, located on the mezzanine and hidden from general view by the ascending flight of stairs, was much more amenable to a little breaking and entering. On the other hand, Victoria was dubious about its contents, which, as far as she could tell in the mahogany gloom, consisted of a jumble of old toys and figurines, several layers deep, and hiding each other, the most prominent among them being a wind-up plastic Snoopy. But, as Scott Alexander would have said, "never think of the possibility of failure".

Because she did not know what exactly to look for, she thought it prudent to allow several days for the completion of her project. So it was essential to find as inconspicuous a way as possible to crack the cabinet open. As it happened, it was free-standing, the back panel, when illuminated by the beam of a flashlight held through the glass, revealing deep gouges, as if it was made up of several boards. Perhaps a board could be removed, then replaced. The hitch was that the cabinet was too heavy to swivel around. But then, Victoria thought of those moving casters that her roommate Maggie had once used to rearrange the living room. Borrowing the car, she made a trip to the hardware store in Saint Yves, and after much gesturing, and rummaging through shelves and drawers, and enthusiastic appeals to the shopkeeper's expertise, and enthusiastic disregard for his worsening temper, she got what she was looking for, all for a few francs, which when you thought of it, was an extremely conservative investment.

But, hard as she tried, she could not lift even one corner of the cabinet by the quarter inch needed to slip one of the casters under its leg. Again, she regretted Heinrich's desertion. He had turned out to be a cow, after all, and although she accepted that being a cow was a perfectly legitimate life choice, although she fully appreciated the usefulness of cows in the general scheme of things, in this particular instance she couldn't help wishing that her ex-partner had modeled himself after a more forceful animal. As to her, she was rhinoceros through and through. However, three o' clock approaching, she had to suspend her charging for that day. When Franny came home, Victoria was lounging on one of the downstairs sofas, a sketch pad in hand, a saltine cracker held between her teeth.

In the middle of the night she had another brainstorm. What she needed–literally–was leverage. And what tool, so common that even Victoria knew how to use it, was designed for the very purpose of providing leverage? A tire jack, of course! She could hardly wait for Franny to vacate the premises the next morning to check whether the rented Peugeot was equipped with one. In fact, she was so impatient that she got up to attend her departure, explaining that she felt much better, but that she thought she would take it easy another day or two.

From the edge of the terrace, her chin resting on her hands laid flat on the banister, she watched the crew come together below. Apart from Franny, demure in overalls and sneakers, an incongruous Scarlett O'Hara straw hat in one hand and a hamper full of home-made sandwiches in the other, there were four people in the courtyard, two women and two men. Among them, Victoria had no trouble identifying the boss from the way the others turned to him while he maneuvered a tractor around the yard. He was an unimpressive little man with a busy demeanor and an effeminate voice, although he did have good hair. It was hard to believe that he was the owner of the chateau. In fact, Victoria realized she had run into him a couple of times before, once when he disturbed her sunbathing with his power lawnmower, another time when she saw him carry some cases of empty bottles into the basement. She had assumed he was some kind of handyman and had had half a mind to approach him to see if he would be interested in a well-paid moving job. She was glad now that, because of the limitations of her French, she had given up on the idea.

Really, she couldn't be faulted for mistaking the owner's identity. If she had been in charge of casting the role of Lord of the Manor, she would have picked a very different type of man. But to each her own. Though he did not strike her fancy, he obviously tickled Franny's. Victoria had suspected that much from her roommate's excited explanations of various aspects of grape-picking and wine-making, from the way she kept referring to the landlord–first as "Monsieur Degency" and then "Hughes"–from her dreamy looks here and there. And now that she saw them together, it was clear to Victoria that he reciprocated her feelings.

When Franny got to the bottom of the stairs, Hughes had been concentrating on lining up the tractor with some kind of trailer that stood in the open barn. She had walked in the direction of a blue van, stopping on the way to plant kisses on the cheeks of the other three crew members. But in spite of the racket made by the tractor's engine, and without a look in her direction, the landlord had somehow become aware of her presence. He jumped off the tractor, retrieved a paper bag full of tomatoes from the barn and intersected her path just as she prepared to heave the hamper onto the floor of the van. He dropped the tomatoes in the hamper, and with his other hand on the handle next to hers, helped her lift the basket in one smooth movement. It was the kind of coordination you saw in old married couples. And yet Victoria was pretty certain they had not had sex yet. Interesting. It did make sense to her that these two bland, unassertive people–not cows exactly, but small, innocuous animals like rabbits let's say–should get together. Victoria wished them all the best. In any case, their preoccupation with each other was bound to be good for her plans.

At last the courtyard was deserted. Victoria, still in her pajamas, tripped down the stone stairs and opened the trunk of the Peugeot. There, underneath the spare tire, was the object of her desire! It took her a while to figure out how to operate the jack, then how to place it under the curio cabinet so that she could lift it at the appropriate spot. But towards noon, she had managed to wedge a caster under all four legs. With delicious apprehension, she grabbed the edge of the cabinet on one side and pulled. Silently, miraculously, the cabinet pivoted forward on the checkerboard of tiles.

The back was in fact divided into two panels, each made up of several vertical slats of unequal sizes, tongue-and-grooved together and framed on all sides by thicker boards. The slats must have shrunk over time, and the tongues has sprang free from the grooves in a couple of places, so that Victoria's best bet for prying the cabinet open without incurring visible damage was to saw through one of the loose slats at the top and bottom. This, however, turned out to be easier said than done. A thorough search of the kitchen, pantry and laundry room having yielded no other power tool than an electrical drill, and the barn being padlocked, Victoria had no choice but to go shopping, although this time she decided to avoid the local hardware store, instead driving all the way to Orange's *hypermarché,* where she could window shop without fear of arousing suspicions. Unfortunately, any suitable electric saw was beyond her budget, while a mechanical saw would require the patience of a Monte Cristo. Back at the house, she pushed the cabinet back in its place, leaving the casters under its legs. She was stymied. "Sleep on it!" she finally advised herself. And sure enough, the solution came to her that very night, in the form of an injunction to "tear along the dotted line". The drill would make the dotted line and she would tear along it.

This was her assignment on Saturday morning, September 22, 2001. Suddenly, she was on a tight schedule: the couple who had rented the chateau were supposed to arrive in the afternoon with their two kids, and the place would soon be crawling with people, which would put a crimp in her activities, kids in particular being unpredictable, likely to pop up like jacks in the box at the most delicate moment. Displaying grace under pressure, she methodically continued to puncture the dense board at close intervals. She had selected the widest slat, on the bottom panel, even though it required more drilling, because she wanted the hole to be big enough for any of the cabinet's contents to slip through. The cabinet itself had three shelves, and if Victoria had calculated right, she would have access to the two lower shelves. There was bound to be something worthwhile there.

It wasn't only Victoria's plans that the Fischbeins' imminent arrival was jeopardizing. Poor Franny, assuming she would remain mistress of the house, had ventured earlier in the week to invite the harvest crew to dinner on Saturday night. She had planned a potluck buffet on the terrace, and had already bought the various cheeses, pates, salami, and olives that would clog her guests' arteries. The greengrocer, who was taking part in the harvest, was in charge of salads. The baker's wife, who was also the Sheriff kid's mother, was bringing pizzas, while the other woman on the team had promised to contribute a pear tart. As to Degency, restored for one night to his own position of master of the house—Franny must have been looking forward to that—he would of course provide the wine. All in all, a cozy little family affair. Then, not only had the Fischbeins announced their intention to usurp the role of hosts, but it looked as if it was going to rain. The party was still supposed to happen, but it was probably going to be uncomfortable. The demands of her own project permitting, for one should never allow anything to distract one from one's charging, Victoria was very willing to stand at Franny's side on this trying occasion.

"Bang!" went the hammer as it slammed down on the handle of the screwdriver, whose point Victoria has inserted in one of the drill holes. The loudness of the noise, reverberating through the vast stairwell, took Victoria by surprise. She put down the hammer and screwdriver and tip-toed upstairs to the large window overlooking the terrace. In the tiered expanse of gravel, lawn, bushes, vineyards at her feet, nothing was stirring, not even a leaf. The entire landscape looked like the painted backdrop of a stage deserted for the intermission. Only the horizon showed signs of preparations for the next act: there the gray sheet of the sky was being overlaid with lurid purple banners, from which issued muffled drumrolls. A thunderstorm was coming, no doubt about it. Victoria tip-toed back to her work.

"Bang! Bang! Bang! Bang!" The board was much harder to dislodge than Victoria had imagined. She had to resort to another round of drilling, knocking down a couple of objects on the shelves in the process. At last, with a wrenching sound, the top of the board split apart from the frame, an inch-wide splinter shooting out and barely missing Victoria's left eye. She moved the screwdriver to the sides of the board, using it as a crowbar to further bend the board outward until she could grab it with her gloved hands, and shaking it back and forth to loosen the bottom seam, finally managed to pull it out. By then there was enough sawdust on the floor to fill a cat box. Always with an eye to the possibility of interruptions, Victoria lay the missing board and tools on top of the cabinet and ran to the pantry to get a broom and dustpan. Only after she had swept the whole area clean did she venture to look inside the cabinet, into which light now fell from both sides.

What the figurines had in common was that they were all wind-up devices, as revealed by the butterfly keys in the back of their stands. There were ballerinas, clowns, magicians in oriental costumes, soldiers in red coats and furry helmets, birds in cages, dogs ready to perform tricks. A memory stirred, of the Nutcracker performance Victoria had attended, courtesy of some Hollywood charity, with a group of other needy kids during one of her stints in foster homes. They had traveled by bus to the newly opened Orange County Performance Arts center, where she had been dazzled as much by the modern luxury of the décor as by the old-fashioned magic of the ballet. After the show, the kids had filed into a reception room where each one was handed a paper sack of Christmas goodies. Victoria had held her pretty red and gold bag tight all the way home, even as her seatmate ripped hers and ate its contents. What she prayed for, snuggled in the tissue paper, was one of those mysterious sugar plums that even the rich girl in the ballet coveted. She imagined it as big as an egg, lilac in color, with a shimmering coat of crystallized sugar all over its surface and a gooey texture. And when she bit into it, it would be more than delicious, it would be magical. How disappointed she had been when apart from snack-size candy bars that looked like leftovers from Halloween, the most exotic thing the bag had yielded was an orange.

An orange, in southern California! After that, Victoria had stopped believing in magic. After that, she had opted for material success, for lifting herself by her own bootstraps.

Now again she had her hand in the party favor bag, but this time there was a cornucopia of goodies to choose from. After a few minutes of indecision, Victoria finally selected the biggest and most intricate looking one and carefully pulled it out of the cabinet. It was a figurine of a young lady in a pink and blue-striped crinoline dress with big puffy sleeves and a bolero vest, and a blue flounce held by pink bows at the bottom. The tiniest straw hat adorned with a blue ribbon was tilted forward on her loosely gathered hair, which was real human hair as far as Victoria could see, and the tiniest pink shoe peeked under her dress. She was turned sideways on the stand, a miniature butterfly net in one porcelain hand, the other hand sheltering her eyes, her torso bent slightly forward, as if she was looking for butterflies on a sunny day. The figurine was no more than ten inches tall, the stand adding less than a foot to the total height of the object, and everything about it was exquisitely detailed, from the features of the face to the embroidery on the vest. Even as a still miniature, it looked as if it could fetch thousands of dollars, at least in the US, if the Antiques Road Show was any guide. But did the mechanism work?

Quivering with anticipation, Victoria wound up the key on the stand. Nothing happened. Ah! there was also a little lever. She depressed it, and felt a shiver of gears engaging through the metal of the stand. Suddenly, a yellow butterfly popped up on a metal stick no thicker than a hair from a hole in the green mossy ground cover at the girl's feet. It started zigzagging along an intricate track, going up and down and even flapping its wings, which were no bigger than confetti. And then the girl was set in motion, grabbing the net with both hands and waving it in front of her until the butterfly came within reach, at which point she bent forward and dropped the net over the butterfly. But in her sudden movement, her hat had tilted out of balance, while one of her legs had shot backward, the pink shoe now dangling from her foot at the heel. To prevent her hat from falling, she let go of the net with one hand, causing the net to jerk up, and the butterfly to fly away. At that point the girl regained her balance, turned towards the front of the stand, and amazingly, she made a face, closing her pin-hole sized eyes and opening her speck of a mouth while her shoulders performed a tiny shrug of resignation. As the mechanism wound down, the girl returned to her original position, and the butterfly disappeared back into the ground.

"Oh! my God! This is it! This is it!" Victoria repeated under her breath. The toy's performance had jerked her completely out of the imperative mood. It did not occur to her to wonder how much her elation owed to the gorgeous price the toy was likely to fetch, and how much to its gorgeousness *tout court*. There was no room in her conscious mind for the appreciation of sheer beauty, which does not mean that sheer beauty did not affect her all the same. She would have loved to wind the mechanism again, if only to assure herself that she hadn't dreamed the amazing act, but she suddenly grew afraid of breaking something. Just thinking how close the drill bit had been to the butterfly catcher's head made her break out in a cold sweat.

When she recovered from her trance, her first thought was to spirit the figurine away into her bedroom. She carefully deposited it at the bottom of the armoire, making a tent around it with one of her long dresses. Then, as best as she could, she restored all the other toys to their original positions, dusted the shelves, fitted the missing board over the hole, held it in place with duct tape, pushed the cabinet back against the wall, shined the wood and cleaned the glass front, then swept up the remaining debris and mopped up the floor. She was in the process of wringing out the mop in the kitchen when she heard a car pull up into the lower courtyard. She tripped back upstairs to make sure the mezzanine was in pristine order. The casters were still under the cabinet legs, but otherwise everything looked untouched.

CHAPTER 13

▼

PLUS ON EST DE FOUS, PLUS ON RIT

(The More The Merrier)

The visitor did not fit Victoria's expectations: first, he was half an hour early, and second, he was alone, a tall, square-shouldered, square-jawed man in his mid-forties wearing a light-gray suit, a pale-blue shirt with fashionably square collar tips and a yellow tie with small blue designs. He was sitting at the wheel of an Alfa Romeo convertible whose color matched his tie and whose top was down in spite of the threatening weather, looking at himself in the rear view mirror while he combed his hair, which was dark and wavy. By the time he was done with it, his part was so immaculate it would have given Cary Grant a fit of envy. He then smoothed his eyebrows with a moistened finger, ran a hand on his chin as if to check for stubble, adjusted his tie, laying it flat against his torso in the gesture of a man who is trying to hide the beginning of a paunch, pulled his shirt cuffs out of his jacket sleeves, looked at himself again, and satisfied with his grooming, relaxed back into his seat, his hands playing drums against the dashboard. He seemed to be waiting for someone else, and as that someone could not be Victoria, she remained hidden behind an urn at the corner of the terrace.

Time passed. Victoria went back inside to fetch a magazine, picked up a lounge chair and settled noiselessly at her observation post to await further developments. From the courtyard below came sounds of whistling, of various radio stations being tried and found wanting, of gravel being kicked, of the padlock chain on the barn door being shaken. At last, another car was heard approaching. It came to a stop and its engine was killed. Suddenly, the parking lot was alive with homey pandemonium: car doors banging and slaps on the back, "Why, Phil, you're here already!", "How're you doing, buddy?", "Mommy, he kicked me!", "Isaac, honey, remember to use your words!", "She started it!", "You guys, keep it down!", more gravel kicking, and finally a kid's howl of pain that drowned all the other noises. Victoria peered over the banister.

"Hey, I can see why you brought the twins along. Al Qaeda is no match for the little buggers," commented the Alfa Romeo driver.

"No kidding!" replied the other man, pulling a bulging suitcase out of the trunk of a BMW SUV. A woman who must be his wife squatted next to a plump little girl of about six in pink ballet tights and faux-fur white jacket, rubbing her knee and saying "There! There! It's all better now," while the girl went on screaming, and her brother, a plump boy sporting polyester cargo pants and spiky haircut, looked on with unabashed animosity. Peace had barely been restored among the kids, and the adults, after exchanging the standard remarks about the maddening confusion of the Charles De Gaulle airport and the disappointing weather, were considering what their next step should be, when another car pulled into the parking lot, an Audi sedan with a woman at the wheel and two girls peeping morosely out of the back windows like princesses under the spell of a wicked witch.

The new woman unfolded out of the Audi, presenting to her American audience an intimidating sample of Parisian upper-class femininity: keen and polished in a way that you couldn't pinpoint, much less hope to emulate, every detail of her appearance, from the short Liza Minelli type of haircut to the chocolate brown leather pants, knitted shirt and high heel boots that could have figured in a Ralph Lauren ad, having an air of familiarity about it, and yet the whole look transfigured by some kind of paradoxical gloss, made in equal parts of fastidiousness and nonchalance.

The Parisian took in her surroundings at a cool glance, as if inspecting them for some slight fault of taste or upkeep. In fact, she was assessing the social standing and likely rights of precedence of the other visitors. That they were American, she had no doubt. The quantity of luggage spilling out of the SUV was a sufficient clue, not to mention the ludicrous way the little girl was dressed, her outfit clearly assembled without any adult supervision. The make of the car, as well as the fact that most of the luggage was unloaded, were at least an indication that these were not yokels from Kansas attracted by the sign planted at the crossroad by that detestable little councilman, and blithely intent on using a private property as a photo op. Having assured herself that the risks of lowering herself were minimal, the Parisian strode towards the Alfa Romeo driver, who stood admiring her.

"Sorry to disturb you," she said. "You must be my husband's new renters, isn't it? Permit me to present myself: Christiane Degency." She held her hand out, and the Alfa Romeo driver, in a fit of dazzled confusion, kissed it. She spoke English with a heavy French accent, but without any self-consciousness.

"Enchanté, Madame. Philip Shaw. And these are my friends, Amanda and Charles Fischbein."

"Just call me Chuck!" the SUV driver threw over his shoulder as he unloaded a golf bag from the trunk. He then ambled over to mash Christiane's hand, the only one among the adults to be unfazed by her glamour. He was a burly man with a booming voice, the manner of a bear and the kind of face that would guarantee a temp gig as mall Santa every year. He was dressed in jeans, short-sleeved polo top and huge sneakers, the thinning of his salt-and-pepper hair compensated for by a short pony tail and a well-trimmed beard and moustache. It was the correct image for a Berkeley entrepreneur.

"And these are our children, Isaac and Sarah," added Amanda in a matronly sing-song. Tall, long-legged, squarely built without much of a waist or butt, she might have been called an Amazon but for a certain awkwardness in her movements that suggested femininity had not come easily to her. Her face on the other hand, under a mass of curls that looked untamed, but that she spent much time every day shaping with a low speed dryer, and got highlighted every month at a toney salon, had an air of benign entitlement. Her entire outfit, from the polar fleece jacket to the Birkenstock sandals, seemed to have come from a Lands End catalog. She advanced towards Christiane Degency, her arms around her children, nudging them forward in a gesture reminiscent of a gift bearing magus. This was her usual way of introducing herself to strangers, thereby establishing her primary identity as a mother of twins and at the same time pawning off the conversational burden onto the two tykes, with often unexpected results that she was the only one to find "darling". Her interlocutor in this case was at a loss as to how she should respond to her gesture: was she supposed to shake the tots' grimy hands, kiss their snotty faces or offer her own children in exchange? Fortunately, she was soon relieved of her indecision by Isaac planting himself right under her nose and shouting:

"Do you want to see what I would do to a terrorist? OK, watch me!" Without any further encouragement, he took a karate pose, let out a blood curdling yell, and started performing a chopping and kicking routine. He had defeated several imaginary opponents by the time his father suggested that now was not the best time for a wrestling demonstration. Meanwhile, Sarah was arguing in the same sing-song as her mother's that she was not in the mood to be polite, and that no one had a right to force her. Both Fischbein parents being thus busy negotiating with their children, Christiane Degency bethought herself of hers.

"Eh! Bien, qu'attendez-vous? Sortez donc vous dégourdir les jambes pendant que j'appelle votre père!" she ordered in a low voice, holding the Audi's back door open. The girls emerged reluctantly: first a slender, grave looking pre-teen with a thick black braid that hung past her waist. She was wearing an updated kilt, rather short with fat pleats in a navy blue, lavender and white plaid, an updated navy blue twin set, and updated oxfords with waffle soles. She was dark and erect, like her mother, but the long face with its preoccupied look belonged to her father. She stood close to the car, and after uttering a barely audible "Bonjour Messieurs, bonjour Madame …", concentrated on the gravel at her feet, in which she drew obscure symbols with the tip of her shoe. Following her, her sister wiggled out of the car, a five year-old blond cherub dressed in a purple jumper.

"Maman, est-ce que je peux aller voir le jardin?" she asked cautiously.

"Oui, mais emmène ta soeur, et ne t'éloigne pas," answered Christiane, as the little girl started toddling towards the stairs, soon followed by her sister, who seemed resigned to her babysitting role. The Fischbein children, intrigued, started after them.

"Well, where are our hosts? A stiff drink right now would hit the spot!" Phil remarked, his head tilted towards the sky, in which thunder heads were growing by the minute. He was going to have to pull the top up on the car, damn it, which would ruin the charm of the romantic spin he was planning.

"Let me call Franny," said Chuck.

"I will phone my husband," said Christiane.

They had pulled out their cell phone at the same time, as if preparing for a high tech duel. Indeed, since they were unknowingly trying to reach the same number (for Franny, lacking a cell phone and predicting that she would be out in the fields at the time of the Fichbeins' arrival, had given them Hughes' number) they had to compete for the line. At last the arrival of the two sets of visitors was conveyed to their respective host, and a few minutes later, Hughes and Franny burst upon the scene. Red-faced and out of breath, they paused under the arch to stare in disbelief at the assembled group of adults, Hughes zeroing in on his ex-wife and Franny on Phil, their astonishment echoed in the look of curiosity, mingled here with approval and there with apprehension, with which the others took in the well-matched couple in their picturesque stone frame.

A new round of introductions was effected. Christiane pecked Hughes' cheeks, and Phil hugged Franny lustily, flattening her nose against his chest in the process. Then Franny took refuge between Amanda and Chuck while Hughes motioned his wife to the side.

"Vous vous êtes fait couper les cheveux," Hughes gasped.

"Quel sens de l'observation, mon chéri! Qu'en pensez-vous?" tossed Christiane, pivoting on her heels to show all three hundred and sixty degrees of her haircut.

"Vous savez fort bien ce que j'en pense," he hissed, and she shrugged back in answer. "Mais peu importe. Ce que j'aimerais savoir, c'est pourquoi vous ne m'avez pas prévenu de votre arrivée."

She made a sign with her hand for him to lower his voice, and their conversation went on in whispers, anxious and angry on his side, stubbornly detached on hers.

"What's the matter?" asked Amanda, her interest piqued by the spectacle of this aristocratic spat.

"Hughes' ex-wife wants to drop the girls off with him for a few days while she deals with the funeral arrangements of an aunt on the Riviera. But this is really the worst possible time for Hughes to be dealing with family emergencies. He is very busy with the harvest, and he has no room for two children in the cabin where he is staying while he rents out the chateau."

"Oh! so she is an *ex*-wife. I got the impression from her that they were still married."

"No, no. They got divorced *two* years ago!" Franny had unconsciously stressed the "two", as if the number by itself could reduce the personage of the ex-wife to insignificance, but the tension in her voice belied her confidence. One glance at Christiane had made her feel completely inadequate as a woman. And then there was the formal "vous" that the ex-couple used to address each other. To Franny's knowledge, one said "tu" to one's intimates. Was this some special etiquette rule that pertained to the rarefied stratum of French society to which they both belonged? And how many others might there be? For the first time in ten days, she wished herself back in Berkeley, where her lack of sophistication could pass for normal. As to Hughes, he had reverted in her mind to the status of complete stranger.

"Well, why don't we invite them to stay with us? I am sure there are enough rooms for everyone, since all our other guests have cancelled. What do you think, Chuck?" proposed Amanda, whose hospitality was famous in her little corner of the world. Besides, she was looking forward to sharing quarters with a French vicomte (for Franny had not been able to resist telling her of his title), anticipating the interest that would accrue to her capital of good will in the shape of fascinating tales at school bake sales and soccer games. Chuck, whose domestic tranquillity rested on agreeing with his wife on most things, thought that it was the right thing to do. Westerners should stick together in these dangerous times, he added, half-facetiously. Only Phil had some objections, but given that he was a last minute guest himself, he refrained from voicing them.

Chuck was therefore dispatched to relay the hospitable proposal to the still huddled Degencys, and after many protests and counter protests, it was accepted. And then Christiane agreed to stay on for dinner, which would allow her to finish her trip to the Riviera after the weekend traffic had thinned out.

The children now reappeared on the stone stairs, the blond cherub, whose name was Héloise, gamboling at their head, and Clarisse, the grave pre-teen, dutifully bringing up the rear. Héloise espied her father in the courtyard below and ran down towards him, crying excitedly:

"Papa, papa, j'ai trouvé une jolie grenouille!"

"Ne cours pas dans l'escalier! Et tiens la rampe! Tu vas tomber," warned Christiane, upon which the girl did slow her pace to a half-trot. At last she reached her father, still busy discussing new lease terms with Chuck. She pulled his sleeve, whispering loudly: "Regarde, papa!"

"Héloise, voyons, on n'interrompt pas les grandes personnes!" Hughes scolded, immediately contradicting his words by turning around, bending down and picking the girl up, rocking her on his arm while he resumed his talk with Chuck. The cherub settled down on her father's chest, one hand on his neck, the other still clasped around her prey, ready at the first break in the conversation to perform a little show and tell. In the background, Christiane could be heard muttering: "Vous ne faites que l'encourager!"

Meanwhile Clarisse stood back, her hands clasped behind her, waiting patiently to be noticed. It was Chuck, made uneasy by the girl's restraint, who brought the conversation short, allowing Hughes to greet his older daughter.

"Eh! bien, ma grande, quelle bonne surprise! Viens embrasser ton père". He held out his free arm, and she dived into its embrace.

"Tu es sur que ça ne te dérange pas?" she cried. "Je peux t'aider, tu sais. Et je m'occuperai d'Héloise, n'aie pas peur."

Something about the girl's anguished tone and the passionate way she clung to her father made Amanda Fischbein avert her gaze. She didn't need to understand French to guess what the poignant scene was about. The legacy of divorce, she assumed, promising herself that she would never let it happen to her family. As to Chuck, he had fled back to the SUV, out of which he now pulled a folded scooter, a deflated plastic raft, a bag of Barbie paraphernalia and a cooler filled to the brim with the kids' favorite snacks, in case they couldn't be purchased in this foreign land.

There was a third round of introductions, as Hughes wanted Franny to meet his daughters. Afraid that the girls would read too much in their father's gesture, Franny tried to be as non-committal as she could. She forbore to claim that she had heard a lot about them or to look for signs of family resemblance, and resolutely eschewed baby talk. As a result, she feared, she must have come off as terribly cold. The girls' response was polite, which was all that could be expected under the circumstances, although in Clarisse's eyes, Franny detected a note of emotional awareness that touched her to the quick.

Now it was Victoria's turn to make her appearance, prompting a fourth round of introductions. She was at her most exuberant, greeting everyone like long lost relatives, particularly the Fischbein children, whom she declared adorable. Sarah at least wasn't mollified.

"I need to do number one," was her only reply.

Victoria immediately offered to escort her to the bathroom. Héloise, at whose request Franny had translated this exchange, also evinced a need to pee. So back up the stairs the children went in single file—this time minus Clarisse—with Victoria figuring as the Pied Piper.

They were no sooner out of sight than a blue van drove in with Pierrette at the wheel and Savia in the passenger seat. In the back sat Chérif, who had let himself be drafted for the weekend, notwithstanding his doubts as to the Moslem propriety of picking wine grapes. A few seconds later Guillaume arrived on foot. The courtyard being full, he had parked the tractor and its dump-bed overflowing with grapes outside the gate. Hughes and Franny led a fifth round of introductions, after which the first drops of rain forced the group to focus on logistics. It was decided that Guillaume would drive the tractor to the Cooperative while Hughes and Franny took Savia and Chérif back to the village and Christiane did the honors of the house to the new American guests. Franny ran upstairs to get her umbrella. When she returned, she was detained by Phil, who, speaking no French, seemed a little flummoxed by the general agitation. He was holding her by the arm, apparently pleading for explanations when Hughes called across the yard, his voice as clear as a bell:

"Franny, tu viens?"

Franny excused herself and ran towards the Mercedes, trying to pass off as a sign of exertion the flush that had spread on her face at being called "tu" by the vicomte. On her way, she met a look from Christiane that suggested she was not the only one to have noticed that small detail of address. It was a look of surprise, but not, as far as Franny could tell, of hostility. "Go ahead," it seemed to imply, "I wish you luck." As she fastened her seat belt, Phil was busying himself with the roof of the Alfa Romeo, swearing at the mechanism under his breath.

They first drove to the bakery, where they deposited Savia and Chérif and picked up their pizza order, managing to score a couple of extra pies to accommodate the unexpected guests. Then they stopped at the Cooperative, where Guillaume was waiting for Hughes to unload the grapes, two tractors in line behind him. Fortunately the rain was holding off. On the way back, they were silent for a while, thankful for the interlude of peace before what promised to be a hectic night, what with the upcoming storm, the multiplication of children, ex-marital tensions, Victoria's uncertain status and Phil's troubling presence, and above all the difficulty of bringing together three separate groups of people who did not speak the same language. But Franny's mind never remained at peace for very long.

"Pourquoi m'avez-vous tutoyée dans la cour?" she found herself asking.

"Did I? Do you mind?" He looked at her from the corner of his eye, and smiled.

"You're not supposed to answer a question with another question!"

"I am not?"

"Quit it! You seem so smug suddenly. Do you enjoy having two women to order about?"

"Order Christiane about? Believe me, I stopped trying a long time ago."

"Is that why you call her 'vous'?"

"No, that's just an old custom. But I would rather not follow it, now, with you."

"Because you can order me about?"

"Yes." There was that yes again, a full bar worth of musical notes, playful and serious all at once, as frustrating as a koan. It suddenly occurred to Franny that this was the way to take it: as a koan. That there was nothing to sort out or establish or protect against, just a moment to enjoy, with this man that she liked very much, no matter what his secret quirks might be.

"OK, I give up!" she laughed, laying her hands with the palms up on the seat in a gesture of submission.

They were going over a bridge. On the other side, on the right, the shoulder widened to create a small parking area under a bower of overhanging hazelnut bushes. Hughes slowed down and pulled over.

"What's happening?" asked Franny.

"Je veux justifier le tu," he answered, bending toward her, and before she knew it, they were kissing, tentatively at first, then more and more comfortably, until they were in complete earnest.

How long did it last? Five minutes or thirty seconds? As is the case with earthquakes, it was hard to tell. Long enough at any rate to give them a taste for more, and also to start a little wave of panic in both of them. What were they doing? What were they committing themselves to? How where they going to pursue whatever it was under the nose of a dozen people, including his children? A ploc ploc on the windshield stopped them before either the hunger or the panic could spin out of control. It was starting to rain again.

"Back to the grind!"

"On n'est pas là pour s'amuser!" they said at the same time, both colloquial in the other's tongue as they pulled away from each other. Hughes turned on the headlights, started the windshield wipers, and merged the car back onto the road.

They were astute enough to suspect that their sudden *passage à l'acte* must have had something to do with Christiane and Phil's presence. On Hughes' part, the temptation to show that he was no longer in thrall to the woman who had jilted him was an obvious motive. He had also refused to take at face value Franny's assertion that Philip Shaw was only a client, as was Chuck Fischbein, of the technical writing firm that employed her. She had been too perturbed by the news of his arrival, and Phil had assumed too much of a right to monopolize her. There was something unresolved between them, maybe one of those seduction attempts that Franny had deplored. Reflexively, Hughes had set about forestalling a potential rival's move, or to look at it more altruistically, about protecting her from a cad. As to Franny, not having been the initiator of the kiss, she did not have to wonder about her own motives, although, human nature being what it is, the gratification of being the object of a contest between two men may have played a small part in her yielding, another part being straightforward sexual attraction, and another, least plausible perhaps to a male reader, a form of kindness, the instinct to give others what they seemed to need—which unfortunately was rarely as encompassing as Franny imagined. Many times, Franny had in this way become the victim of her own good heart.

However tangled the web of their respective intentions, it had led to a simple, undeniable action. A kiss is a small Rubicon over which you cannot jump back. Alea jacta est, they both thought, all considered, as they drove back towards the chateau in a driving rain.

In spite of the umbrella, they were drenched by the time they reached the front porch. They went into the kitchen to put down the soggy pizza boxes. Overhead, the Fischbeins could be heard clomping about. They had taken over the east wing as Franny had predicted, selecting the room with the canopy bed for themselves, and getting Phil to help with the moving of a box spring and mattress down from the third floor into the adjacent dressing room so that Sarah could sleep next to them. Isaac for his part was not afraid to stretch in napoleonic splendor on a high dark bed with posts topped by sphinxes, in a room that could have held his entire first grade class (true, it was a very small class, since the twins were enrolled in a private school).

Héloise had made straight for her old room, from which Hughes gave up extracting her, though for a number of reasons, he would have felt it more appropriate for the Degency family to retire to the attic. As to Clarisse, she was sitting on the bench in the mezzanine, her hands folded in her lap, waiting for her father's instructions in spite of her mother's suggestion that she take up whatever room was still unclaimed. Franny, remembering the poster of Britney Spears on the door of her armoire, guessed that the bedroom she occupied must have been the girl's and offered to move. Clarisse shed on her a look of grave thankfulness but declined. She did not want to disturb anyone, she said, and she was beyond Britney Spears anyway. So she was given the nondescript room, and Hughes, feeling obliged to keep an eye on his daughters, picked the office room, the master bedroom being occupied by Victoria. For his part, Phil, mindful of his romantic designs, had decided to sleep on the third floor, as far as possible from noisy kids and prying adults. He would soon come to see this decision as a strategic mistake.

The room assignment puzzle thus solved, luggage was brought up, linen was distributed, suitcase contents were put away. Hughes went upstairs to one of the locked rooms, which contained his personal effects, to retrieve some dry clothes. Franny took a shower in the bathroom attached to the master bedroom while Christiane used the yellow bathroom to freshen up. As she scrubbed off field dust and dried grape juice, Franny had an attack of sartorial anxiety. It had not previously occurred to her to worry about what to wear at the harvest dinner as it was supposed to be an informal affair, little more than a picnic. But somehow, Christiane Degency's presence had changed everything. Now it seemed that khaki and denim were out of the question, that even the lavender dress wasn't elegant enough. It seemed that what was required was something silky or gauzy or sparkly or low-cut, the problem being that Franny did not own any such piece of clothing. Perhaps Victoria wouldn't mind lending her some item out of her more flashy wardrobe. She was several sizes bigger than Franny, but she owned a number of stretch tops that might elevate Franny's one pair of black linen slacks to the level of dressy. Wasn't that what girlfriends did for each other in TV sitcoms? When Franny came out of the bathroom, Victoria was busy writing in her diary, oblivious to the Grand Hotel comings and goings around her. She did not however seem very receptive to Franny's request for help, and pointedly vetoed the idea of investigating the content of the armoire right then and there. With uncharacteristic terseness, she said she would think about it, more or less shooing Franny out. Franny went back to her room chastened, afraid she had committed a faux-pas.

Fifteen minutes later there was a knock on her door. It was Victoria, her mood apparently improved, holding in the palm of her hand a tiny sheath made out of tie-dyed bubble-stretch fabric that could fit any size of woman. The dress was scoop-necked, and on Franny at least, it had three-quarter length sleeves and just cleared the top of her knees, clinging fetchingly to her every curve. Because of the air trapped in the fabric's bubbles, it was even warm enough for a rainy night. Accessorized with matching earrings and bangles, also brought by Victoria, and Franny's own pair of patent leather sandals, the outfit radiated a sort of California chic that made both women proud, let the Parisian try her darnedest.

Franny paused on the mezzanine, listening to the symphony of noises wafting from open doors and mingling pleasantly in the stately stairwell: the release of a suitcase lock, the banging of a dresser drawer, the flush of a toilet, a few notes on the piano, glasses clinking, vegetables being chopped, adult voices whispering and laughing, and a boy's cry of anguish: "Mommy, I can't find my Game Boy!". The bustle completely transformed the atmosphere of the chateau, making its huge space unthreatening, even cozy. The ghosts whose invisible presence had chilled Franny when she first arrived were still lurking behind the hanging portraits and amid the strange bric-a-brac, but even they seemed to be glad of the change of pace. Having grown up as a single child and spent much of her adult life alone, Franny was not used to sharing quarters with a crowd. Yet right now, at that particular distance from her fellow human beings, within earshot but out of sight, her hand on the gracefully curved railing and silver glinting on each side of her face, she felt perfectly at home. It was only a momentary feeling, however, as she became aware of a chill in her back, although this time it had nothing to do with ghosts. Someone had carelessly left the mezzanine window open, and rain was puddling on the tile floor. Franny pulled the casement closed, re-arranged the folds of the drapes, and prepared to plunge into the evening's maelstrom.

When she arrived downstairs, Christiane and Phil were sitting kitty corner at one end of the dining room table, sipping on drinks and talking of Monte Carlo. The china cabinet, locked until now, stood wide open, its lower half revealing a fully stocked bar. Phil's tie was bunched up in his jacket pocket, and Christiane was shedding a new coat of lipstick on the crystal edge of her glass, otherwise the two looked very much the same as when they had arrived. In the kitchen Franny found Guillaume, who had brought the tractor back and was busy assembling the makings of a ratatouille. Hughes was there too, in black jeans and finely checked cotton shirt, casual yet subtly dressed up (Christiane's influence on him too?), washing salad greens in the sink.

"Est-ce que je peux vous aider?" asked Franny.

"Pas de femme dans la cuisine!" teased Guillaume. "Cooking is a man's job!"

Just then Chuck burst upon the scene, radiating cologne and good humor.

"You guys need a hand?" he boomed over Franny's shoulder. "I am an ace with the chopping knife."

"Absolument. Here, can you slice these tomatoes?" said Hughes, without turning around.

"OK, my friends, put on your sunglasses. The sparks are gonna fly! And you, little lady, you'd better get out of the way. You heard what the man said. Besides, you're much too elegant for kitchen work," said Chuck, grabbing Franny by the shoulders and pushing her gently aside. Hughes still failed to turn around. Did he regret what had happened in the car?

"That's reverse sexism!" Franny cried, anxious under the play-acting, causing Christiane to raise an eyebrow and Phil to shout: "I am going to report this to the Labor Board! Here, Franny, why don't you join the leisure class? Have a drink, relax." And he held out a chair for her on the other side of Christiane. But Franny was too nervous to sit down. Fortunately, Victoria had just entered the dining room, wearing flowing black pants and a gold tunic, her hair elaborately coiled, seemingly ready to attend the Oscars. She poured herself a glass of Port and took the chair offered by Phil, then, bending confidentially toward him while completely ignoring Christiane, she beamed her most enthusiastic smile and purred: "So, Phil, what do you do when you're not tooling around France in that little Alfa Romeo?"

Just then the phone rang and Franny ran to get it. It was Savia, announcing that she wouldn't be able to come to the party. She was very sorry, but Hacene had a late delivery to make, and it was raining too hard to come on bicycle.

Franny offered to pick her up, but she emphatically declined. Franny suspected that the husband had vetoed the dinner, intimidated by the large gathering of strangers. She was fully expecting a phone call from Pierrette, also excusing herself because of an uncooperative spouse, when the door bell rang instead. It was the first time Franny heard it, she realized, and, as had been the case with the phone, she was the only one to make a move to answer it. Somehow, she had been handed the role of *maitresse de maison*. For now, she didn't mind.

Gérard and Pierrette stood on the porch under a gigantic black umbrella. Pierrette, perky in a stretch mini-skirt, her face tense with social good will. Gérard, lanky, a hangdog expression at odds with the military crewcut, broken nose and prominent jaw, an ironed plaid shirt his only concession to formal dress. He would have looked quite at home in a NASA control room, thought Franny. Indeed, he was apparently some kind of nuclear engineer, which meant that within easy commuting distance of her pastoral eden operated one of those dangerous plants she had spent quite a bit of time fighting against in the eighties. Yet even in Gerard's presence, Franny could hardly bring herself to worry about it. Everyone in Saint Yves, including Hughes and Guillaume, seemed to take nuclear power so much for granted, and Gérard himself seemed so benign, without a hint of radioactive glow ... Was her lack of concern another demonstration of the banality of evil, she worried, and then the twins came tumbling down the stairs, followed by their mother, and the decibel explosion prevented any further thinking.

Kisses, handshake, a spot for the dripping umbrella, directions to the kitchen for Pierrette, who was carrying the pear tart, her husband's hand, surprisingly huge and knotty, reluctantly letting go of her waist.

"Phil, can you pour Gérard a drink?"

"Sure, what will you have?"

"Comment?"

He didn't speak English. Fortunately Christiane came to the rescue. Before long, Gérard was seated at her side, a glass in one hand, the other combing through his crewcut at intervals as if he was afraid his hair might have grown an unmanly curl in the last few minutes. However, *l'alcool aidant*, he was soon relaxed enough to venture a few remarks about the deficiencies of the government, a perfectly innocuous topic since the ruling *cohabitation* of socialists and gaullists permitted a convenient vagueness as to which party should be blamed for the sorry state of everything. Amanda, who although she did not speak French, was able to pick up words like "gouvernement", "transparence" and "laissez-faire", thought that talking politics was no way to engage a conversation with a stranger, without even the courtesy of a few preliminary questions about the other person's job, family or place of origin.

On the other side of the table, meanwhile, the Americans were following their own conversational rules, which did mandate extensive biographical inquiries. In this case, Phil and Amanda having known each other for a long time, Victoria was on the hot seat, and she was quite happy to embroider on her story of semi-orphaned childhood, cinematographic ambitions and frozen bank assets. What tactless prying, Christiane couldn't help thinking.

Even after the rain had forced the celebration inside, Franny had held on to the idea of a buffet, afraid that a sit-down dinner might strike too formal a note. But now, seeing her guests comfortably ensconced around the table, which was long enough to accommodate twice their number, she started having doubts about the wisdom of attempting to dislodge them. Against Guillaume's orders, she went into the kitchen to consult with Hughes, who, still too busy with salad making to look at her, teasingly reminded her that sitting down for a meal in France was, far from a formal occasion, in fact a daily ritual. On the other hand, he was definite on the propriety of grouping all the children together at the far end of the table, under Clarisse's supervision, so that they would not bother the adults. So this was how Franny set the table with Pierrette's help, Christiane wordlessly contributing a damask tablecloth retrieved from the depths of the linen closet.

"A table!"

"Let's hit it!"

Franny reviewed the food laid out on the table: tomato salad, cucumber salad, green salad, radishes, pizzas, ratatouille, various *charcuterie*, cheeses and olives, crusty bread and wine from the chateau's cellar. A feast for the Californians in the group, with their vegetarian leanings, but probably inadequate for the French, for whom, if Franny remembered well, a major meat course was the linchpin of any meal. At least the menu had the advantage that all its dishes could be served at once, sparing the cooks repeated trips to the kitchen. The American love of convenience had prevailed in this one respect.

Chuck sat himself next to his wife and Pierrette next to her husband. Then Guillaume, seeing that the table was split by nationality, bravely took his place on the American side, while Franny sat opposite him on the French side, quickly joined by Hughes. Clarisse, familiar with the routine, settled at the head of the children's area, with her father on one side and Héloïse on the other. Isaac perched himself across from Héloïse without a fuss, but Sarah was firmly opposed to being shoved from the limelight. She made her disapproval so loudly known that Chuck and Guillaume ended up moving down the table to make room for her next to her mother, this game of musical chairs, performed with outward cheerfulness, being accompanied by many unspoken comments.

Typical American brat! thought all the French adults.

You go, girl! cheered Victoria.

Not worth fighting over, Chuck inwardly reasoned.

That kid needs a good spanking, was Phil's private opinion.

Well, how would they feel being relegated to the end of the table? Amanda bristled under her breath.

As to Héloise, she silently resolved to try the pink girl's tactics at the first opportunity.

These soliloquies completed to everyone's satisfaction, they were about to dig in when Sarah manifested herself again, declaring that there was nothing she liked on the table, not even the pizza, too thin and skimpy on the cheese, according to her. Amanda went to the kitchen to fix her some scrambled eggs, and in the interval of embarrassed silence, the door bell was heard to ring again. Franny and Hughes exchanged a look, the first since their return from Saint Yves, the chatelain's gray eyes telegraphing all at once that he had no idea who could be at the door, that it was his turn to answer the bell, that he approved of the dress and well remembered their kiss. He had a knack for switching abruptly from abstraction to attentiveness, and for packing loads of meaning in the smallest word or gesture. Was it his true self, or a seduction trick? Whichever it was, Franny feared it was working on her.

The latecomer turned out to be Chérif, scrubbed and with his shirt tucked in, his hands stuffed in the pockets of a black leather jacket that was too big for him, a box of chocolates under his arm. He had decided to come on his own, catching a ride in his father's delivery truck. The chocolates were a gift from Hacene. As he stood next to Hughes, his shoulders hunched, reviewing the group under lowered eyebrows as if he already regretted his boldness, Franny was struck by how much he resembled the other native men with his spare stature, narrow face and vaguely sad look. In a couple of generations, if all went well, nobody could tell a Beur from a Frenchman. If all went well, for as the events of the previous week had shown, there were no end of unexpected ways for things to go wrong.

By the time Chérif had taken off his jacket, unburdened himself of the chocolate and shaken hands with Gérard, who surprisingly seemed to have met him before, Clarisse had added a place setting for him between her father and herself—which caused Amanda to feel sorry for the girl's desperation to please. At last, everyone was seated, and the meal started in earnest.

From that point on, the French faction completely dominated the evening's proceedings. It was a sight to see, how upon the first mouthful, these people, who earlier had seemed embarrassed with themselves and shy with each other, suddenly expanded and relaxed, how their faces became animated, how their elbows and hands flew, how their voices rang across the table, in turn grousing, ironic, appreciative, exuberant–yet never histrionic; how in short they became the mythical *bons vivants* in whose existence Franny had refused until now to believe. There was something to stereotypes after all: it was around the dinner table that the French were truly themselves. For how long, though, Franny couldn't help wondering. How long before the combination of TV, fast food, cyberspace surfing and the frantic pace of living that was supposed to be a badge of modernity blew the institution of the sit-down meal to smithereens, as had happened in the US, in fact?

It wasn't just culinary traditions that would be lost, but a specific art of dinner conversation in which everyone excelled, from the Parisian professional to the country housewife. As to the children, they were clearly expected to learn by listening until they were sure they could make a valuable contribution. The blond cherub, having at one point misjudged her own conversational readiness, was silenced by a definitive "Ne dis donc pas de bêtises, Héloise!" on the part of her mother.

One thing that distinguished this conversational style, it seemed to Franny, was its predilection for topics of general interest, starting of course with food: the first half-hour of the meal had been devoted to encyclopedic disquisitions on the part of the natives about the geography, history, preparation and gustatory merits (but not the health quotient) of each item on the table. This reminded Franny of the dinners at the cousins' in Chatenay Malabry, except that what had bored her to tears twenty-one years ago she now found thoroughly endearing. What had changed? Was the atmosphere in Saint Yves more convivial? Was she just more interested in food? Was beauty entirely in the eyes of the beholder?

Also interestingly, the dinner conversation eschewed private exchanges between neighbors, each remark pitched instead to the entire assembly, with full expectations of being interrupted, contradicted or laughed at. Last but not least, Franny admired the clever transitions the natives took turn in fashioning from one topic to another to keep the conversation lively. There was never an awkward silence or a jarring sense of a change in direction. But suddenly you realized that you were no longer talking about cheese pasteurization (a sacrilege!), but about *Le fabuleux destin d'Amélie Poulain*, the latest movie by Jean Pierre Jeunet (magical or gallo-centric?).

It was a contagious style, and after a while, with a little translation help from Hughes, Guillaume and Franny, the Americans found themselves plunging into the verbal torrent.

True to French form, the meal lasted for hours, stretching beyond dessert with coffee, liqueurs, chocolates and even, horror of horrors, a couple of cigarettes (Pierrette and Christiane) and cigars (Phil and Chuck, as delighted as truant children by their host's offer), all the adults seemingly stuck to their chair, their elbows supporting more and more of their weight, the bread crumbs, lettuce leaves, bits of cheese, chocolate wrappers, wine stains, stray grapes on the tablecloth looking more and more esthetically arranged, and the conversation still going strong.

"… un parc d'attraction, là, sous tes fenêtres, tu t'imagines?"

("There's apparently a secret plot by the mayor and the prefecture to develop an amusement park right around here …")

"Ben, il faut bien que les jeunes s'amusent. Tu préfères qu'ils se shootent?"

("Why a plot? Aren't the locals looking forward to more employment opportunities and higher tax revenues?")

"Bon, si tu trouves ça amusant de se donner le mal de mer sur les montagnes russes … Et puis, il y a le reste: la Mac bouffe, les embouteillages, les canettes de Coca dans la forêt, et notre paysage, notre beau paysage, ça ne te gêne pas de le voir transformé en Disneyland?"

("Apparently not …")

"C'est un groupe américain qui va acheter ça?"

"Oui, apparemment. Mais entre Grévin et Six Flags, moi, je ne vois pas la différence."

"Bah si, quand même. Au moins le bénéfice resterait en France."

"Ce que Guillaume veut dire, je crois, c'est que quelle que soit la nationalité des propriétaires, les parcs d'attraction ne satisfont pas aux critères du tourisme durable. Ils polluent trop, ils ne s'intègrent pas a l'environnement …"

("A question of sustainable development, according to Hughes …")

"Et pourquoi est-ce qu'on fabriquerait de faux châteaux, quand on en a de vrais qui tombent en ruine partout? Des montagnes en carton pâte en dessous du Mont Ventoux? Des rapides à l'eau de javel à coté des Gorges du Tarn? C'est pervers, tu ne trouves pas? Et puis, pendant ce temps-là, on apprend aux gosses à préférer le toc, à compter sur les frissons qu'on leur donne à la petite cuillère sans qu'ils aient besoin de lever le cul de leur chaise."

"Vous avez raison, Guillaume. Ce genre d'amusement préfabriqué ne fait qu'atrophier l'imagination des enfants."

("… And high tech entertainment is bad for children's imagination.")

"I agree with Christiane. Chuck and I refuse to buy all that plastic computerized shlock that passes for toys these days."

"Except for the Game Boy."

"I know, I know, but sometimes the pressure is overwhelming. Try saying no for the thousandth time while your kid is screaming in the aisle at Long's."

("Il est difficile de resister aux colères des enfants quand ils veulent un jouet.")

"My sister Nanette, she cry always to get what she want!"

"En tout cas, on ne peut pas laisser la mairie prendre une telle décision en catimini. C'est l'integrité de notre région qui est en jeu. Sans parler des fonds publics qui vont être consacrés à un tel projet, vous pouvez en être sûrs."

"Et sans parler des dizaines d'hectares, y compris ceux que tu convoites, qui vont être recouverts de bitume …"

("This amusement park will probably be subsidized by tax payers, and it's going to be located on land that Hughes wants to acquire for his vineyard.")

"Est-ce qu'ils ont le droit de faire ca?"

"Il suffit de faire rezoner le terrain. Et apparemment Malefoi a des copains à la SAFER."

"Est-ce que les compte-rendus du conseil municipal ne sont pas publiés sur l'Internet? Ils sont bien soumis eux-aussi à la transparence, non?"

"C'est bien beau l'Internet, mais la seule chose qui va les empêcher de nous faire un coup fourré, c'est qu'on se pointe en masse à leur reunions …"

("Guillaume is urging Hughes and Gérard to attend municipal council meetings to make sure there is public debate about the proposed amusement park.")

"Think globally. Act Locally."

"Well, Phil, we thought you were asleep …"

A little later. Sounds of banging on the piano drifting from the faraway music room, and then music, a piece from the Anna Magdalena Notebook, painstaking, light-fingered, lovely. Franny, whose consciousness has been absorbed in the contact of Hughes's arm against hers, notices that the children, including Chérif, have all left the table, vanquished by travel fatigue, heavy stomachs, or the failure of all their attempts to draw the adults' attention. Amanda looks around, seems to also become aware of the children's absence, turns to Christiane.

"Is this Clarisse playing? She is very talented. Has she been taking lessons for a long time?"

"Four or five years, n'est-ce pas, Hughes?"

"Pardon?"

"Peu importe ..."

"Sarah has been taking piano lessons for a year already. We think it's very important to start early. As you probably know, studies show that musical training fosters children's cognitive development."

"Fosters?"

(Franny, too tired to translate, lets the two women work out their language problems.)

"Speeds it up, you know?"

"Why speed it up?"

"To give the child an edge ..."

Christiane raises an eyebrow.

"I mean an advantage."

"An advantage over who?"

"An advantage in life, in general."

"You mean over children whose parents can't afford music lessons?"

"Well, I don't think of it in those terms. But why do *you* give Clarisse piano lessons?"

"So that she can play."

"What Christiane means is that we feel music is important in and of itself. It's one of the highest human achievements, and to pass it on to our children is a sort of sacred duty, don't you think?"

It's Hughes, once again taking the edge off somebody else's argument. He can be quite the diplomat. But who is included in the "we" he has just used?

"That goes without saying," Chuck replies. "We Americans love classical music too. And we do more than pass it on, by the way. Think Aaron Copland, Leonard Bernstein. And Charles Ives, Philip Glass, John Adams? You get my point. It's just that *we* like to kill two birds with one stone: upholding civilization *and* making our kids more competitive."

"You mean that you feel obliged to use self-interested rationales to justify pursuing the common good?"

Franny recognizes Robert Bellah's influence again. She feels prompted to throw in her own two cents.

"But *what* about the children whose parents can't afford music lessons? Don't they have a right to share in the achievement?"

"Ah! Your ancestors' passion for equality asserts itself ... You're right of course, Franny, and I for one fully supported Jack Lang's efforts to make musical education available to all."

"French factory workers will soon be forming orchestras?"

"Hopefully, yes …"

"A Marxist paradise … I am all for it."

"Le music avant toute chose! Who is Jack Lang?"

"A former minister of education. A socialist."

"Why, Phil, we didn't know you spoke French!"

Still later. Guillaume and Gérard, their acquaintance firmly established on a "tu" basis, have retreated to the billiard room where, the food and wine euphoria having dissipated, they have both reverted to their normal laconic manner, punctuating the clash of balls with mere "pas mal!" and "ah! celle-là, je la vois pas". Amanda and Christiane have gone to round up their children for bed, while Victoria is giving Pierrette a tour of the upstairs. Phil is still sitting at the head of the table, the part in his hair a little mussed. The subject of terrorism has finally come up, and Chuck is addressing Hughes.

"… I don't see why the French object so much to the terms President Bush used. Isn't the hair splitting just a reason not to get involved, so as not to stir up your own Moslem populations? I mean, what's so wrong with the word 'crusade'? Isn't what we are witnessing an actual clash of civilizations? Isn't Bush's only sin that he is willing to call a spade a spade?"

"Well, I would say a lack of diplomacy is a pretty big sin on the part of the most powerful man in the world. When you carry a big stick, it is a good idea to talk softly. People in general, not just Arabs, have no affection for bullies. But in any case the idea of a clash of civilization is a gross oversimplification of a complex set of problems."

Hmm, wonders Franny, what happened to Hughes' own diplomatic skills?

"You don't think that the attack on the World Trade Center was an attack on Western Civilization?"

"I believe that the concept of Western Civilization is an outdated myth, like the concept of race. There are as many differences–and similarities–between, let's say, contemporary French and American cultures as there are between contemporary American and Japanese cultures."

"You are cheating, by picking a westernized country like Japan."

"Which countries are not 'westernized'?"

"The Arab countries, precisely!"

"So you think that the entire Arab world is behind the recent terrorist attacks?"

"No, of course not, not directly, although it's pretty clear that there is broad support for them in the Arab street. Didn't you see the jubilation in places like

Pakistan and the West Bank? It doesn't matter if Western Civilization is a myth, the Arabs believe in it to the extent that they want to destroy it. And that means you and me."

"Perhaps their grievances are more specific than hostility to Western Civilization. For instance ..."

"I know what you're going to say. American imperialism, Israeli settlements, etc. I am not defending the policies of the US or Israel, but I think you are deluded if you think these are the root causes of Arab hostility. After all, American policies have done more harm in South America than in the Middle East. But you don't see Chilean terrorists flying airplanes into buildings. What you refuse to look at is the role of religion. I mean, Islam is pretty clearly built around the idea of sacred war, which makes the idea of 'moderate Moslems' an oxymoron."

Does Chuck realize that Chérif is a Moslem, worries Franny. At least, the teen is out of the room.

"I think it's simplistic to derive the behavior of a large group of people over time from a few paragraphs in a religious text. If Islam is a warrior religion, you can just as truthfully say that Judaism is a racist religion."

Chuck is stunned. Does Hughes realize that I am Jewish, he wonders. He has heard about French anti-semitism, but to be confronted with it is another matter.

"What do you mean when you say that Judaism is racist?"

"Only that it asserts the superiority of a people on the basis of their ancestry. You belong to God's chosen just from the fact that your mother was Jewish, not because you converted."

"But you can convert to Judaism."

"But you don't have to."

"Then are you saying that Jews are intrinsically racist?"

"No, that is exactly the point. Historically, Jews have been no more racist than others, even though their religion would seem to predict that they would be. The same goes with Moslems. They are overall no more aggressive than others, even if their religion dictated that they should be."

"Then how do you explain the history of Arab conquests?"

"No more extensive, and no more bloody, than the history of European wars."

"And what about their current predilection for suicide bombers?"

"A confluence of many historical, political, social problems resulting in humiliation and desperation. To reduce them to the influence of religion is a convenient way to avoid trying to solve them."

"So what do you think should be done?"

"Ah! that's a discussion for another day."

"Amen!"

"Why, Phil, getting religion all of a sudden?"

Amanda has returned, towing Sarah, who won't go to sleep without a kiss from her father. Christiane, fortified by a new coat of lipstick, is ready to tackle the last leg of her journey south. Then Gérard, Guillaume and Chérif emerge from the billiard room, Victoria and Pierrette from the stairs. As the adults lounge around the table, chatting desultorily before separating, Héloïse appears in the doorway, barefooted and in her nightgown, a hand clutched against her chest. She looks around, sees that the pink girl is still up, locates her father, finds that he is not currently occupied, and decides that the time for show and tell has at last come. She sidles up to Hughes and opens her hand.

"Regarde, papa!"

On her palm sits a small green and yellow frog, looking a little squashed, but still alive, its heart beating visibly in its tiny chest. It stares up meditatively, in the manner of frogs, and then, smelling the scent of freedom, makes a mad hopping dash across the table.

"Oh! my God!" cries Victoria, echoed by a "Yuck!" from Sarah.

Tiens! une grenouille, qu'est-ce qu'elle fait là? wonder the French grownups.

"Héloïse, voyons," scolds Christiane, "ne pose pas tes animaux sur la table!".

Hughes finally notices his daughter. "Ma petite puce, je te croyais couchée!" he exclaims, lifting her into his arms.

She can't possibly have held on to the creature since we came inside, Phil wonders.

"I don't understand," Amanda whispers to her husband. "Don't they teach their children not to be cruel to animals? The poor frog could have died."

"Don't worry, Madame," Guillaume whispers back, "it's not an endangered species."

Very, very late. All the French dinner guests have gone home, the children are fast asleep, and so are the Fischbein parents. Even Phil, overcome with jetlag, wine and foreign jabber, has given up for now on the private interview with Franny that he has been looking forward to ever since Amanda, taking pity on his new state of bachelorhood, invited him to join them at their French retreat. Sprawled on the narrow bed of his third story bedroom with his arms and feet dangling over the edge, his parched mouth agape, the part in his hair blown away, he dreams that he is adrift on a stormy sea and that sirens are beckoning from the depths. The only light in the chateau is the one that filters underneath Victoria's shutters.

The rain has let up, only temporarily it seems, the starry holes in the cloud cover fast getting patched up. Indifferent to the weather, the crickets are giving their nightly outdoor concert, attended by Hughes, who has gone down to divert the flow of water away from the filled-up cistern, and by Franny, who is merely watching him.

"I was surprised to see Chérif at the dinner," she muses. "There was no one among the group that he could relate to. I had a feeling, the first couple of times he came for English lessons, that he had a crush on Victoria. But tonight he didn't seem to be paying her any attention. I hope he didn't catch any of Chuck's stereotyping of Arabs. He is a strange kid, don't you think?"

"How strange?"

"I don't know. Shy and brave at the same time. Surly and sweet. Hip and old-fashioned. I can't put my finger on it. I guess he is just a regular teenager, unsure of his identity. Did you notice that he seemed to know Gérard from before, although neither of them made anything of it?"

"Well, this is a very small village. Everybody runs into everybody else sooner or later."

"I guess. You seem to be protective of him, even though he barely acknowledges you. Is it because of your relationship with his mother?"

"That, among other things."

"What kind of things?"

Hughes straightens up, wipes his hands against each other, peers through the darkness above the beam of the flashlight held by Franny.

"It's a long story," he says. "And your teeth are chattering from the cold. Let's go to bed. It can wait till tomorrow." He takes the flashlight from her, wraps an arm around her shoulder and guides her towards the steps. Something in the sureness, the unhurriedness of his gestures towards her obliterates all her mistrust. He acts like a one woman man, she realizes, and suddenly she feels as if she is that woman, secure and unhurried too.

"But now I am really curious," she protests, her head irresistibly nestling in the crook of his neck, "I don't think I can wait till tomorrow!".

"OK, then, but let's go inside before you catch your death."

A few minutes later they are sitting across from each other at the kitchen counter, sipping on lime tea that he has brewed from leaves of his own trees. She is still wearing the corduroy jacket he lent her. Through the doorway, the sight of his rain slicker hanging from the rack in the hallway fills her with quiet elation, tangible evidence that he has moved back in, where he belongs.

"So?"

"What I am going to tell you is confidential."

"You can count on my discretion."

"All right then. A year ago, the Hamzaouis were living in a tough Paris *banlieue* where Hacene was completing his baking apprenticeship. There were a lot of tensions between gangs at the school that Chérif attended. One day a French boy lost one of his favorite CDs. For some reason, he became convinced that Chérif had stolen it and accused him of the deed in front of all his friends. Chérif denied it but the other boy wouldn't let go. He tried several times to start a fight, until one day, in the school bathroom, Chérif lost his temper and punched him in the nose. There were no witnesses to the scuffle, but the French kid must have felt thoroughly humiliated. He went home, got hold of a can of gasoline, came back to school, sat down in the middle of the yard, dowsed himself with the gasoline and lit a match to it right in front of his schoolmates, including Chérif, who, ironically, was the only one to have the presence of mind to throw a jacket over the flames. Unfortunately, by the time the fire was put out, the other boy had suffered third degree burns over sixty percent of his body."

"How horrible, for both of them! But to attempt suicide over a stolen CD? Even if the French boy was crazed with humiliation, I would have expected him to direct his anger outward, by gunning down Chérif's gang, say."

"The Columbine syndrome. As it turned out, the boy had another mediatic model in mind. A rambling suicide note was found in his bedroom, where he accused the Arabs of racism (against the French), and proposed to immolate himself in protest, like the Buddhist monks at the time of the Vietnam war, who had been featured in a recent TV documentary. The theft of the CD came to light, and Chérif found himself going from the status of hero to that of criminal. The school authorities, in concert with the police, hushed the whole affair for fear of inflaming ethnic sensitivities ..."

"Hushed the whole affair? How could they? In the US, it would have been on the ten'o clock news that same day."

"Well, the 'public's right to know' about every gory *fait divers* isn't quite as paramount here. In fact, the story did surface a couple of months later, after the would be martyr recovered enough to decide that he would publicly commit the rest of his life to improving relations between French and Arabs. He wrote a letter to Chérif, with copy to a TV network. And although Chérif's parents felt manipulated, they made their son go to the hospital. The meeting was duly taped. It made for an edifying scene of reconciliation, but Chérif was traumatized by the sight of his disfigured classmate, especially as he felt that he was partly responsible for what had happened. The Hamzaouis were so disturbed by the affair that they decided to move to a quieter place. That's how they ended up here."

"What a burden to carry at such a young age! I would never have guessed. And how is the other kid doing?"

"He is doing OK, considering what he went through. He has received many skin grafts, and is still wearing a compression suit, but he has returned to school. He writes to Chérif from time to time, and is making good on his promise to improve Franco-Arab relations by dating the daughter of a Imam."

"You seemed to imply that there were still other reasons why you feel protective of Chérif."

"You're very attentive. I guess on some level I feel responsible towards Algerians, because in a way I owe my land to their labor."

"How so? I thought that this property had been gifted to your ancestor by Napoleon as a reward for military prowess. Wasn't that before Algeria was colonized by France?"

"It was. But properties seldom remain in the same family for centuries. By the end of the eighteen hundreds, the Degencys had lost most of their land. Some of them emigrated to the colonies to start over, among them my great-great-uncle, who ended up building a little wine-growing empire in Algeria. It was his son, my Uncle Freddie, who re-acquired the chateau and the land around it at the time when it was getting clear that the *Pied-Noirs* were going to have to leave Algeria."

"And Uncle Freddie willed the place to you?"

"To my brother Hervé and myself, yes, as he did not have any children."

"And does Hervé help you with the winery?"

"No, he has other cats to whip—I mean other fish to fry. I am buying his part back little by little."

"Trying to build a little wine-growing empire?"

"No, I couldn't if I tried, but anyway I don't want to. I just want to make a decent living doing something that I like and that I feel right about."

"I'll drink to that!" says Franny, raising her cup of tea. "While I think about it, is your name De Gency or Degency?"

"Degency, in one word."

"No particle?"

"No particle. As a matter of fact, a 'de' or 'du' or 'de la' at the beginning of a patronym, whether attached or detached, has no special meaning other than to indicate that what follows is a place name."

"No difference between Dupont and Du Pont?"

"No difference, really."

"I always suspected that much."
"You were right. Seul le mérite compte."
"I'll drink to that too."

CHAPTER 14

▼

INTO EACH LIFE, SOME RAIN MUST FALL

Ce n'est pas tous les jours dimanche

The day dedicated to the sun (in English) and to the Lord (in French), Sunday/dimanche emerges out of the night very unpromisingly in either respect, with a dense pillow of bituminous vapor pressing down on the lurid glare of an aborted sunrise, a sight suggesting satanic rather than divine influence.

Mais n'exagérons pas. If there ever was a landscape more apt to repel feelings of gloom or evil, it's this one. Even under the choked light of a wet dawn, a sense of serene cheerfulness emanates from the bright green of the hills, the one snowy peak (bare white limestone, actually), and the caramel hues of the buildings that even the rain can't manage to discolor. And as always the air is practically fizzy with wholesomeness, whiffs of mold, fungi, pine resin, faded lavender stirred up by the rain giving it an additional antiseptic quality. As to the plumes from the cooling towers of the nearby nuclear plant, they are not visible from here. Besides, they only contain water, and are therefore non-toxic—as long as there is no accident.

Undeterred by a lack of cooperation of the elements, several roosters on over-time have been busy for a while amplifying the distant jingling of church bells that proclaims the holiday. So far to no avail, it seems. The blank façade of the chateau, its one unshuttered window, above the central door, reflecting the leaden sky in a such a way that it resembles the eye of a blinded Cyclops, persists so markedly in showing no sign of life that a fox, returning late from a hunting spree in the vineyards, ventures to take a shortcut across the graveled terrace towards his den in the woods. Not that its safety would be in any way compromised if every guest in the house stood alert on the porch. Even Héloise's certain attempt at capturing it would be purely motivated by affectionate curiosity. But the fox's survival so far has relied on stereotyping humans.

The first one to wake up is Clarisse. The pealing of bells has reached her ears through pillow down and tangled hair. She sits bolt upright and thinks: "Mass!" She must attend mass today, like every Sunday, or risk being denied permission to take her first communion next spring, already two years late, though it is not her fault, as the *aumônier* made clear, just absent-mindedness on the part of her parents at the time of enrolling her in catechism five years ago, when she couldn't be expected to know any better. And really, even if she could wish that Papa and Maman had not been so distracted by the slow death of their love for each other, which is one of those mysteries that faith encourages us to accept, and for which she is sure that they will eventually find forgiveness with a little help from her own prayers, she is rather happy that her religious instruction has been delayed. She remembers the odd sense of ridicule she used to feel (but never express, for one must always be kind) in third or fourth grade when her initiated classmates showed each other the pictures they had drawn in their catechism notebooks of Jesus holding a red heart in his hand, or lambs with matchstick legs and sun rays darting around their heads. She did not understand then the difference between literal and figurative. She owes this crucial conceptual tool, and the return to the welcoming arms of the Church that it has permitted, to her friend Eugénie, who now lives in New Caledonia, alas. But she has found a whole new set of friends, boys and girls, among her peer group at the *aumônerie*, and she is the *aumônier's* pet, because she has decided to prepare for communion of her own free will.

There is so much forgiveness in God's heart that Clarisse knows she would probably be forgiven for missing mass today. But she is determined to attend all the same, even if Papa can't take her, even if it turns out that this isn't the week for the mass to be celebrated in Saint Yves and she has to walk four kilometers to Mirésol. (In these days of scarce vocations, priests have to rotate their services between several parishes. Fortunately, Clarisse has taped the rotation schedule inside the cover of the phone book in the hall downstairs). She did hike to Mirésol last July, albeit accompanied by Henri, Papa's farmhand, while she was staying here during the two weeks that Papa had not rented the chateau. And Papa said he was proud of her, even though he doesn't go to church himself.

Poor Papa! He has to work so hard now that he doesn't get a salary! Several times, Clarisse heard Maman on the phone say that he was squandering his life and that he was going to end up a homeless bum. To Clarisse, she just says: "Oh! ton père, tu sais ...", which sounds even worse in its vagueness, implying that he is too weird for words and that she washes her hands of him, making him Clarisse's exclusive problem (for Héloise is too young for such responsibility). And Clarisse does what she can to help him, when he lets her. The best thing she can do, she has figured out, is to avoid spending money so that Maman won't ask for more alimony. Thus, she has stopped requesting things that her allowance can't buy, such as catered birthday parties, ski trips, pagers, webcams and CD burners, new bedroom furniture, the latest Naf Naf fashions. As to her allowance, having also renounced Britney Spears, Harry Potter, Japanese Mangas, pains au chocolat and nail glitter, she is able to save most of it, just in case it might become handy. The funny thing is, she does not feel deprived at all, but rich in her difference, uplifted by the idea of Christian sacrifice.

The idea of walking to church by herself appeals to her, and not just as a sacrifice. In fact, she loves the sense of adventure it gives her. In Paris, she rides the metro to mass, clutching her ticket all the way in case there is a control, her handbag tucked under her arm to ward off pickpockets, her gaze riveted on the zooming tunnel for fear of missing her station. When she emerges on the square, she tries to guess which of the passersby are heading like her towards the majestic building, which is in Romanesque style, her favorite because of its old-fashioned simplicity. And then she is inside, a cool dot of holy water on her forehead, organ music reverberating through her bones, darkness and light, call and response, the smell of burning candles, everything safe and predictable in the love of God. She can't wait to be able to walk up to the altar, to kneel in front of the priest in white cassock who will place the golden host on her tongue and bend the chalice to her lips, deeming her worthy to receive the body and blood of Christ–figuratively, it goes without saying, as much as the aumonier's words seem to be saying the opposite.

Clarisse's goal in life is to be a perfect Christian: to do her duty in all things, whether it is to attend mass every Sunday, practice the piano daily, take care of her sister when both Maman and the au pair are away (except on Sundays, when religion trumps babysitting, and Héloise is shipped off to Mammy), stay at the top of her class, or love both of her parents even if they don't love each other (though Clarisse has a secret preference for Papa). Also, in increasing order of difficulty, to trust in God, to love her neighbor, to understand the Trinity, and to avoid the seven deadly sins–pride is the only one that has tempted her so far, but it promises to be a lifelong challenge.

One thing troubles her as she tip-toes to the bathroom to splash water on her face, brush her teeth and re-braid her hair. Not the distance, not the rain that has just started pattering again on the window pane, not the necessity of wearing undignified rubber boots, not the note she is going to have to leave under Papa's door to let him know where she is going. She is remembering last week's Gospel reading in Church, which concerned the parables of the lost lamb and the prodigal son. Jesus claimed that the repenting sinner is much dearer to His heart than the just who has no need to repent. Is it possible, is it fair, that through her very attempt at leading a blameless life, Clarisse might incur God's neglect?

While Clarisse ponders her first theological paradox, Amanda is having her own spiritual crisis of sorts. She woke up more than an hour ago, as she has every hour throughout the night, and this time she knew she wouldn't get back to sleep. She looked at her travel clock, incongruous looking on the marble top of the gilded nightstand. She tried to compute the time in Ohio, where she woke up last, was it yesterday? but couldn't remember if she should add or subtract. It is true that she has never been very good at math, and dreads the time when the twins will start algebra, which will be all too soon, the private school they attend being naturally very competitive. For fear of waking Sarah, who has insisted on having the door to her bedroom left open, she has been lying motionless ever since, staring at the shepherdesses in bowers draped over the bed canopy and listening to Chuck's peaceful snoring. And having finally landed here, the site of her dream vacation ever since she read Peter Mayle's books, and not in a run of the mill bed and breakfast but a bona fide chateau, with the lord of the castle himself asleep only a few yards away, she has found herself strangely dissatisfied.

Her gloomy train of thought started with a simple wish for the New York Times, which in her mind is forever associated with Sunday, even though in the last few years, because of the frenzy that attends the raising of twins, it has often been removed from the beloved blue plastic envelope, as exciting to spot among the azalea bushes as an Easter egg, only to be dumped in the recycling bin. The unread paper, its crisp pages still perfectly folded, is for her the most poignant symbol of her renunciation of the life of the intellect, which is why she hasn't been able to bring herself to cancel her subscription–that and the fact that her yard would be the only one in her neighborhood ungraced with a blue package on Sunday morning. If she were truly honest with herself, she would acknowledge that her renunciation predates the birth of the twins by a good fifteen years, that it was soon after she gave up on an uncertain academic future, instead parlaying her M.A. in History from UC Berkeley into an administrative position in that department, that she started skipping the more intellectual material in the Times, concentrating instead on the Styles and Travel sections, where you could catch up on the latest lifestyle trends before they hit the West Coast. But as long as she was single, she at least read the news headlines, whose compressed, vaguely gothic font made them look more serious than those of the San Francisco Chronicle. Keeping up with current affairs is a must when you are trying to snag a professional husband. Otherwise, she hardly needed the New York Times' editorials to bolster her political views, which, for all her finally marrying a capitalist entrepreneur, and his subsequent turning into a millionaire, have remained staunchly liberal, per family and regional tradition: strong on civil rights and a woman's right to choose, committed to welfare programs, education, the environment and world peace, and supportive of Israel, albeit more and more uneasily.

The news has been a downer for a long time, apart from the small blip of the first Clinton election. Genocide, global warming, AIDS, the endless emergence of dictatorships, the persistence of hunger, Republican victories. And now the horror of mass terrorism on US soil. How could you persist in wanting to bring children into such a world? But how would the world persist if you didn't? Hence the desire to cocoon, to shut out the general misery. Married at thirty nine, Amanda could not afford to ignore the ticking of her biological clock. Semi-consciously, she had settled on Chuck because as a computer nerd he seemed more likely to remain faithful, a quality that his predecessors in Amanda's heart, Phil among them, had sorely lacked. As to Chuck, he had settled on Amanda mostly because she would have him. So after a suitably romantic honeymoon (London, Paris, Venice), they immediately undertook to get pregnant. It took three increasingly panicky years, from a social schedule regulated by the thermometer, through fertility drugs and crying jags over every invitation to a baby shower—which she nonetheless gracefully accepted, always bringing the most expensive gift—to the first steps towards a private adoption, for life to finally adhere to its rightful script: a boy and a girl, a complete family in one fell swoop. Ironically, although the hurried timing of their efforts to produce children never gave Chuck and Amanda much of a chance to revel in their couplehood, they came out of the ordeal loving each other. So much for our convictions about the right way to achieve intimacy.

Motherhood, however, has failed to deliver the expected sense of plenitude. Like many women, Amanda secretly experienced pregnancy as an assault on her bodily integrity. She felt the same way about breast feeding, yet in her anxiety to provide her brood with the highest level of immunity, she kept it up all the way through the twins' first year in preschool, by which time the kids were treating her chest like a vending machine. And of course, caring for twins has forced her to give up on working, at least until … well, she doesn't know exactly when they'll be ready to do without her constant presence, or for that matter if she herself will ever again be ready to tackle the challenge and discipline of a paying job. Paradoxically, the spiraling schedule of shopping, carpool, doctors' appointments, slumber parties, parent-teachers conferences, soccer matches, ballet recitals, visits to the zoo, the park, the Exploratorium, story-telling, finger painting, doll dressing, Lego building, and demands to "Watch me, watch me" from her offspring every time she stops to think have made Amanda feel lazy, incompetent, and to tell the truth, bored.

Home decorating and entertaining have been her therapy. Already in her college dorm, she had discovered how a couple of embroidered cushions, a Christmas cactus, a pink lampshade and a few colorful mugs, like the red shawl in *A Little Princess*, could transform a dingy room into a welcoming nest, attracting a coterie of friends for confidential rap sessions. In the last ten years, Chuck's business ascension, culminating in the acquisition of an authentic Bernard Maybeck house in the Berkeley Hills, has expanded the scope as well as raised the stakes of her favorite hobbies. When you entertain captains of industry, both your home décor and the food you serve start transcending the mere domain of pleasure to enter the realm of signs, charged with making statements about your success, sophistication and innovative spirit that politeness prevents you from making yourself. (In Berkeley, clothes are mercifully exempt from this semiotic rat race). But the need to keep up with the latest developments in taste, whether in wall coverings (is rag-rolled paint already passe?), furniture materials (is chrome making a comeback?) or finger food (where are we on the tapas craze?) while rearing twins has forced her to rely more and more on the initiative of decorators and caterers, depriving her further of a sense of autonomy and creativity. Besides, the effort to maintain a well-appointed home is rendered somewhat futile by the expanding tide of toys, melted crayons, juice stains, lollipop stick and macaroni art that washes farther day by day over every one of its surfaces.

At least, until last night, she felt sure of her talent as hostess, which consisted of assembling the right mixture of guests, and then making sure that they circulated to maximize networking opportunities. Now she isn't so sure. The most shocking aspect of last night's loud, disorganized, argumentative gathering is that it was somehow exhilarating, as if disagreements did not matter, as if people did not need any coaxing to be perfectly at ease, as if she was free to be herself.

Amanda feels a pang of regret about having brought the twins on this trip that was supposed to be Chuck's and her first vacation away from them, a sort of second honeymoon. But after last week's attack, it was out of the question to leave them behind. They have been traumatized enough as it is. Now the darlings are safely asleep a few feet away from her, for which she is grateful. In a few minutes, though, they will wake up, and all of her attention will again be devoted to feeding, clothing and entertaining them. Having been raised as a princess (without any sojourn in an attic), Amanda has no doubt that the same treatment is due to her offspring. In any case, she has no choice: these days, any less reverential attitude toward her children would mark her as an unfit mother. And so, like many of her contemporaries, on the verge of middle-age she has made an uncomplaining and unheralded journey from self-centeredness to self-sacrifice. But it has not fulfilled her.

Meanwhile Chuck has blossomed. His growing clout as CEO of a successful software company that markets inventory control applications, his happiness as a family man, even the added girth he has acquired have somehow made him sexy. Amanda knows from the moist looks and cooing tones of some of his female employees and clients that he must be subject to temptations. So far he hasn't given her cause for complaints. At home he is easy-going, patient with the kids, and amorous enough with her, but he is seldom there, and Amanda is painfully aware of her own handicaps as a graying, sagging, unstimulating wife. She feels that the next nine days will be crucial to rekindle their love, but how is she going to do it with the kids around all day and Sarah's door open all night?

"Mommy, I want waffles!" cries Sarah, right on cue. Sarah has woken up hungry, like every day, and strange surroundings are not likely to distract her from her appetite. Nor does she stop to wonder about the effect of long plane rides on time and date. She knows today is Sunday because Daddy said so yesterday. And to her Sunday is synonymous with waffles. Big fat steaming waffles, crunchy on the outside and gooey inside. They have to be just the right shade of golden, no white valleys, no charred peaks allowed, and Sarah has to separate them herself (otherwise Mommy tries to give her only half a sheet), laying them out in four equidistant quarter-moons with their curved edges right against the walls of the plate, the best arrangement for soaking up strawberry syrup—it has to be strawberry, or the whole thing is ruined. Mommy always pours the syrup, she says it's because Sarah's hand is too small, and she could break the bottle and hurt herself, but Mommy does it all wrong: she dribbles the syrup in irregular squiggles, leaving some areas dry, so Sarah has to wait for Mommy to answer the phone or tie Isaac's sneakers, and then Sarah does it right, filling every hole in the waffles to the brim. Sometimes, after one of her parents' parties, she is lucky to find a left-over of whipped cream in the fridge. Then, to make everything pretty and fair, she dumps a big glop of cream exactly in the center of each piece of waffle, and pours a little more syrup over the top. Sometimes, Mommy sees what Sarah has done, and she is angry, but Sarah doesn't care. She is a big girl now, she is in the first grade, and nobody can tell her how to fix her own breakfast.

Unbeknownst to his mom, Isaac is also astir. He woke up with his eyes on the bed post, and spent some time admiring the cool creature with boobs and claws and wings on top of it, all carved out of wood, which he knows is better than plastic, he'd love to have a bed like that at home, it'd scare the heck out of that sissy Benjamin, who doesn't want to be called Ben, well excuse me! why does Isaac always have to invite him? And it's real high, and yeah, pretty bouncy, you could, like, use it as a fort or a wrestling platform, do a double somersault and crash on the bad guys, like that! Sweet! He lands on his back on the hardwood floor, is a little stunned, picks himself up. And then he remembers: it's Sunday, and that means Power Rangers!

There is no TV in his room, so he ventures down the stairs to go look for one. His quest is untainted by anxiety, as he has never been in a house that did not contain at least one TV set, or that did not have access to ABC Family. At Grandma's, you have to push different buttons to find it, but that's no problem. Isaac is a wiz with the remote control. Nor does the language barrier he has experienced since landing occur to him as an obstacle. Isaac is used to hearing people such as the gardener or the housekeeper babble incomprehensibly, and on TV too there are lots of channels in other languages that Isaac groups under the heading of "Mexican", but this mediatic Tower of Babel is just something you zap through on your way to the real stuff—by real, Isaac is just starting to understand that he means American. Never mind that all his favorite shows in fact come from Japan, their domestication generally achieved through the simple device of dubbing, or in the case of Power Rangers, through a complete remake. There is nothing in them that strikes him as alien, just as Clarisse was in no way put off by Harry Potter's Britishness. Under the radar of parental vigilance, children's imagination from Tokyo to San Francisco has already been globalized, at home in a universe that seamlessly integrates the monarchic social order and pagan sorcery of old fairy tales with space age technology, the glue binding the whole being the violent resolution of conflicts, with team spirit and environmental concerns thrown in for good measure.

Isaac searches in vain through the obvious places: all the rooms with sofas, of which there are quite a number here. Then he thinks of the kitchen, which is equipped with a TV at several of his friends'. Following the same reasoning, he even tries the downstairs bathroom. Still no luck. At last he spots a small set on the floor of the pantry, where Franny dumped it to make use of the stool on which it previously stood. The set has two car antenna-looking things and a weird plug with round prongs instead of the flat ones he is used to. Isaac finds an outlet with matching holes and plugs it in. There is no remote control, no cable hookup that he can see, but that does not discourage him. As a child of the electronic age, he has full confidence in a trial and error approach to making things work. And indeed, the third button he pushes causes the familiar zap that indicates the TV is on. A few more seconds, and an image of men in black playing violins appears. Isaac pushes another button, and now he sees Sabrina the teenage witch, except she is also in black and white, like some of the old shows on TV Land, and she speaks Mexican. Another touch of the channel button. This time he gets a picture of Arabs crouching on carpets, again in shades of gray. He hits the channel button again. Snow. Again. More snow. Again and again. That's it. Three channels, all black and white, all in Mexican. And no Power Rangers. What a bummer! His eyes stray around the room. He sees the cooler full of emergency snacks. He retrieves a bag of Cheetos and settles on the cold tile floor to watch Mexican Sabrina.

Sunday, what a bummer! No way to transact any business today, Victoria realizes in the midst of her morning stretch. Last night, having partaken sparingly of the feast, she had one of her productive brainstorms. She came up with the idea of using the Internet to find out how to best dispose of the wind-up butterfly chaser. The beauty of global means of communications is that you no longer have to be hindered by language barriers. But since, to her knowledge, there is no computer in the house, she will have to repair to the local library, which is closed today, as is everything else in this neck of the woods. Well, if you get a lemon, make lemonade, she concludes. As she wishes to stay here a few more days, she should in any case strive to make herself useful to the Fischbein family. Today she will offer to take care of the twins, and while she is at it she'll include the Degency girls, because you can never have too many friends. She starts thinking of indoor activities she might organize for the kids, for it looks as if it's going to be a rainy day.

The three men in the house wake up with both a hangover and a hard-on, but from that point on their trains of thought diverge. Chuck, disregarding the jackhammer going at his head, reaches over toward Amanda, then remembers Sarah in the next room. Did he just dream that she asked for waffles? In any case, he can scratch the nooky idea. He sighs, remembering Sundays before the birth of the twins, lying in bed with Amanda, the New York Times between them, business and sports sections for him, book review and magazine for her, and often, particularly during her fertile period of the month, their rolling right over it in their enthusiastic transports. How he got to love her solid hips, her studious face yielding to giggles, and above all her miraculous availability! Marriage turned out to suit him to a tee. Of course, children change a lot of things. But if they make a dent in your sex life, they also bring you another kind of joy, the purest Chuck has ever known, as it is attained without any striving. Watching Sarah attempt a ballet pose, or Isaac a wrestling hold, the unself-conscious grace of their little bodies shining through the awkwardness of their movements; listening to them earnestly negotiate roles in a "pretend" game; or lying next to either one of them as they fall asleep, cozy and trustful, he gets flooded with irresistible waves of wonder and gratitude. To him, unexpectedly, children have acted less as a source of responsibility or pride than as a sort of spiritual guide book, teaching him how to recover the innocence of childhood.

"Holy Mackerel!" the thought strikes him for the first time with full force, "We're in France!" France, the land of pleasure par excellence! He intends to honor it by doing absolutely no work. He has not even brought his laptop, only a couple of trade magazines to catch up on, and of course his international cell phone. Nine days, the longest real vacation he has taken in twenty-five years, except for his honeymoon! A long, hopeful vista of fine dining, wine tasting and afternoon siestas opens before his still closed eyes. And then there is Hughes Degency, a little bit of a hot head, but copacetic over all, and a likely mine of useful information about the wine business, on which Chuck has had his eye ever since he sold his company for a tidy bundle to a German conglomerate nine months ago. He has been retained as acting CEO, but working for a big bureaucracy takes the thrill out of being a leader. Besides, he wants to get out of the high tech business, which has become too hyped up for its own good. He was prescient enough to trade his NASDAQ shares against short term bonds just before the bubble burst, so now he has a good deal of capital to invest in a new venture. Why not a winery? There's something cosmopolitan about it that he likes, and profits are apparently through the roof.

Phil's reaction to the contradictory appeals sent by his head and groin is one of intense self-pity. For what has he done to deserve waking up on a Sunday in a bed too small for him, relegated to the attic to suffer the twin afflictions of a smashing headache and a throbbing penis with no one on hand to minister to either? He envisions a bleak near future of spanking the monkey and fixing his own hair of the dog, and it's enough to make him want to throw up. To top off his misery, it sounds as if it is still raining, which makes the rental of the Alfa Romeo look like a uselessly extravagant expense given that he is shortly going to be saddled with a double load of alimony, and considering the precariousness of his position as vice president of marketing in a venture company that's run out of venture capital. At least the plane ticket will come off as a business expense because of the conference he just attended in Monaco.

What do women want? That is the question. No, that's not it, since they make no bones about stating that what they want is fidelity. As if that was the best a man had to offer. An exclusive contract on his cock. Theirs, even when they have no use for it. That and a lavish lifestyle, of course. Downright demeaning, when you think about it. But then why do they go after guys like Phil, the charmers, the extroverts, the adventurers, the studs? Each one of his girlfriends and wives for the last thirty years has stolen him from the previous one. Shouldn't that tell them something? Are they attracted by the promise of fun, on which he thinks he has delivered every time, or do they in fact aspire to the triumph of turning him into a dull, sexless homebody like Chuck Fischbein?

Women believe in a zero sum theory of love. But as Camus said (in translation, as Phil flunked his one semester of college French): "Why should one love rarely in order to love fully?" The trouble is that women don't read Albert Camus. But he has been Phil's hero, his spiritual guide, ever since *The Stranger*, with its unabashed paean to carnal pleasures, its endorsement of human contradictions and its call for a self-created moral code, rescued him from his Presbyterian upbringing. For a long time, his love of Camus extended through a halo effect to everything Gallic. These days, though, he has more of a love-hate relationship with the French. He still appreciates their hedonistic outlook, but he is getting exasperated with their arrogance. What else to call the pretense of shopkeepers that they don't understand his English, or the snubbing of American cultural products from Disneyland to Schindler's List? And then there is their unsporting disregard for free trade shown in actions such as the banning of American beef on the pretext that it contains hormones, or the demand that genetically altered corn be labeled as such, or the persistence of farm subsidies. And now, to add injury to insult, they are expressing only lukewarm support for a military retaliation against the Taliban, hinting that somehow the US might be to blame for the irrational hatred of Islamist lunatics. In the last week, Phil has become quite a patriot.

Phil's attraction to Franny, however, predates his political realignment. For it was a French book she read while eating her lunch in the Spider Global Designs' cafeteria that first piqued his interest. *Le Destin des immigrés*, by some obscure sociologist called Emmanuel Todd. He still remembers the cover, a line drawing of a multicultural family in front of the Eiffel Tower, and how her face, tentative but for those blazing dark eyes, emerged above it when he asked if he could sit at her table. Which shows two things: first, that he has an excellent memory when it comes to women, and second, that contrary to his soon to be ex-wife Cynthia's assertions that he thinks with his dick, it wasn't pure lust that caused him to engage Franny in conversation, since he had no idea what she looked like at the time, her top half hidden by the book, the bottom half by the table. Of course it didn't take long for a connoisseur such as Phil to establish that her body was quite fine underneath the zipped up jacket and bulky pants. But don't we all conduct discreet physical appraisals of the people we meet? And honest to God, it was her mind he wanted to get to know.

As it turned out, she was translating the web site of one of his accounts, so they got to see quite a bit of each other during the next few months. She was an intellectual, like Phil, so of course she was like a fish out of water among the philistines of the high tech world. And then she seemed so self-contained, so efficient, so focused, qualities that Phil finds all the more attractive for their lack in himself. Through the padded walls of her cubicle, the rapid-fire tapping of her fingers on the keyboard was enough to make him stiff. He asked for regular progress reports. She asked for his editing help. He joked, she laughed, they exchanged books. When he started having problems with Cynthia, he confided in her. She was full of compassion. One thing led to another, and one evening found them groping in his office, he at full throttle, she coyly ambivalent. The janitor's vacuum cleaner interfered, as it often does, and she fled. The next day he apologized, and curiously, she apologized too. Taking this as a sign that she shared his feelings, he was looking forward to a repeat performance when she announced that she was leaving on a four weeks' vacation. It had been approved by her boss several months before, so there was nothing Phil could do.

Anyway he has managed to catch up with her, thanks to Amanda's generous heart, and as a free man, more or less. But it seems that in the meantime the Degency dude has put dibs on her. She can't seriously be thinking of getting it on with the pompous jerk, a fine sample of French arrogance. Anyway, there is nothing Phil likes better than a good fight. It's that good ole American competitive spirit, the only missing ingredient in Camus' philosophy. But before he can duke it out with the landlord he must get hold of some Ibuprofen.

Like Chuck, Hughes pays no attention to his hangover, which is slight anyway, so astonished is he upon waking up to find himself swathed in sensuous luxury. Instead of the funky flannel of his sleeping bag, he feels the cool smoothness of lavender-scented linen sheets. Instead of the glare and blare of the morning through the unshuttered window of the hut, a velvety dimness against his eyelids, a muffled call of roosters. Ah! he remembers, he is lying in a real bed, in the comfort of his own house, his little American asleep across the hall, how he wants her right now! He sees himself–the small detail of the intervening corridor being overlooked–striding naked into her room, discerning her recumbent shape under frozen white billows. He scoops her up, her body still wrapped in the sheet, her throat making a small sound between a moan and a purr, her arm falling across his back. He brings her to his own bed, she lies there with her arms spread, still asleep, smiling, a strand of dark hair across her eyes. He unwraps the sheet, uncovers the throbbing birth mark on her collar bone that fascinates him so, pulls the resisting sheet further down. A lovely mother-of-pearl rise, warm and soft to the touch, then, stirringly, a contrasting crescent of café-au-lait tumescence, crowned by a most definite, most definitely succulent chocolate button–he suddenly understands why he has been fascinated by the birth mark. He is eager to pursue his exploration, from the edge of the rib cage, where strength meets defenselessness, across the stomach's undulating plain, towards.... He stops himself, aware that Héloise is liable to barge into the room any minute with another one of her enslaved pets. It is his fault for not teaching her to knock, but then again he has been alone ever since she was old enough to be taught, and well, he has had very little time for erotic fantasies. Also he does not feel quite right about using Franny this way. After all, he has no idea what her body really looks like, and he would rather wait to experience the real thing. For it seems it is no longer a question of if, but only of when. And for a few seconds, he is content to bask in that knowledge.

A gust of wind shakes the shutters, followed by a hard pelting. Is it hail? *Bon Dieu* let it not be hail, just now when more than half of his grapes are still waiting to be harvested. Rain by itself is worrisome, as you can't pick wet grapes. Today is Sunday, which is a day of rest anyway. But if it continues to rain, tomorrow may turn into another forced holiday, which means he will have to send his three new workers home, and they may not come back. Well, that's what you get for choosing Mother Nature as your boss, he reminds himself. He'll take her over Jean Claude Trichet any day.

He jumps into his jeans, pushes the shutters open. It's just rain, big hard swollen drops hammering at the exposed dirt of the butte that bars his view. He leans out the window towards the east, where the worst storms come from in this area. Through the parasol pines, he sees the salmon remains of an attenuated sunrise.

It does not look too bad, in fact. But he'd better check the weather forecast on Yahoo.

As a secular Californian, Franny attaches no special meaning to Sunday. To her, the only meaningful time distinction is between work days and weekend, with vacations falling under the weekend umbrella, as they are rarely much longer—except in the present case. In fact, she is amazed at how easily she has adapted to being idle for an extended period of time, twelve days already, although Hughes merely guffawed when she gloated about this achievement yesterday. It is true that the law here mandates five weeks of vacation per year. It is also true that lately much of her leisure has been occupied with picking grapes.

In any event, Franny isn't thinking about the day of the week as she wakes up from one of her nightmares. In this one, she has just had sex with a man she barely knew and suddenly remembers she already has a lover, except that his name escapes her. She knows these dreams represent a fear of losing control, and that they don't really impugn her character. For if Franny has in the past yielded to sex against her better judgment, she has never been polygamous. But the dream still leaves a bad taste in her mouth.

She turns on her other side, not ready to face the day. Rain is pounding against the shutters. Chuck and Amanda must be depressed, and Hughes must be worried about his grapes. Hughes ... Phil. Franny laughs. No, she isn't in any danger. She knows what she wants, although she foresees it's going to be hard fending off Phil, forever hopeful, forever unwilling to take no for an answer. She can't believe she nearly let him seduce her. With a little distance (and Hughes' proximity), his neediness and volatility appear in sharp relief, canceling out his charm, his wit, his handsomeness. But her very change of heart is disconcerting. Will the scales fall from her eyes in Hughes' case also?

Last night she felt that they were each other's helpmates, the bond between them unstated, serene, expressed somehow in the clouds of steam that rose from their tea cups to mingle invisibly above their heads. And at the same time she could feel the raucous, turbulent pull of desire, like an uncouth guest that everyone ignores. It was the loveliest mixture of sensations she has ever experienced. But of course unstable, as eternal as it seemed. What would have happened if Amanda had not interrupted their tête-a-tête to get a glass of milk for Sarah? Probably, given the circumstances, nothing more than a good night kiss. Hughes, thank God, is not like Phil, who would have made love on his desk, with the janitor's vacuum cleaner banging against his office door. Even under the sway of her attraction to him, Franny was repulsed by his theatrics, guessing that they had more to do with his self-image as a sexual buccaneer than an uncontrollable passion for her. And still it wouldn't have stopped her from yielding if he hadn't been married. It wouldn't have been the first time Franny had sex with a man for fear of hurting his feelings. Is she unique in her weakness, or is this dynamic a common form of emotional rape?

Hughes's desire cradles her but it lets her breathe. How does he do it? He does not seem to have thought a great deal about "relationships" (a word he detests, and which has no exact equivalent in French); he even admits, without being able to say more, that his "negligence" played a part in the breakup of his marriage. Does he mean he took his wife for granted (another expression without a French equivalent)? Franny could see it, for even with her he is not always attentive. He tends to assume that she will play a supportive role in his endeavors. Dare she admit on her side that she finds this thrilling, although she suspects that at one point she will rebel?

How complicated is desire after all! How much more to it there is than a reasonable checklist of affinities (although those are not lacking in the present case, but they were never lacking either with each man that Franny has been attracted to over the years). All Franny knows for sure since last night is that she does not have to be afraid of Hughes, that he is no vile seducer. In fact, she is starting to think that if seduction is to occur, it will need to be her doing. Luckily, she feels up to the task.

Héloise has not yet learned the days of the week. All she knows as she rubs the sandman's grit out of her eyes is that she is at Uncle Freddie and Aunt Giselle's, who are in heaven now, and so Papa has to stay here to guard the house. She is pretty sure this means there isn't going to be any school today, because it would take all day just to drive there, and then there would be no time to dance with the music and to make bread with flour and water and to pet the rabbits, and that makes her sad. On the other hand, it must also mean that Héloise isn't going to spend the day at Mammy, where you can't touch the furniture, where you have to lie down forever on a slippery bed in a dark room that smells like dead flowers while Mammy plays cards with her friends, and where the only pets are some gold fish you can't touch either. And that makes her happy. Here, at Uncle Freddie and Aunt Giselle's, there are so many fun things to do. For instance you can count the legs on the baby frogs in the pond. Sometimes they have two legs, sometimes three or four, or even five if you're really lucky, though Clarisse says that's not possible. Or you can pull the tail of the lizards on the wall because even if it breaks, they'll grow another one. You can make the eyes of the snails go in and out like the car antenna. You can look for pigeon eggs, you can ride the pony. Oh! no, the pony is in heaven too, she had forgotten. But there is still

Uncle Freddie's magic butterfly lady, and the ticklish little hairs on Papa's face, and the Ka-boom Ka-boom of his heart inside his chest. Héloise is so eager to get in on the fun that she starts dressing by herself: a pair of pull-on shorts, a wool sweater without buttons, and of course rubber boots, for rain is falling outside, and that means loads of snails.

She reaches up to the door knob, she pulls it down slowly. The door opens with barely a creak. She peeps into the dark corridor. All the other doors are closed, the coast is clear. She starts down the stairs, clutching the banister like Maman says. She gets to the mezzanine, and decides to look in on the butterfly lady.

A few seconds later the walls of the chateau resound with a terrible cry. Doors open, exclamations fuse, a flurry of footsteps is heard down the stairs. Hughes, bare-chested, Franny in her bathrobe, Clarisse in boots and rain slicker, Victoria in sweat pants, all rush to the mezzanine. Amanda emerges from the maze of the east wing, pulling on a silk kimono. She has heard the cry but knew immediately that it did not come from either of the twins. She stops at the top of the stairs, reluctant to interfere in someone else's family affairs, but ready to lend a hand if needed. She is joined by Sarah, who guesses that the frog girl must have done something naughty again and looks forward to her "getting it".

"Héloise, ma puce, qu'est-ce qui se passe?" cries Hughes, kneeling next to his daughter, who is howling, her face pressed against the glass door of the curio cabinet.

"La dame aux papillons. Elle est partie," she manages to articulate in between sobs.

"Quelle dame aux papillons?"

"Là, là," she points to the lower shelf of the cabinet with a plump finger. "La dame aux papillons d'oncle Freddie."

"What is she talking about?" asks Victoria, a little worried.

"Some butterfly lady that has supposedly disappeared," volunteers Franny.

Hughes peers into the dimness of the mahogany cabinet. There is the usual collection of wind-up toys, including the plastic Snoopy, which, because it looks so out of place, is the only one that has ever attracted his attention in all the time he has spent at the chateau, first as a summer retreat, then as a main residence. Is it possible that one toy is actually missing? He tries the door, it is locked as always. He isn't sure where the key is among the bric-a-brac of the attic. The curio cabinet was not even inventoried when he co-inherited the chateau with his brother Hervé. Hughes is tempted to dismiss Héloise's despair as the result of a bad dream, except that she is known for a photographic memory. She was only a little over two when Freddie and Giselle died within weeks of each other, but she talks about them as if they still lived in the east wing, as if only yesterday Freddie had given her a pony ride and Giselle had baked a miniature apricot tart just for her. Could Christiane have removed one of the toys last night to take it back to Paris as a surprise for the girl? It wouldn't be the first time she takes something without telling Hughes. But that's impossible, she only carried her handbag when she left. Could one of his summer guests have swiped the object? But then the door would not be locked. Besides, they're all wealthy Americans and Brits who have no use for old toys. Hughes gives up trying to solve the mystery and concentrates on comforting Héloïse, whose cries are compounding his headache.

"Ne pleure pas, mon petit bouchon. Je te promets qu'on va la retrouver, ta dame aux papillons."

"Et en attendant, qui veut des croissants? Who wants croissants?" calls Franny, trying to distract the little girl by an appeal to her stomach. It works.

"Moi! J'en veux deux," hiccups Héloïse, springing up from her father's lap.

"Qu'est-ce qu'on dit?" replies this parent, holding her back by the arm.

"S'il vous plaît."

"S'il vous plaît qui?"

"S'il vous plaît Franny."

Hughes lets her go, and she toddles over to Franny, still a little woozy from her recent convulsion. She looks up at her, as if to evaluate the seriousness of her proposal. And then, out of the blue, she puts her arms around Franny's legs. Instinctively, Franny returns her embrace. Hughes looks on benignly.

"I'll go get the croissants," offers Victoria. "Just give me the car keys." And in no time she is out the door.

"I want waffles!" Sarah proclaims from the top of the stairs.

*   *   *   *

When Hughes and Franny meet again downstairs after getting dressed, Clarisse is in the process of opening the front door on her way to mass. Hughes vetoes her walking to the village in the rain, so Franny offers to take her, with the result that it is agreed they will all drive to Saint Yves after breakfast.

They find Héloïse and Isaac watching TV on the floor of the pantry, the empty bag of Cheetos between them, their face and hands smeared with Red No. 5. The sight of his daughter snacking on unauthorized junk food upsets Hughes. But, in Amanda's presence, he has to limit the expression of his displeasure to a frown and a wagging finger, all the while anticipating the myriad ways the American children might corrupt his offspring in the next few days.

In the kitchen Amanda is frantically searching the cabinets for a waffle iron, while Sarah hangs on to her kimono sleeve, making unequivocal demands for strawberry syrup. Chuck appears, sans ponytail, and sets about fixing omelets while Hughes brews coffee and Franny, helped by Clarisse, clears the counter of last night's dishes. Phil in turn makes his entrance, in off-white band collar shirt and drapey tan pants, his damp hair freshly parted, but his face a little the worse for wear.

"My kingdom for an aspirin!" he begs, looking pitifully at Franny, though it is Amanda who pauses in her search for the waffle iron to produce the needed remedy. Fifteen minutes, a glass of orange juice and a couple of pain killers later, he has recovered enough to set about making a fire in the dining room, the one household task in which he feels competent thanks to his early boy scout training. The fire is welcome, as it is a little chilly in the house because of the rain.

Victoria returns with the croissants, and the whole gang gathers around the dining room table to eat breakfast, except Sarah, who has turned a deaf ear to all reasonable explanations about the unavailability of waffles and refuses equally to be bribed with fruit loops or animal crackers. As for the croissants, she would spit on them if she did not guess that this would be carrying things too far. Shocked by such bad behavior, and impatient with the adults' ineffective response, Clarisse feels compelled to try a little psychology.

"Miam, miam," she suggests as she put a piece of croissant in her mouth.

"Yuk!" answers Sarah, who is already familiar with this ploy.

"Waffles are for babies," Clarisse then tries, mustering all the resources of her seventh grade English. This second tack does accomplish something, as Sarah is so disconcerted by hearing the strange girl address her in her own language that she runs out of the room crying, and Chuck stops Amanda from running after her.

"She won't die from missing one meal," he drawls. "You're always trying to ration her food. Here she is helping you."

And so breakfast proceeds in peace, punctuated by the crackling of logs in the fireplace and Sarah's intermittent sobs in some distant parlor.

It's been a long time since Hughes and Franny attended mass. Franny was baptized at her mother's insistence, but was discouraged from any further involvement with religion by her father's blistering contempt for "childish superstitions". As to Hughes, unexceptionally for a Frenchman, he lost his faith during his teens and never looked back, going through the motions of a church marriage and his daughters' baptisms with the amount of spiritual commitment one devotes to signing an insurance policy. But as it is raining when they drop Clarisse in front of the church, they go in, and as the parishioners are lining up behind the font, they fall in line and cross themselves.

There is nothing exalting about the building, which was erected in the nineteenth century at the same time as the village, burnt to the ground during the Terror, was resuscitated a mile from its original location. Its vault is white-washed, its windows mostly clear glass, its organ no more than a harmonium and its plaster statues mass-produced, including Saint Yves, in black robe with a square white collar and judicial black hat. All the same, Hughes and Franny soon find themselves hypnotized by the ritual. Perhaps it is no more than the familiar mise en scene of mystery so dear to Clarisse. Perhaps it's the mellow, forgiving voice of the priest, or the sense of community one gets from acting in concert with a group of people. The recent terrorist attack may contribute something to their receptivity. The miraculous aura of their mutual attraction certainly does. Whatever the cause, the presence of the divine is so palpable that it renders moot the abstract question of God's existence. And really, what could be more urgent, more appropriate, more fulfilling than attending mass on a Sunday morning, they both think at the same time? Of course, as they live in a modern age of easy distractions, the chances of their becoming regular churchgoers are fairly slim. And perhaps all we can aspire to now is an intermittent faith.

As to Clarisse, she is ecstatic about having led those two stray lambs back to their Shepherd. Only Héloise wishes that the mass were a little shorter, or that at least she could have brought her frog.

A few pews back, Patrick Malefoi sits with his wife and two children, but he isn't concerned with spiritual matters. What he wants to know is whether Degency is getting it on with his American guest, and whether his sudden piety is a political move. His suspicions are confirmed when at the end of the service, he sees the priest lunging through the crowd to shake Hughes's hand. Right, he thinks, currying favor with the local authorities.... And he is willing to bet the little American is loaded. Probably a tree-hugging rabbit-food eater to boot. Together they'll buy all the land around the village and turn it into a macrobiotic commune. And did the priest make any effort to shake Patrick's hand, although Patrick attends mass every Sunday? Of course not! It's like the parable of the Prodigal Son the priest talked about last week, a piece of dogma Patrick is inclined to reject. Not too worry. As plebeian as he is, the tobacconist has a few aces up his sleeve.

As they return to the car, Clarisse spots Chérif, astride the retaining wall in front of the médiatheque, busy mouthing the words of a rap song that comes over his earphones. There is a group of teenagers around the fountain on the square, but he pays no attention to them, or they to him. It makes Clarisse sad, so she waves to him. He waves back, and then, amazingly, after a moment of hesitation, he jumps off the wall and shuffles over. A short conversation ensues, at the end of which Chérif accepts Hughes' invitation to spend the day with them. Patrick Malefoi watches the Mercedes back out of the parking lot and revises his prediction: a macrobiotic commune crawling with Algerians.

Phil had his heart set on a visit to Lourmarin, where Albert Camus is buried. But it is too late to undertake the long trip today. Chuck is in favor of going out to lunch, Amanda of a little sightseeing. Hughes, Franny, Chérif and Clarisse are amenable to both, Sarah and Isaac to neither. Héloise has her own plans, which she does not feel necessary to share. Victoria is at everyone's disposal. At last it is decided that Victoria will babysit the younger children while the rest of the group drives to a restaurant Hughes has recommended, and then to the castle of Le Barroux, which is nearby.

The restaurant is in the midst of nowhere, but its parking lot is full, muddy Citroen tin cans cheek to jowl with gleaming BMWs. The rain having stopped for the time being, they take the risk of sitting on the terrace under a white parasol that flaps feebly in the breeze, its canvas weighed down with water, between a quartet of retired farmers and two Belgian women with a German shepherd. Although they have driven no more than twenty miles, the landscape around them has none of the sunny openness of the hills around Saint Yves. On each side of the road mountain shoulders rise abruptly, grim jumbles of gray rocks that seem ready to shake off the few tufts of dark green huddling in their crevices, their savagery only tamed by the gentle clinking of dinnerware and sedate murmur of conversation on the terrace. For eating here entails none of the raucousness the Americans noticed the previous night. Are all the diners afflicted with a combination of jetlag and hangover, or do other etiquette rules prevail? In fact, the loudest patron by far is Phil, who has launched into a hilarious account of his youthful encounter with Existentialism.

The food turns out to be excellent in a way that's mostly familiar to the Californians, featuring the staples of goat cheese, tomato coulis, polenta, aioli, grilled fish, braised meats and pureed vegetables, all arranged on the plates like jewels, and presented by the waiter with the usual mixture of deference and complacency. More exciting are the foie gras, rabbit stew and cheese tray offering a dozen smelly choices. What is truly remarkable though is the price of the meal—

the menu consisting of two hors d'oeuvre, entrée, salad, cheese and dessert cost-
ing no more than a single a la carte dish at any decent restaurant in the Bay Area–
and the fact that the clientele is by no means limited to urban professionals. It's
mind-boggling to think that all over France, in every town and village and scenic
gorge, there are similar restaurants offering sophisticated fare to ordinary people,
for whom eating well is a sacred pastime on a par with spectator sports, with as
little assertion of status involved. And yet they are not obese.

They take their time about it too. Franny is reminded of Edith Wharton's
quip, quoted by Hughes during their first conversation, about Americans being
more eager to get away from their pleasures than to get to them. She can see that
when it comes to eating at least, the French exhibit none of this trait. They sit for
hours, waiting for the succession of courses without exhibiting the least sign of
impatience, as if they were not haunted by the possibility that there might be
more fun things to do out there. Even Clarisse and Chérif are bearing bravely
with the slow trickling of the afternoon, although neither says much, Chérif in
particular seeming preoccupied with the position of his hands, elbows, napkin
and silverware. Hughes clearly expects nothing less from them than this polite
abnegation, which to Amanda seems barely short of child abuse, but which
Chuck admires with a certain wistfulness. Yet determined to do in Rome as the
Romans, both Fischbeins sit and eat and sip their drinks and chat softly like old
French dining *habitués*. By the time coffee is served, they have been converted to
French idleness.

It is Phil, frustrated by Franny's recurring bouts of inattention to his sallies,
and eager to expend some of his boundless energy, who snaps his fingers to
request the bill, in English, to the embarrassment of his friends. The waiter however gives no sign that he has been addressed in a foreign language. He brings the
bill, and gets the tip he was hoping for.

The Château du Barroux is one of the countless fortresses that cling to every
suitably steep hill in many parts of France. Unlike the Chateau Degency, it sports
round towers, square towers, crenelated parapets, covered galleries, spiral stair-
cases, chilly chapel, overhanging latrines, and the narrow openings slanted for the
convenient aiming of arrows and boiling oil at potential invaders that particularly
fascinate Chérif, especially when he learns that some of the potential invaders the
castle was originally built to defend against were the fierce Saracens, in other
words his ancestors, who in fact conquered half of France, then were repelled, but
who apparently were not completely wiped out, since according to Hughes, some
of them found refuge in isolated vales, where they created villages, and little by
little merged with the general population, so that when you think about it, some

of the people who look askance at him in the village are, unbeknownst to them, his cousins.

The castle seems to have emerged intact from a medieval time capsule, but that turns out to be an illusion, as in fact it was converted into a residential palace during the Renaissance, retrofitted as a fortress under Vauban, pillaged by revolutionary hordes, rebuilt in the early nineteen hundreds, and finally set on fire by the retreating German army at the end of World II, this last indignity underlined by the tour guide, who is much too young to have any feelings about it, to the mute consternation of the lone German tourist among the group, who is old enough to have taken part in the destruction. The chateau's current state of preservation is in fact the work of restorers, the *patrimoine* of France providing work for as many of them as there are fitness trainers in the US. The problem is, Amanda reflects as she reads the English version of the visitor's pamphlet, to what state do you restore such an architectural *mélange*? It's an issue she faced during the remodeling of her kitchen, but here it seems a real conundrum, calling into question the very concept of authenticity. Yes, Franny has to agree, the search for authenticity, like the search for wilderness, is dubious at best in such an old country. Or is it everywhere?

What impresses Franny is the erudition of the guide, a nineteen-year old girl in tube skirt and Doc Martens who rattles off historical minutiae at breakneck speed in an ornate syntax and without any joke, and the nonetheless rapt attention of the visitors, most of whom, from their accents, seem to be locals, parents with their children, lively groups of seniors, who could have been expected to be blasé about the overabundance of ruins in their neighborhood. When asked about this, Hughes opines that these Sunday pilgrimages are less about learning or entertainment than communing with the past and nourishing one's cultural identity, the same purpose served in the US by visits to Monticello or Sutter's Mill. Of course, there are far fewer historical landmarks in the US, hence the attempt to substitute for them with theme parks. But here, as Guillaume remarked, theme parks are not only redundant, they are culturally inauthentic, an assault on the national soul. Yet, faced with a choice between a real chateau and a water slide, Franny suspects that most French youth, as willing to have their cultural identity nourished as they appear to be, would not hesitate long before picking the latter. All the more reason not to give them that choice, concludes Hughes. To Franny, this cultural tyranny seems highly impractical, yet she can't help wishing it to succeed. "Mais peut-être on peut faire les deux," suggests Clarisse, who having for the time being renounced earthly pleasures, is still not willing to ban them for eternity.

As to Phil, what fires his imagination is the chateau's violent history. It echoes a central tenet of his world view, which is that men are nothing more than animals, that war is inevitable, that the cosmos has no vested interest in humanity, and that one should therefore enjoy life to the fullest while one can. And Chuck, regretfully, has to agree.

They get back home to a scene of devastation worthy of the Terror. Muddy tracks all over the hallway, clothes on the stairs, spilled milk on the rugs, tortilla chips on the upholstery, a broken Egyptian statuette, which fortunately turns out to be a plaster replica, and everywhere objects out of place, as if the storm had set up quarters inside. Hughes visibly blanches, a reaction that not even the tractor breakdown managed to elicit. He has rented the chateau to families with young children before, but has not been present while they wreaked havoc on his household, returning only after they left and things were tidied up, and failing to notice the new dents in table legs, the smashed vases swept into the dustbin, the water stains on dressers. As to his daughters, they have been raised to mind the furniture. To Chuck and Amanda, the state of disorder seem par for the course, until they remember that they have not brought their housekeeper. But Phil congratulates himself on his childless state, and Franny is more than a little embarrassed.

The children on the other hand are in fine form. This is a surprise to Amanda, who felt guilty about leaving them to entertain themselves in a strange house without a VCR. They have spent the afternoon building forts under the piano and, under Victoria's direction, making collages out of pages torn from magazines. Then Héloise led them on a snail hunt, the result of which sits on the kitchen counter, a big plastic bucket full of the slimy beasts, crawling and drooling on top of each other to the great delight of their capturers. Amanda, horrified, is about to request that they be returned to the garden immediately, when she hears Hughes congratulate the little sadists, proposing an escargot feast in a couple of days, once the snails have properly disgorged. Chuck, the traitor, is all for it.

Both the fridge and the snack cooler have been extensively raided. There is no more orange juice, milk, bread, or pizza, and not a clean dish in the house. Without exchanging a word, both Franny and Clarisse realize that it is time to get organized. So while Franny dispatches Victoria to the village to get some bread (the bakery luckily staying open on Sundays), makes Phil responsible for the building of a fire, puts Chuck and Amanda in charge of loading the dishwasher and drafts Hughes in the hallway cleanup, Clarisse lays down the law for the younger children.

"No food in the living room," she can be heard admonishing her charges in the faraway music room. "The boots stay in the entrée. The clothes stay in the bedroom. Don't touch the things of my father. Et toi, Héloise, tu devrais avoir honte."

Sarah and Isaac are petrified. They had thought that this was their house, but now they see that they were mistaken, that they have to follow the big girl's rules. Amanda is in a quandary: she feels like protesting the disciplining of her children by a third party, but by so doing, she would herself be disciplining someone else's child. Chuck is intrigued, Phil amused, and Franny secretly thankful. As to Hughes, as he is just then retrieving the mop from the pantry, he has plausible deniability about his daughter's speech.

That night, surprising herself, Franny instigates a discussion of housekeeping, at the end of which a rotating schedule of chores is instituted. The adults are divided into three teams of two persons, which somehow end up consisting of Chuck and Victoria, Amanda and Phil, and Hughes and Franny. Every day, one team will be responsible for shopping and cooking, another for cleanup, the last one for babysitting. Chores can be traded by mutual agreement.

"Like a kibbutz!" exclaims Amanda.

"Or a dude ranch!" adds Chuck.

"A boy scout camp!" quips Phil.

"My old group home ..." muses Victoria.

As to Hughes and Franny, who have no communal experience to compare it to, although less vocal about it, they are the most enthusiastic supporters of the new system.

CHAPTER 15

▼

L'OISIVETÉ EST LA MÈRE DE TOUS LES VICES

(An Idle Mind Is The Devil's Workshop)

Le Lac des Chevrettes reminded Franny of Lake Temescal in Oakland. It was man-made, its filmy expanse, not much bigger than a pond, fed by a trickling creek at one end and kept in place by a earthen dam at the other. It had a narrow beach of yellow sand that looked glued on, a carefully tended lawn sprinkled with shade trees, a few picnic tables, a concrete bathroom, and an asphalt path that started at the parking lot and wound around the lake until it disappeared in the woods on the far shore. Even the fauna looked familiar: mallards (in French: cols verts, according to Hughes), Canada geese (in French: oies du Canada. How had they ended up there?), and black bass (in French: black-bass) stocked for the benefit of anglers. As it was a school day, the humans were few and far between, and those few were no more exotic than the beasts, the only female not wearing a bra being Héloise –a discovery that deeply disappointed Chuck. All in all, the place was neither wild enough nor artful enough to be beautiful, but the gentle slope of the beach provided safe wading for the children and the width of the water gave the adults a chance to do some serious lap swimming. Which was how the group consisting of the Fischbeins, the Degencys and Franny had ended up here. Leisure, like marriage, often requires compromise.

The rain had started again shortly after their return from Le Barroux the previous evening, and had continued throughout the night. Toward nine in the morning, the sun had finally pierced the clouds, but the summer seemed over. The sky was veiled, the temperature in the low seventies. Dead leaves were scattered on the terrace, some of them looking unlike those on any of the nearby trees.

Early in the morning, while Hughes was out checking on the state of his grapes, Phil had again proposed a trip to Lourmarin, but none of the kids were up for the long car ride, and as it was Hughes and Franny's turn to babysit, Franny had had to decline in both their names–she only wished he had talked to her before leaving. Chuck and Amanda had also passed up the offer, unwilling to leave their children behind two days in a row. As to Victoria, she had claimed to have some business to attend to, although Franny found that hard to believe, the only business the Gypsy girl ever seemed to have being to suntan and make quite nice architectural drawings. She had not talked to her Hollywood contacts in days and seemed resigned to the freeze of her bank account and the disappearance of her sister.

Phil had left for Lourmarin on his own after making one last-ditch attempt to lure Franny by taking the top down on the Alfa Romeo and mysteriously quoting Camus to the effect that all of man's unhappiness sprung from hope, and for a second, Franny had felt like yielding to his entreaties. As he had feared, Hughes was forced to send his vineyard workers home because of the humidity, except for Pierrette, who was to help Henri bottle wine in the cellar. When he returned, he found Franny trying to dissuade Héloïse from pouring herself a big bowl of Cocoa Puffs. Franny barely raised her eyes as he strode past the dining room door on his way to the bathroom to wash his hands, but in that short moment he sensed that trouble was brewing.

He promptly completed his toilette and came back to the kitchen, where he snatched the box of Cocoa Puffs from Héloïse's hand, lending a deaf ear to her pointed questions as to why she couldn't eat what the American boy was eating, and set about making toast for everyone. After breakfast Chuck and Victoria, who were in charge of dinner, drove to Saint Yves to do some shopping while Amanda wiped the counters and stacked the dishwasher. Hughes and Franny found themselves alone in the dining room. Franny mentioned that upon getting up, Héloïse had tearfully returned to the theme of the missing butterfly lady. Sarah, who until then had seemed entirely self-absorbed, had shown compassion for the tot by handing over her best Barbie doll. Héloïse seemed to be appeased for the moment, but Franny wondered whether the matter should not be investigated further. Hughes promised to call Christiane in the evening to see if she knew what the girl was talking about.

It turned out he had not forgotten that it was their turn to be on babysitting duty, and had in fact worked out a plan for the day. How about going swimming at a nearby lake in the afternoon, he suggested. He knew that Franny liked to swim, and the kids would enjoy playing on the beach. It was going to be the only day he could spend with his daughters, so they should make the best of it. In the morning, if Franny did not mind, he would like to take advantage of the break in the harvest to repair the broken trellis before the vines got damaged. What could Franny do but agree?

In the end Chuck and Amanda had decided to come along, and they had all piled into the SUV with swimming gear, towels, sunblock, the re-stocked cooler, the inflatable raft, the scooter, the Barbie paraphernalia, a frisbee and various other beach toys. Clarisse for her part was bringing a few pounds of textbooks and school supplies, as she intended to keep up with her class during this unexpected vacation.

"What grade are you in, Clarisse?" asked Amanda, raising her voice as people instinctively do when talking to foreigners. The adults, arrayed in a loose circle, were lounging around on the still damp sand while the younger children built a lagoon at the water's edge. It had originally been Isaac's project, but Héloïse had soon decided to contribute her own civil engineering skills. Isaac, who usually had no use for girls, had tried to shoo her away with a few carefully aimed putdowns (a very pacific child for all his wrestling mania, he never hit anyone but his sister). Alas! He had run headlong into the language barrier. In the end, in the absence of a more suitable partner, he had let her help. Soon, even Sarah was dirtying her hands.

Clarisse raised her eyes from the textbooks spread before her and gave her father an imploring look.

"Allons! Tu dois pouvoir répondre à cette question!" said Hughes.

Clarisse rolled her eyes in protest. She had had only two years of English after all. What if she made a fool of herself? But no help coming from the parental quarter, she had no other choice but to answer Amanda's question herself.

"I am in fourth form."

"The equivalent of eighth grade in the US," Hughes quickly added, not wanting his guests to think that his daughter was behind in school.

"Eighth grade already!"

"I just started, actually. I am one year in advance." Clarisse lowered her eyes modestly, trying to hide a feeling of triumph over having used the word "actually", which made her even prouder than having skipped a grade.

"And what do you study in eighth grade?" asked Amanda.

"Oh! Everything: French, mathematics, history, geography, physic, how do you say ... sciences of life and the earth ... technology, art, music, gymnastic, civic education ... oh! and English of course, and Arabic ... C'est tout, n'est-ce pas Papa?"

"All that in eighth grade! You must go to a private school."

"Non, I go to a public school. My sister goes to a Waldorf school, but Papa does not like it."

"Then it must be a very good public school. In Paris, I assume."

"*Actually*, as my daughter would say," explained Hughes, smiling complacently in Clarisse's direction, "the program is the same in all French schools, public or private."

"Ah! That's true, I heard that France has a national curriculum, something we in the US can't quite manage to do, although we are trying ..." Amanda sighed.

"And I can't figure out why ..." Chuck intervened. "Knowledge changes so fast these days! You can't expect kids to cram down a whole bunch of stuff that will be outdated six months from now. Let the schools concentrate on teaching learning skills. I'll tell you, as a businessman, what I look for are employees who know *how* to learn. I'll take care of the *what*."

"Chuck, you sound so crass! You know very well that there are other things in life besides business!"

Amanda, still smarting from the materialistic way she had come off during Saturday night's conversation about music lessons, was intent on forestalling the possibility of her husband appearing as a specimen of the American boor. In fact, of the two, for all the cowboy affectation that was par for the course in his professional circle, and for all the sophistication that her leisurely lifestyle afforded, Chuck was the one with the more genuine appreciation of high culture. His rattling off the names of American composers at Saturday's dinner had been no fluke. He was extremely fond of classical music and quite knowledgeable about it, although he had never had any musical training, whereas Amanda, who had studied the piano for years as a child, never even touched the CD player and went to concerts only because having a season's ticket to the Symphony was a must in their social group. It was just that she had too many things on her mind to savor the moment, she often thought wistfully.

"And not every field of knowledge is subject to drastic revisions," added Franny.

"Like what?"

"Well, geography for instance …"

"Geography is not subject to revision? Countries split up, forests disappear, populations explode, even continents shift."

"All things we should teach kids. Don't you think it would be good if Americans could at least place Afghanistan on a map before they make up their mind to bomb that country?"

"Do you believe that would influence their opinion? There is no evidence that better educated people make wiser political decisions. Both you and I know where Afghanistan is, and I am willing to bet we don't agree on whether we should bomb it."

"It is true," said Hughes in his diplomatic voice, "that at this point of our evolution as human beings, we still don't have enough knowledge about most complex problems to come up with definitive solutions. But that doesn't mean we should revel in our ignorance. A solid general culture is something we all wish for our children, isn't it?"

"But isn't culture relative? By general culture, you probably mean Western Culture, which is totally abhorrent to your average Arab for instance."

"As a matter of fact, I seem to remember that Clarisse told us she *is* studying Arabic as part of her general culture, didn't she?" Franny interjected.

"Yes, and I find that very interesting," rejoined Amanda in her most emphatic singsong, turning to Clarisse in an effort to deflect the mounting argument. "Is Arabic a mandatory course in French schools, or is it an option?"

"Qu'est-ce que ça veut dire, 'mandatory'?" Clarisse whispered to Franny.

"Obligatoire."

"Oh! non. I choosed it myself!"

"I see. But why?"

"Because it is difficult. It has a different alphabet that I am just learning, and the words change when they are a complement. Papa says it's like Greek, but better because people still speak it. And also last year we studied the Islamic civilization. I like the Arabs because they teached us to make silk fabric and to grow roses and apricot trees, and many other arts and sciences."

"Sort of like ethnic studies in our schools," concluded Chuck. "I thought you guys didn't go for multiculturalism …"

Hughes clenched his jaws. There were so many misconceptions in that one sentence of Chuck's that he did not know where to start refuting it. To make matters worse, Franny now went over to the enemy, as she was wont to do in the presence of her American friends. Hughes understood that she did so out of kindness, but still it rankled.

"So, you don't agree with Bourdieu's claim that the 'general culture' that schools in France are supposed to transmit is in fact mostly a tool for the reproduction of the elites?"

He turned to her. His gray eyes were dark with hurt.

"No, I don't. Do you?"

He was appealing to the truth of her soul, and Franny felt ashamed of having yielded to the temptation of knee-jerk radicalism. There was no doubt in her mind that in the US as in France, the elites by and large reproduced themselves through the selective processes at work in education. In the US it was multiple choice tests. In France it was eight page essays. The result was the same, and as the daughter of a factory worker and a nurse, she objected to it. Yet, thanks in great part to the sacrifices made by her working class parents, she had acquired a liberal education, and if it hadn't brought her that much material success, it had definitely enriched her life and consciousness. She did want that for everyone.

"I don't," she admitted. "I was just trying to give you a hard time."

"Well, you have succeeded!"

There was a lull in the conversation, after which Amanda resumed quizzing Clarisse about her school work. She learned that civic education was some sort of citizenship course where among other things, children were taught that the Social Security system was an expression of the solidarity between the healthy and the sick, the young and the aged. The formulation, distinct from both an appeal to charity and a claim of individual rights, greatly appealed to Amanda (but made Chuck suspect that French schools engaged in wholesale socialist indoctrination). As to citizenship proper, French students were enjoined to think of themselves as members of Europe as well as France. Again, Amanda liked the idea, while Chuck inwardly put it down to mere wishful thinking.

Further discoveries about the French school system were made: that life sciences in eighth grade covered human reproduction and the different types of rocks; that grammar and spelling were big in French class; that all the schools were wired for the Internet and that Clarisse had learned to do spreadsheets in technology class, although she considered that skill less important than reading plays by Molière.

Overall, Amanda was impressed. She wished she did not have to look forward to spending tens of thousands of dollars a year to provide a similar education for her children. At the same time, the scholastic burden on Clarisse's shoulders saddened her, as did Hughes' excessive intellectual demands on his daughter: she noticed how he kept prompting her to elaborate on her answers, interjecting his own questions to test her knowledge and priggishly displaying his own. The girl, however, seemed to enjoy the challenge. It was obviously their preferred way of being intimate, and if a simple "I love you" would have seemed more natural to Amanda, she was willing to make allowances for cultural differences.

Chuck, on the other hand, who had been lending an ear to the exchange while ostensibly perusing the latest issue of *Computing*, found himself put off by Clarisse's quiet aura of intellectual superiority. The businessman, who had never hidden his own smarts, and who, even more than Phil, had competition in the blood, deemed the girl a little too much of a striver. Perhaps it was the fact that she strove in a direction he was uncomfortable with, although Hughes' intellectual pretensions did not phase him one bit. Perhaps it was her seeming lack of animal spirits that he found unnatural in a youth, although at her age he had spent most of his time immersed in *Popular Mechanics*. Perhaps it was a matter of her being a girl, although his female employees saw him as the least sexist boss they had ever dealt with. Perhaps in fact he recognized his old self too much in her, both in intelligence and lack of social sophistication–meaning that she did not flirt. To his credit, he made an effort to overcome his dislike. When he inflated the raft, he asked her to help him put it in the water. A moment later, she was diving from the raft and kicking water at him, her clear laughter ricocheting on the quiet surface of the lake. Her animal spirits were fine after all.

After that they all went in, Amanda, who did not swim, merely dunking and splashing about with the younger kids, while the men raced across the lake and Franny kept Clarisse company by doing the breast stroke along the shore. Chuck, for all his bulk, was in surprisingly good shape, his stomach taut, the muscles on his thighs and arms well defined. Next to him, Hughes appeared nearly fragile, but his swimming was just as competent. Where Chuck seemed to churn a great mass of water, Hughes sliced through it, a few drops rolling off his elbows at each stroke as if merely to suggest wetness. They reached the clumps of reeds that lined the far shore at the same time, and conscious of being admired by the women, turned over and raced back towards them, feeling similarly pleased with them as physical beings. Indeed, both Franny and Amanda looked better in swimsuits than fully dressed; Franny because clothes tended to make her look skinnier than she really was, Amanda because they hid her best features, which were long legs and voluptuous flesh tones.

"You seem a little prickly today," said Hughes, absentmindedly brushing sand off the back of Franny's hand. After the swim, Chuck and Amanda had rowed the boat to the other side of the lake, moored it, and disappeared into the trees for a while. Upon their return, a little flushed but extraordinarily relaxed, they had lured all the kids on an expedition to the nearest village in search of ice cream, the park being bereft of a food concession. (The French have no business sense, Chuck opined.) The beach was by now deserted except for a couple of widely spaced fishermen on their right, and a local woman a hundred yards to their left who kept herself busy knitting while watching her two tots splash around in the shallow water. It was not the first time Franny had observed a disparity in the way French men and women occupied their leisure, or more exactly how it seemed that French women did not have any. It was men you saw straining up the winding roads on racing bicycles. It was men who played *pétanque* on the village square, men on the tennis courts built outside of town by the EDF, men jogging, men hunting in the woods while women shopped, cooked, cleaned, watched the kids. The French were in dire need of a Title IX, thought Franny, her irritation compounded by the fact that her general observations dovetailed with what she was noticing in Hughes, which was that he seemed all too ready to use her as a surrogate wife. And they had not even slept together!

"So, are you prickly today or am I just imagining it?"

Franny, who had been lying on her stomach with her face buried in her towel, raised herself on one elbow without withdrawing her other hand from Hughes' grasp. Hughes could not see her eyes behind the thick straight lashes, but her face seemed uncharacteriscally withdrawn.

"How would you say that in French?"

"Est-ce que tu es de mauvaise humeur? But wait, *you're* answering a question with another question."

"I just wanted to know if I was a 'tu' or a 'vous' today."

"Ah! tu es de mauvaise humeur … Tu veux me dire pourquoi?"

He turned her hand over and rubbed her palm with his thumb, following the creases in it as if he was trying to read her future. Her body responded to the loveliness of the sensation though her mind refused to acknowledge it. Suddenly he underwent one of his barely perceptible changes of affect, this time from quizzical to fair-minded.

"I think I know why you are prickly. Shall I tell you?"

The curtain of lashes rose, but her eyes remained opaque.

"I am all ears," she said.

"You're annoyed that I left you in charge of the girls this morning. You are starting to think that I am a male chauvinist pig."

"Well, are you?"

"Yes, of course," he laughed, changing tone again, "but I am in no position to play that role with you!"

"And if you were?"

"Ah! Then we would have to work it out. It's a challenge I would welcome. But that's not where we are right now. Right now we are in a situation that makes both of us uncomfortable."

"How so?"

"For one, you are a paying guest. I should not have agreed to your working on my harvest."

"*Actually*, as your daughter would say, it's an interesting touristic concept. Some people pay big money to take part in archeological digs or clean up rain forests. Why not a grape picking vacation, with chateau accommodations no less?"

"That's a very generous way of looking at it."

"It isn't, trust me. I found the experience very rewarding. Besides, I didn't actually pay for my board here, as I was supposed to trade it against translation services for Amanda."

"All right then. We'll leave it at that. But now we are living under the same roof, and in a way I am your guest too. So when I go out, you may feel obligated to look after my daughters, even though in fact the girls are used to being here on their own, and Clarisse is old enough to handle any emergency. If she doesn't know what to do, she knows she can call me on my cell phone. And so can you, by the way."

But what about Isaac and Sarah, thought Franny. The babysitting shift was supposed to include them too. On the other hand, of course, Hughes was the only one of the adults at the chateau who was not on vacation. Some allowance had to be made for that.

"It's no big deal, really. In any case, remember that we are functioning as a kibbutz. Your children are my children, and so on."

"I'll go along with that idea too. But I still feel in your debt, which is hard to bear for a male chauvinist! And then I am in the middle of the harvest, which means that after today, I will have even less time to devote to my family and to you all. I don't want you to end up doing more than your share of the housekeeping chores, because that's sure to make you prickly." He wove his fingers through hers, spreading them apart, then pressing them together. She could feel the dry heat of his skin, the suppleness of his knuckles, the chafing of a few grains of sand.

"I really don't mind taking care of housekeeping chores. In fact, I find that I do enjoy playing innkeeper or camp director or den mother or …"

"Maîtresse de maison …"

"… or whatever else we may call that function. It's just that …"

"You don't want to be taken for granted."

Franny couldn't help laughing. How could he hit the nail on the head so perfectly, when the expression "to take someone for granted" did not even have an equivalent in French?

"You have such a command of the English language!" she teased.

"On some topics I am better in English than in French …" he replied thoughtfully. And he meant it. It wasn't the first time he noticed how having different idioms at his disposal channeled his thoughts in new directions. Additionally, speaking English had a way of refreshing topics that his marriage with Christiane had made trite and hopeless. But Franny was not like Christiane anyway. For one thing, she was fair-minded.

"So can we agree that from now on, as den mother you will let me know if I am remiss in my chores?"

There was something about his way of putting it that bothered Franny, but his good will was so obvious that she had to let it go. He held out his hand, and she shook it, sealing their agreement. All her irritation was gone. In retrospect her complaints looked petty, paranoid even. But he had not seized on that point. On the contrary, he had done something that she had never known another man to do: he had admitted being sexist, and in so doing he had made sexism seem bearable, not an intractable evil but a slight accident of birth that could alternatively be corrected or tolerated, like a gap between your front teeth. He had been able to see how his behavior would look through the prism of her past experience with men, and instead of chiding her for stereotyping him, he had sympathized with her fears. Better yet, he had come up with a plan for laying them to rest. If men could see how effectively this approach can disarm a woman, her cynical self whispered, they would all adopt it. Yet somehow she knew that in Hughes, it had come from the heart.

She was disarmed. But she was sad too. He had talked to her as a friend, no more. In fact, he seemed to be warning her not to expect anything else from him. Wasn't that what he meant when he said that he was in no position to play a macho role with her, or when he hinted that he would be too busy to spend time with her for the rest of the week? His handshake, concluding several minutes of what had felt like a delicate, inspired bit of lovemaking, put a nail in the coffin of her romantic illusions. Only yesterday, she had thought she was up to the task of seducing him. But that was assuming that he wanted to be seduced. Perhaps she had misinterpreted the signs. Perhaps even his kiss had been in jest. She had her familiar sense that the rules governing human interactions must be written in some book she had somehow failed to read, for all her love of literature. At least, in this foreign land, she could be excused for her cluelessness.

But what was she mooning about? In a week or so, she would be gone for ever. Had she in fact considered having a fling with Hughes, in spite of her firm opposition to such things? She reminded herself that flings were not worth the risks to heart and health. Thank God, he felt the same way.

"How long are you in France for anyway?" he asked, as if he had read her mind.

"My plane leaves on the ninth of October."

"That's a week after the end of your stay here. What are you going to do for a week?"

"I was thinking of traveling around before going back to Paris. Can you recommend any place that would be nice to visit this time of year?"

"Stay here. There is no better place in France. And traveling is overrated."

"Here? In Saint Yves? Where would I stay?"

"At the house."

"Aren't you renting the chateau to another group of Americans?"

"They cancelled."

"Isn't that bad for your finances?"

He frowned. They had never broached the subject of his cash flow, never even alluded to their encounter at the cabanon, where he felt he must have cut a poor figure playing Brahms in the wilderness. But she must have guessed that he was in debt up to his neck. The directness of her question, which he was sure no French woman would ever have asked, had the paradoxical effect of setting him at ease. If she did not feel that poverty was shameful, why should he?

"Yes, but I'll manage. So will you stay?" He was the one looking away now, his hand, seemingly of its own accord, patting the sand into little mounds, then flattening them out.

"As a paying guest and den mother?"

He flinched, making her wish she could take back her words. She must have sounded crass and tactless. But what did he have in mind? She could not assume that he meant her to be his private guest. He turned to her and saw that she was biting her lip. She was just insecure. He relaxed.

"As neither. As a lover, hopefully."

Franny was left speechless by his boldness. Was this a typical sample of French courtship, or was it just him? And what did it matter anyway? She could respond in any way she saw fit.

She agreed to stay. Hughes explained that he did not think it would be a good idea for him to become intimate with a new woman while his daughters were staying at the chateau. He was incapable of dissembling, and he did not want the girls, particularly Clarisse, who was very attuned to him, to be alarmed by signs of something momentous happening to their father that they could neither comprehend nor help make safe. And he wanted them to get to know Franny for herself. But Christiane was supposed to pick them up on Thursday. After that ... After that, if Franny was agreeable, he would love to take her into his bed, or whatever bed was available. And after that ... After that they would see. It was a good plan. Reasonable and rational. And while they were being so reasonable and rational, they dealt preemptively with the issue of STDs, which turned out to be an easy one, as Franny had been tested for HIV after her last romantic disaster, and Hughes had slept with only one woman since 1987. As to contraception, thought Franny, this was France, where, in case condoms did not please, it was easier to get a hold of RU486 than to find a lawyer in the US. After that ... they would see.

They felt so reasonable and rational about their plan that they shook on it. Somehow their arms got entangled, and before they knew it, her body had been dragged under his, one of his hands was nestling her head against his chest, the other one was enfolding her waist, his thighs were warm against hers, he was kissing her eyelids, her nose, her lips, her arms were around his neck, they were breathing into each other. At which point they heard a car horn. The SUV was back on the parking lot, and the children were running down the path towards the beach, where they found the couple discussing Bourdieu at arms length of each other.

The sun was gliding down towards the dark tangle of trees on the far shore of the lake. The misty veil in the sky had lifted, and in response the milky film on the water had dissolved, revealing a serene mirror of saturated turquoise and emerald hues in which the concentric waves spreading out around a couple of meditative ducks commingled, causing some upside-down pines to perform a quiet belly dance. On the beach, the lengthening shadows sketched a landscape of miniature dunes over which scarlet dragon-flies hovered. While no one was watching, a small miracle of light had metamorphosed the humdrum landscape into a scene of exquisite beauty. Franny felt blessed, but also a little scared by the evidence that grace should be so protean. For metamorphoses cut both ways. You might hike toward a beloved peak, remembering its carpet of wild flowers, the waterfall tumbling over mossy rocks, the ocean of blue overhead. But when you got there, the flowers might have given way to nasty Japanese thistle, the waterfall might have dried up and fog might obscure the view. She was reminded of how she had hated France in the past, and how she loved it now. She thought of Jean Jacques Rousseau finding a factory in the middle of what looked like a primeval forest. How were you supposed to stick to any course of action when reality was so changeable? What had Rousseau himself done? All she remembered was that he had not given up on hiking.

She went for a last dip in the lake while Chuck, Clarisse and Isaac threw the frisbee on the lawn and Hughes gave a swimming lesson to Héloise and Sarah. Apparently unperturbed by the fickleness of nature, the chatelain was in an excellent mood, his normal air of preoccupied efficacy replaced by one of relaxed confidence. Still, he did not deviate from what Franny would end up referring to fondly as his relentlessly pedagogical attitude towards children. In this case at least, the strategy bore fruit. Within twenty minutes, both girls were able to stay afloat for a second or two.

Back at the chateau, the group dispersed for a while. Chuck set about roasting a couple of herb-marinated chickens while Victoria followed his instructions for braised fennel. The kids were dispatched to the garden to pick tomatoes, and Hughes went down to check on the wine bottling. Instead of going around the building to the rear entrance of the cellar, he used the door located under the hallway stairs, the one that has stirred such fearful imaginings in Franny on her second night. The door was still locked, but only to prevent the children from tumbling down the steep stone staircase and cutting themselves on a bottle rack, Hughes explained as he showed Franny the hook above the door where the key was kept. He reminded her of his early offer to show her his *cave*, but she declined for the moment, eager to wash the pond scum from her hair. When he came upstairs half an hour later, he was carrying a computer. He put it down in its old place in the second floor office, connecting its modem wire to a phone jack under the desk. The computer was for Clarisse, who had arranged to get her homework from a classmate via e-mail. This is when Franny understood why the phone line had been occasionally unavailable during her first few days at the chateau: it had been used to connect the PC to the Internet.

Phil showed up as the adults were taking the *apéritif* on the terrace—more out of principle than strict enjoyment, as the evening was far from balmy. He regaled them with his adventures in literary fandom and the antics of French drivers, his boisterousness barely masking a forlorn mood that pulled at the women's heart-strings.

After dinner Héloise and Isaac undertook some construction project out of wooden blocks, although from the look of the odd mixture of plastic farm animals and tin soldiers that soon littered it, their collaboration had apparently stopped short of agreeing on the building's function. Meanwhile Hughes taught Franny, Chuck and Amanda how to play *belote*, the card game made famous by Pagnol's movies. In the music room, Sarah danced to a Clementi sonatina played by Clarisse. Phil traded quotes with Victoria.

As she was drifting off to sleep, Amanda realized that Sarah had not had a tantrum all day, and that Isaac had not missed his lost Game Boy. Then she thought of her escapade in the woods with Chuck. It was at that moment that she made a decisive turn towards francophilia.

CHAPTER 16

▼

THINK GLOBALLY, ACT LOCALLY

It was well past midnight by the time Gérard left the plant. The evening shift supervisor had called in sick, and the staff being pared down to a minimum according to the new lean and mean paradigm, Gérard had had to substitute for him, which meant that he had worked for sixteen hours straight. Fortunately the double shift had gone very smoothly, so he still felt wide-awake in spite of the late hour. Not that the plant was completely trouble-free, of course: the yearly maintenance on reactor number two was three weeks behind schedule, and the Association pour la Sureté Nucléaire had recently demanded that EDF post an incident report regarding the seismic deficiency of the racks that held spent fuel assemblies in the cooling pools–a design flaw which had been identified more than a year ago and had still not been fixed. These problems, not being operational, were however not in Gérard's bailiwick. One thing you learned working inside a meticulously designed, immensely complex, and potentially dangerous engineering system was not to worry too much about issues that fell outside of your responsibilities, because in each department, there was at least one person you could trust to handle them before they degenerated into a catastrophe. If only one could be as confident about the world at large....

Gérard opened the car door, tore his badge from his shirt pocket and tossed it on the passenger seat, asserting through this small ritual that he was again his own man, even though he was still within the plant's security perimeter. He started the engine and let it idle while the fan cleared the night dew from the windshield. Above the ring of ground level lights, the plant's buildings loomed darkly: the two containment domes, sort of Brutalist mosques, complete with minaret looking chimneys; the gigantic tool boxes of the turbine buildings; various other cubes that housed machines and administrative offices; and his favorites, the bobbin-shaped cooling towers, exhaling their own weather into the navy blue sky. Underneath the purr of the car engine, he could discern the plant's electric hum. To Gérard, to the extent that he thought of such things, it was the sound of celestial harmony.

As soon as he had passed the guard house, he floored the gas pedal, mechanically taking note of the time it took to get to a hundred and thirty kilometers per hour. The reward for working late was that he could get up a good speed on the first stretch of the road home, which was mostly straight. He loved to zoom into the abyss of the night, driving fast enough to be forced to steer seemingly ahead of the information conveyed by the headlights. During those moments life became a pure abstraction, the closest thing to eternity. At the first bend he turned back into a family man.

Everything was fine on the home front. Gérard could no longer understand his lapse from manly self-control only a week ago, when he had interpreted a mere break in his routine as the death knell of his marriage, but he did not regret it either, as it had led to a deeper understanding with Pierrette. As for her working outside the house, it had turned out to be no big deal. With only one kid living at home, and the dog out in the yard all day long, the house did not need that much upkeep. So what if the floor got vacuumed and mopped only once a week instead of daily? You could hardly tell the difference. For the rest, every member of the Chemineau household had long been trained to pick up after themselves, except of course for Gros Bébé.

Dinner was not an issue either. They could either cook it together, which actually made the evening livelier, or they could go out, which they had done once already. Pierrette's colleague Guillaume had turned them on to a couple of very nice restaurants within a ten kilometer radius, plus you could always fall back on the pizza from the bakery in Saint Yves, so much better than the gooey, artificial tasting stuff sold at fast food franchises, as they had discovered at the Degency place on Saturday.

His pride was not even stung by his demotion from the status of sole family provider. Pierrette, far from using her new earnings to assert her independence, was going to put them all into their housing savings account, so they would be a little closer to being able to buy their own home–only a little closer, as she was not making much, and that was just fine with Gérard, who if he was no longer bringing home all the bacon, was still pleased to contribute the lion's share.

Most importantly, there was no shame attached to the career Pierrette had picked, which was lucky when you thought of it, because with her lack of formal education and non-existent CV, she might have seemed limited to jobs as domestic help or sales clerk. But winery work was respectable, part of the noble tradition that made France unique. Gérard was proud that his family would contribute to this heritage, even if the financial benefits were negligible. For it appeared that Pierrette would continue working at the Chateau Degency beyond the harvest and bottling period under a sort of apprenticeship: Degency's vineyard overseer, who was getting on in years, was willing to train her in everything he knew, from pruning to operating the machinery, with a view that she might be able to replace him one day.

Gérard's fears had revealed themselves to be groundless even in the small matter of the dinner at the chateau. Contrary to his expectations, Pierrette's aristocratic boss was just a regular guy, wound a little tight maybe, but courteous and unassuming, and not at all flirtatious with other people's wives. In fact, upon first entering the dining room, Gérard had assumed that the vicomte must be the tall guy with the chiseled profile, brilliantined hair and starched shirt who held a scotch in one hand and had his other arm wrapped around the chair of an icy brunette straight out of Vogue. Then the guy had opened his mouth, and he had turned out to be American–Philip Something. The icy brunette was Degency's ex-wife, and *she* definitely looked the aristocrat, although to be honest she had made an effort to be hospitable, the problem being that the effort showed. He could see why the marriage of those two hadn't worked. What could poor Degency have thought? He was much better off with that little American girlfriend of his, a mite of a woman, but shapely, with a nice *minois chiffoné*, a warm manner and a brisk way of getting the dinner table ready–the same type of woman as Pierrette, come to think of it.

The chateau was also very different from what he had imagined, big, but not at all cold or ostentatious. Truth be told, it was a little funky: Gérard was sure he had espied some dust bunnies in the corners of the dining room. When it came to furniture, he and Pierrette had a number of Louis Philippe pieces inherited from her grandparents' farm–simple, solid oak and walnut buffets, armoires, sleigh beds and dressers polished to a high gloss that could compete quite favorably with the dull, rickety and mismatched stuff owned by the vicomte. And according to Pierrette, who had visited the upper floor, the place was completely lacking in electronics. Degency was obviously struggling financially. Inheritance taxes must have long eroded his family's wealth, and going organic was probably costly. Quitting his banking job may not have been altogether a wise move–at least Gérard would never have recommended it. But it didn't seem out of character. Soft-spoken and restrained as he appeared, the vicomte had a touch of the quixotic–that was where his social class showed. Generally, Gérard had as little patience with aristocratic utopias as with the crassness of the *nouveau riche*. But in this case he wished Degency luck, if only because he wanted to see his wife happy.

He had not had much chance to chat with the other American couple at the dinner, because they did not speak French, but at least they had put to use every single word of the language they knew, and in return Gérard had requisitioned his rusty English. He had managed to exchange a few words about American football with Chuck, and Amanda had written down the recipe for Pierrette's pear tart, a laborious process as the Americans didn't use grams, and Pierrette had had to convert the proportions into cups and tablespoons. Gérard was hoping the result would be edible. Anyway, apart from their size–Chuck looked like a linebacker, and his wife was taller than Gérard–which caused him to worry about the fate of Degency's dining room chairs, there was nothing objectionable about the Fischbeins, and they seemed to have taken a genuine liking to the Chemineaux: "it was nice meeting you" they had declared at the moment of parting, which in the Chemineaux' world was an unheard of emotional outburst on such short acquaintance.

Obviously, there were good, unpretentious people everywhere, even in imperialist countries. Perhaps it was just their ruling class that was evil? Or it may just have been a product of historical circumstances. After all, France had been an imperialist country at one time. In any case, Gérard was close to being able to claim that *he* wasn't anti-American, since he could count Americans among his best friends.

But it was Guillaume that Gérard had found the most *sympa*, the greengrocer's general outlook and demeanor–a common French mixture of bottled-up indignation and laidback cynicism–being close to his own. He was from the area but barely had a trace of southern accent, because like Gérard, he had lived in many different places. He was smart, funny, his background and occupation placed him on the same rung of the social ladder as Gérard, and he seemed to know how to have a good time. Gérard would have worried about his working in close proximity with Pierrette, even though he was younger than her, because he knew there were plenty of men who went for older women, and Pierrette, let's face it, was luscious even at forty-two. Fortunately, Degency had managed to get a crew together for the rest of the harvest, and Guillaume had gone back to his shop. But that also meant Gérard would not get the opportunity to see more of him, and that was unfortunate.

Another positive outcome of the Chemineaux' new domestic arrangement was that Gérard was able to spend a little time alone with his daughter in the evening as both of them got home before Pierrette. Now tête-à-tête does not necessarily mean heart-to-heart, particularly with a girl. Gérard did not expect Chloé to suddenly start pouring out her teenage soul to her father. If she had, he wouldn't have known how to react. His approach to parenting had been to provide for his children's comfort, to give them instructions on what to do, which was basically to get good grades in school, and what not to do—to get afoul of the law or make babies, and then to stand back and watch them grow, lovingly, humorously, and sometimes warily, but without excessive demonstrations of his feelings or prying into theirs. His approach was vindicated by the results: all three kids had turned out fine—hard-working, reasonable, emotionally balanced—although Gérard knew that this success was at least half Pierrette's doing, and she was much more demonstrative than her husband. In a way, the very intensity of her involvement, by allowing him to remain somewhat aloof, had robbed him of a certain amount of intimacy with his children. But now that she wasn't always home, he found himself wandering into Chloé's bedroom, patting her curly head, asking her what she was doing, playing video games with her, and generally being awed at the thought that this poised young lady had come out of his loins. He had in fact done all those things before, but in his wife's absence they felt more natural. And Chloé, in her non-committal adolescent way, seemed to welcome the increased attention.

Through those low-key schmoozing sessions Gérard had discovered that Chloé had a Japanese boyfriend. It was strictly an Internet romance so far, but now the boy was proposing to come to France for a visit. The two had "met" in a Franco-Japanese chat room, an extension of their respective language coursework, and had soon begun a private conversation. They communicated every day through instant messaging and visual telephony, which, thanks to DSL, did not cost any more than if the boy had lived in Saint Yves. Gérard now understood the purpose of the webcam perched on top of the computer.

It was mind-boggling to watch in real-time the face of a boy who lived on the other side of the world, to see the parents walk back and forth in the background, the father removing his tie, the mother carrying a tea tray, and to know that his own face was being displayed in a living room in Osaka, warts and all, behind

Chloé's shoulder. Gérard had even exchanged a few words with his Japanese counterpart, in English of course, which was the language also used by Chloé and Kenzo. (But didn't that defeat the whole educational purpose on the online friendship? Oh well, English was fast becoming the universal language anyway.) The father was a doctor, the mother stayed at home, the whole family seemed to be polite and respectable, in short, Gérard had no objection to receiving the boy. The kids might end up getting sexually involved, but Chloé was pushing eighteen, and her mother would be sure to talk to her about contraception and HIV. Afterwards Kenzo would return to Japan, and a long-distance affair would on the whole interfere less with the kids' studies.

As much of a chauvinistic stick-in-the-mud as Gérard admitted himself to be, he was in fact tickled pink at the idea of his daughter turning into a cosmopolitan. Towards the Japanese, he felt nothing but respect: they worked hard, they did not make a lot of noise, they were not interested in warfare, they had a very old, very sophisticated civilization, and they gave the Americans a run for their money in the economic arena. But it was more than the nationality of Chloé's love interest that he approved of. Her online friendship gave him a glimpse of a possible future for mankind—as a global family united in peace, collaboration and understanding. That was if mankind didn't blow itself up first.

As he rounded another turn, Gérard became aware of something nagging at the back of his mind. Something he had passed on the road. Something that shouldn't have been there. It was the second time in two weeks that his internal alarm went off while driving around the plant. He was probably just being paranoid because of the recent terrorist attack. Still. He slowed down and rewound his visual memory tape of the last minute or two. A car parked on the shoulder. No, two vehicles, a sedan and a van, next to some field tilting up gently towards the horizon, where a quarter moon was caught in the web of a high-voltage pylon. It was impossible for both vehicles to have stalled or run out of gas; it was unlikely they were both serving as shelters for a little night romance, not parked so close on a main road, not in this un-picturesque place. What else then? The presence of the pylon worried him. There was probably an innocuous explanation to the sight, but better safe than sorry. Instinctively, Gérard turned into the first cross road, backed up and came back around, slowing down as he passed the two vehicles, and again getting the impression that something was fishy. He drove another kilometer towards the plant, then turned around again, and stopped his car twenty meters behind the two suspicious vehicles. He turned off the headlights, opened the window a crack, and concentrated his senses.

The cars were empty, but they had not been for long, as indicated by the pops and crackles of cooling engines under their hoods. The field on this side of the road was planted with corn, the swaying of its foliage in the night breeze producing a swoosh similar to the drag of a wedding dress. But over these harmless noises, Gérard soon perceived more ominous sounds of trampling on dirt and snapping of stalks that suggested several people were moving through the field. It seemed they were going in the direction of the pylon. Terrorists! Gérard felt his shirt pocket for his cell phone. It wasn't there. He patted his back pockets, the crook of the passenger seat, the inside of the glove compartment. Merde! He had left the phone at the office.

His hand on the ignition, he was about to drive back to the plant to alert security when he noticed that the intruders had stopped moving and were instead hammering at something in the middle of the field, a good distance from the pylon. Then, through the silvery black vegetation, a green glow appeared. It rose above the canopy of leaves and turned into the white light of a storm lamp, suspended from a hook in a wooden pole. Three other lamps were lit in the same manner, illuminating a square patch of ground about ten meters on each side. Gérard could now hear muffled conversations, laughter, even a few notes of a song. Terrorists or pranksters? Then the edges of the illuminated patch started swinging violently. To the accompaniment of a wheezing sound like that of a scythe, sheaves after sheaves of corn stalks were falling, creating a ragged hole in the inclined plane of the field. In a flash, Gérard understood was he was witnessing: environmental activists were destroying a test plot of genetically modified corn.

A flurry of such incidents over the summer had been reported on the news, but Gérard had paid scant attention. Not that he was indifferent to environmental concerns, but to him the Greens had forfeited any right to being listened to by stridently opposing nuclear energy, when it was obviously cleaner than any viable alternative. They were like the boy who cried wolf, equating every bit of scientific progress with mankind's perdition. Though of course even the boy who cried wolf had been right at last. The mad cow episode had certainly shaken people's faith in modern agriculture. And behind much "scientific progress" there were big multi-nationals who cared only to increase their profits, the health and livelihood of the rest of the population be damned.

Gérard wondered what Guillaume, who was a staunch advocate of organic farming, would think of the presence of a genetically modified crop on the commune's territory, whether he would applaud its stealthy destruction, whether he might in fact be one of the activists doing the mowing. The idea occurred to him to pay the greengrocer a visit in the next few days. He would not be hard to find as there were so few shops in Saint Yves. But first Gérard would have to gather some facts so he didn't sound like an idiot. The future of food was well worth investigating anyway.

Reassured that the nuclear plant was in no danger of terrorist attack, Gérard started his car and peeled away from the scene. Strangely, the people in the field had not seemed to hear him, unless they were just not very worried about being caught in the act. He got back home around one AM and managed to tiptoe upstairs without waking Gros Bébé. A fine guard dog they had. In the bedroom Pierrette was fast asleep on her side of the bed, a ray of moonlight that had squeezed through a slit in the shutters drawing a fluorescent bar through her hand open on the pillow, making it appear as if she held a magic wand. Gérard undressed in the dark and slipped under the covers, shifting his body until it comfortably spooned his wife's. Without a hint of movement or a change in her breathing to indicate that she had woken up, Pierrette whispered:

"Tout va bien?"

"Tout va bien," answered Gérard, clasping her more tightly.

*   *   *   *

The next day at work, Gérard took advantage of some idle moments to conduct a Web search on Genetically Modified Organisms. He found out that although the French government had suspended all testing and commercialization of GMOs in 1998, following the legal precautionary principle which prohibits products and techniques with the potential for causing great harm, even in the absence of proof of their nefariousness, the decision was reversed in 2000 by the Cour d'Etat, bowing to EU pressure. Under the new transparency paradigm, the French ministry of agriculture was supposed to make available a list of all GMO testing plots, but as it was dragging its feet, NGOs had picked up the slack. Gérard visited the site of Les Amis de la Terre, clicked on the Provences/Alpes region of the map, and there, under Vaucluse, he found the following entry:

Type de plante: Maïs (Monsanto)

Lieu: Saint Yves

Année: 2001

It turned out it wasn't just genetically modified corn that was being tested in the area. Tomatoes, lettuce, soy beans, tobacco, rape were undergoing their own Frankenfood transformations right under the nose of blissfully ignorant citizens. They were often planted in the middle of a field devoted to production, the patches unfenced and unmarked to avoid detection by environmental activists. Regulations had been established to prevent cross-fertilization with regular crops, but often they were not enforced. Gérard dug deeper and ran into stories of transgenic field contamination in Mexico, of engineered resistance to antibiotics, of allergic reactions in humans, of false pregnancies in pigs, of deformed chickens, and even if the Internet was notorious for conveying unreliable information, there was enough material there to scare the pants off you. Plus there was the incontrovertible issue of the commodification of life forms, with companies like Monsanto and Aventis taking patents on recombinations of genetic material that had taken nature and/or mankind eons to evolve. And finally there was the prospect that, contrary to the humanitarian assertions of agribusiness representatives, the GMOs, like the Green Revolution before them, would mainly achieve the ruination of Third World farmers, who would be faced with a choice between paying exorbitant prices for the new seeds or losing in the competition against them.

All this and more Gérard discovered from his desk within a couple of hours, in Web pages that came from all over the world. The Internet was a wonderful thing, but it wasn't for the faint of heart: with knowledge came responsibility.

On his way home, Gérard, who had promised to take care of today's food shopping, decided to do it in Saint Yves instead of the supermarket in Mirésol. First he stopped at the bakery, which he had never visited before. Monsieur Hamzaoui was behind the counter, his dark skin sprinkled with flour. As there were no other customers in the shop, the two men exchanged a few words about the weather. Gérard told Monsieur Hamzaoui that he had met his son. The baker's face darkened further. What had Chérif done now, he wondered. Gérard reassured him, congratulated him on his pizza, got interested in the new oven that sparkled through the open back door of the shop. Monsieur Hamzaoui ended up giving him a tour of the bakery, and Gérard was impressed. It had never occurred to him that there was so much technical knowledge involved in making bread. He bought a scrumptious looking round loaf, grabbed a few of the flyers left by the organic milling company. He told Monsieur Hamzaoui he would hand them out to his colleagues and neighbors. Monsieur Hamzaoui's face brightened a little as he shook Gérard's hand. He knew there were hundreds of people living in the EDF cité. And he desperately needed new customers, as about a third of the villagers were still inexplicably shunning his bread in favor of the puffed-up, tasteless cardboard sold at the grocery. Hacene suspected it was because he was Algerian. Around Paris it wouldn't have mattered, as half of the mom and pop shops there were held by immigrant moms and pops (and their extended families). But here people were backward. They probably needed convincing that bread made by an Algerian wasn't going to poison them. The problem was, Hacene was not the convincing type. All he could do was to work hard and hope for the best.

In the greengrocer's tin shack, Guillaume was arranging a display of locally produced pâtés and preserves. Another handshake, another chat about the weather, at the end of which Gérard got down to brass tacks. Did Guillaume know that Monsanto was testing transgenic corn in their backyard? No, he didn't. Gérard told him of his discoveries, and also of the existence of a campaign coordinated by a number of environmental groups, including Greenpeace, ATTAC and La Confederation Paysanne (José Bové's organization), to help municipalities pass ordinances against the open field testing of GMOs on their territories. Gérard had printed the letter advertising the campaign as well as sample ordinances and deliberations. Guillaume was starting to look over these documents when Madame Malefoi entered the store. Guillaume wrote Gérard's phone number on the sheets, stuffed them in his pockets, told Gérard he would call him as soon as he had read them, and turned to attend to the tobacconist's wife.

When the phone rang that night, Pierrette went to answer it, as usual. But then she handed the phone to Gérard with a look of surprise. Ordinarily, the only calls Gérard ever got were from work, or, but very rarely, from one of his sisters. Gérard talked for a long time in conspiratorial tones. After he hung up, he explained to Pierrette that he was about to get involved in local politics.

CHAPTER 17

▼

AIDE-TOI, LE CIEL
T'AIDERA

(God Helps Those Who Help Themselves)

Sitting astride the peak of the roof with his back leaning against a chimney pot and his shoelaces undone, Chérif is composing a rap song. So far he has written one verse, which reads:

Sa natte m'éclate
C'est la pendule de mon coeur, j'en pleure, malheur
Quand je grimpe derrière elle à quat' quat'
Les doigts me démangent de la défaire
De voir ses cheveux couler comme une rivière
Bas les pattes kim'fait l'papa
Le propriétaire
C'est moi
Tout dans l'regard, pas dans l'blabla
Il prétend que la thune ça l'intéresse pas
Mais moi, pas con, je sais bien qu'pour lui plaire
I' faudrait que je sois dans les affaires

It is his best rap to date, yet he is unhappy with it. He thinks that it hardly does justice to the feelings of awe, adoration, perfect devotion, hopeless and eternal longing that stir for the first time in his breast. There is so much more to say about her bewitching braid, not to mention her angelic face, bent in its own shadow as if behind a veil; her hands fluttering dove-like over the piano keys; her pillowy voice; the dimples at the back of her knees. Somehow the tyranny of the rhyme, unless it is the superficial cynicism that is part and parcel of being hip, has caused him to veer away from the glorification of the beloved's many charms into an admission that she is way out of his league.

As a matter of fact, his predicament does have literary echoes. Isn't the unattainability of a woman endowed with all perfections the essential theme of the poetry of courtly love? How ironic, how appropriate too that the resolutely modern, American-born idiom of rap should be a vehicle for reviving a genre originated by Chérif's putative ancestors in Moorish Spain! Not that he is aware of the lineage, although it was duly brought to his attention in seventh grade–not once, but twice, as he had to repeat that year–when French students are supposed to read *La Mort du Roi Arthur* per national curriculum dictates. But it is possible that however inattentive Chérif may have been at the time, he has absorbed something of the lesson through that osmotic process that is the secret weapon of propagandists of all ilks. Thus, for better and for worse, in and out of school, cultures keep cross-pollinating each other.

Frustrated with his expressive powers, Chérif tells himself that he still has time to tame the muse in following verses. And his prospects for winning his lady are not completely bleak either. The thing is, at fifteen Chérif already has a business plan.

He raises his eyes from the spiral notebook and surveys the landscape shimmering in the afternoon haze. It looks so different from the way it did only a couple of weeks ago, imbued as it is now with knowledge! The wobbly green lines that run down the slopes are vineyards, from which you get grapes, from which you make wine, from which you can make enough money to live in a castle. The spastic green dots are orchards: cherries, apricots, figs, almonds, olives, hanging from the trees like Christmas presents–not all right now, in fact, but still–just waiting to be converted into cash. You can make baskets with the osiers that grow along the river valley. The leaves on lime trees are used for brewing tea, those on mulberry trees for raising silk worms. Purple lavender is squeezed into perfume, yellow sunflowers into oil. Even the wild-looking stretches of chaparral teem with valuable commodities: fodder for goats and sheep, thyme, rosemary, mint, fennel seeds, blackberries, elderberries, juniper berries, there isn't one fucking useless thing growing out of the dirt around here!

Cool. But what has really won Chérif over to the Eight Four–apart from the radiance of his darling, to whom he owes his new botanical awareness–what gives him hope that in time he may become as respectable as the Chemineau dude, or even as the castle owner, is actually invisible to the eye, which is just as well as far as Chérif is concerned. With prophetic aptness the green atomic mushrooms that crown the hilltops have turned out to harbor the king of all fungi: the black truffle, ultimate dining status symbol for every aspiring stockbroker, high-tech entrepreneur, soccer star and drug dealer, which sells for up to 2000 Francs a kilo on the market at Carpentras, apparently a hush-hush kind of trade with no paper trail, pretty much outside of the law. In other words, a "bizness".

Ah! Those *ploucs*, they are sly ones after all. Riding their muddy tractors in their patched up blues, getting the government to pay for their gall bladder operations, stringing proverbs as if common sense was their only asset, and all the while they're sitting on a gold mine! And the cops don't even bother them. Chérif can't see much moral difference between dealing truffles and dealing *kif*, except that truffles typically don't grow around the projects, and you have to make do with available resources. Chérif is loyal to his homies. He will always defend them, always be one of them in his heart of hearts. But he is starting to see how he might find his niche here.

In the paved courtyard below, among the scrappy oleander bushes and potted geraniums, in a cardboard box lovingly attended by Nanette, is the key to his future success, the magic sword with which he will perform the deeds that will dazzle the mistress of his heart: a little puppy, half-Labrador and half-mutt, which Chérif is shortly to start training to hunt truffles. Nanette does not know this. She thinks she has just managed to wrangle yet another goodie from her parents. This in itself is cause for rejoicing: for once Chérif has outsmarted her. He is sure that if he had said the dog was for him, the Father would never have allowed him to keep it.

He mulls over a second verse. Maybe he should go back to the beginning, that stormy Saturday afternoon long long ago when he first saw her. He had let his mother drag him to Monsieur Degency's vineyard on the promise that he could keep the money he earned. When the crew got back to the parking lot, it was full of fancy cars and people yakking away in English. There was a girl standing in the background looking at her feet. Right away, Chérif felt something different in the air, like when a door opens behind you. As he jumped down from the van his knee hit the side of the door. She looked up at him for a second and a smile that seemed to come from far away fluttered on her lips. Then she turned away and her braid came into view, thick, heavy and shiny, dangling all the way to her waist. In a heartbeat, he was smitten.

He feels as if she is the first person he really saw. Normally, when he meets strangers, he is too busy figuring out what they want from him, too worried about how they're judging him, to pay attention to them for themselves or take pleasure in their company. Normally, his instinct is to fight or flee. Even "nice" people like Monsieur Degency and his girlfriend Franny don't put him at ease: they always try too hard, pretending not to want anything, pretending that they aren't judging him, when in fact they want the most, they are the harshest judges. But Clarisse–there, he said her name–she was just there, smiling on him from her ivory tower, beautiful and complete and undemanding, and instantly he wanted to give her everything.

In a dream, he came back to the castle for dinner that night. In a dream, he tagged along on Sunday when they went to visit another castle. The whole time he felt like a knight undergoing an ordeal: part of him was wracked by fear of showing bad manners or saying the wrong thing, and another part was wallowing in his torment, offering it up to her who knew nothing of it, who just smiled on him as if she took it for granted that he belonged to her.

He didn't see her again for the next two days. Now that the other Americans had arrived, Franny had no time for tutoring lessons, and Chérif couldn't think of another excuse to throw himself in Clarisse's way. But on Wednesday afternoon, it being a half-day at school, he found himself pedaling towards the castle. The gear cable on his bicycle needed adjustment, and he had to ride standing up on the last part of the hill, conscious that he was going to look like a chump by the time he got up there, red faced and sweaty in his torn cutoffs. And then he thought how ridiculous it was to be chasing after a thirteen-year-old girl from a hoity-toity French family. (He figured she must be thirteen, since she was in fourth at school). On the other end, his own mother had not been much older when she was promised to the Father, and what about Romeo and Juliet? Plus, he wasn't chasing after Clarisse. He just wanted to bask in her aura, which was so much more restful than trying hard to get some action, then wondering why he wasn't getting any. With Clarisse he didn't have to wonder.

He threw the bicycle to the ground and climbed the stairs two by two. The terrace was a blinding white, empty except for an abandoned badminton net, the few flecks of shade huddled around the foot of the trees. The front door was open, but no sound was coming out of the house, and not much was happening outside either. The cicadas had not sung ever since the last storm, either drowned, or finally busy stocking up for the winter. Only a couple of birds were tweeting back and forth pitifully from both ends of the row of trees, like kids arguing after a nap. On the far side of the house, some clothes were drying on a line. Chérif recognized one of his mother's sheets and felt ashamed. What the heck was he doing here after all?

He tip-toed over to the balustrade, attracted by the cool scent of mowed grass wafting from below. As he peered down into the garden, his heart leapt in his chest: right below him, Clarisse, in shorts and tank top, was lying on her stomach, studying. How alien she looked suddenly, all that slim tanned flesh suggesting a more worldly, more dangerous femininity! The other kids were scattered around the lawn, the two little girls busy making lavender wreaths, the boy pretend-fishing with a stick in the basin. Victoria, the wild American chick, was sitting cross-legged in a deck chair, also making a wreath. She was the first to spot Chérif.

"Hi, there!" she cried blithely, as if his face peeking among the stone vases was the most natural thing in the world. She was odd, that one: super-friendly one minute, completely oblivious the next. Chérif had watched her interact with the other people at the castle. At first he had thought she was just dopey. But then, he had started to suspect that she was the kind of person who makes an effort to get in your good graces only when it suits their own private agenda–kind of like his sister. Still, she had rescued him from the cops, and there was nothing in it for her that he could see.

Her cry had attracted Clarisse's attention. She squinted in his direction, recognized him and waved him over, smiling like a queen from her carriage, herself again.

"J'en ai marre d'étudier!" she said, slapping her book shut. "Tu as envie de faire un tour de la propriété?" All casual, but inviting too, as if she had been waiting for him to lay off the cramming. Then she turned to the American kids, her voice taking on that fakey enthusiasm of the kindergarten teacher:

"Sarah, Isaac, do you want to see the land of caramels?" Chérif may have only got an eight in English last year, but he could tell her words to the kids weren't an exact translation of what she had said to him. She was just humoring them to get them to go along. It worked.

"Is it like the gingerbread house?" Sarah asked, all excited. "Is there a wicked witch there?"

"You'll see!" Clarisse answered mysteriously.

"Are the caramels for free?" Isaac said.

"You'll see!" Clarisse answered again.

They had to wait while the kids went to the bathroom and Victoria got her backpack ready. Sarah decided to stuff her pockets with white pebbles–to find the way back, she explained, and Clarisse translated, rolling her eyes at Chérif on the sly–and Clarisse's sister Héloise started doing the same thing, like she was playing *Jacques a dit*. Isaac ran back down to the lawn and grabbed his fishing rod to use as a walking stick. Finally they were on their way.

As Chérif goes back over it, the hike unfolds in his mind with the episodic dreaminess of a video game adventure, complete with scary scenery, magical objects and feats of prowess. Indeed it *was* a quest with a prize at the end, although he did not know it at the time.

First they climbed the hill behind the house. It was hard going, what with dirt crumbling under your feet and roots that looked like snakes snagging your ankles, but Chérif didn't let it bother him. When they got to the top, they found themselves in a field planted with trees that came right out of the bare dirt. Clarisse asked him if he knew what they were. Of course, he had no idea. They were cherry trees, she said, in French and in English, and the sound of the words immediately struck him as poetic, though he did not mention it: Clarisse, Chérif, cerise, cherry, it was a sort of rhyme pattern. Too bad the cherries had all been picked. He would have loved to climb a tree to give her some.

A little further there were some apricot trees, also picked clean, but even without fruit on them, she had no trouble identifying them too. OK, it wasn't so surprising she knew the names of everything around–after all it was her property. But she never sounded boastful about it.

As they walked, she went on pointing out various plants. It was weird, but each time she named something, it was like it stepped forward from the surrounding green blur and answered: "Present!" with a face all its own. Here and there she would translate for the Americans, using a tiny French-English dictionary she carried in her pocket. But mostly she talked to Chérif – Héloise, unfazed by the language barrier, pretty much stuck with the twins – and mostly he listened. Sometimes they would walk side by side, and he kept imagining that he took her hand, and he felt hot and dizzy, but in a good way. Then the path would narrow and he let her walk in front of him so he could catch her if she fell, and her braid would swing and the dimples at the back of her knees would throb, and he felt like slipping off the glittery tie that held the braid together to let her hair cascade down freely, and he felt even hotter. But of course he would never have dared.

They went through a forest. A lot of the trees in there turned out to be oaks, although they didn't all look the same, some tall with scalloped leaves, some bushy with spiny leaves. The way you recognized them was from the little brown heads covered with knit caps–called acorns–that dangled from their branches. The oak tree was another thing that dude La Fontaine had written about, some kind of contest with a reed where the reed had come out on top–as if. But La Fontaine had left out the best. It was Clarisse who told Chérif about the truffles that grew around oaks, how you found them with dogs, and how the people who knew the best spots, her father's farmhand Henri among them, kept them a secret.

In the middle of the forest there was a clearing with a hut and a pile of stone shaped like a bomb. When she saw the hut, Sarah grabbed Clarisse's hand and asked in a whisper if that's where the wicked witch lived, and Clarisse answered no, a kind magician lived there, and when he played his clarinet all the animals came and held hands with each other. Sarah wanted to wait for him, but Isaac wanted to get to the caramels.

They went down into a *combe*, which is a rocky ravine, normally dry, that turns into a torrent when it rains. Clarisse showed him the piles of dead leaves stacked neatly behind every rock by the last storm, and Chérif realized with a chill that, safe as it looked now, the combe was a place where you could drown if you happened there at the wrong time. Fortunately there wasn't a cloud in the pale blue sky. While they were puzzling over the leaves, Héloise caught a lizard that looked like the original model for Godzilla. She wanted to give it to Sarah, but Sarah just shrieked when she saw it. Isaac was game though.

At the top of the next hill the view cleared. They were looking down on a small abandoned vineyard surrounded by woods. On the far edge there was a round tower with a sloped roof. It had a door, but only one window at the top, mostly walled over except for some round holes.

"Does a princess live there?" Sarah asked. On his mother's head, that girl had fairy tales on the brain.

Before Clarisse could answer, they heard a huge flapping sound that echoed around the hills, and a tornado of birds rose from the vines, splattering the sky with white wings, then swooping down over the tower, and finally coming to rest on the roof, where they cooed peacefully.

The birds were pigeons and the tower was called a dovecote. The vineyard and the dovecote belonged to Clarisse's father, but Henri was the one who raised the pigeons. It turned out that pigeons, which Chérif had always thought of as flying rats, were very good to eat. Of course these pigeons were much prettier than the ones that scrounged around drunkenly on the Parisian asphalt: they were all white and plump, like the peace dove.

As soon as she saw the pigeons, Héloise unglued herself from the twins and ran down toward the dovecote. The rotten door was stuck shut but she managed to push it ajar and disappeared inside. By the time the rest of the group caught up with her, she had climbed a decrepit ladder that was attached to a central pole and was rummaging around one of the hundreds of holes in the interior wall of the tower, which were nests for the pigeons.

"Héloise, descends, tu vas tomber!" Clarisse cried. It was like talking to a deaf person. The girl had probably figured out from watching Sarah that not understanding French had some advantages, so now she was pretending she didn't. Again, Chérif was reminded of his sister, who was also an ace at playing deaf to get her way. The Koran taught that women must submit, but obviously the Prophet had never run into your modern type of female. Maybe it was just as well things had changed. It was more fun this way.

At last Héloise found what she was looking for and climbed down the ladder. She was holding an egg, white like a regular supermarket egg, but much smaller and kind of longish. Everyone, including Victoria, stared at it as if it was a diamond or something. Even Chérif had to admit it looked kinda cool. Sarah said that it wasn't nice taking eggs from a nest. So Héloise offered her the egg, and after nodding no a few times, Sarah accepted it. Then Isaac decided to get his own egg, and Chérif had to grab him away from the ladder. Finally Clarisse asked Chérif to put the egg back in its nest.

Another hill, another combe. They ran into a dirt road that wound through a pine forest. Around a bend, they looked up and saw the most amazing cliff. It was layered, from light tan at the top to blood red at the bottom, and all dug up with gullies, reminding Chérif of a piece of raw meat torn from some huge beast, with the bushes that covered the top layer acting as fur.

"On arrive à la carrière," Clarisse commented. "Regardez par terre. Sarah, Isaac, Victoria, look at the floor!"

"The land of caramels!" exclaimed Sarah.

Chérif could see what she meant. All around them, the ground was covered with sheets of very fine, perfectly smooth sand in the same colors as the cliff. The rain had washed the sand down from the rocks above and spread it on the valley floor like multi-colored frosting, making the trees that stuck out of it look fake, like cake decorations. The contrast between the savage cliff and the luscious valley was so awesome that Chérif felt compelled to come up with a simile:

"C'est marrant, ici" he blurted out, "en bas, c'est comme une pâtisserie, mais en haut c'est comme une boucherie!" He could have kicked himself, it sounded so lame as similes went, but Clarisse understood.

"Ah oui, tu as raison. Je n'y avais pas pensé."

"But it's not real caramel!" Isaac complained.

It turned out the reason the cliff was torn up was that it was a quarry: people around here used the colored sand to make plaster to cover the houses–another way to make money. The quarry didn't belong to Clarisse, though.

Victoria got the idea of using the sand to make sand pictures, so they stopped to collect samples of it into plastic baggies she had brought along in her backpack. She had even brought a garden trowel. (And a Swiss Army knife, and a sketch pad, and a water bottle, and some biscuits, and one of those maps with squiggly lines to mark the relief. She was well equipped, that one.) When they had enough, they retraced their steps on the dirt road, which Clarisse said led back toward the chateau. Chérif was amazed. Without her, he realized, he would have been completely lost. The little girls had of course run out of white pebbles a long time ago, and Victoria was clueless with the map.

Farther on, as they were going through some more vineyards, they found zillions of ripe blackberries winking at them from a mess of brambles on the road embankment. A free snack–except for the thorns. The kids really got into it, gathering big handfuls of berries and then scooping them into their mouths all at once, as if they had never tasted fruit before. And to be honest, it was a brand new experience for Chérif too, to be eating something that had not been bought in a store, and sweet, too. They were so busy picking berries that they stopped talking, and for a while all you could hear was the sleepy chirping of crickets, with an "ouch!" or an "aie!" here and there when somebody got stung by a thorn.

All of a sudden, in the woods they had just come out of, gun shots were fired. Chérif barely had time to be thankful they were on open terrain when he heard a galloping sound coming towards them. Something black and hairy shot out of the trees and charged in their direction, kicking rocks every which way. It was as large as a big dog, but stocky and short-legged, and it had a long nose and … tusks. A boar! One of Chérif's bête noires! Because the road was sunken at that spot, the boar had no other choice than to go by the group of humans. The kids were all out of reach on the embankment, but Victoria was standing right in the middle of the road, drinking from her water bottle, her back to the beast, oblivious to it. Finally, she heard it, turned around, and instead of moving out of the way, she froze. Without thinking, Chérif jumped down from the embankment and ran towards Victoria with both arms outstretched, his momentum propelling both of them into the ditch on the other side of the road just a fraction of a second before the boar charged through the spot. It was such a close call that Chérif had felt the beast's breath on his leg.

The force of the push had caused Victoria to lose her balance; she fell to her knees, and Chérif tripped over her. As he raised his head over the rim of the ditch, he had a last glimpse of a skimpy little tail and a flurry of hooves disappearing into a dip of the terrain.

The kids had their mouths open, but for a while no sound came out of them, the purple berry juice on their lips making a sort of picture of their fear. Finally they all scrambled down and gathered around the fallen pair. Clarisse helped Chérif up, but he was in such a shock that he failed to register the thrilling touch of her hand until it was over. Then they both took care of Victoria. She wasn't hurt apart from a couple of bruises and scratches. The cookies in her backpack were smashed, but the sand baggies were intact.

Finally the kids got their tongues back.

"It was the evil king," Sarah decided. "The magician turned him into a pig."

"Il était beau, le rhinocéros!" Héloïse mooned.

"Watch how I'll kill him if he comes back!" Isaac bragged, brandishing his walking stick like a spear.

Meanwhile Victoria kept repeating: "He was charging right at me!" as if she thought the boar had a personal grudge against her. She had lost all her goofy, gawky, super-friendly varnish. For the next five minutes, she sat on the embankment, her arms around her knees, her eyes glazed over. Clarisse and Chérif exchanged some worried looks, like parents over a sick kid. It was clear that the two of them were now in charge. It was a nice feeling. So, to give Victoria time to recover, Chérif did some martial art stuff with Isaac while Clarisse wiped blackberry juice from the little girls' mouths. Finally Victoria stood up and they went on their way.

"Tu es un vrai héro!" Clarisse whispered as soon as they were walking again side by side. It was the first time she had said something about him. He felt flattered, but uncomfortable too. She seemed to be referring to more than the little push he had given Victoria. Did she know about the burning incident? And if so, what else did she know about his past? Was she judging him too? It was scary to realize that she had her own thoughts. For a few minutes, he felt a tightness in his chest, a wish to escape. Then the mere action of walking, punctuated by her calm round voice, got the better of his feelings of inadequacy and suspicion, lulling him back into a state of stunned bliss.

At the bottom of the hill they came to another dirt road. On the right, on the other side of a big rock shaped like a tooth, the road ran along a long stuccoed wall with a gate in the middle. On the left the road ended at a stone cottage and a few scattered outbuildings. At last Chérif knew where they were: they had reached the bottom of the castle grounds. The cottage was where Henri the truffle hunter lived. He was there, just returned from picking grapes with Degency's crew. He was an old guy with crinkly blue eyes and gnarled hands, wearing the old-fashioned blue canvas outfit of peasants, complete with the cloth cap. He was the kind of person that Chérif would normally have blown off. But mindful of his manners in Clarisse's presence, and knowing what he did about the old guy's money making schemes, he paid him respectful attention.

Clarisse introduced everyone, and Héloise asked where the puppies were. So they walked over to a barn where a sandy-haired dog with floppy ears was nursing four little balls of fur on a blanket thrown over some straw. Henri picked up one of the puppies and gave it to Héloise to hold. And when Héloise was ready to put the dog down, and Sarah and Isaac had had their turn at petting it, Chérif asked if he could hold it too. It was the smallest of the pups, and it had a different color from the mother, a sort of mottled chocolate. But it was very cute, and it seemed to take to Chérif right away, licking his hand and looking up at him with big wet eyes as if it knew him from somewhere. It turned out Henri wanted to get rid of it because the mother's pregnancy had been accidental–in other words she had been a slut. Chérif went on petting the puppy while Clarisse and Henri chatted about the weather, his health, her mother, and so on. Here and there, *mine de rien*, Henri would grill him about his family and school work. But rather than being intimidated, Chérif imagined that the old dude might be a descendant of those Saracens that had colonized the area a long time ago, and therefore practically family.

So, by degrees, they came to an agreement that with the Father's permission, Chérif could take the puppy home that very night. He was then emboldened to broach the subject of training it to find truffles, and Henri, perhaps softened by Clarisse's tale about the boar, hinted that he was willing to help.

"Eh! ça peut se faire. On en reparlera, té, si ca te chante encore dans deux mois. En attendant, il faut bien l'élever, ce petit. Le Labrador, c'est comme les femmes, ça demande beaucoup d'amour. Et alors, tu sais ce qu'on dit, aide-toi, le ciel t'aidera," he said. That old peasant was quoting La Fontaine too!

They re-entered the castle grounds through the lower gate. The key was hidden in a crack between two stones on the gatepost, which did not strike Chérif as being very smart. It was the kind of key he had only seen as an icon in video games: with a long straight shaft, a heart-shaped loop at one end and teeth like a big molar at the other. It looked too rough for Clarisse's hand, but she managed to unlock the gate without any fuss.

They meandered through the garden, stopping to eat figs and to pick mint for the kitchen. Before they got back up to the terrace, Clarisse gathered everyone around her, and made them all swear in two languages not to tell the grown-ups about their adventures in the forest. Otherwise, she explained, they would no longer be allowed to go on walks by themselves, and that would be sad, wouldn't it? She had spoken in her most reasonable voice, but there was no way to avoid noticing that the perfect girl could be quite sneaky. Chérif found the thought a little shocking, but, to tell the truth, kind of exciting too. Later, he would wonder what exactly she had wanted to hide: that there were boars in the woods, that she had left the castle grounds without permission, or that she was hanging out with him?

The ride back down the hill was a blast. Standing again on the pedals, the wind drying off his sweat, the bike slicing silently through the green, he felt like a kamikaze pilot, except that he was plunging towards life, not death. At night, after he and the Father brought the puppy home, he dreamed that Clarisse gave him the key to the castle gate. He woke up rich with hope, and with another feeling it would take him a few more years to name: gratitude.

The fact that the puppy Henri had given him was a mutt and the runt of the litter did not bother him. He understood that he would have had to pay a lot of money for a pure bred dog. And as a one meter sixty-five Arab-Berber mix, in other words a runty mutt himself, he had no prejudice against them. From what he read on the Internet during study period in the school library the next day–his first independent Web search ever, the techno teacher would be proud if he knew–any type of dog could be trained to hunt truffles anyway. What counted was an affectionate nature, and that, Pidou already showed signs of possessing. Nurture would do the rest, with Henri's help. As to Clarisse, she would leave in a couple of days, but she'd be back, because the castle was hers. In the meantime, Chérif was going to get busy becoming worthy of her if he could.

At the side of the house, the Father is loading baskets of bread into his delivery van. Chérif shoves the pen into his pocket, tucks the notepad into the back of his jeans and crawls on the roof towards the attic window. He is going to give his parent a hand without being asked, for a change.

CHAPTER 18

▼

A LITTLE DRAMA

Un coup de théâtre

"Frankly, I am a little puzzled at the way the French treat their children," Amanda mused, peering through the cloudiness of her pastis as if the key to all Gallic mysteries might be hiding at the bottom of her glass. It was *l'heure de l'apéritif*, an institution with nuances that distinguished it quite brightly from cocktail hour in Amanda's mind—less an expedient aimed at drowning the day's stresses in alcohol than a celebration of loquacious tipsiness; not merely a way station for the appetite on the road to dinner but rather a refined strategy to prolong the pleasure of its anticipation. It was a cultural artifact Amanda intended to import to Berkeley if she could, name included; all that was required, apart from the drinks, olives and mixed nuts, was to *sit*, preferably outside (which was already a problem, Berkeley nights tending to be arctic), preferably in front of a view, at a good distance from the children and around adults who liked to converse. But would the transplanted ritual thrive, would it ever achieve its present perfection under a different sky? Amanda doubted it. She was just starting to suspect that translation in general is a hopeless task.

The present was indeed perfect: a balmy sunset, summer having unexpectedly returned; pastis and roses on the wrought iron table; two more than adequate conversationalists at hand in the persons of Franny and Phil, and the shortly expected return of two more: Hughes and Chuck, who were crowning a hot day of working in the vineyard with a game of tennis on the EDF courts in Saint Yves—a reckless feat of male one-upmanship at Chuck's age, but Amanda wasn't complaining: if the trend held, her husband would still have plenty of energy for her tonight, after Sarah crashed and her door was discreetly shut.

From the open kitchen window, intermittent clashes of pans, gushes of water and yelps of pain signaled that Victoria was attending to dinner. At the other end of the house, various wrestling and piano noises issued from the music room, where the children were putting the last touch to some kind of entertainment program they had worked on all afternoon in great secret—with some help from Franny, who had been on babysitting duty that day, and also from the L.A. waif, who in many ways was just a kid herself. In front of the vacationers, the orderly succession of pinkly glowing gravel, feathery acacias, ornate balustrade and coral-washed sky had the feel of an operatic stage set. For a penny, Amanda would have launched into a triumphant aria. But supreme contentment being more or less inexpressible, she instead opened the topic of French parenting.

That after only a week in a foreign country, Amanda should venture an opinion about any aspect of its culture may seem foolhardy. On the other hand, the Berkeley matron was a very conscientious tourist: under her impetus, the last four days had been packed with opportunities to observe the natives. As anchor of a small party which reconstituted itself according to mood and circumstance—Amanda, Phil and Franny, Amanda and Chuck, Amanda and Franny, Amanda and Phil, or all four Berkeleyites, at times even joined by the elusive Victoria—she had visited roman chapels, gothic cathedrals, cisterian abbeys, walled cities, quaint villages, wineries, museums, antique shops, craft studios, botanical gardens. She had shopped at open air markets, waited in line at the post office, sat at café terraces, watched *pétanque* games on village squares, driven on the *autoroute*. Better yet, she was sharing quarters with a native family. And everywhere she had been confronted with the shock of difference, which is after all the main point of tourism, this serendipitous form of ethnological inquiry. But, unlike many ethnologists, whose observations tend to be forced into some doctrinaire theory of the impeccable—if doomed—fitness of primitive cultural arrangements, and unlike many other tourists, whose hidden agenda is to prove to themselves that they live in the best country in the world, Amanda had no ax to grind: she was prepared to admit that the French did some things better, some things worse, and that often the better or worse was just a matter of taste. Moreover, she was willing to be tentative in her conclusions, to modify her hypotheses to fit new data. Cultural analysis was just great intellectual fun. Still, when it came to the raising of children....

"In what way?" asked Franny, eager to share her own reflections on the subject. In the last few days, she had warmed up considerably to Amanda, who, at the few office parties, company picnics and political fundraisers where the two had met in the past, had merely struck her as a typical yuppie housewife: a gossip, a snob, a feckless mother—worst of all, an SUV driver. (On her side Amanda had filed away the knowledge that this reserved yet presentable young techie spoke excellent French.) But if those irritating traits were still in evidence, they were now mitigated by others. For one, Amanda was genuinely kind: her hospitality towards both Hughes and Victoria had been just one example of her unfussy generosity. What touched Franny the most though was that surrounded as she was by family and friends, including life-of-the-party Phil, Amanda actively sought her company, including her in all her outings, helping her with her chores when Hughes wasn't available, and—most flatteringly—asking for her opinions about everything. It turned out the reason Amanda loved to talk to Franny was that she was trying to re-engage her mind after six years of dealing with infants—she had actually confessed that much, although perhaps using different words—and Franny highly approved of her effort.

"Well, take for instance the snack issue. Every time Hughes catches Héloise eating a rice cake, he has a quiet fit. But he sees nothing wrong with the girls downing chocolate eclairs or rhum baba at dinner. I would think the former is much healthier than the latter, don't you agree?"

"Funny you should mention it. I just had a conversation with Hughes about it last night. For him, the issue is not health food versus junk food, but snack versus regular meal, the four o'clock *goûter* counting as a regular meal for kids, which is why he had no objection to the ice cream cones when we went to the lake. By the way, there is no French translation for "health food". Any food that is part of French culinary tradition, even if it's loaded with butter and sugar, is assumed to be healthy—in moderate quantities. It's processed foods that the French are suspicious of—by processed food they don't mean cheese and pâté, but anything whose recipe was developed in a lab as opposed to a kitchen. To tell you the truth, I agree with them there. I just read a book called *Fast Food Nation,* have you heard of it?"

"Is that the one that links fast food to the epidemic of obesity? I caught part of a Jim Lehrer Newshour segment about it a while ago."

"Hmm, I didn't watch it. Actually the book covers much more than the health repercussions of fast food. It also shows how fast food has transformed agriculture, labor practices ..."

"Marxist propaganda!" Phil interjected, clownishly pounding the table with his fist. Lately, he seemed more than ever given to such out-of-turn pronouncements. Amanda gave him a maternal pat on the arm, at the same time shooting Franny the one-eyebrow-raised glance signaling that the psychology of the individual thus patted will be delved into in an upcoming female-only confabulation.

"Anyway, there is a chapter in the book about the "flavorists" who make fast food attractive by adding chemically manufactured smells to it, like a "beef" aroma to French fries. The manipulative implications by themselves are truly scary."

"Well, I would be the last one to defend McDonald's. But what is wrong with snacking per se? Every pediatrician tells you that children should eat in small quantities many times a day."

"I am not sure the pediatricians can be relied upon to be completely free of influence by food manufacturers. The main problem with snack foods is precisely that they are always available. Children get used to eating all day long, as a pastime, as a pacifier, whether they are hungry or not. The easiest way to limit caloric intake, probably, is to restrict eating to certain supervised times, in other words regular meals. Mind you, this is my opinion, not Hughes'. For him, it seems it's more a matter of tradition: meals are an important ritual, and he doesn't want his children to ruin their appetites for them by snacking. Funnily enough, recent statistics seem to be bearing out traditional wisdom: as French children are getting lured by TV advertising into eating more and more snacks, they are becoming fatter. It's probably just a matter of time before France finds itself in the throes of an obesity epidemic. After centuries of bechamels, defeated by Mars bars. Pretty ironic, don't you think?"

Amanda twirled the pastis in her glass, reflecting on her own unsuccessful efforts to limit her children's caloric intake. Both twins were overweight, and in spite of the pediatrician's assurance that it was all part of normal growth patterns, Amanda couldn't help but worry. She had been plump herself as a girl and had suffered the usual taunts in consequence. She did not wish that kind of trauma for her offspring, particularly for Sarah—thanks to the current fashion for baggy pants and oversize tee-shirts, a boy's heft was less noticeable. It was all very well for Franny to talk about "easy ways". She did not have any children. But what could you do when your kids refused to eat anything green, or red, or raw, or chewy, or bitter, or with any kind of smell? Every pediatrician (in whom, unlike Franny, Amanda had full faith) told you that forcing a child to eat what's on his plate is a sure path to future eating disorders, not to mention a cause of strains at the family table, which, given the stressful nature of your husband's job, you were inclined to avoid. The same pediatricians also told you that forbidding any kind of food was bound to make it all the more attractive to children. So at dinner you ended up feeding them hotdogs and pizza, and in between meals you let them snack on Gold Fish crackers. Also, more often than you cared to admit, you rewarded them for some small act of childish cooperation with candy. To Amanda, who had herself been raised on junk food, there was an inevitability to it, an unavowed normalcy.

She had noticed that since the imported snacks had run out four days ago, the kids seemed to be doing fine without them, gorging instead on blackberries, figs, almonds and unripe pears that, following Héloise's example, they scavenged in the garden like blooming little hunter-gatherers—she wondered whether Hughes was aware of this surreptitious snacking, but you could not argue against the healthiness of fruit. It was the same with other things Amanda had believed the twins could not do without: the old black and white TV, still on the pantry floor, had not been turned on in days; Sarah had hardly taken out her Barbie and Isaac had completely forgotten about the misplaced Game Boy. Instead, the kids played with sticks and stones, rambled over the garden, built forts, caught insects. At night they fell asleep without asking for a bedtime story. It was as if, inside the pampered, finicky, sophisticated, bored shell characteristic of modern urban mid-dle-class childhood, the seed of a primitive *joie de vivre* had remained intact all along, just waiting for the right conditions to sprout lustily. Mostly, Amanda was glad to see her kids turned into happy little savages, although at times she felt a certain dread, echoes of *Lord of the Flies* reverberating in her head. She reassured herself with the thought that the playmates under whose influence this metamor-phosis had occurred were the daughters of a vicomte—at least you couldn't say that the twins were slumming.

But the best development from Amanda's point of view was that Sarah had stopped demanding special dishes at dinner. Under Clarisse's watchful eyes, she ate what she could and left the rest on her plate without a fuss. Was there a lesson there? Of course at home, there would be no Clarisse, the lure of fig trees and blackberry bushes would be replaced by the attraction of candy racks and fast food franchises. Again, Amanda was confronted with the difficulty of translation.

"I don't know, but expecting children to wait for hours to be fed when they're hungry seems to me part of a more general pattern I have observed, which is that the French don't make much allowance for children being children. You notice how in restaurants, in stores, even in the street, parents constantly shush their kids, constantly stop them from running around, how they forever seem to be force-feeding them knowledge that is beyond their developmental stage, like that tot at the *Musée du Petit Palais* yesterday, getting a lecture on chiaroscuro, poor thing!"

Shockingly, this evocation of borderline child abuse caused Franny to burst out laughing. "Relentlessly pedagogical," she said "is how I put it to Hughes. And you know what his reaction was? He just beamed!"

"That's another thing I notice. The French seem so cocksure in their role as adults, as if every one of them felt they could teach Dr. Spock a thing or two. Remember the teacher at Senanques, how he pooh poohed the African girl's scruples about entering a Catholic church? He didn't have the least doubt that visiting the church was good for her, and so he basically bullied her in—which in the US would be considered culturally insensitive. It's interesting in a way, but because I don't understand the language, I find myself paying a lot of attention to people's tone of voice, and what strikes me about the way the French talk to children is how bossy and sarcastic they sound, as opposed to empathetic. They don't seem to try to put themselves at the kids' level."

"You mean they don't pretend to be kids themselves!" Phil exclaimed, flinging an olive pit across the terrace, and watching it with satisfaction arc above the balustrade and disappear into the garden below. "There's nothing specifically French about it. That's the way my parents were, and I was raised in the Midwest. If you ask me, kids nowadays could use a little more of that kind of parenting: eat what's in front of you, speak when you're spoken to, do what I say when I say it, not after half an hour of namby-pamby negotiation, and a good slap on the butt from time to time. It worked for me!"

"I'm not sure it worked that well ..." Once again, Amanda patted Phil's arm while shooting Franny a knowing glance. Far from objecting to the condescending gesture, Phil seemed to have spoken at least in part to provoke it. It struck Franny that he was himself very much a spoiled child, in spite–or because?–of his supposedly strict upbringing. Only his successful businessman aura had previously prevented her from seeing that aspect of him. But it explained why she was having such difficulty fending him off. For the last four days, with Hughes away in the vineyard all day, he had been pressing his attentions on her—without committing himself to a direct sexual overture—through literary allusions, off-color jokes, exaggerated gallantry, comico-tragic tales of his youth, half-cynical, half-rueful references to his defunct marriage segueing into bathetic disquisitions on the immensity of the cosmos, and again and again, his hands on her neck, her shoulders, her waist, her knees, patting, sliding, squeezing, as tenacious and irritating as a wasp at a picnic table. But as he always took care to paw Amanda to an equal extent, including in Chuck's presence (though not Hughes'), and as

Amanda blithely tolerated it, Franny felt obliged to do the same. Not that, left to her own devices, she would have found it much easier to make him keep his hands to himself. Underneath the layer of reflexive flirtatiousness, below even that of a possibly real attraction to her, Franny sensed in Phil a fundamental insecurity that she was loath to aggravate by a verbal rebuke. Then again, even the outright rapist is fundamentally insecure. Being afraid to hurt *his* feelings might be taking empathy a little too far.

"I share your impressions, Amanda, but Phil has a point when he reminds us that authoritarian parenting is not exclusively a French phenomenon. And on the other hand, we should probably avoid over-generalizing from our limited observations. For all we know, parenting styles in France may vary by region, or social class, or they may be evolving as they have in the US, just a little later, under the influence of the same economic forces."

"Spoken like a Communist!" Phil exclaimed, loud enough for the word "Communist" to bounce incongruously across the dignified terrace, the first syllable, loaded with intimations of the "K" in Klu Klux Klan, coughed out like a mouthful of poisoned potato, which was always how the word was pronounced, in fact, but Phil's buffoonery made the effect more distinct. In the last few days, one of his more frequent jokes had consisted in flinging political epithets at Franny. And as strange a courting maneuver as it may seem, Franny understood it to be just that. What it meant to convey was that, alone among men, Phil had been able to tap into her mind's secret springs, and that far from being scared by her bluestocking, red-dyed intellect, he found her the cuter for it. But Franny sensed that as his courting was making no progress, his desperation was turning into hostility.

"Well, maybe it's the other way around. Maybe it's because French parenting does not encourage independence and initiative that the French economy lags behind?" Amanda had phrased her hypothesis as a question, because if on the topic of child rearing she knew herself to be at an advantage against two childless interlocutors, when it came to economic matters she was conscious of straying into less defensible terrain, her main authority on the subject being Chuck. Still, she had dared float out an original idea, and she felt exhilarated. This was the life of the intellect!

"Or we may be deluded in our conviction that the American economic model is the best. If you look at trade deficit, for instance, we are not doing that well. In many ways, it seems that for the last twenty years, we have flourished basically by borrowing money from other nations so we can buy their goods. You could call that economic parasitism, which is not a model every country should or could emulate."

"See what you did," Phil cried, gesticulating in Amanda's direction, "sending the innocent alone into enemy territory? She has been brainwashed! It's gonna take weeks of de-programming when we get back to the US. Maybe she isn't even free to leave. Maybe we'll have to kidnap her."

Although neither Amanda nor Phil was looking at her at that moment, Franny felt herself blush. Her several allusions to private conversations she had had with Hughes since their arrival had not been inadvertent. She did want Phil to register that he had been supplanted as a love interest and that he was wasting his time pursuing her. But she wasn't ready to be thought of as having thrown her lot with the landlord or his country. Yet it was impossible to defend herself against the playful accusation without making it sound serious, and therefore plausible. The fact was, Franny suddenly realized, it was true.

"Down, Phil, down!" Amanda was saying peaceably.

Immediately, Franny realized another thing: Amanda and Phil must have been lovers in the past. This was what gave their joshing its innocuous cast.

A sound of car engine was heard, followed by voices on the stone stairs, sportive, companionable, projecting confidently into the pixelating dusk.

"... when you consider the marketing benefits of being able to print on the entire surface. To me, it's a no-brainer."

"To me, artificial cork would be on the order of sacrilege. Or as you would say, it looks cheap."

"Or too American?"

"That too!" (chuckling)

"So, you care about image after all ..." (more chuckling)

The three people on the terrace shifted their attention to the approaching voices, the way they would have at the theater to a new scene beginning off-stage. Indeed, for the last few days, Amanda had felt as if she was both spectator and actor in a play–a light, sophisticated comedy of manners straight out of PBS–a perception that paradoxically gave her a sense of enhanced reality. Meanwhile, thoughts of terrorism had receded in her mind to the point where they seemed like mere specks on a motel rug, which might turn out to be fleas, but until they moved, you did not intend to give them a closer look.

A pair of heads, then torsoes, then legs rose above the violet gravel. Hughes and Chuck paused at the edge of the terrace, catching their breath, their pose, at that moment, irresistibly suggesting a male beauty contest–each man a poster-boy for a certain national ideal of manhood, the contrast between them only enhancing their respective sex appeal. On the left, Chuck, regal in bermuda shorts, tennis racket wielded like a club, sweat dripping into his beard; short-necked, round-shouldered, arms akimbo, hips tilted forward, butt held high and stomach proudly projected, legs spread so that they gave the impression of being bowed, although they were not. A florid, deadpan face, in which gold-flecked eyes twinkled behind thick glasses. An ox, a locomotive, he made you think of G force and steel bridges and barbecues, of walking on the moon and rolling in the grass and making rash purchases with your credit card, of being sure that the pie in the sky had a slice for you. And as a woman you wanted to bask in that mesomorphic glow; you wanted to be taken off your feet, to be squeezed, to be crushed, to surrender—of course if you were married to the guy it wasn't quite that torrid.

On the right, Hughes, darker, more economically built, less sweaty. Dressed in proper tennis shorts, freshly laundered, but hanging on his narrow hips as easily as if he never wore anything else. Standing with his weight resting on one leg, his racket tucked under one arm; straight-spined, flat-bellied, torso tilted forward from the waist, head to one side, his whole body looking slightly off its center of gravity, as if leaning into an imperceptible wind. Long muscles, acute bones, giving a sense of anatomy as a neat mechanism, of a strength based on sinew rather than blood. His expressive face dominated by eyes full of wondering, impatient life. An egret, a Calder mobile. Watching him reminded you of dovetail joints and passing clouds, of electric arcs and first-aid kits and Champagne; of being dressed for the occasion, of having a cellar under the house and old photographs in the attic, of looking before you leapt, of caring about fairness; of fencing and spooning and taking one's time, holding forth and holding on and holding some things sacred. And as a woman you wanted to glue yourself to him, to kiss slowly with soft mouths, to buckle and tumble and lay on lavender-scented sheets, to surrender—if you could ever get a moment's privacy.

As different as they looked, Chuck and Hughes had much in common. They were both alpha males who did not strut their power, who had in fact hidden reserves of shyness, Chuck's Achilles heel being a dread of speaking in public, and Hughes' a suspicion that he was a misfit. They had both gotten the best education their country had to offer, Hughes at the ENA, Chuck at MIT. They were both entrepreneurs, although Hughes would have scoffed at the term (he thought of himself as a born-again *paysan*). They were both brainy, Hughes' intelligence tending towards the speculative, and Chuck's towards shrewdness, per the predilections of their respective cultures—of the two, in spite of his air of sophistication, Hughes was the more innocent. When it came to ancestry, the French aristocrat and the American self-made man were not that different either: the first Vicomte

Degency had been a blacksmith before joining Napoleon's army; as to Chuck's forbears, they included German bankers, Polish estate overseers and even an Austro-Hungarian courtier. Anyway, mathematically, half of the people of European origin are said to be descended from Charlemagne.

And so, in a matter of days, and against their own expectations, the two men had struck up a friendship. Chuck's decision to take part in the harvest had in this respect been a stroke of genius. It had given Hughes the pleasure of expounding on his farming philosophy and practice, and Chuck, tuning out what he considered the excesses of French romantic impracticality, had learned much he wanted to know about managing a vineyard. He was already starting to have some business ideas, which he diplomatically kept to himself until the time was ripe. Meanwhile, without his knowledge, through exertion and bantering and moments of stillness, sifting dirt through his fingers, shaking hands with the staff at the Cooperative, driving the tractor on sycamore shaded lanes, pouring wine from old barrels under the cellar's medieval vault, he was being seduced by the life of a Côtes du Rhône vintner. Before the week was over, he would be as religious as Hughes on the concept of *terroir*.

"OK, you guys," called Amanda in her matronly singsong, "enough shop talk! How was tennis?"

"He beat the crap out of me!" Chuck answered equably. "But, heck, tomorrow is another day."

Hughes looked modestly at the ground, shrugging off his victory. As he raised his head again, his eyes met Franny's for the briefest moment, telegraphing both his pleasure at seeing her and his concern for how her day had gone with the girls in his absence. She responded with a nod of welcome and reassurance, but he also detected a flicker of some dissonant emotion in her ardent eyes. Mirth, lust, irony, annoyance? He noticed anew the tight muscle in the angle of her jaw, a feature of hers he found a little daunting, belying the message of yielding conveyed by her lovely, blurry, lopsided smile. Something in the way she leaned on her bent-back hand, the torque of her crossed legs–silky thighs, round knees, dainty ankles poised as if for a flight, a dance, or a wrestle–hinted that she was restless.

"How about playing doubles the next time? Franny, I know that you play. How about you Amanda? Phil? Victoria?"

Everyone turned towards Victoria, who had appeared at the kichen window.

"I don't play," she cried. "But I need Chuck's help. I have no idea how to cook those duck breasts!"

"Coming, coming," answered Chuck, bounding up the porch stairs like a two hundred and twenty pound puppy. "Did you remember to pick some figs?"

"Yeah, yeah!" came the answer from the depths of the kichen.

"No tennis for me, I am afraid!" said Phil with a big flourish of the arm. "I'll have to do with petanque. Herniated disk, very nasty looking Xray, you don't want to know ..."

"I haven't played in years ..." Amanda demurred.

"Nor have I," lied Franny. "Oh! please, let's do it. It'll be fun. Besides, *we* don't care about winning, do we?"

Her feminine lofty indifference to competition thus appealed to, Amanda had no choice but agreeing to play. Hughes looked at Franny again, and was happy to see that the sharp glint in her eyes had dissolved. He was getting good at figuring her out, he thought self-congratulatorily. And really, he was looking forward to playing with her. She was fit, she was nimble, she would probably make a good tennis partner, with a little coaching from him if needed.

"Oh! and tonight, after dinner, the kids are putting on a show. Isn't that darling?"

Darling, Hughes seriously doubted it. He couldn't understand the American kids' obsession with public performance, nor the way their parents indulged it, as if their lisping attempts at drama, ballet or gymnastics naturally bore the marks of genius. Not an hour went by, it seemed to him, without the twins interrupting the adults' conversation with a demand to "watch" them make a spectacle of themselves with some incoherent stumbling about that the kids obviously took for serious entertainment. And far from chiding or ignoring the twins for putting themselves forward so immodestly, far from being embarrassed by their ineptitude, the Americans (with the exception of Phil), rewarded them with doting smiles and extravagant praise. In Hughes' view, this gave them a false sense of their merits, encouraging laziness by fostering the illusion that art was easy. In Hughes' view, one should not dare to present oneself in front of an audience until one was absolutely sure one's skills were up to par. He, who had had many years of training, and still practiced regularly, never played his clarinet in public. He expected Clarisse to show the same reserve.

He had had a conversation with Franny about this strange performance mania, in which he had argued that it was a sign of narcissism—it turned out they had both read Christopher Lasch. And while generally agreeing, Franny had suggested that maybe the French pushed *la peur du ridicule* a little too far, thereby stifling young people's creativity and diminishing their *confiance en soi* (she had stayed away from the term "self-esteem", which was too fraught with pathetic connotations even for her). Hughes had had to admit that for all its supposed crassness and pandering to the lowest common denominator, American culture had for the last thirty years or so been more vibrant than French culture even in its higher manifestations, such as literature, music and cinema. But if the solution consisted in treating every kid as a budding Shirley Temple, he wanted none of it.

"By the way, the kids needed some props, so we unlocked the attic in the east wing. Héloise assured me that she had your permission. I hope that's true?" added Franny.

"It's all right, provided an adult is present. Did you find the costume trunk? We used to raid it for pirate and princess outfits on rainy days when I was a child."

"Princess outfits? I thought you only had one brother."

"Yes, but I also had a pretty *cousine*!"

"Where is she now?"

"Actually, she lives in Belmont, California."

"How interesting!" Amanda cut in. "We have some very good friends who live there. Brian and Diane Sandalow. Do you know them?"

It sounded like a silly question, Amanda realized, but in her experience, it wasn't so rare that it got answered in the affirmative. According to the six-degree-of-separation principle, everyone knew someone who knew someone who might turn out to be a valuable connection: a potential business partner for Chuck, playmates for the twins, a source of authentic ethnic crafts or rare Italian marble. This time she drew a blank. A few days later though she would manage to hit pay dirt: Hughes would turn out to have studied under one of her favorite professors. The connection would be a dead end, but it would still be thrilling.

"Going back to tonight's entertainment," she resumed, "we made free to move the furniture around in the music room a little. Don't worry. We did not break anything. And we can put everything back exactly where it was. But it made me think about how this place could use a makeover. I hope you don't mind my suggesting it, but I believe your home is not making the strongest statement it's capable of."

"A statement of what?"

"I don't know ..." Amanda hesitated, confused by the unexpected question and vaguely afraid of having fallen into a conversational trap. She remembered a similar occurrence with Hughes' ex-wife. Another problem of translation was that words like "edge" and "statement" which normally stood quite solidly by themselves, suddenly sounded as if they needed a qualifier. "... It depends of what *you* want it to be."

"I am not sure I want my home to make any statement at all. I am vain enough to think I am an adequate conversationalist. I would not want any competition from my furniture."

"He doesn't care about image!" Chuck shouted from the kitchen.

"But you *have* to care. Your home, like your clothes–and I notice that you pay attention to what you wear–creates an impression about you, whether you want to or not. You might as well try to control it."

"So what impression does my house make?"

As Hughes approached the table, Phil had gotten up, brandishing an empty Scotch bottle in his direction. "Want some?" he mouthed silently, and upon Hughes nodding in the affirmative, he strode towards the house. Hughes excused himself and went to retrieve a folding chair from the other end of the terrace, breezily placing it between Franny's seat and the one vacated by Phil. At last he sat at ease, one arm draped across the back of his neighbor's chair, his thumb subtly caressing the underside of her arm while with a smile, he signaled to Amanda that she had his full attention.

"My impression," said Amanda, "is of a venerable home, built with pride and full of cherished memories, but a little ... how shall I put it ... frozen in time ...

"Then it is making a true statement, and I wouldn't change a thing for fear of making a liar out of it."

"A little bit like the old lady's mansion in Great Expectations," suggested Franny, tongue in cheek, "spider webs all over the rotten wedding cake?"

"I hope it's not that bad!" Hughes jerked backwards, pretending to be shocked, but truly a little astonished. The "rotten wedding cake" had hit home more than Franny could know: he hadn't touched a thing since Christiane had left, apart from carrying the most precious furniture to the attic and locking a few doors prior to renting out the place.

"No, no," Amanda reassured him. "It's very livable. In fact, I am having the most exquisite time here."

"Then why would you change anything?"

"Isn't there always room for improvement?"

"A very American view...."

"No stereotyping!" Franny cut in again. "Besides, it seems to me the French have been quite busy improving things since I was here last, in 1987."

"And making them worse too...."

"You can't bathe in the same river twice...."

"But you can try to swim away from the current...."

Verbal tennis, thought Amanda. She had noticed that conversations between Hughes and Franny often took this sparring turn, which, between a man and a woman, felt a little uncomfortable, and even … unseemly, not a thing to further romance at any rate. The phenomenon was all the stranger to Amanda because she had always perceived Franny as a basically shy, non-confrontational person. The vicomte, as mild as he himself looked normally, must have brought it out of her. And Amanda had to admit that between those two at least, intellectual arguments did not seem to do any harm to a growing *entente*, that in fact, there was something downright erotic about them. Perhaps it was a French version of the more epidermic personality clashes that fed love in American romantic comedies.

"Talking about water …" said Chuck, who had reappeared on the porch, a goblet of red wine for himself in one hand, a tumbler of whiskey for Hughes in the other, a dishcloth tucked into his shorts to serve as an apron. He had turned out to be an enthusiastic cook, intent on making the most of local culinary bounty. With Victoria's fledgling help, he was coming up with sophisticated dishes that outdid the more homey fare prepared by Hughes and Franny (couscous, vichyssoise, stuffed tomatoes …). Franny had always appreciated Chuck as a client: he knew what he needed, he didn't pull rank, he wasn't stingy with compliments. But the last few days had deepened her liking for him, in part because his jovial, confident, easy-going personality shone even more brightly without the trappings of institutional authority, in part because he was a model of a loving husband (a particularly welcome and interesting sight to Franny at that moment) and finally because he got along so well with Hughes.

"… this place could use a swimming pool. A little dip after a day of picking grapes would be just the ticket!"

A cloud passed over Hughes' face. He was conscious of being derelict as a landlord by not providing his guests with a pool—by now an expected amenity of any vacation rental, and even a standard feature on many local farms, where artificially blue concrete basins had taken the place of the old manure pit.

"Ecologically speaking," Franny answered, sensing the landlord's embarrassment and aware of his financial difficulties, "swimming pools are not such a great idea. All that water that you can't even recycle because of the chlorine.…"

"I don't really care for their look either," Hughes added. "A few years ago, my uncle, who used to own the property, proposed to build a pool on the lawn below, where the basin is. He thought it would be nice for the children. But I dissuaded him, because to me, a pool would have ruined the historical character of the place, making it look like some kind of Riviera resort. Of course, this was before I started renting it out in the summer. I realize a pool would be nice for the guests."

"Well, if not a pool, how about a pond?" Chuck mused.

"A pond?"

"Yes, like the lake where we swam on Monday. In California, many ranchers have ponds dug on their land. You can swim in them, but they are also good for wildlife, irrigation, fire fighting. It's a win-win kind of thing: good for the environment and good for tourism. All you need is a source of water and a little depression lined with clayey soil."

"I do have a spring. But, as you know, the soil around here is mostly lime."

"Look, you've got about sixty acres, right?"

"About that, yes...."

"And some of it is not suitable for vines, right?"

"That's true...."

"Well, I bet you if we walked around, we could find a spot somewhere for a pond. Even if the soil is not clay, there are solutions. I know some people in the pond digging business. I could contact them for you."

"It would be marvelous!" Amanda chimed in. "We have several friends who own ranches in Sonoma County, and they swear by their ponds. A pond really adds *cachet* to a property."

Ah! those Americans, Hughes ruminated, his jaws clenching under the onslaught of unsolicited advice. They meant well, but with their boundless ambition, their unflagging optimism, their unceasing concern for "property values"— which was the opposite of the love he felt for his land, as it was based on the perspective of selling it someday—their certitude that they knew what was good for you and that everyone was there to help them, they made his head ache. Still, he had to admit he found the idea of a pond attractive. Reeds, water lilies, cool dark water, the ducks and frogs dear to Héloïse, waiting for you at the end of a walk in the woods, holding hands with someone dear....

"Ponds are great ..." Franny said dreamily, as if she had read his mind.

But of course, he couldn't afford it.

"As to the interior decor," Amanda resumed, "it wouldn't take much to make it more airy, more focused, more comfortable. You have nothing against comfort, I assume...."

"No, comfort is a concept I can relate to."

"Then would you allow me to try re-arranging a couple of things in the *salon*? Nothing that couldn't be undone or that would cost money, of course. I would enjoy it very much."

"Is that something you would like to do too, Franny?"

"Me? I know nothing about interior decoration. But it would be fun to try, if it won't destroy the *historical character* of the place. I'd like to see what Amanda will come up with."

"Ok, then, go ahead. But I warn you the Degency ghosts may object."

"How will they object?"

"I don't know, but they are a mischievous lot."

"Oh! We Americans don't believe in ghosts," Amanda said with a dismissive wave of her hand, on which a new tenth anniversay diamond throned among various other lapidary offerings to the gods of matrimony. It occurred to Franny that notwithstanding the reputation the French had of talking with their hands, it was the Americans in the group who gesticulated most. Later, Hughes would explain to her that in his family (by which he really meant his well-heeled Parisian milieu, but of that he never spoke, for the same reasons he never referred to his title or called his house a chateau), hand gestures had been discouraged.

Though Amanda did not believe in ghosts, the idea that the chateau might boast a few tales of apparitions tickled her fancy. Haunted mansions were definitely a major Old World attraction, but until now, she had thought they were only to be found in England, where, let's face it, the weather was iffy at best. Of course, England had the advantage that the natives spoke English–with just enough quaint variations of accent and vocabulary ("queue" and "boot" and "lift" and "as well") to make you feel deliciously abroad. But the language issue in France had turned out to be minor after all–Amanda had discovered that a few well meaning words of French and a humble attitude were enough in most cases to unlock the natives' own proficiency with English. Besides, her French vocabulary was increasing day by day. And then, there was the food. All in all, France was looking more and more like the ideal vacation destination.

A smell of burnt duck fat drifted out from the kitchen.

"Better get back to my cooking!" said Chuck, turning back towards the porch. "You guys want some crostini?"

"No, thanks," Amanda answered, "I wouldn't want to *ruin my appetite* ..."

"I should go round up the children for their baths," Hughes announced.

"I'll go with you," said Franny.

Amanda settled back in her chair to watch the first stars make their appearance in the sky, glad to have a few moments alone to savor the spectacle of nature. She had barely had time to make out what must be Venus when Phil reappeared at her side, his third whiskey in hand.

"Makes you feel darn small, don't it!" he blared in an imitation of redneck accent, massaging her shoulder with his free hand.

"What's with the mood, Phil?"

"What mood? Never been happier in my life. Free as a bird, and mankind on its way to blow itself to bits! I just can't wait. More room for the cockroaches is how I look at it."

"You're being manic."

"Hence the recourse to my favorite medicine!" He held his glass in front of her eyes, adding: "Another dose and I'll be as mellow as a wheel of Brie at a Buddhist convention."

"You should watch it with the booze ..."

"You mean I might die of cyrrhosis of the liver and miss the big bang?"

"Honey, why don't you can the Lord Byron act? I know you too well. By the way," here Amanda lowered her voice, "I don't think it's working on Franny either ..."

Phil flopped down on the chair next to Amanda, spilling a third of his glass in the process. "Damn!" he muttered, dabbing the stain on his silk shirt with a paper napkin, then suddenly giving up and heaving the soggy, balled-up napkin across the terrace into one of the urns that crowned the balustrade.

"You'll have to pick that up," Amanda said calmly.

"Yes, Mommy. Anyway, what do you mean about my act not working on Franny? Did you have one of your girly chats with her?"

"No, but I think it's pretty obvious something is going on between her and Hughes."

(Her pronunciation of the landlord's name fell somewhere between hue and hugs. He couldn't have picked a more difficult name for English speakers to pronounce.)

"How do you know? Did you see them fuck?"

"Don't be crude, please."

"So you didn't. And I can tell you: they haven't. I have a sense about those things. The guy is a wuss, your standard uppity Frog, all in the head, nothing in the balls. That may appeal to a French woman, but it's not going to go far with Franny. That girl is more red-blooded than she looks, trust me! What she needs is a *real man*. She is nice to him because she doesn't know how *not* to be nice. Anyway, Degency is too busy fussing about his grapes to make a move on her. As they say, victory goes to the bold."

At that point Sarah's voice pealed over their heads.

"Mommy, I need clean underwear!"

Amanda looked up and saw her daughter's shape outlined in the lit frame of the window on the second floor landing.

"Be right there, sweetheart!" she cried. Then, as she was getting up from her chair with a sigh, embracing in a last glance the serenity of the outdoors, she turned back towards Phil and whispered:

"You won't say I didn't warn you."

"Thank you ma'am!" he answered, reverting to the redneck drawl.

Amanda stopped by the kitchen, where Chuck and Victoria were putting the last touches to dinner: shredded beets *tartare, magrets de canard* in a fig sauce, sauteed potatoes, French beans with shallots, green salad, *plateau de fromage,* and *mille feuilles* from the bakery. All the surfaces in the kitchen were littered with dirty pans and food debris, and Amanda regretted briefly having picked the cleanup shift on the nights that Chuck and Victoria cooked, and even more her choice of a partner in Phil, who was as useless with housekeeping chores as when she had first known him twenty five years earlier. Pairing off with Phil had been her idea: she had wished to downplay her couplehood with Chuck out of sensitivity for the unattached guests. Perhaps she had also tried to generate a certain erotic tension, to suggest independence from her husband the better to reel him back in. In the end, none of her subtle seductive subterfuges had been necessary. The Vaucluse had been a sufficient aphrodisiac. Now she was stuck with the dishes and a fumble-fingered assistant. Meanwhile Hughes and Franny were looking more and more like a serious couple. Amanda consoled herself with the thought that *she* had had something to do with this development: it had also been her idea to take the kids out for ice cream on the day they had gone to the Lac des Chevrettes. The glimpse of the couple engaged in some heavy petting on the beach that she had caught upon their return had been very rewarding.

As she was going up the stairs, she ran into Franny, who was coming back down, water splashed all over the front of the demurely chic, navy-blue knit skirt and sweater set they had bought in Avignon the previous day. Amanda realized that since her arrival at the chateau, she had not seen Franny in slacks once. Did Hughes object to women wearing pants? It would be interesting to investigate. The two women exchanged a few pleasant words, and then Amanda went in search of underwear for Sarah.

A few minutes later, she was passing the still open window on the second floor landing on her way to the west wing's master bathroom, where Héloïse and Sarah were taking a communal bath while Isaac showered in the east wing bathroom, when she heard a murmur of voices floating up from the terrace below. By then the night had completed its descent over the chateau, and the window opened onto an indigo blank, dipped with orange at the bottom from the porch light below, and speckled in the distance, where the garden fell in waves towards the river valley, with whimsical patterns of tiny glowing dots that reminded Amanda of the view of the San Francisco bay from the living room of her house. Naturally curious, Amanda stopped a few feet back from the window, where she couldn't be seen outside, and listened.

The voices were Phil and Franny's, and they seem to be issuing from the western end of the terrace. There the gravel gave way to a flower bed along a crumbled stone wall in the middle of which stood a ruined arch supporting a wisteria vine–the remains of a medieval chapel that had once been part of the chateau, under the flagstone floor of which some Roman graves had been excavated a few decades earlier, according to Hughes. A path went under the arch, leading to what used to be the inside of the chapel but was now a grassy area surrounded by kitchen herbs, oleander bushes and cypresses, the flagstones having been all removed and reused in some other construction project. From the muffled sound of their voices, it must be in that little arbor that Phil and Franny had wandered.

Under what pretext had he lured her there? For as Amanda had feared, it was obvious that Phil was "making his move", his loud whisper, in turn cajoling, piteous and urgent, alternating with Franny's tensely apologetic murmur. Like all intellectuals, the girl has some glaring gaps in her social skills, Amanda reflected: she should have known that apologies are invariably taken by men as a signal to proceed, and that sometimes the only unambiguous response to a sexual advance is a good kick in the groin. Amanda herself had resorted to this strategy more than once during her sorority days. But then it was true that Amanda was five foot ten. What was to be done? It seemed to her that her intervention was required: given that she had invited both Phil and Franny, their welfare was her responsibility. As she contemplated her options, the timer on the hallway lights ran out and she found herself standing in the dark. Thus protected from discovery, she leaned out the window–a somewhat perilous exercise because of the width of the window frame and the additional blocking of her view caused by the wooden shutter–peering beyond the orange halo of the porch light towards the inky mass of the ruined chapel while simultaneously trying to come up with a way to draw the pair's attention. She was still working on an opening sentence when she heard Phil utter a sharp cry:

"What the …" he said, his exclamation followed by a dampened thump, and then a yelp of pain. There was a second of complete silence.

"What's the matter with you?" Phil resumed at last in his loud whisper. "Can't you take a joke?"

"About as well as you can!" Franny answered distinctly. She wasn't shouting, but there was something explosive in her voice that Amanda had never heard before, some unleashed passion poking through her modulated tones. Phil had been right: she was red-blooded after all, though apparently not for his benefit. Had she in fact kicked him in the groin?

Thereupon Hughes' voice rang in the night. Amanda guessed that he must be standing at one of the windows that faced the side of the chateau where the chapel stood. He must have heard the commotion as he went through the master bedroom to get the girls out of their baths.

"Franny, ça va? Tu as besoin d'aide?"

"Non merci. Juste une petite démonstration de judo!" she answered, the anger in her voice subsiding.

"Et lui? Il a besoin d'aide? Tu l'as vraiment étalé!"

"Ce n'est qu'une blessure d'amour propre, je pense."

"Hey you guys, while you parlay-vous, I am getting old on that fucking grass. Can I get a hand up? I think I slipped another disk," Phil muttered.

"I'll be right over!" said Hughes.

As he ran past Amanda on the landing a few seconds later, she called out to him.

"What happened down there?"

"Phil seems to have slipped on the grass," he answered, "Franny does not think it's serious, but would you ask Chuck to come out with me, just in case?"

"Sure," Amanda answered.

By the time they converged on the spot, Phil had in fact managed to stand up. He was rotating on his hips slowly, massaging his lower back, Franny watching him with her arms crossed, her face inscrutable in the shadow of the moon.

"The old spine seems to have held out," Phil said, somewhat sulkily. Then, regaining his boisterous, let-it-all-hang-out persona, "I guess I won't have to call my lawyer in the morning!" he added, "Just what I get for venturing out of the fort at night!"

"Well, at least we've got some fresh parsley for the beets!" Franny said, holding out a few crumpled looking sprigs.

"You've got to watch out for that evening dew," Hughes remarked casually.

"Lean on my shoulder, man," said Chuck. "You ain't fit for the country life!"

"Dinner's ready!" Victoria announced from the porch.

Thus ended Phil's courtship. For once, Amanda forbore trying to obtain the confidence of either one of the combatants. The whole incident had been handled with such tact and sophistication on everyone's part that the only possible crowning touch was to forget all about it. Anyway, she was clear enough about what had happened. But Franny, a judo expert?

The kids were so keyed up over dinner that they could barely eat, except for Clarisse, who never seemed to lose her composure. At last, the table cleared and the dishwasher stacked, they all filed into the music room, where they found motley chairs arranged in two rows in front of a couple of bedsheets which had been draped over a clothesline strung between a door hinge and a window latch. The Fischbeins (Chuck armed with a digital camera) and Victoria took up the front row, acting their spectator parts with ease: sitting back, looking around, chatting animatedly in low voices, while in the back row Hughes stared detachedly at the ceiling moulding and Franny pressed her hands in her lap. As for Phil, he had excused himself, claiming a blistering headache. Behind the bed-sheet, Sarah could be heard giving the troupe last minute stage directions.

"No, you can't use the gun! Only the sword! Princes don't have guns."

"Like that, Héloise. On your tippy toes."

"OK, we're ready. Clarisse, you can play now."

A few chords were struck on the piano, figuring an overture, after which Sarah intoned in her brash singsong:

"This play is called 'The Princess and the Chocolate Forest', written by Sarah Fischbein and Clarisse Degency. Once upon a time there was a beautiful and rich Princess. The king said she had to get married but she didn't want to because she liked to dance a lot and when you're married you are not supposed to dance. Then the king died so the princess told the guards not to let any prince into the castle because she did not want to get married."

There was a pause.

"Your turn," Sarah whispered.

"The prince!" Clarisse whispered back.

"Oh! right. One day a prince climbed the wall and killed all the guards so he could marry the princess."

"Clarisse, j'ai envie de faire pipi!" Héloise piped in.

"Attends l'entr'acte. C'est dans cinq minutes!" Clarisse replied.

"OK," Héloise said with a pitch-perfect American accent.

As strains of Clementi played on the piano, Sarah and Héloise tiptoed in front of the curtain, arms raised above their heads, and started dancing to the music, Sarah in an imitation of ballet, and Héloise, after a few seconds of following the other girl's lead, reverting to the eurythmic movements taught at her Waldorf school. Sarah was wearing a pink Cinderella dress with bows and puffed sleeves, one of the costumes found in the attic trunk, while Héloise's outfit had been improvised from a white muslin chemise cinched under her arms with a sky blue scarf. Both girls were crowned with lavender wreaths, and Sarah's splendor was further enhanced by several strands of plastic beads.

"Aren't they darling?" whispered Amanda, eliciting an emphatic assent from Victoria and a flash of Chuck's camera. Franny, whose insular childhood had precluded such displays, felt irrepressibly moved by the girls' innocent boldness. But Hughes, squirming in his seat, was far from conquered. Apart from his general objections to children putting themselves recklessly forward, he realized that he felt specifically repelled by Sarah. It was the sight of her outfit that had crystallized his feelings, the dress having been worn by his pretty cousin Marie-Catherine many years ago. On Sarah, though, it looked sad and frumpy, the seams of the bodice bursting around her plump torso, the puffed sleeves strangling her sausage-like arms, the rosy hue of the fabric only drawing attention to what was not flower-like in the girl: her goggle eyes and pale eyelashes, and the limp curls of her sandy hair, obviously the object of her mother's blind vanity. If Sarah had been plain and shy, he would have felt compassion for her. If she had been beautiful and commanding, he would have been disarmed. But the contrast between her lack of attractiveness and her bossy self-assurance shocked his sense of propriety. At heart, his reaction was not one of snobbery or male chauvinism. On the contrary, like Chuck's unease with Clarisse, it arose from an unconscious identification with the object of his dislike. What Sarah's unwarranted confidence suggested to him was how unrealistic our perception of ourselves may be, how for instance his intelligence might be mere bookishness, his authority mere social privilege, and the courage he had needed to quit a salaried job for the chancy business of winemaking mere stubborn folly–as Christiane had opined. These self-doubts, most often unacknowledged, had accompanied him all his life. And perhaps they were no more than the passing uncertainties that affect us all. But in him, they translated into the intense dread of ridicule mentioned by Franny. As he watched Sarah dance, his superciliousness masked painful visions of some future time when the girl's delusions of grandeur would be shattered by an unsympathetic world. He did notice though that Clarisse was acquitting herself quite respectably of the Clementi, and that Héloise seemed to be having a good time.

The piece of music concluded, Sarah came forward and announced that she was the princess, and that Héloise was her sister. Immediately, various warlike noises, accompanied on the piano by a cacophony worthy of John Cage, were heard from back stage while the curtain shook to indicate off-stage combat. Then

Isaac stepped forward, his torso wrapped in tin foil, an old French army helmet, also wrapped in foil, on his head, holding a foil-wrapped stick as a sword. So that's how the roll bought the previous day had been used up, thought Chuck as he took another picture.

"I am Prince Salamek," Isaac said brusquely. "I've killed all the guards, so now I can be the king."

"You mean you can marry me," Sarah corrected him.

"I don't care about marrying," Isaac replied, obviously deviating from the script. "I just want to be the king."

"And to be the king you have to marry me," Sarah retorted without missing a beat. "But first, you have to bring me an egg from the magic dove that lives in the biggest tree in the chocolate forest."

"Oh, all right," Isaac acquiesced, defeated by his sister's superior eloquence.

"End of act I" announced Sarah, and the actors fled behind the curtain.

The intermission lasted longer than Act I, costume changes being apparently required for the next act, and Héloise having to make a trip to the bathroom. To mark its end, the piano emitted a little mood music and the curtain was pulled back on both sides, revealing a scene that even Hughes found interesting. In the middle of an undulating terrain made of pieces of fabric in various shades of brown and beige, some silky, some woolly, some velvety, Sarah, in a black leotard, stood rigid with her arms bent at odd angles, holding brown paper leaves in each hand and carrying on her head a white porcelain piggy bank in the shape of a bird. On her left, a cardboard box had been transformed into a gingerbread hut, its door outlined with M & Ms and its roof tiled with Petits Ecoliers cookies. A river of orange tulle meandered among the hills and disappeared behind the curtain. The collection of odds and ends, in the dim light of a couple of wall sconces, managed to convey the sense of a magical landscape.

"I am the biggest tree in the Chocolate Forest," Sarah declaimed. She blinked, the fluttering of her pale eyelashes among the dark surroundings giving her a strange inward look, a sort of incantatory power. The first scene had been in line with her usual girlish mugging and preening, but this was different: more imaginative, starker, as if tapping into an actual dream. She herself was transformed. As a tree she seemed taller, more erect, her chubby face turned solemn, her pudgy arms taking on the stiffness of branches, her feet planted like roots. At not quite seven years of age, she had discovered the Method trick of acting her role from the inside out.

Isaac now entered stage left, still looking like a plump Don Quixote. Unlike his sister, he was not a natural actor. After a perfunctory gesture of using his hand as a visor to search the landscape, he trampled the woolen hills, jumped clumsily over the tulle river, and without further ado faced the chocolate tree.

"I am Prince Salamek," he said in his blunt monotone. "I want an egg from the magic dove."

A brief argument ensued, the Tree refusing to yield the egg, and the Prince trying to grab it. Under threat, the Tree summoned the forest's boar to its defense, at which point Héloise charged onto the stage head forward, an old grey alpaca sweater thrown over her, brandishing ivory chopsticks and grunting fearfully. After a brave but unequal fight with the boar, the Prince was gored and fell at the foot of the tree. The Tree bent down, and having shed its chocolate leaves over the corpse, it buried it under a velvet bedcover.

The curtain was pulled over the scene for the second intermission. Then the audience was informed by Sarah's voice that an earthquake had struck the chocolate forest, and that the tree had fallen, this announcement underlined by another John Cage fragment on the piano. In act III, the Princess, the pink dress accessorized with a white feather boa to mark the passage of time, made her way to the Chocolate Forest, where the M & M hut lay smashed on its side, and the tree was nothing more than a log from the fireplace. She saw the Prince's hand sticking out of the velvet and opened it; it contained a green Playdoh egg nearly as big as the porcelain dove. Elated at the sight, she kissed his (reluctant) hand, which promptly resuscitated him. To the cheers of the populace represented by Héloise crying "Vive la Reine! Vive le Roi!", and to the tune of Mendelssohn's march, the couple returned to the palace for the wedding, which, however, was not shown, Isaac having categorically refused to lend himself to this ceremony.

"The end," Sarah said simply, and all the actors, joined by the orchestra, bowed towards the audience. Wild applause broke out. Hughes himself was astounded. Over the course of twenty minutes, his embarrassment and annoyance had given way to curiosity, to admiration, and finally to unfeigned awe.

"How much of this is your doing?" he asked Franny after the applause had died down and the camera stopped flashing, as the children, led by Victoria, boisterouly dismantled and put away the stage set.

"Not much. I helped with the costumes, and Victoria built the chocolate hut, but the original idea came from Sarah, and Clarisse did most of the staging. Otherwise, I just acted as translator. As far as the direction went, you can see Sarah was completely in charge."

"And she can act too."

"I know," beamed Amanda, "isn't she amazing? I wonder if I should enroll her in drama classes."

"You notice how she made the best use of her bilingual cast? And how she managed to get Isaac to go along with a girl's scenario?" Franny remarked.

"Leadership," said Chuck, squaring his shoulders. "She's her daddy's girl."

"She definitely has character," Hughes agreed. "And amazing aplomb."

"And imagination," added Franny. "That chocolate forest ..."

"I wonder where the idea of the boar came from," Amanda mused. "It's not an animal she is familiar with."

"A TV show, probably."

"I guess.... Anyway, Clarisse is a wonderful musician. I loved her sound effects. And Héloise is such a cherub. She was right on cue every time. You must be proud of them, Hughes."

"To tell you the truth, I am completely surprised. I feel as if I am discovering my own daughters."

"Isn't it marvelous? It seems that our children and your children bring the best out of one another. I am starting to think that there is something magical, a synergy, as Chuck would say, that comes out of mixing our two cultures."

Amazingly, Hughes found himself agreeing with Amanda again. Yet it would take him another year to agree to play his clarinet in front of his guests, with Franny at the piano.

As had become their custom, Hughes and Franny met in the kitchen for a cup of lime tea after all the other guests had gone to bed, but the night being fine, they decided to take their drinks outside.

"Where?" whispered Franny, her eyes adjusting to the darkness, as Hughes had turned off the porch light to bring out the stars. He pointed his chin towards a gap in the balustrade, where the blue phosphorescence of a half-moon bathed the first step of the stairs that led to the garden below. As they tiptoed across the terrace, the crunch of gravel filled Franny's consciousness. More than any other noise, it seemed to stand out as emblematic of the last two and a half weeks, a sort of leitmotif of her vacation. It was actually more than a single noise, varying as it did according to the weather: langorous in the midday heat, sloshy when it rained, as crisp as fresh snow on a night like the present one. If you listened carefully, you could even identify each of the chateau's inhabitants by the quality of the sound they made treading on gravel: with Chuck or Phil it was like a crashing of waves, the difference being that Phil's was stormier; with the kids, who liked to drag their feet in it, it resembled the rattle of a cicada; Amanda's step sounded like biting into a Rice Krispy treat, and Victoria's like maracas; only Hughes made that neat, urgent, contrapuntal ping that stirred her deeply.

At the bottom of the stairs, he guided her across the lawn to a stone bench carved out of the retaining wall, and they sat down side by side, their bodies turning towards each other by an irresistible tropism. Franny propped her cup on her knees, using it to warm her fingers, and Hughes, leaning back on one hand, laid his cup down at his side, where he promptly forgot it. It was the most privacy they had had since the day at the lake, a fact they both registered with quickened heartbeats. In the kitchen, or in the parlor, there was always the risk of being interrupted by one of the other guests on an insomniac quest for a snack or a magazine. And of course, given their virtuous resolution to wait until the girls' departure before putting their attraction to the test, they had not stepped into each other's bedrooms. But here, out of hearing range of the chateau's windows, protected from prying eyes by the retaining wall at their back and by shaggy poplars on both sides, the unimpeded view in front merely suggestive of the shrouded valley, they were really alone. It was probably just as well that the bench was cold and hard, its back rest hard and bumpy, the carpet of grass at their feet damp and cold. Somehow they both knew that neither one was much inclined towards heroic lovemaking.

Still, they refrained from touching. Instead they chatted companionably about the progress of the harvest and the day's happenings at the chateau, about cultural differences and individual quirks, in no hurry to go to bed in spite of the late hour and the sleep deficit they were accumulating, knowing they would toss and turn much of the night anyway. Above them, the Milky Way streaked across the sky, its attendant crowd of stars, piercingly brilliant in spite of the moon, seeming to scream in ecstasy.

They had been chaste longer than they originally planned, as Christiane, perversely, had twice postponed her return, the girl's departure being now scheduled for the next morning. Yet they had taken the successive delays with as much good cheer as if they had had their whole life ahead of them to make love, instead of twelve, then eleven, then only ten days. In fact, though they did not talk about this, because it would have had the same effect as touching, they were both experiencing delayed gratification as the keenest of pleasures—not a pleasure of the imagination, for they even refrained from imagining anything, but something just as physical as sex, a sensation akin to itchy scabs and upwelling sneezes, throbbing, engrossing, and yet kept under wraps, controlled.

This was something new to Franny. For all her mistrust of men, she disdained playing hard to get. But for Hughes, abstinence had been a frequent strategy in the years before his marriage, evolved from inchoate remains of Catholic conditioning into a clear-eyed recognition that no matter how lightly we have been encouraged to view it in the last forty years, sex does in fact change everything. Sex was powerful enough as a bond to mask a lack of other affinities, so primal that it obscured your partner's personhood. By the time you woke up to both, it was too late. If anything, he was determined to be even more cautious now, as his divorce from Christiane had exposed some fatal flaw in his judgment as to what constituted a likely mate. At the same time, he was aware of being carried forward by sheer lust, against which all his scruples were an insufficient force. So it was just a matter of holding off as long as one could (he had no doubt whatsoever about Franny reciprocating his feelings), which was a delight all its own–his ascetism had a decidedly epicurian flavor.

Strangely enough, Franny, who had a knack for finding reasons to worry, never misinterpreted his physical reticence for a lack of desire or for sexual inept-itude, even though she did not completely buy his explanations that it was neces-sary for his daughters' welfare. When he did touch her, his gestures were so sure, so full of promise, that she gladly yielded all the initiative to him. Of course, as he had all the power, she was bound to chafe a little more–and he happened to love her chafing.

They had been silent for a few minutes, letting in the gestalt of the moment: the rustling of poplar leaves, a sleepy cricket or two, an occasional plop of a frog in the basin. Whereas the motionless stars had previously looked as if they were rushing headlong across the sky, a late jet plane, too high to be heard, and visible only from its blinking lights, now seemed to be laboring through it. The cups of lime tea were exhaling the last whiffs of their sweetish scent–a smell neither Hughes or Franny was in fact that fond of, though it would remain forever asso-ciated in their mind with the thrill of anticipation. As balmy as the evening had been, a chill was now rising from the ground, causing goose bumps to appear on the top of Franny's knees. Without a word, Hughes, who had seemed completely absorbed in the flight of the plane, took off his jacket and wrapped it aroung her legs.

"Bundling, are we?" she asked, slyly alluding to the old Puritan practice of let-ting a prospective couple sleep in the same bed with a board between them.

"Pas pour longtemps!" he answered. As usual, he had understood her refer-ence. Reflexively–perhaps as a check on the power he exerted over her–Franny kept testing his knowledge of her culture, and he kept passing her tests with fly-ing colors. Of course, he had spent a couple of years as a student in the US, and had returned a number of times on business. Anyway, all over the world, people were much more exposed to American culture than the other way around. And the more they knew, the more they objected to, but Franny didn't mind: overall, she shared Hughes's objections, and where he clearly misinterpreted or generalized too widely, she felt free to set him straight.

Her own views of French culture had undergone a revolution in the last two weeks, or rather it was her feelings that had changed. Traits that had previously irritated her now seemed touching, or at least inextricably linked to others that she deeply respected: parsimony to conservation, rigidity to a sense of traditions, melancholia to humility. And then, France was a place where a woman did not risk her chance at happiness by being intellectual.

Certainly Hughes did not begrudge her the right to voice educated thoughts and opinions on any subject. In fact he expected a great deal of intellectual fluency in a mate, to the extent that it was the bread and butter of all social intercourse in his world. In his world, names like Lyssenko, Keynes or Tavernier were tossed about in conversation with the same easy familiarity as car makes. The surprise was that people steeped in such an homogenous culture should manage to disagree on anything.

At first, given his past experiences with UC Davis coeds, Hughes had been surprised to find Franny's mind so well furnished—his first spoof of T S Eliot had been his own kind of test. Since then he had taken it for granted. In his mind, she was French Canadian, as if that explained everything. He was more intrigued by the discovery of commonalities with Chuck, who was American through and through, although there again there was the complicating factor of his Jewishness. When it came to a prospective lover, what he worried about were compatibilities of temperament and emotions, the dynamics of give and take, of disclosure and evasion, about which he felt completely in the dark. In the last few weeks, he had confirmed for himself that he liked power, and also that he liked to have his power challenged. In what way, to what degree, and whether it was even fair for him to like both of these things, or just egotistical, he was still at a loss to say. He did know that he did not want to be egotistical or unfair, and he sensed that Franny would not let him. That was a good start.

But to Franny, their intellectual affinities were manna from heaven. Until now, she had believed that a compatibility of "taste", "breeding" and "understanding" (and how tantalizing were the very words!) was something to be found only in the novels of Jane Austen. In the real world (that is *her* world), even in an academic Mecca like Berkeley, intellectual concerns were compartmentalized and only skin-deep, often abandoned when no longer needed to advance a career. In the real world, you talked literature with English professors, economics with economists, education with teachers, movies with film students, music with musicians, and work and mortgages with everybody else. In the real world, even intellectual men did not like intellectual women. Oh! it did not stop them from pursuing you, even if you made no effort whatsoever to play dumb; on the contrary it seemed to goad them on. But if you paid attention (which unfortunately you didn't always do) you could tell, even at the height of courtship, by certain impatient looks and good-natured putdowns, that your intelligence made them uncomfortable, though it was only after they had got you to bed that they suddenly realized how wearing, how anxiety producing dealing with a woman who thought might be in the long run. By then you had something at stake, so you did make some effort to dumb yourself down a little, but they, supposedly so obtuse, could no longer be fooled. With Hughes, for the first time in her life, she felt that her mind was given full room to stretch, not as an expedient of seduction, but as a medium of intimacy, so that even before they had gone to bed, she found herself as comfortable as if they had reached the stage in a relationship when you can resume wearing your fuzzy slippers.

Hughes by himself was fine, she was nearly sure of it. But he did come with baggage in the shape of children. Whatever his real reasons for deferring sexual intimacy till after their departure, Franny had to admit that it had left her free to relate to Clarisse and Héloise as just one among several adults, a limited responsibility that suited her fine given her lack of experience with children. But what about a possible future? Héloise, independent, adventurous, quietly willful, with adorable bouts of indiscriminate clinging and a still intact respect for authority, was for now a breeze to deal with. Even her strange obsession with the butterfly lady had abated after a few days, probably just an expression of longing for her mother. Christiane, duly consulted about it, had suggested that the girl was merely referring to some toy she had played with at school. It was Clarisse, who seemed to have come out of the womb fully raised and who beamed on everyone equally a sort of Christian forbearance, that Franny paradoxically worried about. There was something heartrending in the way the girl doted on her father as if *she* were the adult, in her diligence with her schoolwork, her abnegation in front of the other kids. Franny, like Amanda, (they had talked about the subject), suspected that she was suffering from a certain amount of benign neglect from her parents, a neglect that her self-sufficient façade only contributed to perpetuate. It had been exhilarating to watch her come out of her controlled persona that afternoon as she threw herself into the spirit of childish invention and unself-conscious exhibition that the staging of the play demanded. Franny felt that the girl should have more opportunities to let her hair down, but feared that might be going against Hughes' child rearing philosophy. Dimly, she perceived that Clarisse was the glue that kept the disjointed family from falling apart completely, and she foresaw painful dramas in store when the girl ceased to accept that role.

"You said tonight that you felt as if you were discovering your own daughters. How so?" she asked, pursuing aloud her meditation.

"I am not sure I can put it into words. It wasn't so much that I discovered new aspects of their personality or that I was surprised at their talent, although I did not expect them to be so confident on stage, or to even want to take part in a play."

"La peur du ridicule ..."

"Exactement ... It was more like a realization of their autonomy as fully-formed persons ... It made me feel proud, but also a little anxious and a little guilty."

"Guilty?"

"In the last three years, since I took over the vineyard, I haven't seen much of them. I know that Clarisse in particular misses me, and Christiane is not always the warmest parent. I need to find a way to spend more time with them."

Franny brought her feet up on the bench and buried her chin between her knees.

"Are you looking for a stepmother for them?"

"Perhaps. Would that be terribly male chauvinistic?"

"No. I guess it would be practical."

"Let me assure you that the thought did not occur to me until tonight. And even now, it's the last thing on my mind in connection with you."

"Is it?"

"Yes!"

It was another one of his long, multi-layered monosyllables that in one fell swoop gave the best possible answer to all her contradictory questions. No, his feelings for her were not utilitarian, but yes he liked her enough to envision a future with her. Franny raised her chin to look at him and in so doing caught a flash of his hand in the dark. It seemed he had been about to caress her head, but had been stopped by her own movement. For a second, she felt like collapsing against this chest, like seeing what would happen next. But in the spirit of clarity, she laughed at him instead.

"You make so much of the shortest words," she said. "George Bush *fils* could use a few lessons from you."

"I'm afraid he'll do well enough without them," he answered, his hand, back in its resting place at the back of the bench, still burning from an independent urge to creep under the corduroy jacket towards the crevice between her knees.

"But back to the stepmother question. Assuming everything for the best, is that something you would contemplate?"

"Yes," she said.

She wasn't bad at monosyllables either. He couldn't help bending down, and still keeping his hands at the back of the bench for safety, he pressed his lips against hers, softly, teasingly. She let herself respond for a few seconds, concentrating all her arousal on those two square inches of flesh. Then she pushed him away.

"You're sadistic! You know that?"

"By the way, I won my bet about Phil. Did you really knock him down?"

A nod.

"I see now what you meant when you said you could defend yourself. Did you study martial arts?"

Another nod.

"A bon entendeur salut …" he muttered as if to himself.

"Is that a proverb? I don't understand it."

"It means that I'd better remember that for the future."

She peered at his face. He didn't look threatened in the least. She gave up on finding yet another reason to worry.

CHAPTER 19

▼

UN TIENS VAUT MIEUX QUE DEUX TU L'AURAS

(A Bird In The Hand Is Worth Two In The Bush)

The coast was clear, at last. There were a few vehicles in the parking lot: Pierrette's Renault and a van with a coat of dirt all the way up to its windshield, obviously the property of a farm worker. Hughes' Mercedes was there too, because he had driven the tractor out to the fields, but otherwise all the cars that mattered were gone. The BMW, packed with Fischbeins and Fischbein possessions, had left for a day excursion to the coast. The Alfa Romeo had been missing since before breakfast, and it was safe to assume that it would be missing all day as Phil was probably in no hurry to show his face after last night's "accident". The Parisian bitch's Audi had come and gone, carrying away the poor little rich girls. And Franny had followed Hughes in the Peugeot. Now was the time to wrap things up, to make tracks, to charge into the future. But Victoria lingered at the balustrade, feeling uncharacteristically sluggish.

She briefly considered making a trip to the library to see if at the last minute, a crucial new piece of information might justify a change of plan. But first, she did not have any transportation, and second, it was Saturday, so the library was sure to be closed. Its opening hours were so rococo that Victoria could not for the life of her remember them, but even when it was supposed to be open, half the time she found it locked anyway, without even a message on the door to let customers know what the problem was. This kind of frustration happened a lot in France, and not only at government offices, whose employees, all over the world, were basically paid to frustrate you, but even at private businesses. It was part of a whole attitude people had here, a way of asserting that making a buck was not the only thing in life, and from her new vantage point as a nearly French person, and a potential heiress on top of that, Victoria could dig it. Besides, when they *were* open for business, people were remarkably helpful. Not necessarily dripping with friendliness, and far from subservient (except waiters of course, who managed to make subservience a mark of superiority), but proud to share their knowledge, and even willing to get around all the rules and other obstacles they first put in your way when you asked for help–provided you showed the proper spirit of patience and appreciation. It had been the case with the librarian, a young matron with darting black eyes, bleached hair pulled into a French twist, and a whole collection of cardigan sweaters she wore thrown over her shoulders. She had spent twenty minutes explaining, in a mixture of French and English that Victoria had wisely declined to understand, why it was impossible to set up a Hotmail account on one of the library computers, and another twenty minutes setting it up, then showing Victoria how to bring up the browser and send and retrieve messages (all of which she already knew how to do, as her roommate Maggie had let her use her PC at times, but it would have been counterproductive to rain on the librarian's parade).

It had been worth it. Once she figured out how to use the keyboard, which had half the letters in the wrong place, in particular the 'Q' where the 'A' should be, and all the punctuation marks mixed up, and once she made sense of prompts like *recherche* and *précédente*, the Internet had fulfilled its promise: from a little village in the south of France, she had gained direct access to the best American appraisers of antique toys. The library even had a scanner, so she was able to attach a close-up of the wind-up butterfly catcher to the message she composed describing it, asking for an estimate on its price, and requesting advice on the best way to dispose of it. She copy-pasted half a dozen different e-mail addresses in the recipient box, clicked the send button, the blue bar filled the box at the bottom of the screen, and it was done. Without envelopes, or stamps, or even a phone charge, her need had been instantaneously communicated half across the world.

The speed and reach of machines was unprecedented, but human sloth was still an issue. On Tuesday, Wednesday, Thursday, Friday, she returned to the library. On Tuesday it was closed. On Wednesday she found her in-box empty.

Wondering if there was some breakdown on the Internet causing messages addressed to her to be routed to someone else or to languish on a foreign hard drive, she decided to conduct a scientific test by firing off a message to Maggie. But first she had to find her ex-roommate's e-mail address. That's when she found out that there was not one but several Yahoos, that Yahoo.fr could only search the French directory and Yahoo.com was limited to American addresses. And while she was going back and forth between the two sites, she also noticed that their news sections looked different, not just in language but also in content, the headlines on the French site containing more names of other countries, including some that had nothing to do with terrorists as far as Victoria knew. It was a scream, really, to think that with all the world supposedly at your finger tips, you were still looking at it through a small window that somebody else had placed there for their own reasons. It was like being taken to the department store by a brand new foster mother and being told you could pick your own school outfit, but any item you as much as looked at caused her lips to tighten or her eyes to go back in her head, and finally you let her choose because you didn't want to get sent back to the group home, and the clothes she bought were all dorky, so later on you had to filch some lipstick to make yourself feel better. It was like any number of other situations, in childhood and in adulthood, when they tried to make you believe you were in control, but in fact you weren't. Stay loose, trust no one, that had been Victoria's motto before she read her first self-help book. And it still was, deep down.

On Thursday the library was closed again. She had in the meantime discovered that there was a computer in Hughes's room at the chateau, but unfortunately it was password protected. So on Friday she had to make the trip to the village again, and this time she had to walk, because Franny had taken the Peugeot to shop in Orange with the kids. She found a message from Maggy waiting for her, which at least proved there was nothing wrong with her connection. But not a word from any of the appraisers. For half an hour, she yielded to discouragement. Suddenly, none of her most cherished maxims seemed to be of any use. Instead, some older, more primitive ways of making sense of life held sway in her mind: she thought of bad luck signs and voodoo curses and the wheel of fortune, all those bugaboos that hung like bats in dark recesses in your brain carved out by forgotten ancestors, ready to take shrieking flight at the first disturbance.

She recalled her first hint of a feeling of doom, when the angelic tot had pointed her chubby finger at the empty spot in the curio cabinet and bawled her baby blues out. It was just too eerie that of all people, and among the oodles of knickknacks that lay about the chateau, *she* should notice the missing butterfly catcher. If, like the pointer on a Ouija board, the chubby finger had swung around and settled on her next, she wouldn't have been surprised. Fortunately, Hughes and Franny had been too busy trying to quiet the girl down to pay attention to what she was saying. But from that point on, Victoria lived in dread of being found out.

She had quite a job of making sure Héloise stayed away from her armoire, as there was no key on her door, and the master bathroom, because of its large tub, was in daily requisition for the girls' communal baths. To keep things in hand, she ended up spending more time with the kids than her babysitting shifts demanded. And for the most part, until the hike on Wednesday, it had worked to everyone's advantage: Amanda got to check off more items on her touristic to-do list, Franny got to hang out with Hughes, and Phil got to do what he did best, which was to be a useless puppy. Anyway the kids turned out to be no problem. Héloise showed no more sign of paranormal powers, and if any discipline was required, Clarisse took care of it. Like a summer camp posse, they made pencil rubbings of old coins and pressed flowers in books; they climbed on each other's shoulders to pick almonds, took turns zooming down the road on the scooter, waded into the river while teenagers on the bank smoked pot (Victoria went over discreetly to ask for a toke), made topiaries out of a couple of bushes in the garden; they had badminton tournaments and blackberry fights and snail throwing contests. It had turned out to be fun—not much of a consideration usually for someone as driven toward success as Victoria, but if you equated it with the rest that you were advised to take between bouts of charging, then it became a legitimate part of your plan.

The hike was the thing that had really thrown her off. It was one of those airless days when the sky was a muddled white and all your muscles felt liquefied. They had been lounging around on the lawn when Victoria sensed some presence at her back. She turned around, and saw one of the urns on the balustrade metamorphose into a living head, its features indistinct except for a pair of eyes that seemed to be drilling into her, as if they were warning her or accusing her of something. For a second, she thought she was going to pass out. Then she recognized the Sheriff kid and the spell was broken. She had probably just got dizzy from changing focus too fast.

Clarisse wanted to go on a hike, and she agreed, thinking that along the way she might discover a better hiding place for the butterfly catcher than the armoire in her room. That, however, turned out to be a fool's errand. Within a mile's radius of the chateau, there wasn't an old tool shed, an abandoned vehicle, a hole in a tree, a cave, where you could have stashed a precious object and been sure to find it a day later. As she should have remembered, every inch of the land here was constantly trampled by people and animals, and every building was in use. Once, walking around the village, she had spotted a dilapidated house with a huge hole in its wall, through which her attention had been drawn to a sculpted fireplace panel. She had poked inside, only to bump her nose against a work boot. A mason, perched on a makeshift scaffolding, was shoring up the ceiling with reinforced concrete. The house had just been purchased by a Welsh retiree. It was the same all over, Hughes had explained. Barns, watermills, hunting cabins, train stations, sheep pens, were being grabbed by urban northerners in search of sun and peace. Meanwhile the peasants continued to squeeze a living out of every clod of dirt. The Vaucluse was very different from the Nievre in that respect—heavily populated, it was not a good place for freelance antique recycling.

As she was entertaining these sobering thoughts, some black thing had materialized in the middle of the road. At first, because of an intervening bump in the terrain, she hadn't seen its legs, so it had looked to her like another disembodied head, this one very shaggy with a weird curly smile and eyes that were mere slits in the fur, yet potent like eyes always are. Again, she had an unsettling sense that some otherworldly but strangely familiar spirit had risen to admonish her. Suddenly the ground was shaking under her, and some beast was upon her, charging through as if she hadn't been there, and she realized it wasn't charging towards her, but away from something else, and that what she saw in his eyes was not recognition but blind fear. Then she was pushed aside and fell into a ditch, and the beast disappeared down the hill.

Try as she may to be rational about it, Victoria could not help seeing the incident as ominous. OK, so it had just been a boar fleeing from hunters. You couldn't blame it for that. Self-preservation was the first law of the jungle, literal or figurative. And though it was Victoria's first encounter with a real wild animal (except behind bars at the zoo, and that only once on a kindergarten field trip; her only clear memory of it was that she had needed to pee the whole time), boar sightings were apparently not that rare in the area, according to the librarian. But that she, whose whole philosophy revolved around the idea of enthusiastically charging at life, should nearly have lost hers to the panicky charge of a dumb animal, well, it seemed too much of a coincidence. It seemed … what was the word … ironic. As far as Victoria was concerned, irony was the worst kind of voodoo.

So she wasn't that surprised to find her in-box empty on Friday. But as hope springs eternal, before making the exhausting trek back to the chateau, she passed the time by idly surfing the Web, on the off chance that some expert in America, after a long day of attending auctions (for it was nighttime over there), might this very moment be looking at the picture of her toy and jumping up and down from excitement, all sleepiness forgotten, and that the next minute when she'd click on her *boite de reception* she'd be informed she had mail. After a while she thought of entering her own name, McWorruster, in Yahoo.com People Search box. The search did not return any result, which made her a little sad. Well, what did she expect? Her mom had died, and Victoria herself had never had a separate phone listing. She wasn't that attached to her name either. She had read somewhere that America was the only country where you could legally change your name without marrying, that this expressed a uniquely American belief in self-reinvention. It was a belief Victoria shared. In fact, without the least patriotic intention, she had re-invented herself several times in her twenty-five years. Still, to find that of all the billions of pages on the Internet, none of them so much as mentioned your name, that was harsh. It really drove it home that you were alone in the world, which had been Victoria's assumption all along, but obviously there had been a little corner of her mind that had not totally accepted it. For a second, she wished her name had been something like Smith or Williams. Then at least, she could have imagined that some of the people returned by the search engine might be far flung relatives.

But then she remembered Yahoo.fr. So she typed McWorruster in the *Pages Blanches' recherche* box, and lo and behold, the page came back with one entry:

McWorruster Emilie

53 r. Claude Debussy 10399 GODOY EN CHAMPAGNE 03 96 00 05 44

Victoria couldn't believe her eyes. Of all places, to find a branch of her family tree in France! From the very first instant, she was sure that Emilie McWorruster was related to her, if only because the name was so uncommon. Suddenly, she needed to know more. So she expanded her search, going to Google.fr to find all possible references to any McWorruster, and to Emilie in particular. And this time, the Internet came through sensationally.

From link to link, some in English and some in French, from online encyclopediae, university course syllabi, museum catalogs, tourist office blurbs, newspaper articles, minutes of city councils, personal web pages, auctioneers' sites, through text and photographs and maps and charts, she found out that Emilie was the only daughter of a certain James McWorruster, an African-American painter associated with Expressionism and Fauvism (she looked those up too), born in 1895, who had first come to France during World War I as a soldier in the "Harlem Hellfighters" regiment, and returned in 1920 to escape discrimination in his own country. He had lived the rest of his life in France, hanging out in Montmartre with other expatriates (Langston Hughes, Sidney Bechet, Josephine

Baker ... all names that barely rang a bell, but the Internet had a lot to say about them) and being influenced by Henri Matisse and Emile Antoine Bourdelle (more names to look up). He had partied hard, embraced all the fashions, met with moderate success. Then in 1931 he had married a girl from a wealthy family and moved to her hometown of Godoy en Champagne, where he had remained until his death from a heart attack in 1953. He had been rediscovered in the eighties, at a time when the Japanese nouveau riche's insatiable thirst for early twentieth century French art had brought a lot of obscure paintings out of attics and onto the auction block. (James McWorruster had been classified as a French painter until he was reclaimed by American ethnic studies scholars, though the French never ceased considering him one of theirs). As it turned out, Emilie McWorruster (born 1931 ... hmm looked like old James' wedding had been of the shotgun kind) had had a lot of her father's paintings in her attic, completed during the twenty years when as a country *rentier*, he hadn't had to sell his art. And it seemed that, quite hip to the laws of supply and demand, the old lady was letting go of them at a trickling rate. The last one sold, in 1999, at the height of the hi-tech boom, had fetched a cool $288,000. It was a poster-like picture, all in bright reds and yellows and blues, of a naked white woman with a chicken on her head, unless the chicken was supposed to be behind her, it was hard to tell in the general flatness of tone and lack of discernible perspective, and the title: Demain (Tomorrow) did not help either. It was now at some corporate headquarters in Menlo Park, or at least had been as of the last Web update.

As she looked at the Web reproduction of Demain, a memory bubbled up in Victoria's mind, of another picture, this one in pencil, and with exquisite shadowing and perspective, of a black woman, seen through the doorway of a shack, with a chicken on her lap and some kind of tub between her feet. She distinctly remembered wondering whether the woman was about to give the chicken a bath, and the question had that urgency that idle questions can only have in childhood. Where was this? It seemed she had wondered about it over a period of time, and that her curiosity had never been satisfied. Then she remembered an associated feeling, of having a fever, and lying shivering under a crazy quilt, tracing the outlines of the picture among the reflections and greasy fingerprints on its glass cover, as if reconstituting it in her mind could somehow make her well. She must have been four or five, and she must have been living with her mother in the Valley, before social services took her away for the first time. By the time they got reunited, her mother had moved to an apartment in Echo Park, and the picture had disappeared. Victoria had forgotten all about it until now.

But suddenly a lot of things made sense. Didn't the one photograph of her McWorruster grandfather, as an inexplicably black young man, have an inscription on the back that said: Memphis, 1934? And wasn't James McWorruster raised in Memphis? Yes, he was. His biography made no mention of an American son, but it wouldn't be the first time a man had skipped town to reinvent himself free of a family. The American branch of the McWorrusters had probably never heard from him again, and then they had been too busy being poor to find his name in some art magazine. Couldn't the long lost drawing of the woman holding the chicken have been the work of her ... great-grandfather, passed down through generations until alcoholism and ignorance finally robbed Victoria of her only inheritance? The fact that the drawing, in her memory, seemed much more skillful than the $288,000 later painting did not disprove her theory. She knew enough about art history from her one community college class to understand that twentieth century artists had progressively done away with representational skills. And, looking at the illustrations at artcylopedia.com, it wasn't hard to see that James McWorruster had had a thing with chickens.

And then, as a crowning piece of evidence, there was the fact of Victoria's own artistic talent. Ever since first grade, teachers and classmates had complimented her on her pencil drawings and watercolors. Once, when she was no more than ten, she had held a sidewalk sale of her artwork, pinning a few samples of her portfolio on a refrigerator carton she had dragged out of the neighbors' yard. Some guy riding at the back of a limo had made the chauffeur stop the car, walked over to her stand, and given her five bucks for one bitty drawing. Unfortunately, no one after that had shown that much confidence in the market value of her work, and so she had not pursued it as a possible career. Anyway, she had moved too much and struggled too early with mere survival to pursue any career consistently. But she had continued doodling, not even as a pastime, but as relief to some uncontrollable itch. It was her skill at drawing that had got her the job with Ruth. And now, it was going to be her passport into her French family.

All afternoon, as she helped the kids build the set for their play, and all evening, as she cooked, and ate, and watched the play, and later as she lay in bed writing in her diary, waiting to hear the squeak of the front door, followed by two sets of steps padding up the stairs, then stopping for a long time at the level of the mezzanine (the first night she had feared that they were inspecting the curio cabinet, but since then she had figured out they stopped to kiss) then resuming reluctantly up, and gliding along the carpeted corridor, and finally the house falling silent after a last whisper and the simultaneous clicks of two door latches, which was the signal that all was well for one more day, all evening she had thought about how she was going to introduce herself to Aunt Emilie, how she was going to make her case that they were related, how she was going to get herself invited to the Aunt's chateau. For of course, Aunt Emilie lived in a chateau, which was the French equivalent to a house in Malibu. Recently, a plaque commemorating the celebrated *fils du pays* had been dedicated, courtesy of the *syndicat d'initiative* in Godoy, and Mme McWorruster had gracefully consented to open the chateau to tourists in exchange for the installation of a security system paid for by the municipality. (It was amazing how many words were written more or less the same way in French as in English, particularly the long words. It made reading bureaucratic texts a cinch, though it did not help much in conversation, where a word like conversation, for instance, sounded completely different. So how did the two languages happen to share so much? And why were they considered separate tongues, and not mere dialects? Victoria would have liked to know. In fact, since she had started travelling in France, she had found that many things she had previously taken for granted, like language and food and architecture, had become sources of fascinated inquiry. Underneath her strictly utilitarian preoccupations, more and more she could feel the tendrils of a disinterested curiosity poking up. Perhaps, in the end, she might go to college?)

Aunt Emilie didn't seem to have any children, or at least none had attended the dedication ceremony for the plaque. So she might be well disposed towards an unexpected relative. At seventy, she might also welcome the help of a young, enthusiastic, artistically inclined and English speaking assistant in steering the tourists around her abode, making sure they did not touch her precious artwork or spill coffee on her parquet floors. She might like to be wheeled around the grounds or chauffered into town. She might be in need of affection. These were all tasks Victoria felt qualified for. Plus, and this showed that she had been on track all along, the two weeks she had spent within the sphere of a French Vicomte were bound to have imbued her with a certain refined *je ne sais quoi* that would incline the rich old lady to see her as a fit companion. It was not that Victoria had consciously studied Hughes' mannerisms. Unlike Franny & Amanda, she did not engage in objective cultural analysis. She could no more describe in detail in what way Hughes showed *class* than how she knew that his ex-wife was a bitch or Phil a puppy. When it came to human sciences, her understanding was instinctive, her learning kinesthetic. After a few days of being steeped in an aristocratic *milieu*, she just automatically started opening her mouth less widely, cocking her head in a certain way, making fluid instead of staccato gestures, using words like *milieu* and *class* and *je ne sais quoi*. It was a gift she had always had. She wasn't particularly proud of it—not exactly the gift of an actor, as she had discovered in her one drama class, more the tricks of a chameleon—but she relied on it heavily in her quest for success.

Fortified with this careful review of her assets, Victoria was able to fall asleep. But the next morning found her inexplicably apprehensive at the idea of actually talking to her relative. Perhaps it was her lack of fluency in French, always more of an issue on the phone, where you could not supplement verbal cues with visual ones. Perhaps it was the fact that failure in this case would take on the aspect of an intimate rejection, the sort of disappointment Victoria had not risked for a very long time. Whatever the cause of her anxiety, dialing Emilie McWorruster's number was probably the bravest thing she had ever done.

But in the end it had been so easy.

"Allo?" a smoky, querulous voice had asked at the other end of the line.

"Madame McWorruster?"

"Que lui voulez-vous?" the voice had asked suspiciously.

"Je m'appelle Victoria McWorruster," she had thrown like a buoy into a hostile sea.

And the voice had replied: "Ma cousine!"

After that they had switched to English, and within fifteen minutes, they had arranged to meet the next day in Godoy. It seemed that Aunt Emilie had learned from some biographer about the existence of her father's first wife and son, and had subsequently done her own research, which had revealed the existence of one great-grand daughter. But due to Victoria's peripatetic habits, she had not been able to trace her further than the Jewish Home for Girls where Victoria has spent half a year during her teens . She was unmistakably excited at finding her alive and well and already in France, especially after the recent terrorist attacks, which she seemed to think might have decimated the entire American population. They did not talk specifically about inheritance, but Victoria got the distinct impression that it was a subject that weighed on the old lady's mind. In any case, for once wishful thinking was vindicated by reality: Emilie was, truly, amazingly, family. Until she had been called "ma cousine" (but wasn't "niece" more accurate?), Victoria had not realized that she did not believe her own memories.

As she put down the receiver in the hallway, she heard a rustle of fabric behind her. She turned around and saw Franny tightening the belt of her bathrobe, or more exactly guessed at what she was seeing, as her vision had suddenly gone blurry.

"Something wrong?" asked Franny, instinctively moving towards trouble, as she always did. That's how Victoria figured out that the blurriness was caused by tears.

"No, everything is right!" she cried, and threw herself in Franny's arms.

So she recounted the conversation she had just had, and Franny held her hands and said she was really happy for her. She had even heard of James McWorruster. At that point Victoria realized she'd better come up with a reason for going by the name of Victoria Brown before, so she said that Victoria Brown was her business name, and Franny accepted her explanation without batting an eye. It flashed through Victoria's mind that the reason Franny seemed so unfazed by the new information might be that she had never quite believed her previous accounts of herself, but she rejected the idea as implausible. Then Hughes came down, and he also knew of her great-grandfather. Amanda thought she had read something about him in the New York Times, and even the Parisian bitch, when she showed up an hour later, said that she had seen an exhibition of his work at a Parisian gallery. Just like that, Victoria was famous.

No one mentioned the fact that James McWorruster had been black, which automatically made Victoria black as well, according to the "one drop of blood" theory that Victoria had always rejected. Her mother, who was half-black, had looked vaguely Mexican. Victoria herself could pass for Jewish when it suited her. But she wondered how Aunt Emilie looked, and whether that caused problems in her village. Then she remembered that the French did not believe in the one drop theory either. And the old lady definitely sounded pure French. That's how Victoria intended to sound as quickly as possible.

They looked up SNCF schedules on the Internet and found a train that left from Avignon at 15:53, connecting at Dijon with another train that went to Troyes. After that she would have to take a taxi to Godoy. Franny asked her if she needed some cash for the trip, but she still had her one hundred dollar bill, and she decided that now was the time to spend it. So Franny left her to her packing and went out after Hughes. She was supposed to come back in time to drive her to the train station.

But Victoria preferred to slip out alone. For one, she wasn't comfortable with goodbyes, especially from people she liked, and she had to admit that she liked Franny. In fact, she liked all the people at the chateau. They had been nice to her without expecting anything in exchange (you couldn't count the few hours of cooking, cleaning and babysitting as payment for her room and board, as everyone had chipped in for the various chores). And even though they had much more money and education than she had, they had never made her feel like a pariah. But Franny, Franny was like a sister. It was not even the things she had done, it was not that they had much in common, it was just a feeling, and it seemed to come from the same parts of her mind that had remembered her great-grandfather's drawing. For now, she was willing to trust it.

Most importantly, she did not want to be around when the butterfly catcher was found back in its place in the curio cabinet. For after mulling over the issue at length, she had decided that putting it back was the only thing to do. Whether it was worth a lot or it was worth nothing, she would never know. But she did know that she was no longer a free agent. She had a family, a home, a reputation to uphold, an inheritance to deserve, friendships to keep, all things that were incompatible with theft. She couldn't think of one self-help maxim that would support her decision to give up potential monetary gains in favor of immediate respectability, but then, instead, an old proverb came back to her: A bird in the bush ... no ... how did it go again? A bird in the hand is worth two in the bush. It was not exactly the kind of wisdom that guided entrepreneurs, but it would do.

Victoria sighed, tore herself away from the balustrade. It did not take her long to restore the wind-up toy to its rightful place, as she had left the casters under the legs of the cabinet, and as the back board was held with duct tape. Afterwards, as a parting gift, she vacuumed and dusted the entire second floor, and left her tie-dye dress on Franny's bed with a note explaining that she couldn't face saying *adieu*. She put the note in the envelope, then took it out again and wrote Aunt Emilie's phone number at the bottom.

She was standing in the hallway with her backpack and her guitar at her feet, thumbing the phone directory in search of a taxicab company, when Phil appeared at the door. She told him her news, and he offered to drive her all the way to Godoy. He was getting bored staying in one place, and a long drive with the top down on the Alfa Romeo was just what he needed to cheer up. Victoria gracefully accepted, and half an hour later they were zooming north along the autoroute.

Meanwhile, through routers and switches and servers and fiber optic cables, the following message was making its way across the Atlantic:

From: Grissom & Gross–Auctions & Appraisals
To: Victory01@hotmail.com
Subject: Re: What is it?

We apologize for the delay in answering your query. We have been extremely busy dealing with shipping problems resulting from security measures taken after the recent terrorist attacks.

We are very interested in taking a closer look at the item you described in your message. It is of course impossible to appraise an object over the Internet, but from the information you provided, we think it conceivable that it might be the work of Pierre Stevenard, one of the most famous creators of miniature automata in the nineteenth century.

Authentication will be a complex task, as very little documentation exists regarding Stevenard's creations. But assuming the piece is an original, and in working order (you do not mention that it produces any music, which would be unusual) it might fetch up to $1 million at auction.

Please contact our office at the number listed below for further information. We can arrange for wrapping and shipping services anywhere in the United States. We will be very happy to dispose of the object for you. Our auctions are advertised on the Internet and will give you access to the widest range of buyers.

The message was never retrieved and eventually got deleted from the Hotmail server. By then Victoria was firmly established in Godoy, surrounded by many other art objects that she would inherit within a few years.

CHAPTER 20

▼

CHATEAUX EN ESPAGNE

(Castles in Spain)

When Franny returned from the vineyard around one PM, she was struck by how deserted, how suddenly forbidding the chateau looked. The garden furniture, the badminton net, all the kids' toys had disappeared from the terrace, probably put away by Hughes as rain had been forecast, but still the bare gravel looked bleak. More surprisingly, the front door was closed, and so were all the windows, their small panes at odds in their rippling reflections of an uncertain sky, shards of dishwater gray, sooty blue, taupe, drab, ecru, scattered as in a kaleidoscope, mutely declining to come to a consensus on the weather. Without the relief provided by sun shadows, the yellow façade itself, ordinarily so cheerful with its creamy stone framings and lavender shutters, seemed massively indifferent, like a sentinel barring access to a place you had no right to stand in front of, let alone enter. Franny tried the door handle, and found that the door was locked. For a second, she felt as if the last two and a half weeks had been a dream, and she was only now arriving from a long disorienting journey at a destination not of her own choosing.

"Victoria?" she called out, her voice dampened by the porch overhang. Nothing moved inside. She stepped back a few steps and called again: "Victoria? ... Victoria!" This time she was pleasantly surprised by how powerfully her cry had rung out. Still there was no answer. At last, she remembered to check the urn on the left of the stairs to the garden, which was the designated hiding place for the key. Standing on tiptoe and cursing her small stature, she rooted blindly around the dirt that filled the urn, finding olive pits, cigarette butts, a balled up paper towel, something furry and squishy that she preferred not to identify, and at last the bunch of keys. She checked her watch. Where had Victoria gone, and how, so close to the time when they were supposed to leave for the train station?

She ran upstairs to Victoria's bedroom, where she found the bed stripped, the armoire doors wide open, the backpack and guitar gone, the nightstand and dresser tops free of lotions and potions, earrings and bangles, scarves, hair ties, maps, brochures, sketchbooks, pencil rubbings, oddly angled polaroids of inanimate objects, jam jars full of colored sands, all of Victoria's mysterious bric-a-brac, without which the room looked suddenly so bare than an awful thought flashed through Franny's mind: what if her protégé had decamped after stealing something?

From the beginning, there had been inconsistencies and implausibilities in the stories she had told of herself, all the way to her miraculous discovery of a famous French relative this very morning, which was the story that Franny was most skeptical about, but until now she had interpreted it as a white lie—the gypsy girl's way of accounting for her decision to move on without hurting her hosts' feelings or arousing their concern. Franny thought she had met people like her in the past, although she could not name one, people with no instinct for the truth, who lied spontaneously, not to defraud, but merely to please, to get by, to fit in; people who probably lied to themselves with the same innocence as they lied to others, who lied as much in their self-presentation as through their words, either by taking on the color of their immediate environment or by emulating distant idols. Too benign and too transparent to be called sociopaths, but too gifted to be seen as simply pathetic—the kind of people who seemed to have missed the boat of opportunity by only a few inches, thereby reminding you of the essential unfairness of life. In the end they did manage to endear themselves, half through their real qualities (charm, talent, helpfulness, adaptability), of which they seemed to be unconscious, and half because you felt compassion for their very clumsiness at lying—which they did not seem to recognize either. Or did they? Did they in fact intend to inspire pity, and was that just a means to more devious ends?

How would Franny even know if she had stolen something? Whatever it was must be small. The kind of robbers who used moving trucks would have left more traces of their passage. Besides, according to Hughes, none of the furniture on display was of much value, mostly cheap copies of Louis XV, XVI, and

Empire styles bought haphazardly at *brocanteurs* by a succession of owners for whom the chateau had only been a secondary residence. The few very nice pieces had been shipped back from Algeria by Uncle Freddie, to whom Hughes owed his inheritance. They were Art Deco chairs, consoles, side tables in rare woods, all safely stored in the attic, as Franny has observed the day before while looking for props and costumes for the play. Oh! no! Victoria had been there too! And Héloïse had probably showed her where the key was kept.

Franny ran into the house, skidding on floor tiles and banging her elbows in door jambs. With a trembling hand, she opened the drawer of the dining room buffet. The key was there, in a cigar box, behind napkin rings and candles and decorated toothpicks. She ran up the two flights of service stairs, fumbled with the key in the attic lock, struggled with the door, finally managed to get it open. The first thing she saw was one of the Art Deco chairs. The others were there too, and the side table, the console and all the other furniture, looking startled by her intrusion among their dusty stillness, and frankly shocked at her suspicions. She closed the door, locked it, tried the door again for good measure. What else? The curio cabinet on the mezzanine, the bookcase in the billiard room. No, those were intact too, their doors safely locked, their unbroken glass front revealing the same arrangement of toys and dusty books. Just to be sure she hadn't overlooked anything, she retraced her steps slowly through the entire house, and found everything in order, or in the case of the Fischbeins' suite, in its usual state of disorder, including Amanda's engagement ring in a glass and Chuck's golf clubs on a bergère. In Isaac's bedroom, jammed between the baseboard and the bed, she even spotted the lost Game Boy, which she decided to leave where it was. The kid would have plenty of time to be enraptured by electronic gadgets back in Berkeley.

She had kept her own room for last, figuring she didn't have anything worth stealing except for a few hundred Francs that Victoria had refused to take anyway. There she found the bubble dress and a letter, calligraphed on the reverse side of a lovely sketch of the bench in the retaining wall, the smooth texture of its river stones rendered in exquisite shading, against which a rose bush stood out delicately, its flowers merely suggested in white space, but their shape so precise, so dynamic, that the eye separated every petal. Even if the skill of the drawing, or the strange intuition that had caused the artist to select as its subject the spot dearest to its recipient, even if those things had failed to convince Franny, the phone number scribbled at the bottom of the letter would have done the job. Victoria had not lied after all. She really was the great-granddaughter of James McWorruster, and Franny felt like a heel for having slandered her in her heart.

She went back over the last two weeks, recalling all the times she had dismissed, evaded or pitied the L.A. waif. Was she just as much of a snob as Amanda? And had Victoria sensed her veiled disrespect? Poor Victoria, who, for all her spacey, disjointed personality, had been such a good sport (from the evidence of cross-hatch patterns in the rugs, she even seemed to have vacuumed the entire second floor before leaving), who had only expressed positive feelings, who had unmistakably liked and admired her, who had bequeathed her a slinky dress. How disappointed Franny's father would be if he knew of her condescending attitude, he who believed in universal brotherhood! It was the kind of thoughts you could not sustain for long, and Franny took comfort in the fact that Victoria wasn't in fact "poor" at all. She had a family, a place to stay, maybe even a fortune waiting for her. No permanent harm had been done.

She looked again at the card, noticing a postscript, wrapped around the edges of the main message, and terminated by a smiley face, in which Victoria informed her of Phil's decision to drive her up to Godoy. She lay the card flat at the bottom of her suitcase, where it joined a similar note from Clarisse, slipped under her door sometime before Christiane's arrival that morning. "I enjoyed to speak with you. The play was fun. Please take care of my father for me," it said in magenta ink. And it concluded with "North winds", a queer expression Franny took some time to decipher, finally realizing that it was the wrong translation for "bises"– was it possible that her English curriculum did not include the word "kiss"? In her mother's presence Clarisse had merely shaken hands with everyone, but then Amanda had given her a big hug anyway.

Suddenly Franny was alone, and with several hours to kill before Hughes came back after dropping the last load of grapes at the cooperative. She had been so constantly busy, so constantly surrounded by people in the last week that she had forgotten her first few days of ecstatic solitude. She had not had time to commune with nature, nor to feel oppressed by the chateau's vastness and antiquity. She had not shed tears once. It was as if she had had separate vacations in two different places, and she couldn't tell which one she preferred.

She longed to go for a walk, to reconnect with the landscape she had fallen in love with even before she knew of Hughes' existence. But the weather was unpropitious. A thunder storm was announced; it was no time to wander around the countryside acting as a human lightning rod. Instead she toured the house again, this time leisurely, stopping in every room to assess her feelings about it. At least, her silly fairy tale imaginings had been dispelled by familiarity. She had unlocked every door, inspected every nook and cranny. She had met the landlord and he was no Blue Beard. There were no secrets, no black magic, no ghost, only many accumulated layers of history, some known, some unknown. The cellar with its crossed vaults dated from the Knight Templars, the ruined chapel from the sixteenth century, the rest of the building from Napoleon's time; the west wing's second floor had been remodeled by Christiane. The garden had evolved beyond the reach of passed-down memories.

To Hughes, the place and all its objects was just a given, kept intact more out of duty and pride than emotional or esthetic attachment. What he really loved was the land. But Franny was intensely affected by her environment. And without the bustle of a full array of guests, this house still made her feel blue. On the outside, the building was fine: well situated, with its back nestled against a butte, and its front wide open to the valley; fairly modest in size, simply designed, its austere symmetry relieved by the shallow arches above door and windows and its pastel color scheme. Even the flaking paint on the shutters and discolored patches of stucco on the walls merely conferred it a charming patina. But inside was another matter. Inside it was just too big, too dark, too fusty, too cold, even now, when the thermometer in the kitchen registered twenty-two degrees Celsius (about seventy degrees Fahrenheit, Franny translated mentally, although she no longer needed to), which in Berkeley would have sent you outside in your shorts and tee-shirt, so there was something more to this cold feeling than objective temperature. It seemed to emanate from those massive stone walls, through the plaster and wallpaper and wainscotting and drapes meant to make you forget about them, some tomb-like chill, powdery, moldy and crushing, that promised to be immune to central heating. But perhaps it was all psychological? She did not feel cold in the yellow bathroom, nor anywhere on the third floor, though there was an objective explanation for the latter: the ceilings being lower up there, there was less space to be warmed by sunlight, and additional heat was refracted down by the roof tiles. Otherwise the spot she liked best was the top of the stairs, from which she felt in firm command of a harmonious perspective of curved banister and fanning steps, the mezzanine below, with its bookcase and curio cabinet, and its upholstered bench under the small window opening onto a wall of green, figuring as a sort of aerie, a refuge in case midway down the stairs, you decided you did not feel up to going into society.

The staircase was the pure spirit of the house, lofty, benign, welcoming. Much of the rest, as far as Franny was concerned, was pretentious and ugly. She felt nearly heretical thinking this, but she really hated all that plush, all that damask and tapestry and gilding, all those clashing stripes, all those bowed chair legs, those narrow medallions of upholstery held by brass nails, those flower baskets and eagle talons and laurel wreaths and sea shells and bees that jumped at you from every piece of furniture or wallpaper with the same decorative obsessiveness as the cartoon characters stamped on goods manufactured for the kiddie market. Did Amanda really believe that she could improve the décor without first gutting it?

Gutting it was of course out of the question. Aside from the money issue, and aside from Hughes' attachment to the way things were, Franny had a horror of remodeling projects. Having been raised to respect objects to the extent that they embodied human labor, she could not understand how some of her friends went about demolishing perfectly serviceable kitchens just because the fashion in cabinet facings and countertops had changed. In her own rented duplex apartment, she had over the years engaged in surreptitious decorating, repainting a room here, adding a mirror there, laying rugs over worn out tiles or stained hardwood floors, replacing grungy drapes with roman shades. She liked her place, which was compact, bright, warm and safe. She had never had any real estate aspirations. And mostly this was fine with her. She felt that she was living in accordance with her values and with family traditions, her parents never having owned a home until they retired to Quebec the previous year. But sometimes she wondered at her lack of desire for material things. Was it some kind of repression, some kind of sacrificial bent, some flight from happiness? The fact that the wondering drew tears in her eyes seemed like a clue. (Ah! the tears were back. Why?) Still, her values held.

So wouldn't it be ironic if she ended up living in a chateau? The only way she could stomach it would be if she had to share it with other people at least some of the time. Couldn't they transform the place into some kind of bed and breakfast or *gîte rural*, so that Hughes (and herself?) wouldn't have to exile himself (themselves?) to the cabanon every summer? Better yet, the French equivalent of a dude ranch, as she had jokingly proposed earlier. An elegant resort where people would spend their leisure doing farm work and their kids could connect with nature for the first time. Chicken coops, a bigger vegetable garden. Cherry picking, apricot picking, grape, olives. There would be stuff to do for half the year. A mixture of French and American guests to foster cultural understanding. Perhaps some scholarships so that working class families could experience luxurious living for a change? A worthy tax deductible charity for Chuck, and some useful occupation for his society wife. Pétanque, amateur concerts and plays in the evening. And a pond, maybe. Would Franny be up for it? She thought she would.

Still unthreateningly poised between the status of a fantasy and that of a plan, the idea energized her. She strode purposefully into the parlor, trying to see it with Amanda's eyes. She noticed how the furniture stood at attention along the walls, leaving a desert of floor in the middle, how the paintings were too evenly spaced, how the collection of knickknacks on the mantel piece looked like a Salvation Army display. Groupings, she thought, wasn't that what they advised in the Chronicle Home section? She had no idea how to go about it, but Amanda would. Still there was the darkness, restful on a hot summer afternoon, when entering the house was like immersing yourself in a cool bath, but despair inducing at any other time, like now, with the sky cut into solid gray squares against the window panes. It was definitely going to rain, she realized. She thought of Hughes and his crew, and all the other farmers working invisibly in the surrounding vineyards, hoping they wouldn't get soaked. In a gesture meant to give her wish more room to fly forth, her hands pushed back the drapes on both sides of the window. Something fluttered at her back. She turned around, letting go of the drapes, and caught a glimpse of rose light on the far wall, immediately snuffed out into the usual dull burgundy. She pushed the drapes back again, and the rose tone reappeared, this time echoed in the border of the rug. Ah! changing the mood of the place was just a matter of letting in more light. She was considering looking for a ladder to test her theory by taking down the drapes when she heard a loud plink on the window, more like gunshot than a splatter of rain. And then suddenly it was like machine gun fire. Hail, grape-sized balls of ice pounding the ancient glass, bouncing off the window sill, knocking leaves off the acacia trees, and finally drowning everything else in white noise. Without one conscious thought, Franny found herself deliberately turning the window handle, pulling the casements open, and bending out in the roaring downpour to pull the shutters closed, then repeating the process with every window on the ground floor, then the second floor. She was climbing the back stairs to the third floor when the hail storm stopped as suddenly as it had started. Not one window pane had been broken, thank God! Her knees still trembling, she returned downstairs and looked out through the door glass. The ground was covered with hail stones and stray leaves, but otherwise there was no visible damage. It wasn't even raining to speak of. As quickly as the storm had come and gone, her dread gave way to exhilaration. What a strange occurrence, and how well she had reacted, considering that hail storms in Berkeley were practically unknown. She was as proud of herself as if she had slain a dragon. A few minutes later, as she was undressing in the yellow bathroom to take a shower, she felt a lump in the pocket of her overalls. It was a hail stone, still intact, a tooth from the dragon … Oh! well, her imagination was apparently never going to give up fairy tales.

She had taken a shower and changed into a peasant dress with a row of buttons down the front, pinned her hair up into a French twist, put on some mascara. She had found a copy of *Le rouge et le noir* on the bookshelves in the mezzanine, had curled up on the bench, read a few pages. Her mind had wandered off. The phone had rung. It was only Amanda, announcing that they were staying in the Camargue overnight, but would return in time for the *diner des vendanges* in Saint Yves the next day. And upon hearing that Phil had left with Victoria, "So you guys are on your own tonight", she said with evident satisfaction but no trace of surprise, genially adding: "My best wishes, Honey!" Franny felt herself blush into the receiver, as the prospect of complete privacy rose before her for the first time, and as it occurred to her that she probably owed it to Amanda's social engineering. "Thank you!" she said, a little primly, she feared, but truly thankful all the same. She normally hated to have her private life exposed to prying eyes, but in this case she found it impossible to resent Amanda for her successful interference, or to deny her the pleasure of vicarious romantic expectations. She realized that it was the first time she had been courted in public, and acknowledged that this exposure to the sanction of society may be a good thing, that it may throw a sort of safety net under a new relationship, insuring a minimum of seriousness and suitability. She thought again of the old practice of bundling, of matchmakers, of the social scrutiny trained on lovers in the novels of Jane Austen, and what had previously felt as unbearably oppressive now seemed eminently reasonable. At the end of her thirties, was she turning conservative?

She went back to Stendhal, where it was all illicit romances. Julien Sorel seemed less a hero now than a psychiatric case, but Mme de Rênal was as good as ever. Somewhere in the house, a clock she had never noticed before ticktocked relentlessly. Yellow parallelograms appeared and disappeared on the floor. She got pins and needles in her legs. Where was Hughes? Waiting, that essentially feminine activity, was getting on her nerves. Would it always be so? Was that the price to pay for love, submission to time as a preamble for submission to a man? Her instinct said yes. Her instinct said that no matter how hard we fought for gender equality and reciprocity, there would remain this power imbalance, bound to the core of erotic feelings. But some women, through some quirk of nature or nurture not necessarily apparent, and quite compatible with the most irreproachable heterosexuality, simply couldn't live with it. She suspected she was one of those women, and that all her grievances against men were a cover for that knowledge. She felt like fleeing but knew she wouldn't. Her attraction to Hughes was just too strong, it was the chain that would enslave her ... that and the sanction of society.

Well, how about a drive to Saint Yves? One thing modern women had going for them was their own vehicles. Buy something for dinner, stop by the cooperative, see the preparations for the *fête des vendanges*. If she got lucky, when she got home Hughes would be waiting for *her*.

She checked the fridge, grabbed her denim jacket, stepped out onto the porch, and was greeted by a great heavenly fair. Clouds of every color and description were rioting across the sky, flat-bottomed ones with the kneaded look of dough, tall ones shooting up like rockets; others unfurling like banners, fraying like cotton-candy, puffing themselves up, duking it out with each other, embracing, melting away; and everywhere blue was breaking out in applause, and again there was that beloved clang of wind in the air.

On the square in Saint Yves, a bandstand was being assembled out of aluminum tubing and slabs of padded plywood, and boxes of fireworks were being unloaded from a truck, to the apparent indifference of a cluster of teens dangling their legs from the retaining wall. Other villagers were similarly minding their own business, walking little dogs, carrying loaves of bread, drinking *panachés* at the terrace of the one café. In front of the church, its doors gaping on a seductive dimness (why was dimness seductive in a church, but not in a house?), the curate was checking his watch against the clock in the belfry with the impatience of a Wall Street trader. A fat woman in a square black graduation type cap, and a flimsy purple cape over a gold tunic, was toddling as fast as she could along the street, holding on to the hat, the folds of the tunic getting caught between her legs. From opposite directions two similarly clad men, their capes billowing behind them, and a third one dressed in a gold toga and crowned with vine leaves, were leisurely converging toward the church, joshing amicably. Underneath their costumes, they all wore jeans and sneakers. They were assembling for some kind of religious procession that was to open the harvest festivities, though they didn't seem at all in a religious mood. They must be members of the local *Confrèrie Bachique* founded only a few years before, whose goal was to promote the wines of the region while giving its adherents a pretext for getting happily soused. Later that evening, they were to conduct an induction ceremony for the director of the nuclear plant that Hughes was supposed to attend. Hopefully, they did not expect the event to draw a lot of tourist trade, as Franny couldn't see any sign of a gathering crowd.

Hughes's tractor was not among those waiting in line to drop their loads of grapes into the underground crusher. Had he already left? Or was the tractor overturned on some muddy lane, grapes spilled into a ditch and its driver crushed under the wheels? Wasn't that what happened when you counted your chickens before they hatched, as she had done with her dude ranch fantasy? She hadn't even slept with the guy for God's sake! In a way, if he were to die, he might as well do it now, before the last rampart of her independence was blown to pieces. She would go back to Berkeley, her technical writing job, her contemplative life. She would be spared making decisions. Ah! she was even more pessimistic than La Fontaine, who in his cruel wisdom, had spilled the milk but spared the milk-maid. After all, hadn't he himself conceded:

"Quel esprit ne bat la campagne?
Qui ne fait de chateaux en Espagne?"

And her castle in France was pretty modest, wasn't it? If there was a God, it was blasphemous to think that He could be that jealous of a small wish for earthly happiness. If there wasn't, then no one had witnessed her fit of hubris. She was falling prey to hysterical superstition, as usual. Or megalomania, if you looked at it another way: the belief that her thoughts had a life and death power over another human being. It was ridiculous, and she was going to stop worrying right this minute, even though her heart seemed to be caught in a vise and her legs felt like rubber.

She ducked into the tobacco shop to buy *Le Monde*. The tobacconist was out-side rearranging his display of postcards, whistling *La Vie en Rose* under his breath, like a sarcastic comment on her morbid visions. The coincidence nearly made her burst out laughing.

"Alors, Mademoiselle Franny, les vacances tirent à la fin?" he asked, strolling back toward the counter after straightening a pile of lavender fields and finding the right slot in the carousel for a view of the Mont Ventoux. He was about the same age as Guillaume, dressed casually, but with a certain commercial glaze over his features that made him look older. Like Guillaume, his southern accent was undetectable to Franny. The influence of schooling, or TV?

"Pas tout à fait," she answered, laying a ten Franc bill on the glass money tray.

"Eh bien, vous avez de la chance alors. Parce que chez vous, les vacances, c'est normalement deux ou trois semaines, non?"

He was taunting her with the superiority of French social benefits, no doubt. For a second, she felt like defending her country. But what was the use? Besides, on this issue of paid vacation he happened to be right. In fact, even in this little village, people seemed exquisitely well informed about every failing of American society, and did not hesitate to stick them in your face. In the last couple of weeks, she had run into several people who had spent time in the US, and what seemed to have galled them most was the restrictions imposed by homeowners' associations on the rights of individuals to decorate and garden as they pleased. Which was funny, considering that Franny herself had never been confronted with this type of problem, and given the religious fervor the French exhibited for the safeguard of their own landscape, individual rights be damned. What was even more funny was that even though Franny had voiced many of their criticisms back home, here she kept having the patriotic reflex of wanting to rebut them. It was the same type of reaction you would have if a friend made the mistake of echoing your putdowns of your family. Silly, but deeply ingrained. How much of a problem would it be were she to become an expatriate? For now, it was just easier to pretend that no gauntlet had been thrown.

"Oui, mon patron est très compréhensif," she merely said.

"Et ça vous plait, comme ça, le Vaucluse?"

The question was banal, the local shopkeeper merely assessing the potential for repeat trade. But there was something insinuating in his tone, confirmed by the look he flashed at her from under his eyebrows as he counted out the change. He was making it clear that he knew her interest in the place had some personal component. How had he surmised this? Had Guillaume or Savia blabbed about her relationship with Hughes all over town? Were the natives discussing the couple around the dinner table? Were they making bets about their future? It was shocking, but it was also strangely encouraging. Again, the sanction of society. She was no longer an anonymous tourist, but Mademoiselle Franny, someone whose fate mattered in the local scheme of things. What the tobacconist was really asking was whether she was going to stay. And even if she sensed some murky motives to his curiosity, she was flattered by it, because it affirmed her importance. Of course, as she had already had a crisis over counting her chickens in private, she wasn't about to do it again publicly.

"Oui, c'est très joli, aussi beau que la Californie, dans un autre genre," she answered wickedly. But he wasn't quite defeated yet.

"Vous êtes inscrite au diner des vendanges, j'espère."

"Oui, bien sûr."

"Et vos amis les Fischbeins?" He knew their names too. Suddenly, she was reminded of Defarge, the sinister wine merchant in Tale of two Cities whose shop was the nexus of a spy ring. All that was missing was the knitting wife.

"Eux aussi."

"Et Monsieur Degency, bien entendu ..."

"Bien entendu."

Why was he even asking if they were going to the harvest dinner? She was sure that he had access to the registration list. He seemed, ingratiating as his manner was, to be on some kind of power trip. Hadn't Guillaume mentioned that he was on the city council, and that he was opposed to environmental policies? He must consider Hughes as his enemy then. Was he trying to get to him through her somehow? Ah! of course, internecine quarrels would be the flip side to the coziness of village life. But probably no worse than office politics. She would have to tell Hughes about this conversation. For now, interestingly, she felt more amused than scared.

"Eh bien, vous me ferez bien l'honneur d'une danse?" he asked, oilier than ever.

"Pourquoi pas?" she tossed back airily. "A demain donc." And she sauntered out of the shop with the newspaper under her arm.

She bought some lamb chops and merguez from the butcher's, then made a detour by the greengrocery to say hello to Guillaume. He was not surprised by the tobacconist's inquisitiveness but denied having been the source of his information on the goings on at the chateau, and Franny believed him. She finished her shopping trip at the bakery, where she found Savia behind the counter, looking so innocently shy that the idea of her being a gossip instantly became preposterous. Savia confirmed that Hughes had already brought his grapes to the cooperative. He must have started back toward the chateau just as Franny was parking her car.

There was happily no trace of an overturned tractor anywhere on the way home. Even as she scrutinized the pristine edges of the road, Franny was sensitive to a triumph of dappling effects over the entire panorama: damp stains burning off the tarmac in places, sycamore trunks mottled with absurd topographical precision, sunlit patches and rain funnels leap-frogging randomly across the hills. It was good to see nature doing its thing, completely oblivious to human meanings.

The Mercedes was in the parking lot. Through a gap in the rotten barn door, a sliver of the red dump-bed was clearly visible. He was home.

He was home and playing the clarinet, the Brahms sonata again, this time with piano accompaniment. Who? Franny stopped on the stairs, clutching the iron railing, which felt so cold it set her teeth on edge. There was something tinny, scratchy about the piano sound, and it went on mechanically when the clarinet paused. Ah! it was just a record, one of those Music Minus One type of things. Her hand relaxed on the railing, and the music enveloped her. He was running through the third movement, leaning shamelessly into its dance hall lilt. She had never thought that Brahms could be that sexy. All the things she did not know about Hughes suddenly felt like a gift instead of a threat. She couldn't wait to start the unwrapping process, and at the same time she wished it to never end.

As she walked across the terrace, the music stopped completely. Had he heard her? Had he, while he played, kept an ear cocked for the telltale sound of her approach on the gravel? Was he as familiar with her step as she was with his?

Would he be able to describe it? Would he even admit that he could? The third movement started again. Of course, like any man, he would have barricaded himself in some totally engrossing activity against the vulnerability of anticipation. Still, he had pushed back the shutters in the music room, and the window was ajar.

But how lovely to enter a house alive with music! What a power it had, better than any decorator, to set everything to rights–to adjust the distances, mellow out the angles, enchant the shadows; to lighten your load and fill your cup. As she put the groceries away, Franny was fairly dancing. As long as he played, he was there, he was hers. And then somehow he was here, right behind her, his arms clasped around hers, the clarinet on the counter next to the loaf of bread, his hair damp against her neck. She hadn't heard the music stop. She was still in motion, and for a second she reflexively fought his embrace, mindful of the need to refrigerate the meat. Then abruptly, she let go of her housekeeping mode and relaxed against him. He didn't pull, he didn't grab, there was no franticness to it at all, his body simply molded itself to hers inch by inch until the several layers of fabric between them seemed to have dissolved. Franny recalled the little ode to French male beauty she had composed in her head upon seeing Hughes stand next to Chuck on their return from tennis the day before. Spooning. It was exactly what she had yearned for. They remained like this for an indeterminate amount of time, breathing in concert, completely enraptured by each other's feel and receptivity. At the core of this serene, mystical, supra-sexual trance, of course, was the tangibility of his erection against her lower back. Sooner or later, they both knew, they were going to have to attend to it (and to the reciprocal volcanic eruption in her corresponding parts). But for now they could not imagine a more satisfying position than the one they were in.

"Where have you been?" he said at last, shaking her from left to right ever so slightly, and with a hint of petulance in his voice that she found deeply gratifying.

"I'll give you three guesses," she answered, pointing to the package of meat, on which, per tradition, the butcher had added her purchases in pencil, scornful of the adding machine that languished on the counter.

"Looking for me. Chatting up the natives. Shopping for dinner. It doesn't look like there is enough meat for everyone though."

Even if he had spoken in jest, he was so dead on it was nearly humiliating. How could he be so smug to presume that she had gone looking for him, as if she was an eighteen year old virgin in love with her older, worldlier master, when she was barely five years younger than him, and by all accounts far ahead of him in worldliness (i.e. sexual experience)? She knew better than to rock the boat at this point, though. For one, his conjectures happened to be true. And for another, every woman knew that a man's potency depended on a certain amount of smugness. That was the root of inequality: you had to hand him the power to humiliate you or risk his shriveling up. The question was, was there anything beyond that primal "dance" (the kind of "dance" you performed by walking on hot coals)? He had led her to believe there might be. But even if he hadn't, she might be exactly in the same place, glued to him like jam on a slice of bread.

"What a good detective you are! As a matter of fact, everyone has deserted us. Tonight it's just you and me."

"Par exemple! Et que nous vaut cette désertion inesperée?"

Franny went about recapping the day's happenings, but he was barely listening to her. While she talked, he had slipped his arms under hers, and was running his hands exploratorily over her dress, taking particular note of the row of buttons.

"Hmm," he said, "what would you think of going to bed early?"

"Like when?"

"Like now …"

"Don't you have to go that drinking club meeting in a few minutes?"

"I am afraid I am going to be unavoidably detained."

"What about the future of the Côtes du Rhone?"

"The Côtes du Rhones can take care of themselves."

"You're sure?"

"Hmm …"

She tried to turn around to face him, but he had her pinned to him so tightly that she could barely crane her neck to verify that the head on her shoulder was his. Thus holding her, he started piloting her toward the stairs. It was a mystery how they got to the second floor without ever breaking contact, but somehow they found themselves in the middle of the west wing corridor, still attached from neck to knees.

"Here I get to show my mastery of idiomatic English," he joked, though his voice sounded a little hoarse. "Your place or mine?"

"You've rehearsed that sentence, haven't you?"

"Hmm …"

"Well, let's see."

So they hobbled, sack race-like, to Franny's doorway.

"Too noisy," she said, referring to the rickety iron bed frame.

"And too virginal," he added. "I would start thinking I am a satyr." They hobbled across the hall to Hughes' study.

"Too narrow," he said. Indeed the sleeping accommodations in there were limited to a sort of imperial daybed.

"And too business-like. I would start thinking I am your secretary."

"Let us think then."

He opened his arms and she was at last able to look at him. He did not have any big pimple or gash on his face as she had started to suspect. On the contrary he was freshly scrubbed and shaved, comb marks still visible in his damp hair. His eyes seemed opaque though, his cheeks a little more sunken. A vein beat against his temple. Was he scared? Suddenly Franny was quite satisfied to be a woman. She put her arms around his back and pressed herself against him, delighting in the firm ridges on each side of his spine. They now had full frontal contact. The fit wasn't as good: her breasts were in the way (more a problem for her than for him, obviously), and there were concavities around both of their solar plexi. On the other hand they could kiss.

"Equal time," she said, noticing that her voice was hoarse too. They kissed. They had had quite a bit of practice in the last week, and practice makes perfect. There was still the same leisureliness, the same mutual attuning, the same impro-visational play of call and response. While kissing they were peers. But now that they did not have to stop, they kissed with growing abandon. At first it felt like a conduit of emotional expression, a manifestation of soul, kissing as a quintessen-tially ethical act, the fullest recognition of the other's personhood. What was interesting though was how quickly, without any effort at choreographing the scene, without even a sense of conscious volition, as all they were conscious of at that moment was the desire to kiss forever, how quickly soulfulness descended into pure lust. Lust, as impatient with personhood as it is with clothing, and quite scornful of parity, was not satisfied with closeness, but demanded penetra-tion. And lust was all right too.

"Well, what do you think?"

"Would it turn you off if we went into the master bedroom? If it's any help, I haven't slept there in three years."

"At this point, nothing would turn me off. But what about you?"

"Nothing would turn me off."

"We'll have to make the bed."

"Of course. Comme on fait son lit, on se couche …"

"Let's smooth those sheets then. Let's make hospital corners."

"Let's."

But first they kissed again to give themselves strength. By the time they pulled apart her dress was held together by one solitary button, her hair was undone and his shirt was completely loose. They went to the linen closet, out of the bottom of which Hughes insisted on retrieving the best pair of linen sheets and matching pillow cases, part of Aunt Giselle's *trousseau*. They made the bed: bottom sheet, not fitted, extremely heavy, unfurling over Franny's head with a snap like a sail and a shower of lavender seeds, pull it, no, give some back, I can't tuck in it on this side, hospital corners, remember, how is that done? heck if I know; top sheet, another sail, let me help you, no, no, we'll never get done, tucked in only at the bottom; coverlet, also tucked in, top sheet turned down over it with the embroidery displayed just so, pillow cases, where is the other pillow, ah! here on the floor, how is that? Perfect! Come over here.

They made their bed and lay in it.

Dinner time came and went, the lamb chops remained on the kitchen counter. They had talked about going to Saint Yves to watch the fireworks that were supposed to be shot along the river at ten, weather permitting. Inwardly they both prayed: let it rain, let it rain. It rained on and off, as far as they could tell by the pattering sounds that occasionally registered on their consciousness. At ten the fireworks went off anyway, but all they saw of it, thanks to Hughes having partially opened the shutters, were intermittent glows highlighting in blue the pit of a navel, in red the curve of a hip. From the tender, through the exploratory, the feverish, the deliberate, all the way to the inescapable, the stages of passion blended into one another seamlessly. In between they chatted as they had always done, with the additional ease and fearlessness that only the horizontal position can confer. They did not talk about sex, though, sex being one topic where few people become truly bilingual. The little English vocabulary Hughes knew in that area seemed too clinical to him, and Franny, who had only had one other French lover, thought the few words she knew sounded dirty. Eventually they would develop their own argot, and it would be mostly French. Eventually, because of the demands of daily life, their entire conversation would be carried on in the local language, except when they talked about their relationship, when English would continue to prevail.

They did not talk about sex but they thought about it, afterwards, as they fell asleep in the entangled sheets, and as they woke up fitfully through the night, and as a new day shone on the awesomeness of their situation.

Who would have guessed (but he must have, in some mysterious fashion) that this neat, demure, tightly-wound little person could be such a ball of fire in bed? he marveled, gazing at her face on the pillow. Her body an incarnation of her temperament: athletic (the martial arts training …), combustible, but still wonderfully pliable, with softness and gravity in all the right places. Asleep she looked tense again, her eyelids taut, the straight lashes quivering, the bridge of her nose crinkled, as if she had to fight to keep her eyes closed. Was she dreaming? What did she dream about? He felt as if he was still inside her, but also as if he was standing shyly at her door step. He was suddenly grateful for his divorce, for the chance to fully experience again this tantalizing mixture of knowing and not knowing. It would remain a mixture, he guessed. He was never going to get Franny's complete score, any more than he had fathomed Christiane's. The tantalizing effect would diminish, but hopefully the flats and quavers would continue to strike his heart as pleasing. Hopefully she would continue to like his music too. In any case he was ready to make room for her in his life. He had spent three years in the wilderness, he had atoned for whatever sins of inattention he may have committed. He had returned home, thanks to her. He would try to sin no more.

She was hooked, it was clear. Just the heat of his thigh against hers, the tickling of his breath upon her eyelashes, the dent of his elbow in the bolster were enough to throw her into a rage of desire. He must be watching her sleep, how nice! She itched to grab his face, to kiss his lips, to push back the covers and let him do whatever he might please, and God knew there were many things he was pleased to do, and how much what pleased him pleased her. More than attentive, more than skillful, inspired was what he was. She hoped it had something to do with her, but she was not naïve enough to believe it was all her doing. She was going to have to revise her theories about sexual experience. Maybe duration counted as much as variety. How could Christiane have let that go? It was so sweet of him to have worried about taking her into the ex-conjugal bed. But she didn't mind one bit. Whatever he had learned with other women was of use to her right now. And right now, he was hers, it was amazing how confident she felt about this.

Of course, sex wasn't everything. But hadn't they already established that the other basic compatibilities were there? He seemed to think so. It wasn't even the "Ah! tu me plais. Tu me plais profondément!" he had let go of last night that had convinced her of his seriousness. That could have been pure sexual ardor talking. It was when he had touted the winters in Saint Yves, when in between pruning and replanting, he claimed, there would be plenty of time to lie around, take trips to Paris, fix up the house, play music, lie around. (Did he realize he had listed lying around twice? Yes, he did. What about the girls? Yes, of course, the girls would be there for the holidays. It could be fun, no? And there would still be plenty of time to lie around.)

He hadn't mentioned anything about her having to find work. But there was no way she was going to be a kept woman. For one, he could hardly afford it. And for another, she was already feeling slavish enough toward him without also depending on him for money. But who talks about working in a foreign country talks about work permit, green card, or whatever the equivalent was here, in other words marriage. Ugh! Perhaps she could arrange with her boss some kind of tele-commuting arrangement. A lot of her work these days involved setting up web sites anyway. She was going to check into it in a week, if all continued well. (There, God! No hubris!)

Having come up with a plan, she relaxed back into a sensual mode, trying to define the quality of his physical persona the way you would analyze a wine. His skin: taut, dry, hot. Mostly mineral. Limestone, iron, salt. His breath, herbal, rosemary or thyme, until he got turned on, and then there was a heavier note, musky, peppery. She could smell it now. Ah! she had played possum long enough.

She opened her eyes, already smiling. He was smiling too. She grabbed his face, kissed his mouth, and pushed the covers back to let him do as he pleased.

CHAPTER 21

▼

IT TAKES A FRENCH VILLAGE

(Il faut un village)

It was Chuck and Amanda's turn to find the look of the chateau odd on their return from the Camargue on Sunday afternoon. Again the door was closed, and this time most of the windows were tightly shuttered, except for those in the music room and kitchen, and the smaller ones on the third floor. But their nerves being steadier than Franny's, they did not see the oddity as ominous. On the contrary, the blinkered façade struck them as somewhat rakish, half one-eyed pirate and half winking vamp. It is true that by then the sun had reappeared, lighting sequins on the still wet underside of the gravel on the terrace. They exchanged an amused glance, and Amanda held the children back while Chuck opened the door and bellowed: "Anyone home?"

A door slammed upstairs. Judging that the children's innocent eyes were probably safe, the Fischbeins proceeded to their suite to unload their luggage. On the way up, Amanda found a trail of hair pins on the steps. She picked one up and held it to Chuck with a triumphant look. Her plan had succeeded marvelously.

The twins were a little sad at the loss of their playmates, and a little disconcerted to discover that Victoria's old bedroom was now occupied by Hughes and Franny. But as their parents kept mum on the subject, except to warn them against barging in there as they had been in the habit of doing, they kept their conjectures to themselves. Isaac was of the opinion that they must have fought over who got the biggest bedroom, and that moving in together was the compromise they had hit upon. But Sarah, showing her superior maturity as a girl, told him that he was a dummy, that of course the reason Hughes and Franny had moved in together was that they had got married, but it was a secret wedding and so they were supposed to pretend they did not know about it. Soon after this conversation, Isaac found his lost Game Boy, and Sarah decided to put on a play with her Barbie dolls, but for both of them the rest of the vacation was anticlimactic. Fortunately, those last few days would vanish from their memory. Back in Berkeley, their glowing reports of their French friends and their new interest in nature would in no small part contribute to their parents' plans to put down roots in Saint Yves.

Or perhaps what clinched their decision was the harvest dinner that took place that evening. Earlier in the day there had been a small fair on the village square showcasing the products of local craftsmen: goat cheeses, lavender soaps, olive wood carvings, stained glass windows, Provençal fabrics, clocks with digitized cicada songs for alarms, re-editions of nineteenth century Masonic pamphlets. Franny's attention had been drawn to a wood panel etched with a whimsical map of the village as it had stood on the eve of the revolution of 1789, clustered at the foot of the old chateau, which was shown bristling with the usual allotment of towers and creneled walls, of which only the entrance arch, movingly recognizable with its drawbridge slits and flying buttresses, was still standing. In the corners of the map, various acts of revolutionary depredations were depicted: the burning of buildings, the arrest of the priest, the slaughter of villagers. It seemed like a tendentious piece of art, considering the veneration in which the revolution was generally held in France. Who would want to buy it? But according to Hughes, the revolution was in fact currently undergoing a revisionist assessment, which was probably a good thing, as it was time for mankind to delegitimize violence no matter how noble the ends. Franny heartily agreed, but what about Napoleon? Was the Empire also being reassessed for the great suffering it had caused in the name of spreading the values of the Enlightenment? Yes, Hughes believed the Empire was a fair target of criticism, even though it had made his ancestor's fortune.

The pair had run into the fair by chance, at the end of a hike they had taken right after breakfast through the hills. The walk had led them past the cabanon (where they finally talked about their first encounter), past the dovecote, through the quarry (where Franny recognized Victoria's colored sands), and down a side

street into the village, which they entered holding hands in view of all the villagers. And as the church bells were just ringing mass, celebrated out of turn in Saint
Yves because of the harvest holiday, they went in as if it had been their plan all
along. After mass they ambled through the fair, had a sandwich at the café, and
walked back along the main road. They napped until the Fischbeins' return.

By six o'clock, when the denizens of the chateau arrived en masse at the
square, the fair booths had been replaced by a long line of tables covered with
white paper cloths held with clothes pins. Metal folding chairs were ranged on
each side of the tables, and extra chairs were piled against the retaining wall of the
mediatheque. A caterer's van was parked under the sycamores, its open side
revealing hot plates and refrigerators, a huge open air grill next to it sending its
smoke all over town as an advertisement of the feast. The bandstand at the end of
the square was flanked with wine barrels, and random flowers in bud vases had
been placed at intervals along the tables, otherwise the decoration was nil. But as
soon as the diners started converging on the square, Amanda remembered that
having a good time around a meal was as matter of fact an affair here as vegging
out on the couch in front of the TV in the US. No props were needed.

About a hundred people eventually showed up, all except a handful of them
locals or friends of locals, the tourists being represented by the chateau's American guests and a Scandinavian looking male trio (father and sons?) from the
municipal campground. But not all the locals were French. The Welsh couple
who had bought the last remaining ruin in the village were there. He was a big
lumbering man with a shock of gray hair and a gentle, somewhat nerdy manner.
She was tiny, rotund, deeply tanned and creased, expansively jeweled and gaudily
dressed, her low cut dress showing off a very impressive cleavage for a woman in
her sixties. She seemed determined to outdo the French in Gallicness, and was
actually succeeding, as evidenced by the number of people who greeted her with
kisses on both cheeks as she wove her way through the crowd, leading her man
and rolling her R's with great gusto in both English and French. The pair had
spent the last twenty five summers traveling through France, and had finally
achieved their dream of retiring in Provence. They had nothing good to say about
the British, which probably accounted in no small measure for their popularity
with the French.

There was also an American couple originating from California. He was a
retired professor, slightly built, keen-eyed, and with the ruddy complexion that is
as good as a passport in a wine-growing region. She was quite a bit younger,
beautiful in the manner of a Byzantine icon in her flowing long dress. She was
still tethered to a teaching job in Ohio, which she loathed, but currently on sab-

batical. They had bought their house on the outskirt of the village many years ago and spent every summer here. They both spoke a very decent French as far as Amanda could tell, had the kissing routine down pat, and seemed to be considered honorary natives.

For the rest, a lot of seniors, some of the old men still wearing those caps with the embedded visor familiar from black and white postcards you found in toney stationery shops in Berkeley, their wives in small print dresses buttoned down the front, the fabric stretched to bursting around their thick waists. But also a fair number of young families, women in their twenties already with a couple of kids, svelte and sharp-faced, dressed in tight jeans and clinging tops, men who would have looked at home on a ranch in Montana, but more voluble. Hardly any teenager, probably off somewhere with their peers, determined not to be caught dead attending some hokey adult function. A kaleidoscope trained on the crowd would have displayed more black, red, purple patterns than back home, although here like there blue denim, khaki twill and white cotton jersey dominated. People presumably from all walks of life, but no indication of status differences. A community, thought Amanda, suddenly aware of how rarefied her social world had become. Thrillingly, many of the faces were already familiar to her.

She saw Guillaume, his arm around a ravishing young Asian woman, about whom, frustratingly, neither Hughes nor Franny knew anything. Gérard and Pierrette came by to introduce their daughter Chloé and a couple of nuclear plant workers. Then there was that sarcastic little man from the tobacco shop, his mousy wife and surly children in tow; the debonair postmaster; Hughes' farmhand Henri, leaning on his cane, chatting good-humoredly with the baker's son, Chérif, and petting the kid's Labrador puppy. Several vintners Chuck had met at the cooperative, ranging in age from twenty to eighty. The butcher, the grocer, and even the Arab baker, as dour looking as ever, impossible to connect such a face with bountiful bread and luscious pastries. Standing at his side, but a few inches back, his wife Savia, exuding enough shy sociability for two. Franny, bless her heart, was going to teach her to drive next week, which may not go over so well with the husband. (Weren't women in Saudi Arabia forced to use a chauffeur?)

"A table! A table!" the cry was relayed through the crowd.

People lined up in front of the caterer's van to pile their paper plates with boar stew, merguez, puffed potatoes, salade niçoise. Big loaves of organic *pain d'epaûtre* had been provided by Monsieur Hamzaoui, wine by the cooperative. And then everyone was seated, the kids relegated again to the end table, but this time, lured by Chérif's puppy, they made no complaint. By sheer coincidence, it seemed, Amanda found herself sitting next to the other American woman, Laurie, who turned out to be a treasure trove of information about local real estate, touristic attractions, quality crafts, four star restaurants, village gossip. Amanda got so absorbed in conversation that she missed the two most salient events of the evening, both having to do with the Hamzaoui family. She later comforted herself with the thought that without Franny and Hughes' explanations, she might have failed to comprehend their importance, but still, she regretted that her future tale of the *fête* would not be entirely an eyewitness account.

Event number one was that when the first toast was proposed, Monsieur Hamzaoui was observed to raise his wine glass, clink it against his neighbors', put it to his lips, and actually sip from it. According to Franny, a perceptible shiver propagated itself along the table. The Moslem baker had drunk wine! It took one second for the villagers to digest the sight. The next instant they were ribbing him about it, claiming they now understood why his bread tasted so good, offering to fill his glass again, and generally making themselves obnoxious in a good-natured way. And lo and behold, not only Monsieur Hamzaoui bore their sarcasm with great composure, but people swore his dour mien melted, and that by the end of the evening he was as tipsily mellow as the best of them.

And this may have explained the second event, which was that when Guillaume invited Savia to dance, Monsieur Hamzaoui did not object. The pair waltzed a few turns around the dance floor, Guillaume mugging while holding his partner chastely at arms' length, Savia blushing and chuckling behind her hand, her pencil-pleated skirt sashaying like a debutante's. She soon claimed dizziness and came back to sit demurely next to her husband, but the lesson was driven home: not only the Moslem baker drank wine, but he let other men handle his woman. These two facts did more than the Vicomte's patronage could ever have done to dissipate the villagers' prejudices against him. By the end of the week, every housewife in Saint Yves would be buying their bread at the bakery. A year from now, Patrick Malefoi would go out of his way to rally Hacene to the side of the Modernes. He would get a non-committal answer. It was rumored afterwards that the entire scene had been orchestrated by Guillaume (or by the Vicomte, according to other sources), that without prodding the Hamzaouis would not even have attended the harvest dinner. None of the principals ever confirmed the theory.

Amanda slow-danced with the postmaster. Franny let the tobacconist teach her to tango. Sarah practiced her ballet steps with a couple of little girls, and Isaac wrestled with Chérif's puppy. Hughes held court with other cooperative members, translating the debates for Chuck while necking with Franny shamelessly.

The band played on into the night, alternating accordion tunes with electric rock. Everyone got drunk from wine, food and noise. Everyone felt they belonged.

Alas, nothing lasts for ever. A few days later, the Fischbeins were on their way back to San Francisco. As the plane entered the layer of clouds above Charles De Gaulle, and the last piece of French land disappeared from view, the recent terrorist nightmare returned to Amanda's consciousness. It was ironic, though, that from her point of view, the September 11 attack had had positive consequences. Franny, stranded in France on her own, had found love. And because of that, the Fischbeins had become intimate with a French vintner, which in turn had opened new business and lifestyle opportunities. Should one then passively condone atrocities because they happened to have a silver lining, or worse, plan atrocities with the silver lining as a goal? No, it was unthinkable. There was talk in the Bush administration of going to war with Afghanistan in the name of the fight against terrorism, and as a side benefit to unseat the totalitarian rule of the Taliban. And after Afghanistan, Iraq, Iran, North Korea? Amanda promised herself that as soon as she was back in Berkeley, she would become involved in the peace movement.

Franny stayed. Her boss did retain her as a contractor for the time being, and soon she was translating French web sites into English. With Amanda and Chuck's support, she convinced Hughes to open the chateau as a *gîte rural bio* five months out of the year. Amanda volunteered herself as interior decorator, making several trips during the winter to oversee the remodeling efforts, during which the twins stayed home with Chuck. The next summer, the whole Fischbein clan were the first guests of the refurbished *gîte* while they looked for their own place to buy. By then francophilia had become somewhat of a risky political choice (though not in Berkeley, thank God), but the Fischbeins were not deterred.

Chuck formed a partnership with Hughes to buy and develop Monsieur Rosetti's land and to market the Chateau Degency wines in the US. He also took responsibility for getting the pond dug. He was determined to wean himself from the software business within a few years, and to become a full-time *vigneron*. The state of the hi-tech economy only strengthened his resolve.

Thanks to the growing ranks of environmental activists in the village, Gérard having enrolled several of his colleagues in the cause, the theme park plot was defeated. In the same vein, a municipal resolution was passed banning the open-field testing of genetically modified corn on Saint Yves territory. Alas, it was declared illegal a few months later, and testing continued, with unknown consequences as of this writing.

It was of course Héloise who noticed the return of the butterfly lady during the next Christmas vacation, which the girls spent at the chateau. The strange comings and goings of the toy were the object of some bemused speculation for a day or two on Hughes' and Franny's part, and then were forgotten, until the furniture in the mezzanine was pulled out to allow the walls to be repainted. The drilling work at the back of the curio cabinet was discovered, and speculations resumed. But as nothing in the end had been stolen, the matter was dropped again. Amanda did suggest that the contents of the chateau should be appraised, but between the additional work involved in the expansion of the vineyard and the easing of his financial difficulties, Hughes saw no immediate need to establish the exchange value of his *patrimoine*.

Imperceptibly, over the next year, Chérif became one of the chateau's habitués. He went on truffle hunting expeditions with Henri, became handy with paint brushes and pruning shears, occasionally even took the vacuum cleaner from his mother's hands. When the girls came back for a month in the summer, it seemed natural to see him hang out with them, or more exactly with Clarisse, Héloise's attention being focused on Pidou. Returning from the vineyard, Hughes more than once found the pair lying prone side by side on the lawn, their heads supported by their elbows, Clarisse earnestly pointing at something on the textbook in front of them while Chérif's eyes tracked the swaying of her braid. On rainy days, they could be heard practicing their English with the guests in the music room. They also spent a fair amount of time text-messaging each other. She was helping him with his school work, Clarisse had explained, an endeavor that met with her father and stepmother's complete approval.

Franny did have an occasion to make use of the phone number Victoria had left her, when the gypsy girl's travel diary was found in a nightstand drawer in the master bedroom, forgotten there in the haste of packing. Victoria was delighted to hear that her friend was living in Saint Yves and invited her to stay at her chateau in Godoy en Champagne whenever she pleased. She had no use for her travel diary, which represented a bygone part of her life. So Franny deposited it in the basket of postcards in the dining room, where it joined the Italian travel diary that had so moved her in her first few days in Saint Yves, and where it would stimulate the imagination of future visitors.

Glossary

Aumônerie	Catholic youth center attached to a school.
ANPE	Agence Nationale Pour L'emploi. French equivalent of EDD.
Babylon	Youth slang designating middleclass society
Bouvard & Pécuchet	Main characters of a novel by Gustave Flaubert. Symbols of mediocrity and stupidity.
Beur	Slang designation for children of North African immigrants.
Bouillie bordelaise	Organic pesticide.
Cabanon	Hut or cabin in southern France.
Céline, Louis Ferdinand	Major twentieth century novelist.
Consigne	Luggage room.
EDF	Electricité de France. State owned energy consortium.
ENA	Ecole Nationale d'Administration. Prestigious training ground for French politicians and executives.
FNAC	Fédération Nationale d'Achat des Cadres. Large store chain specializing in books, CDs, DVDs and electronic equipment.
Gawris	Youth slang designating the native French.
Harki	Algerian who fought on the French side during the Algerian war.
HLM	Habitation à Loyer Modéré. Subsidized housing project.

Jacques a dit	The game Simon says.
Kif	Hashish.
Les rêveries du promeneur solitaire	Book by Jean Jacques Rousseau.
Marcel	Youth slang designating the native French.
Médiathèque	Modern public library.
Métèque	derogatory term designating immigrants from parts other than northern Europe.
Noblesse d'Empire	Class of people whose nobility title was conferred by Napoleon. Noblesse d'Empire is considered by snobs to be inferior to old nobility.
NTM	A rap group.
Pavillon	Suburban middleclass house.
Plouc	Slang for peasant.
Quincaillerie	Hardware store
RATP	Régie Autonome des Transports Parisiens. Parisian public transport authority.
RMI	Revenu Minimum d'Insertion. Welfare stipend.
SAFER	Société d'Aménagement Foncier et d'Etablissement Rural. State controlled association regulating agricultural land sales.
SNCF	Société Nationale des Chemins de Fer Francais. State controlled railway company.
Teuf	Cop.
Thune	Slang for money.
Verlan	French equivalent of pig latin. Very old form of pseudo-language using syllable reversal, still widely used by modern youth.